CASSIE STEWARD

Number Thirty-Two

Front cover image © Eddie Linssen, Alamy Stock Photo

Back cover image © Venera Rustamova, Alamy Stock Photo

First edition

ISBN: 978-1-7395287-1-3

Cover art by Nuria Zaragoza
Editing by Claire Beesley

This book was professionally typeset on Reedsy.
Find out more at reedsy.com

For Jesse Blue,
who taught me how to love from the top of my head to the tips of
my toes.

I

Part One

Anna

ONE

Anna, 2022.

Anna answers the door in one of her dead husband's faded and holey oversized t-shirts. An unidentified mustard-coloured stain takes centre stage, running from her collarbone to her navel.

She runs a hand through a matted mass of white hair, and peers out suspiciously through sunken, squinting eyes. Two young men stand on the step, each of them shifting awkwardly from one foot to another in their ill-fitting suits. *More bloody Mormons*, she thinks, *come to save my soul.*

'You're fifty years too late,' she mutters under her breath as she sighs and starts to close the door.

'Mrs Carmichael?' asks the one with the shaving rash.

She stares at him blankly and starts picking at a scab on the inside of her nose. His eyes are too close together. His ill-fitting suit suggests he's borrowed it from his father. He should be in the library studying, not on people's doorsteps.

'We're from the bank, Mrs Carmichael. We called on Monday to discuss your mortgage arrears, but seemed to get cut off. With you being such a long-standing customer, the manager asked us to come and see you personally.'

Somewhere in the depths of her consciousness she has a vague recollection of sitting at the telephone and announcing loudly into it that fine, she was leaving, packing up and going. It had been more a display of belligerence than a proclamation of true intention. Her hearing isn't what it was, of course, nor is her patience. There are so many telephone calls these days from strangers trying to sell her things, or asking her if she's had an accident. She'd presumed it had been another of the same ilk and left the phone dangling from its hook accordingly.

He looks like a shrew, she thinks, or a vole. Yes, a vole. He needs a few healthy meals and some time outside, a good dose of vitamin D.

She inspects the crust she has picked from her nostril and flicks it down onto the tiles. She catches sight of her thick, yellowing toenails and the wiry hairs sprouting from her big toe, and sighs. They may as well come in. They'll only come back another day. And things will only be another few days older.

She turns on her heels and walks back down the hallway, leaving the door wide open.

The two young men follow her through.

The light bulb went some months ago now, and there are any number of flyers and circulars heaped on the floor where they'd fallen to their final resting places over the last year. There will be some bills somewhere in there too, she supposes. But without the light, she can't possibly begin to search for them. Not amongst all the other things: the boxes, the broken bike, the unidentified objects that render her narrow hallway even narrower. She should really just tape the letterbox over and be done with it. There are enough things crammed into her house. She doesn't need any more.

She hobbles down the hall to the doorway to her right and into her living room, scraping her jagged nails along the peeling walls as she goes. Perching herself on the arm of the sofa, she studies the lads as they take in their surroundings.

What must they be thinking? She inwardly chuckles, appraising the piles of junk, the detritus of the last week's meals strewn over the various surfaces. All chipped crockery and half-eaten week-old toast, stiff in decay, starting to rot... a bit like her.

I wasn't always like this, she wants to tell them. She glances across to the photographs on the sideboard and sees her younger self smiling back at her through a layer of dust. She stands and walks over to it, almost slipping on a rogue dish. She wipes away a small circle in the dust so that she can see herself in the photo more clearly, then replaces it on the shelf.

She turns to face the young vole who is looking increasingly overwhelmed. His sidekick hasn't taken his eyes from the clipboard in his hands, which he is gripping so hard that his knuckles are turning white.

'What's all this about, young man?'

'You're in arrears, Mrs Carmichael. We've tried to call, sent letters,' he says, gesturing towards the hallway, home to the heaps of unopened post. 'We've come to discuss setting up a payment plan... our manager, she looked through your account. You've never missed a payment, until now, for over thirty years. You're only a year away from being mortgage free. We want to do everything we can to help you avoid a repossession order.'

The word repossession manages to pierce through Anna's internal fog. The rusty and cobwebbed cogs begin to click and whirr as she processes the gravity of her predicament.

'Oh dear,' she says. 'I don't have any money.'

He nods slowly, seemingly having lost the ability to speak, perhaps on account of the stifling smell of stale smoke that enveloped him immediately upon entering the room. Or perhaps at the sight of the sheer amount of junk strewn across every surface. Or perhaps it's the fact that the thin streaks of sunlight coming through the curtains have revealed Anna's old t-shirt to be so threadbare in places that it is almost completely see-through; and she isn't wearing a stitch underneath it. That brown stain that his eyes had been stuck on wasn't a stain at all, but a large, angry looking nipple.

She follows his gaze and he turns a strange shade of purple. Even his ears.

'Oh,' she says. 'I'll go and get dressed.' And heads for the stairs.

She sighs again, wishing she'd had the foresight to bother sanding and painting the banister a couple of years ago when she'd been toying with the idea of redecorating, breathing some life into this poor neglected pit. Houses are like marriages, she's realised since. You neglect to do a few bits of upkeep, you cut a few corners because you're tired or you can't be bothered, then you turn around one day and suddenly the roof has fallen in and you're buried under a pile of rubble.

The boards creak wearily underneath her as she crosses the landing towards her bedroom. She catches sight of herself in the floor-length mirror, propped up wonkily against her teak drawers, and cackles. Poor young vole.

Goodness me. I need a haircut, a good haircut would banish a few years. I should start using that cold cream before bed again, I used to be so meticulous. What has happened to me?

She sits down on the edge of the bed and nestles in where the mattress has dipped, a little concave she spends most of her time in these days.

How did it get to this? This house, this bloody house, these bloody walls... and the echoes and the memories and their voices and the smells and...

I'm rotting away, slowly away, the house is decaying and it's taking me with it.

'Fuck it,' she whispers, and lays down, closing her eyes. It's just exhausting. Life is exhausting.

When she wakes up at 7pm, it's dark and the vole and his friend have gone.

TWO

Neighbour, 2022.

Anna wakes early the next morning wrong-footed. She hasn't slept well, her dreams an ugly mish-mash of faces from the past, each one contorted in anger and pointing accusatory fingers. The nightmares are routine, she has spent so many nights laid side to side with them that they aren't enough to unsettle her on their own. But last night, everything had felt wrong, even more wrong than it usually did.

The house had been too quiet, the air too humid, rendering restful sleep impossible. Each time she eventually nodded off she would startle awake only minutes later as though she'd been bitten.

By 8am, all thoughts of rest have been chased over the horizon and the only thought that is clear is this one: I must get out of this house.

The need to escape has become a compulsion, urgent enough for her to forfeit her morning coffee, thick with sugar.

She throws on her coat and steps onto her porch, feeling a

physical weight lift as the cold air meets the corrugated flesh of her cheeks.

'Good morning, Anna!' comes a voice somewhere to her left. She turns toward the voice, milky eyes blinking from the shock of sunlight. 'Beautiful day today, isn't it?'

As her eyes adjust, Anna can see that the voice is coming from Arthur Maxwell and that yes, indeed, it is a beautiful day. The type of day she'd loved, once upon a time: clear blue skies, leaves crunching underfoot, clouds of breath. Arthur is smiling at her over his glasses as he pours a jug of warm water over the windscreen of his mother's car and scrapes it with a credit card.

His mother had lived at number thirty, conjoined with Anna's, almost as long as Anna has lived in number thirty-two, and had become a dear and trusted friend in those years. Not that she had had the pleasure of many friends, but Margaret Maxwell had been one of the very few people through the course of her life who had been consistent in her kindness.

'Yes, yes it is. Tell me Arthur, how is your mother?'

'Oh,' he smiles sadly, 'you know.' Anna doesn't know. 'She's fine. Still ticking, just about, you know mum. The doctors told us she wouldn't see Christmas, but here we are, almost there. She'll outlive the lot of us I should imagine. I'm just on my way to visit her, actually. You should come along sometime, I know she'd love to see you.'

Anna's shoulders prickle with that inconvenient feeling of guilt she normally pushes to one side and dismisses whenever thoughts of Maggie creep up on her during the day. If she's being honest, the thoughts come less and less now. She has pretty much chosen to forget about Maggie altogether.

The idea of Maggie, old and sick in a home somewhere,

9

surrounded by other old and sick people, makes Anna feel distinctly uncomfortable. She can't picture it, and doesn't want to.

In the early days there had been phone calls. They'd chatted away about this and that for an hour a night or more, until Maggie's pressing for a visit became more frequent. The very idea of seeing her like that had filled Anna with dread, and the more Maggie had pushed, the further Anna had retreated until eventually the calls had dwindled away completely. Just another thing to feel dreadful about.

Anna studies her bitten nails, her chapped and flaking fingers and then makes a snap decision. 'Shall I come with you, then?' she asks as she looks directly at Arthur, who looks something bordering on alarmed. His mouth has dropped open slightly and he pushes his glasses back up his nose as he recovers his composure.

'Absolutely,' he says as a smile begins to curl up onto his lips. 'Are you sure? Were you not on your way out somewhere?'

'A few errands,' she lies. 'Nothing that can't wait. I'd like to come.'

He's pleased. An inane grin splits his face as he walks down the driveway out of next door's gate and into Anna's front yard where he leans over and offers her his elbow to take.

He nods towards the ground, saying, 'Here, hold on. It's very slippery.'

If he noticed that she has stepped out in a pair of entirely inappropriate Birkenstocks, he is too polite to say so. He always did have beautiful manners, even as a boy. Maggie had been lucky with her two, especially Arthur. He had always been wonderful with her, doing all the right things, in just the right order. Flying the nest but always remaining on hand for a leaky tap or a blocked drain. Things that had made Anna act and feel scornful towards him on more than one occasion, she acknowledges, guiltily.

Anna takes his outstretched arm and lets him help her down the path and into the car.

'It needs a run,' he tells her. 'I have no idea why she refuses to sell it. I've offered to buy it from her myself... I know where to pick my battles, though.'

Once she's safely inside, he pours the rest of the jug across the windscreen and puts it to one side in the tiled porch, then hops into the driver's seat beside her.

'Ready?' he asks, and starts the engine without waiting for an answer.

Now they're moving, Anna has started to second guess her decision to come along. She stares out of the window at the huge sycamores that line the pavements of their street. She is transfixed as they drive past harassed nannies herding pre-schoolers along the pavement, teenagers perched on walls with dark eyeliner and lip rings, a smartly dressed man talking on his mobile phone as he tries to navigate the frost.

All these lives going on all around her, only yards from the fortress she's been festering in for all these years. The concept is shocking to her. When did she become this grumpy misanthrope? She is still miles away when Arthur breaks the silence.

'So, Anna, how is everything? Are you OK? We haven't seen so much of you. Mum asks after you often. She'll be so thrilled to see you.'

Anna stiffens. If she hadn't known Arthur since he was a young boy she might have interpreted his comments as digs, but she knows him better than that. It wouldn't have even crossed his mind.

She takes a deep breath.

It was the October of 1969 when the Maxwells had moved in next door. Arthur had been five and his brother, Teddy, a year older. Anna had watched with curiosity from her bedroom window as they'd helped their mother and the removal men carry bits and pieces into the house connected to hers.

The boys had seemed slight, a couple of mini whippets with their long, skinny limbs and sallow faces. Both wore glasses and had tufty, mousy hair sticking up at odd angles. The older one a little uglier, missing a few front teeth. Maggie had been on form that day, steering the ship, bossily pointing and gesticulating to the boys and a couple of brawny men as they teetered around with an endless stream of furniture and boxes.

She was a commanding woman, in every sense. Raven beehive, lashings of mascara and her signature red lipstick. She'd seemed impossibly exotic to twenty-year-old Anna. She had felt something close to trepidation as she'd watched this woman in her boiler suit and floral headscarf, the vibrant colours seeming at odds with her bossy tone and barked orders.

It had been early afternoon when the last box had gone indoors and Maggie had waved the van off. Anna had been so busy curtain twitching that she hadn't realised the time.

She'd flung on her coat and run out of the door, dashing down to the end of the street and towards the school gates. The last to arrive again.

THREE

Moving in, 1969.

Maggie surveyed the scene and let out a loud sigh. Boxes were stacked one on top of the other almost up to the ceiling, marked only by room. She inwardly cursed herself for not adding more detail, it just hadn't seemed important at the time. The move had been impulsive, a knee jerk reaction and ever since she'd had the offer accepted on number thirty she had been running on autopilot.

She knew that there was a logical way to begin. But it had been a long and fraught day, and the enormity of the task threatened to overwhelm her. She reached into her pocket and took a swift swig of neat gin from her hip flask to conjure up some courage.

This wasn't her first move, but it was her first solo move, a thing she hadn't imagined in a million years she'd ever have to do. Even after she'd found out about the affair. She had truly believed that her expertly choreographed dalliance with a partner at Walter's firm would serve as a wake up call for

13

him, forcing his hand in ending his juvenile fling. Not give him a way out of their marriage. How had she been so stupid?

So here she was, just her and her boys in her new house in West Dulwich. Half the size of their detached family home in Holland Park but still big enough. And far enough away that there was very little chance she'd bump in to Walter and that dimwit little Russian secretary, who no doubt thought all her Christmases had come at once, when she tucked herself into Maggie's marital bed. She still found it incredulous that Walter - stuffy, repressed, ordinary Walter - really couldn't conceive of Oksana, almost half of his age, being in love with his money rather than him. She had only worked for him for nine months prior. To Maggie, the whole thing seemed ridiculous. Humiliating, and just ridiculous.

'She loves me, she makes me feel like a man, again!' he had yelped, just before he'd slammed the door on their life together, trunk in hand, and gone to stay at Oksana's studio flat in Earl's Court eight weeks ago. Even amidst the pain of the situation, Maggie had not been able to stifle her laughter. A man?! He would struggle to fight his way out of a paper bag. The sight of Maggie's sanitary towels in the bathroom cabinet had made him blush and stutter like an awkward pre-teen who had been caught peeping on a neighbour. Such was his embarrassment that she'd had to start hiding them in the linen cupboard, even after twelve years of marriage and two children.

He hadn't needed a wife as much as he'd needed somebody to mother him. She hoped Oksana was well versed in council tax, mopping, stuffing pheasant and starching white collars just so... not to mention navigating his periodic bouts of stress induced irritable bowel and walking the treacherous tightrope of friendship with the serpent he called mother.

Walter was nothing if not a creature of habit, a very particular creature of habit. He wouldn't even be capable of identifying an iron in a line up, never mind working an oven. Sure, these oversights wouldn't matter now, but Maggie would bide her time until the honeymoon period ran dry and the reality of living with a twenty-year-old really began to sink in. When final notices started turning up, his dear mother didn't get her annual Fortnum and Mason hamper next month and he didn't have a single pressed pair of trousers in the house of a Monday morning, that's when he would realise Maggie's worth. She was sure he didn't miss her yet, but she sincerely hoped he missed the boys by now, who were more bewildered than even she was by the turn of these swift and brutal events. New house, new school, what a bloody mess.

She ascended the steep and creaking stairs in search of the boys, seeing everything afresh as she went. This house was a far cry from the last which had been so sterile and void of personality, all white marble and glass panels. Walter had always liked things minimal, and for years Maggie had fought off her natural magnetism towards good, solid antiques with stories to tell, and pretty vases and ornaments. Things Walter had referred to as her 'tat'.

This house could be a real family home, floor to ceiling nick nacks and family photos. Not the huge and uniform black and white family prints they'd had done on Kensington High Street every year, but the real moments: sports days, boy scouts, birthday parties, barbecues. Anything she damn-well liked.

The idea of having so much autonomy was at once nerve-wracking and exhilarating. So many of her worldly belongings had gone into storage when she had first moved in with her husband, just until the renovations were finished he had told her, remaining there ever since. Many of the boxes she had yet to open would be a surprise to even her, and that part she was looking forward to. But first, the essentials.

She reached the top of the stairs to be greeted with another pile of boxes deposited haphazardly on the landing, marked either 'Arthur' or 'Edward', and a round of giggles.

'Where are you?!' she demanded. 'Have you chosen your bedrooms yet?! We need to get cracking or you'll be sleeping out here in an empty box each.'

Two little heads peeped over the top of the cardboard and descended into another round of giggles, then a few serious sounding whispers and some nudges.

Ted, the eldest, cleared his throat. At six, he was the dominant one. Arthur was more introverted and shy like his father, although thankfully the calm and easy going manner that comes with being a younger brother had cancelled out the rigidity and seriousness that he might have otherwise inherited from his dad, too.

'I want that room,' Ted announced, pointing to the door to his left, 'the big room. But Arthur is being a baby again, and doesn't want any of the other rooms and doesn't want to sleep by himself because he's *scared,* but he's not staying with *me.* I'm too big now to share a bedroom. I need my own space.'

Maggie looked down at her second born with sympathy and affection. It struck her once again how young and ill-prepared he was for all of this upheaval.

'I don't think so,' she said, folding her arms. 'The big room

16

is mine. You take your pick out of any of the others and we'll get to work finding your bits and pieces, in amongst this chaos.'

She had barely finished speaking before Teddy had charged off to inspect the rest of the rooms, propelled by the fear of ending up in a bedroom smaller than the one his brother might get.

'And you,' she said to Arthur, placing a hand reassuringly onto his shoulder, 'you and I can have a sleepover together tonight, and tomorrow we can choose you a bedroom and you don't even have to sleep in it if you don't want to, but we've got to get your name plate on one of the doors, haven't we?'

'Thank you, Mummy,' he whispered, as he nuzzled his head into her waist.

***

It wasn't until the next day at the school gates that Anna and Maggie met properly.

Maggie stood in amongst the usual flock of mothers who were hanging on her every word, thrilled to have one of the Kensington set in their midst. Domination of the PTA coven was no mean feat for her first day.

She watched as Anna dragged Louie down the road by his elbow, launching him through the gates as the bell rang. She waved frantically and blew kisses at him as he ambled over to join the end of the line as his class snaked inside, one by one.

As Anna turned to walk back, Maggie extracted herself from her new fan club and followed her down the road.

She watched with amusement as Anna stumbled over a milk bottle on the front steps and lost one of her mules, her long coat falling open to reveal her pyjamas covertly underneath.

'Bollocks!' Anna said, possibly louder than she might have thought she had, as she stretched her left leg from the top step and tried to hook back the rogue shoe with her toes. Mission completed, she looked up and met Maggie's gaze from her own front step, cheeks reddening.

'Fancy a coffee? I'm Maggie.' she had said, and that had been that.

It was the first of thousands of morning coffees they would go on to share through the years after the school drop off, becoming almost a ritual. Over a decade's age difference and an enormous class divide sat between them (Maggie hailing from old money in Chelsea, Anna from a council estate in Catford) the gulf was filled quickly and easily with the kinship that comes about from becoming a single mother and meeting another of your own.

Anna found Maggie to be unexpectedly easy going, as generous and funny as she was outrageously posh. She found her upfront, no-nonsense approach to life comforting, and she sought her counsel on all matters from there on in. Maggie gave her a glimpse into another world, the one many of the other school mothers inhabited. Anna was Maggie's loyal confidante in return.

FOUR

The Cedars, 2022.

Arthur turns the car into a long, narrow driveway flanked on either side with oak trees as old as the red brick building itself. The house sits at the top of a vast expanse of perfectly manicured lawn, with a huge duck pond close to the bottom.

'It used to be an asylum, Mother tells me. A very macabre history, apparently,' Arthur says absentmindedly as he parks the car as close to the door as he can.

Anna realises she hasn't responded to anything he might have said for the entire journey, and hopes he assumes she's simply not heard him. The only real benefit of old age is the myriad excuses it provides for rudeness.

He helps her out of the passenger seat and they walk companionably through big white double doors into a large reception room. The Cedars seems more like a country club than an old people's home, the only giveaway being the smell of disinfectant and mothballs. She lets herself be led by Arthur, who smiles warmly at a receptionist he's on first name terms with as he signs them in.

'She's in the lounge, in her usual spot,' the girl tells him.

They walk down a long and echoey corridor for a few minutes until they reach an enormous room with a huge head height fireplace at one end, and three sets of white gilded French doors leading on to a decked veranda. Various sofas and armchairs are dotted around, inhabited by various bodies, some awake, some asleep.

There is the low hum of chatter which stops as they enter, until someone stands up at the French doors furthest from them and starts waving manically. Arthur picks up the pace until they get closer, enveloping the small waving maniac into a hug. Then he steps aside and gestures at Anna as though he were presenting a prize at a gala.

Anna and Maggie lock eyes for the first time in two years.

'Bloody hell, Anna Carmichael. I was starting to think you'd copped it in your kitchen and been eaten by the cat. But here you are, looking like *you're* the one who's seen a ghost! Pull up a chair, the service here is magnificent.'

She winks as she presses a button hanging on a red string from her wrist. A young girl in a pale blue tunic arrives almost instantly, and Maggie continues, 'Nicola, darling, we need coffee! Proper coffee, in the cafetieres. My very dear friend is visiting, and she won't stand for any of that instant crap any sooner than I will!'

And Anna knows she is forgiven.

The girl smiles warmly. 'Of course, Maggie, how exciting. I'm sure we've got some of those scones left over, too. Give me two minutes.' She squeezes Maggie's hand, turning to Arthur. 'And tea for you, Arthur?'

'You know me so well, Nicola. Thank you. I'll come and

help you, actually, I'll only be in the way here. I daren't get too embroiled in whatever cunning scheme these two concoct in the next five minutes!'

Anna watches him as he follows the girl back out of the double doors, engaging her in animated conversation.

'We've gone full circle, Anna. The dependents are the caregivers now. They forget we wiped their arses for years, trying to impress the nurses with their condescending jokes. He's only helping so he can flirt with her over the cups and saucers, mark my words.' Maggie grins.

Anna is mesmerized by the almost imperceptible changes in her friend. The frailty is new, as is the incessant quivering of her hands and wrists. But these things are tempered by the directness in her sharp chestnut eyes and the signature beehive. It is white now, lacquered to such an extent that it could easily be an attempt at an avant-garde headpiece. Even here, surrounded by walking-frames and adult diapers – most of her contemporaries stinking unabashedly of piss – she is impossibly glamorous.

The heavy gold Van Cleef's that have always dangled from her ears now pull her papery lobes down so low that they look as if they might fall away at any given moment. As translucent as licked Rizlas. But the familiar sight of them brings Anna comfort.

She could never have imagined her fiercely independent friend finding any happiness in a place like this. Living this life. At first, Maggie had fought tooth and nail against 'the regime' as she'd called it when she'd gleefully regaled each day's small rebellions in those early phone calls. Her voice had expressed her utter disgust towards those 'spineless, simpering, weasel sons of mine', for putting her here in the first place. But now, as Maggie sits before her, Anna recognises a contentedness in her friend that she herself does not possess, even with her relative freedom.

'So, here you are, not dead yet. To what do I owe the pleasure?' Maggie's shrewd eyes skewer Anna to her seat.

'I want to say I've been busy, but it'd be an outright lie,' says Anna, and they both cackle. 'What's happened to us, Mags? I swear I've woken up one day, an old woman, in an empty house. Even the cat's dead. And I'm next! With not a soul to gnaw on my bones afterwards.'

'No, darling. Not that it's a race or anything, but *I'm* next. The doctors tell me so every week, but the reaper is running late so far.'

They sit in a comfortable silence until their coffee and scones arrive, each lost in their own thoughts.

'They're kicking me out of the house.' Anna tells her as she smears a giant glob of clotted cream onto her scone, pausing for effect.

'The ghosts or the bank?'

'Well, both I suspect. Apparently I've run out of money.'

Maggie considers this for a moment. 'Well, good. Sell up and get out of there. There's years in you yet. A fresh start on the coast, perhaps, or up sticks to a lovely little apartment somewhere sunny, the world is your oyster.' She leans forwards. 'Or if bedpans and bingo are your thing, I could do with a comrade here for when I stage the uprising... viva la revolution!'

They both chuckle.

'Really, Anna,' Maggie continues, giving Anna another beady eyeing, 'get it valued and sell up. It's time to move on and lay the ghosts to rest. You've punished yourself enough.

Time is finite, take it from me. Go and find a way to enjoy it whilst you still can.'

Anna recognises the sincerity in her friend's eyes and is relieved to be swept away in her pragmatism. Maggie had always had a way of turning a disaster into an opportunity. The rest of the hour passes by in a blur of nostalgia and gossip and before they know it, visiting time is over. With profuse promises to come again soon, Anna hugs her friend goodbye.

And with a throat full of Rive Gauche, silently thanks a God she doesn't believe in for blessing her life with this person who has anchored her through so many storms.

She is silent all the way home, and concedes that perhaps there is a lot to be said for the kind of life where there are no chores, no responsibilities. Carte blanche to read, sleep or just sit, picking and flicking your nose all day.

For so much of her life Anna has been a flightless bird, intermittently falling into others' nests by chance, until the twigs slowly dry out and disintegrate from underneath her and she is forced to move on. She may have spent the largest portion of her existence between the same walls, but the lives she has lived within them have been vast and plenty.

She falls into a deep and contented sleep downstairs on the chesterfield that evening, cracked lipped snores echoing up the walls. A glass of red wine keels precariously in her left hand, slowly trickling down her wrist, to spread across her lap like violent murder.

FIVE

Help, 2022.

The woman's heels click-clack up the tree-lined street at as brisk a pace as the height of them will allow. She has tried, through the years, to quell the rage she feels at the inequalities that meet a woman in banking at every turn. The pay gaps are outrageous, of course, and casual misogyny is par for the course. But the silly, sexist rule of the mandatory high-heeled shoe is a step too far. Physical discomfort should never be mandatory in this day and age, particularly when it is an affliction foisted upon only the staff who drew the short straw in the genital lottery.

She isn't a graceful woman, nor is she a woman who sees any benefit in the lunch time salon slots many of her colleagues dutifully run off to every week. No, she is all function, all business.

She counts the house numbers as she goes. It's a beautiful street, quiet and suburban. Flanked on either side by towering red brick semi's, each of them perfectly aligned, they differ only in a very few aspects: the colour of the front door; the choice of hanging basket; and the brand of sports car parked in front.

This certainly isn't the type of road that she would usually visit on this type of business. She rarely conducts this type of business herself anymore, full stop. But when she'd viewed the account and seen the age of the client, their previous pristine payment record, and the tweedle-dee and tweedle-dum deputies the client had been assigned, returning from their visit stating the client had 'gone to bed', she'd decided to make an exception.

The affluence of the street means she is optimistic, until she reaches number thirty-two and her heart sinks. Its shabby exterior is juxtaposed entirely with its pristine counterpart, number thirty, who's tiled path is gleaming and who's chrysanthia is in full bloom, meticulously pruned and swaying softly in the breeze.

Anything that ever bloomed on this side of the iron railings has long since departed, leaving only a skeleton of dry and splintering stem and barren soil. The rusting gate creaks loudly as she opens it and underneath her, the Victorian tiles are chipped and uneven, weeds sprouting freely between them. The door paint is flaking and the stained glass is dull with grime.

Anna, disturbed from slumber on her sagging couch, startles awake at the sound of knocking on her door. Hesitating, wondering if she'd heard correctly, the smart rat-a-tat comes again. It sounds authoritative, unignorable. She shambles to the door to find a smartly dressed woman smiling a cracked, red-lipped grimace at her.

'Good morning, Mrs Carmichael, I'm Polly Parker from the bank. May I come in?'

'At least they've sent a grown up this time.' Anna says, watching as Polly offers an even tighter smile.

Polly from the bank follows Anna down the unlit hall, Anna chuckling inwardly as she sneaks a glance at this well-dressed stranger navigating the assault course of junk stacked up between the front door and the kitchen.

Nevertheless, Anna feels compelled to sweep the crumbs from her kitchen table to the floor with her sleeve and gestures for Polly from the bank to sit down. Which she does – to Anna's amusement – by perching on the edge of the chair while fixing that tight smile firmly to her face.

Anna tries to see her home through Polly from the bank's eyes. Although the woman is attempting subterfuge, she can't hide her dismay at being landed with this particular role.

Polly is meticulous about hygiene. She can scarcely conceal her disbelief at the unsanitary living conditions. Every area of space is covered in objects, thick with dust and cigarette ash. Mould blooms above the tiles and along the wall. The space is eerie in its half light from a backyard so overgrown that a towering tangle of shrubbery blocks out nearly all the natural light that once lit it up at this time of afternoon.

After a moment's hesitation, Polly seems to decide she has no choice but to engage with her surroundings, and sets her briefcase down, locating a file within it. 'So, Mrs Carmichael, the last four months of mortgage payments have—'

'I know,' Anna cuts in, folding her arms. 'They told me.'

'I see. So I'm here today to discuss—'

'I don't have any money.'

'—your options.' Polly is beginning to look flustered. She starts rubbing at her eyes, perhaps on account of the dust. 'Can you tell me a little more about your circumstances, Mrs

Carmichael? You've been an exemplary customer of the bank for over thirty years, but we can only be so lenient.'

Anna sighs. How many times does she have to tell these people that she doesn't have any money? She has no means with which to pay them. It's not rocket science.

'I can defer the payments so far or see if you're eligible for a payment holiday. We can extend the mortgage term to bring the payment amounts down. There are lots of things we can do. But we need to ascertain your circumstances, ways and means of paying back the debt and the time frame in which you can do so.'

Anna is silent, tight lipped and rheumy eyed, looking into the distance somewhere above Polly's head. Polly glances down at the file in her hands.

'I see that previously the payments were debited from one account which is now empty. Do you have any income at all? Any pensions, state benefits? Any assets?'

Anna continues to stare blankly. She doesn't know about any of these things. She has never been frivolous, there has always been money in her account and she has never needed to understand how it got there. Until now.

'Any family who may be able to help?'

'No,' Anna croaks, wringing her hands. 'They're all gone.'

She nods in the direction she has been gazing. Anna watches as Polly turns towards the collection of dusty portraits hung on the wall behind her. A man, a wife, two children. The woman shudders, the hardness in her eyes somersaulting between surprise and sympathy.

Well, good, thinks Anna, as Polly continues to crane her neck. *Life hasn't been kind. Not to me, anyway. If you were me, you wouldn't bother brushing your hair, either.*

'If you don't pay the money, the bank will start a repossession order.' Polly says a little more gently as she turns back to the table. 'So we need to find a way to stop that from happening.'

'My husband… he was the one who dealt with all of this stuff, the house, the bills, anything like that. I wouldn't know where to begin. Before he died, he'd set it all up to tick over and I've never had to worry about it until now. I've never earned a penny. I've only ever been a wife and a mother. A redundant one for the last thirty years as it goes—' Anna pauses, giving herself a mental shake. 'You're not here for an old woman's sob story, of course. But the crux of it is, I don't have any money. I'm going to have to sell the house.'

Polly glances up from the files. 'You're the sole owner of the property, is that right? It says you paid cash in 1966? And then took out a mortgage on it in 1985?'

'We needed some money,' says Anna. 'My son was in trouble.'

The women jump in tandem at the sound of another knock. Arthur stands behind them at the back door, his tatty check shirt smeared with dirt, waving a pair of shears aloft. Anna shuffles towards the door and opens it.

'Mum's asked me to give the lawn a mow and trim the hedges and I was going to see if you wanted me to cut back some of yours too, now that I'm on a roll…' his voice trails away as his eyes run over Polly and a spark of recognition ignites, but for the life of him, he can't place her. 'Sorry! I didn't realise you had company.'

Polly stares back at Arthur and then back towards the photos on the wall and the blood drains from her face.

'I suppose you better had,' replies Anna, appraising the

wilderness where her back garden once was. 'If I'm going to sell the house I suppose people prefer a garden to a jungle.'

Arthur looks from Anna to Polly, his mouth slightly open, which Anna thinks makes him look rather foolish.

'Mrs Carmichael, I'd better be going.' The sound of Polly from the bank's chair scraping on the tiles as she stands startles them all in the thrumming silence. 'I'll be in touch next week. In the meantime, have a think about how you would like to proceed. As I said, there may be options available to you that you aren't aware of. Selling the house isn't a choice you should make lightly, and should only be a last resort. There are other avenues we could explore first if you would like to…' Her gaze has wandered back to the photo on the kitchen wall again and she has to force her eyes away. 'I'll see myself out.'

Anna and Arthur hear the front door slam closed behind her.

'What did she say her name was?' asks Arthur, and Anna shrugs. 'You're moving?' Anna shrugs again.

***

The next day, Anna awakens with a renewed sense of purpose.

'You're not dead yet,' she tells the pallid little old lady in the mirror, who looks as though she very well might be. 'It's time for a wash, and then we're going to tackle this, one room at a time.'

The watery, red-rimmed eyes squinting back at her take on a determined look and she straightens her back. It's time, she's decided, before she ends up a heap of forgotten bones underneath a pile of expired Next catalogues.

She and Arthur had sat at the kitchen table with their heads together until late into the evening, plotting her next move. It had been a surprisingly enlightening process: the more options Arthur gave her, the more reasons she found to debunk them.

Now that she has floated the idea of selling up and starting again, the more she finds herself drawn to it. It no longer felt ludicrous even saying the words aloud.

There hasn't been any kind of potential in her future for a long time now. And so, decision made, Arthur had moved from sounding board and voice of reason to more of a project management role, to her great relief. Anna has never been a comfortable decision maker. She's never needed to be and she's more than glad to defer to a man.

She lowers herself slowly into the warm water lapping at the sides of the chipped avocado bathtub, almost slipping on the layer of limescale. Laying back with only her face out of the water, her heart thumps unsteadily in her ears.

I loved this suite forty years ago, she thinks, *it had been so modern.*

She'd been so proud of it back then, perpetually littered with garish plastic bath toys, wet towels adorned with various characters covering the floor. Whoever buys the place will almost certainly rip it out with no thought for the little heads of soft downy hair that have been lathered up in here. The splashing, the squabbles, the laughter.

There's no time for melancholy, she silently admonishes herself, and realises she has no shampoo, mentally adding it to her shopping list. Oh, well. It's still cleaner than it was before.

By 11am she has bathed, dressed, been to the corner shop

and back and is sitting down at her kitchen table eating a slice of toast topped with the very last smear of crystallised honey. Today is already the most productive day she's had in the last six months, and she's feeling rather pleased with herself.

She decides that she will do a tour of the house and try to see it as somebody else might. Distance herself from the clutter; all those belongings, all those memories. She will appraise and be brutal.

She watches the strange, shaky fingers that unroll the first bin bag, all age spotted and bent at odd angles and can hardly believe that they are the same hands that could play a sonata upon request at a dinner party.

The back bedroom seems to be the most logical place to begin, in that it's been unused and thus undisturbed for over a decade, and any possession she hasn't bothered about in ten years shouldn't be something she ought to be troubled by parting with now.

The first obstacle is the door. Jammed, of course, stuck fast. Anna pulls and rattles the handle with all of the strength she can muster, but concludes it is she who is likely to break far more quickly than a slab of solid oak.

After a full twenty minutes wrestling with the brass handle and muttering expletives, she reluctantly admits defeat, not altogether sure she hasn't dislodged her shoulder in the process. She turns her back to the wretched door and begins down the hall in the opposite direction. There is a sudden creak and the door swings slowly open.

Bloody typical.

With a deep breath, she pushes the door fully open and quickly scans the room. It is, of course, exactly as she left it over two decades ago but somehow the sight of it still punches the wind from her gills. She wants to turn on her heels immediately and slam the door shut. She has toyed with the idea of bricking over the door more than once over the years. *No*, she admonishes herself, *it's time*.

This room, this is the biggest hurdle. The rest will be a walk in the park after this. With a sharp intake of breath, she straightens her back and walks purposefully across the room to pull open the curtains.

The room is the biggest bedroom in the house. South facing, high ceilings, original wooden floorboards and fireplace. This room was the main reason she fell in love with the house all those years ago. She can remember the moment exactly. As soon as she'd walked into this room, she knew.

The perfect room for her beautiful baby boy to dream, to play, to grow. More than enough room for a chair to rock him to sleep in the early hours. Space aplenty for train sets and toy cars and anything else his tiny heart desired. Huge sash windows for them to see the sun rise together after a sleepless night.

She had known it then and as she'd looked down into his huge blue eyes, she felt he had known it too. And so it was.

She's not sure she could stomach seeing that same optimism in another young woman's eyes as they surveyed the room. A diamond in the rough compared with the rest of the house which she has let slip so badly. She imagines she may have to restrain herself from screaming.

As she surveys the sparse room, she can vividly remember its many guises through the years. It has morphed from a talc scented nursery into a little boy's kingdom overflowing with toys, and then onwards into a grungy teenage lair.

32

When she'd first moved in, she'd spent hours on a ladder in her dad's old overalls, painting the walls sage green whilst four month old Louie had sat babbling at her from his bouncy chair in the corner. She had loved it. She hadn't given a second thought to the fumes, you didn't in those days. The first night she had put him to sleep in his cot by the door, she had whispered softly to him: 'This is it, now, our very own home, just you and me. We'll be very happy here.'

As she looks at the scratched and abandoned wooden bed frame in the corner, she feels a physical pain in the pit of her stomach. What a transient and whimsical thing happiness is, she thinks. No matter how solid you think the bricks and mortar are, evil has a way of burrowing through even the tiniest of holes, permeating the walls and sucking the life out of a home before you've even noticed.

The sage green had lasted five or six years and during those years the room mainly smelt of talcum powder and milky sick, a smell which still stirred intense feelings of longing in Anna all these years later whenever she met an infant.

Louie had been everything Anna could have asked for as a single, teenage mother: easy going, smiley, happy to go along with Anna in anything she did as she fumbled her way through.

He never seemed to mind that she was clearly an amateur compared to all the other mothers in the park with prams. These mothers were almost always much older than Anna, expertly put together and huddled by the gate discussing so-and-so's drunken antics at last week's golf club social, whilst she sat on her favourite bench smoking roll ups and cooing at Louie whilst he laughed and waved a stick around.

Anna wasn't – couldn't – be included and she knew it. She

didn't have a husband who played golf. She didn't have a husband, full stop. She didn't have a car she could moan about the cost of repairs on, she didn't have a cleaner who had neglected to dust the skirting boards again. She had ended up in her lovely house in this affluent area entirely by chance.

She knew that these ladies all speculated every time she locked the heavy yellow door behind her. Second-hand clothes hanging off of her tiny teenage frame topped with wild blonde curls entirely at odds with her formidable Edwardian semi.

She didn't begrudge them their whispers, but she certainly never threw them any scraps to chew on, either. More than anything, she knew better than to be anything less than grateful to have quite suddenly found herself with the ways and means to give Louie a proper home.

She knew first-hand how life had the ability to pull the rug from under you without warning. She had felt emboldened by the gossip, and the solitary existence she shared with Louie had truly been a gift. No expectations, nobody to answer to, the freedom to get things wrong and then to be able to right them without judgement.

And time. At that stage in her life, Anna had had endless time. Time to spend with her son, to talk to him. Hours to while away making shapes in flour on the floor, time to teach him to count the worms they dug up in the garden, finger painting, covering the kitchen and themselves in margarine in numerous failed attempts at shortbread. And time to clean it all up again. Yes, she had been lucky and she'd known it.

Thinking back, these were truly the best days of her life, the days when Louie needed her as much as she'd needed him. He'd tethered her and given her an important purpose. He taught her just as much as she taught him. He never went to the local nursery or a pre-school like all of the other children on the street, no matter how outstanding other parents claimed them to be. Quite selfishly, Anna simply couldn't bear to be parted with him for so many hours a day.

By the time school came around, the lack of socializing hadn't been to his detriment. He beamed his way through his first day after an inconsolable Anna waved her curly blonde-haired boy through the gates. He was academically advanced in almost every way and could read before his peers could count. He was top of the class and his undemanding and easy-going demeanour meant he was popular with teachers and students alike. That first week, he came home with two invitations for tea.

It was at that point that Anna had realized that a new stage in his life had begun, and it was time for her to move forward, too. She needed something else to devote her time to. Life was out there, going on all around her and it was time for her to re-join it.

Anna wipes a stray tear from her face and smiles sadly. Those beautiful days seem like only yesterday, yet were so long ago. It's scary how life seems to go so quickly that it basically just sneaks up and overtakes you when you get to a certain age. And Anna knows she has long since passed that threshold. If she stays here in this house, she's essentially admitting defeat and waiting to die, whereupon some poor soul would have to come in and try to create some order out of the haphazard twists and turns of her material memories. Far better to do it herself.

The realisation dawns that once again it's time for Anna to

re-join life, the outside world. To find a new way, grabbing any scraps of happiness that may be possible out there in her final years.

Her eyes run over the built-in wardrobes, the antique bureau and the matching drawers and bedside table. Viewings-wise, there's nothing to be done in here beyond a hoover, a mop and a dust. There are no belongings on display, to all intents and purposes this room is an empty husk of what it had been and could be, and that's probably just how an estate agent would like it.

Most of the possessions that had a home in this room have been sold or disposed of long ago. Everything that is left is sealed up in three boxes and one suitcase, hidden up in the attic and for that she is glad. She couldn't face that today.

Satisfied, she closes the door behind her on her way out, leaving the curtains open for the first time in twenty years.

Exhausted, she retires to bed shortly thereafter and dreams of tiny, sticky fingers gripping hers tightly, listening to the heavenly sound of little lungs breathing, curled in next to her the whole night through.

***

First thing the next morning, she calls next door's number, a number she has dialled thousands of times and knows by heart, enlisting Arthur as her unofficial aide in her house clearing mission. He deposits cardboard boxes in various sizes onto her porch before he leaves for work. A note stating that he is available for any and all odd jobs, furniture moving and tip runs from here on in, is left on the kitchen table.

Boxes to her left and bin liners to her right, Anna is on her knees in her tiled hallway, sifting through the huge pile of mail, most of which she bins without opening. That done, she wheels her old powder-blue Raleigh out of the front door and props it up against the wrought iron railings, thanking it profusely for its years of loyal service.

'It's not you, it's me,' she tells it. 'A small gust of wind and I wouldn't stand a chance. I couldn't even hoist myself up onto you anymore, I've shrunk.'

She pats its wicker basket affectionately and returns inside to tackle the console table and drawers. She owns, she discovers, more sellotape, envelopes and allen keys than any one person ever should.

At the bottom of the very last drawer, she finds an ancient Filofax marked '1971', stuffed with letters, notes and appointment cards. She pulls a photo, edges curled, out of the side pocket, and a five-year-old Louie grins back at her in black and white. The photo marked the end of his successful first year at St Winifreds.

SIX

School, 1969.

At the mid-point of Louie's first school year, the headteacher, Mr Kilpatrick, summoned her for a meeting in his office. All that morning she had been back and forth to the toilet, stomach swirling with anxiety. She shuffled into his office full of fear and trepidation, plagued by paranoia and a terrible sense of foreboding. She must be in trouble. Louie must be in trouble. They were on to her.

She sat down on the chair in front of the headteacher's heavy mahogany desk and barely dared to lift her eyes from her fingers, twisting in her lap.

'Mrs Carlton,' he started, in his heavy Glaswegian drawl. 'Louie has come to my attention recently – well, to everyone's attention as a matter of fact – on account of him being so advanced compared to his peers in many of his subjects. We have been discussing between us whether it might be beneficial to move him ahead a year, to a class and a curriculum he might find more challenging – and therefore more rewarding – and we'd like to know your thoughts.'

A thousand thoughts flooded Anna's consciousness at once. Wasn't he too small to go into the next year? The year three children looked so much bigger than him. What about sports, that wouldn't be fair, would it? What about the friends he'd made?

Anna already hated the rate of knots he was growing up at, and here this man was, trying to push the hands of time even faster! This pompous man, with his bulbous nose and port wine cheeks, ear hair splaying out at all angles…didn't he know that Louie was still a baby?

'Um…' Anna struggled for words, then felt a comforting hand on her shoulder. She turned her head towards it.

Miss Lang, Louie's teacher from last year, smiled encouragingly at Anna. 'Louie is reading at a level of almost two years ahead of the other children. He's doing basic maths while the others are still learning to recognise numbers. He's so sociable, he makes friends easily. I think he will fit really well into Mr Parson's class and get much more out of it.'

'Are you sure he won't struggle? It seems so grown up. He's so small…'

Miss Lang sat next to Anna and spent the next half an hour talking her through all the minute details of the transition, dispelling her worries one by one. Mr Kilpatrick spent most of the thirty minutes pinching the bridge of his nose in obvious irritation, adding nothing but the odd grunt of acquiescence. Louie's academic career was plainly much more important to Miss Lang, who slowly won Anna over with her patience, warmth and intimate knowledge of Louie's school life. It was quite obvious why Louie had adored his teacher, and Anna left the room feeling much the same.

As the double doors had swung closed behind her, the cool air had assaulted her senses. She dashed across the tarmac and out of the gates, and was banging on Maggie's door within minutes. A stiff drink was what was needed, 11am be damned.

She didn't wait for Maggie to come to the door, she never did. A round of warning knocks was manners enough. She went straight through and plonked herself down at Maggie's kitchen table. Maggie swiftly dried her hands on a tea towel and sat down opposite her, back straight and eyes wide with expectancy.

'They want to move him up a year! They say he's too clever. They say he isn't challenged enough,' Anna breathed, still slightly bewildered at the unexpected turn of events. She'd been so convinced that something terrible had been going to happen that she'd been bordering on hysteria. Now she'd had a chance to digest it, she didn't know whether to laugh or cry.

'Bloody hell! That's great, you've a genius on your hands. He'll be in Arthur's class…hopefully jolt my boy into the land of the living. He's away with the fairies, he is.' Maggie laughed affectionately.

'Arthur will look after him, won't he?'

Maggie reached over and squeezed her arm.

'It's more likely to be the other way around, let's be honest. Arthur doesn't know his arse from his elbow most days. God bless him!' and they'd both laughed. They spent the rest of the day speculating about their boys' future careers over a bottle of Merlot, cackling well on into the afternoon until they both staggered, pink cheeked and half cut, to the school gates to walk the subjects of this great debate home.

By that April, Louie had a term under his belt in his new year group and just as Miss Lang had predicted, it had been a roaring success. He settled in among his new classmates with ease, made lots of new friends and had taken the challenge in his stride.

He was enjoying the work, and Anna had felt relief at having made a good decision on his behalf. He'd soon earned quite a reputation amongst the parents too as the veritable child prodigy, and his social calendar was far fuller than Anna would have liked.

Off of the back of this glowing prominence, Anna found that she in turn was becoming more accepted and included among the mothers, with most of them now stopping to trade small talk at the gates and local grocers. There was even the occasional invite to coffee mornings.

While always acutely aware of handling the olive branch being presented to her delicately, she found reasons to graciously decline each time. She still viewed the group with an air of distrust, knowing far better than to lay herself down as a slab of cold ham during one of their many gossip banquets. There were far too many skeletons in her closet already, even at the tender age of only twenty-one.

But with this new time, she found she was left with a large amount of empty space in her own life.

It was Maggie who alerted her to the fact that other girls her age were living lives much different to hers, particularly in London. It wasn't the 1950's anymore, there was far more freedom to be tasted nowadays. Women weren't stuck at home baking bread or darning socks. They had jobs. Lovers, even.

'He isn't a baby anymore,' Maggie told her one day across

41

the kitchen worktop. 'You're allowed to have fun, you know, to be young. You've done the hard part. Think about it – you could be anything you liked. You could go out. Meet someone maybe.'

Anna had balked at the thought at first. But as the weeks went on, the idea pushed its way to the front of her mind more and more. Until she found herself sneaking glances at young men across the freezer aisles, scanning them for wedding bands and trying to conjure up images of what they might look like naked.

Seed firmly planted, it was no great surprise to anyone when Anna received her first invitation to dinner. The only real surprise had been where it came from.

It was the annual school fete. A day which the other mothers treated with great reverence as they embarked upon laborious logistical planning sessions and jostled for pole position within the hierarchy of the St Winifreds set. There were myriad ways to peacock one's status, philanthropy and skills at these events.

Preparations would begin many months before in some households: the real queen bees would have prime position in the tea tent, manning the raffle or the tombola. The next tier belonged to the mothers at the trestle tables, basking in the accolades of their homemade jams and baked goods. At the lower end of the pecking order were those at the bric-a-brac stalls or overseeing the games.

Anna regarded the whole thing with utter disdain, and it would have been her preference to shun the day entirely for a glass of wine and a barbecue in the garden, but Louie's excitement was palpable. The children had spent the last few weeks of term making garlands and wreaths.

As they arrived side by side with the Maxwells, even Anna couldn't fail to appreciate the work that had obviously gone into the day. The Victorian building on its slate grey tarmac and the surrounding fields usually hotch-potched with pale faces and small bodies in matching slate-grey uniforms, was a kaleidoscope of bunting dancing in the breeze. A thousand tropical butterflies.

Squeals of delight fell from the mouths of the children zig-zagging around the maze of stalls, clutching ice creams and cakes. Families lolled around on deck chairs and blankets, spread out across the grass, chatting easily as the early summer sun beat down on their eggshell skin, heat flushing up collarbones and necks. Even Mr Kilpatrick had managed a smile today, in his silly boater hat.

All three boys made an instant getaway, loudly greeting their friends. Maggie and Anna browsed the stalls, giving out perfunctory greetings before they found themselves a spot on the field. Settled on the grass, they sipped at homemade pink lemonades.

Maggie, an old hand by now at these kinds of things, had brought along the prerequisite hip flask full of Cinzano which they clandestinely slopped into their lemonades all afternoon like a couple of wayward teenage girls. Anna, all elbows and knees in her denim cut-offs and ringer tee, Maggie in her loud paisley maxi dress and huge bosom.

As the afternoon wore on and the sun began its descent, the women realised they were as pissed as farts and had missed every one of the organised games scheduled. They pushed themselves up onto unsteady legs, and hooked arms, staggering across the grass in search of the sons they hadn't set eyes on for hours.

They clumsily navigated the sea of stalls, litter and sweaty bodies, hair stuck to necks and legs indented with blades of grass. The boys were to one side with the children of the other last stragglers, sat in a circle on a huge Moroccan style blanket singing giddily along to a man expertly playing knick knack paddy whack on a banjo. The man, Miss Lang and Miss Harper sat with their backs to them, leading the singing. The children were rosy with enthusiasm as they clapped their hands and knees in the right places.

Satisfied their charges were in good hands, they continued onwards to try and negotiate another couple of lemonades for the road as people wearily packed down stalls into the backs of estate cars. The stall owner glowed with pleasure as she informed them that, unfortunately, she had sold out hours ago, and she really had no idea quite how popular it would be.

'Next year, I'm going to have to make up double the batch!' she crowed as she wiped her brow and wound the window of her car up, the epitome of martyrdom.

Anna barely managed to conceal a vermouth belch with the back of her forearm as she started back towards Maggie to inform her of the unfortunate turn of events on the pink lemonade front. She looked left and right, seeing two's and three's per person, the sweltering summer dusk doing nothing to aid the recovery of her composure. She tried again more slowly and finally spotted flashes of tell-tale red and gold paisley fluttering from behind a tall tree to the far right of the playing field. As she got closer she could hear loud snorts of Maggie's laughter, and smelt the strangest smell.

Maggie was deep in conversation with the banjo man, passing a giant, sweet-smelling roll up between them. As she approached, Maggie stuck her head out from behind the tree. Mascara had sweated off in greasy rings around each eye, her cheeks were flushed and her beehive was leaning off to one side to such an extent that it might take the rest of her down with it at any moment.

'It's Anna!' she slurred in a loud stage whisper to Mr Banjo. Anna heard him laugh, and picking up on the discretionary air of the occasion, she slipped behind the trees too, wanting in on the secret.

'This iss my friend, Anna! Sh-she's Louie's mum, the child genius.' She continued, throwing out some ta-dah arms.

Anna bowed theatrically and the man looked amused. 'Who's your friend?' she nudged Maggie in an uncharacteristically brazen way, at which Maggie disintegrated into raptures.

'This is Mr Carmichael. Teddy's teacher,' Maggie went on. 'HE'S SINGLE!' she added in her stage whisper, attempting a wink that came off more as a blink. She sauntered off, hips swaying unsteadily across the field as Anna and Mr Carmichael spent a few silent minutes watching her go.

'Grayson, call me Grayson,' he said, extending a hand for her to shake.

She took it and grinned, brushing the ringlets of damp hair out of her eyes and behind her ears.

'Do you want some?' he proffered the giant roll up, which she took, being quite beyond rolling herself a cigarette at this point. The heat of the thing hit the back of her throat like a sandblast and she spent the next five minutes with her eyes watering, frantically trying to suppress a violent coughing fit as he carried on. 'I know Louie, he's a great kid. Bethany, uh, Miss Lang tells me he's very gifted. You must be very proud.'

There wasn't much Anna enjoyed more than listening to people wax lyrical about Louie, but she found that when they did so with a sing-song Scottish lilt, a strong jawline and waves of jet black hair, she enjoyed it even more.

'You don't look like a teacher,' she told him, and this made him laugh.

'So I'm told,' he replied, as he took a long draw on his suspicious cigarette. 'It wasn't the plan. I thought I was going to be a musician, you know, a composer, something like that. I started doing lessons for a few kids and enjoyed it. My dad back home, he knew Mr Kilpatrick and the rest is history. I like the kids. It's not like work. Although I'm winging it a bit on the maths front, the clientele are too young to realise so far. Don't tell anyone.'

Anna laughed, enchanted by this odd man. She lent her weight onto the closest tree, having been hit with a disquieting rush of dizziness and nausea.

She only managed to mutter, 'I won't', before she stalked off into the dusk to find her friend.

A pair of gently lined Angus eyes followed the length of her unsteady journey towards the wrought iron gates, where Maggie herded her and three boys deftly down the road and into the distance.

SEVEN

Mr Carmichael, 1969.

Anna had been successful in pushing all thoughts of her embarrassing liaison with Mr Carmichael out of her mind in the weeks that followed, run ragged by her restless four year old throughout the summer holidays. It was with a sigh of relief that Anna ferried him back to school when the next term began, having run dry of ways to stimulate his increasingly active mind.

As they began their walk towards home that first afternoon back, Louie chattering animatedly about his classmates' various exotic vacations, she heard her name being called in a familiar soft Scottish lilt. She stopped in her tracks and closed her eyes, the warmth of a thousand suns shining down on her, fingers tingling with anticipation.

As she swung around he was making a beeline for her, weaving his way through parents and children.

'Anna,' he said again, the same coy smile playing on his lips, leaning in closer. 'I was hoping I would bump into you today.'

Without the haze of the alcohol, Anna immediately saw

exactly what the other mothers must see in Mr Carmichael. He could only be mid-thirties, with hair falling in long black waves, a few stray greys at the temples, light crinkles around his eyes whenever he smiled. For just a second, the world stood still. She didn't notice the hawk-eyed gazes of the other mothers boring into her back, or Louie impatiently pulling at her hand.

Mr Carmichael, however, had. He glanced quickly over his shoulder and raised his hand to someone in greeting, before leaning in towards her and looking her dead in the eye; a co-conspirator.

'Could I take you for dinner one evening next week?' he said in a low voice, fingers lightly touching her upper arm.

She was stunned into silence with his confidence, and the electricity tingling up and down her arm from the spots his fingers had brushed. His eyes searched hers expectantly, and he raised his eyebrows as if to say, *well?* and stole a quick glance behind once more.

'Yes,' she finally said, 'Friday?'

'Friday at 7? I'll pick you up.'

She nodded in agreement and staggered away as a million questions criss-crossed around her mind. Where were they going? What should she wear? Was this *really* a good idea? Would Maggie have Louie? Of course she would. What the bloody hell would she wear? She'd have to buy something. What would they talk about? Would they kiss? Would they have sex?

Only being narrowly missed by an angry cyclist as she crossed the road snapped her out of her reverie, the cries of 'fucking blind bitch!' echoing down the road.

Friday at 7. She almost felt like hugging herself.

***

By the time 7pm had rolled around that Friday, the only thing Anna had left to be terrified of was the entire thing being an anti-climax. It had been built up to such an extent, dissected and speculated over to such a degree by both herself and Maggie, that every possible scenario had been explored at length.

Even the boys had been caught up in the excitement, Louie particularly. All three of them approved enormously, branding Mr Carmichael 'cool' and 'so awesome'. They had asked all kinds of questions, top of the list being would Mr Carmichael be coming over to see the model railway?

'He'd be very impressed, he'd probably like you more.' Teddy had told her very seriously.

At Maggie's insistence, Anna had visited the salon in town that Maggie frequented for a trim, blow dry and manicure. She was plucked, preened and oiled to a degree she hadn't realised was possible.

Anna viewed her new shaggy cut with awe, having no real idea how Swedish Jonah had fashioned this out of her chronic bedhead which she couldn't usually (and didn't often try to) get a brush through.

A short, emerald-green shift dress with strappy platforms had been the unanimous final decision on the outfit front, after having tried on what had felt like Maggie's entire wardrobe at least twice. Maggie advised Anna that it revealed just the right amount of her slender bronzed legs. Formal enough for dinner, trendy enough for a club.

She had sat for over an hour as Maggie had painted jet black kohl around her eyes and glossed her lips. She didn't even look like herself. She was magnificent.

'You are a vision,' he had whispered in her ear as he'd helped her into a black cab, and the hairs on the back of her neck had stood on end.

The evening had been perfect. They went to Ronnie Scott's, a little place in the middle of Soho that Anna had never heard of, for dinner and lots of drinks. He introduced her to jazz music – the love of his life – over oysters and champagne, a hat trick of firsts. He was interested, attentive and looked her straight in the eyes.

As the evening wore on and their confidence grew, they shared intimacies, glimpses into the people they were and had been, thighs and fingers meeting. They talked and danced until the early hours, until they tumbled through the front door of number thirty-two, and straight into her bed where they had stayed entangled until the birds sang in the sunrise and they gave in to sleep.

***

Less than a year after that first evening at Ronnie Scott's, on a cloudless day in August 1970, Anna was once again sat at Maggie's dressing table, eyes closed as she was powdered and glossed by her friend. This time, however, she was in white.

Grayson had gotten down on one knee only a few months prior, a rather unconventional proposal in the middle of a busy Brockwell Lido. Louie had been splashing around with a couple of school friends he had bumped into, Anna had been reclining on a sun lounger in her two-piece, enjoying what she had thought to be a companionable shared silence. Grayson had perched on the end of the lounger and taken hold of her hand.

'Anna…' he had said suddenly, 'who is Louie's father?'

She'd been waiting for this question to come for some time now, having concocted many different scenarios and excuses in her head to suit the narrative, to whip out when the issue finally reared its ugly head as it had always been destined to do. However, in real time, the weight of truth felt much heavier on her shoulders than she had accounted for.

'You want to talk about this here, in front of all these people?' she had hissed from under her huge sun hat.

'I need to know,' he had replied, solemnly.

'Peter Bennett. His name is Peter Bennett, and he doesn't want either of us. He never did.'

After a few torturous minutes of silence, Anna bracing herself for an onslaught of questions, she tentatively peeped out from under her sun hat, ready to face an inevitable expression of distaste. Grayson nodded, stood up and asked his next question.

'Ice cream?'

'Yes, please.' She had replied gratefully, and that had been that, case closed. And off he went to the ice cream kiosk. Louie's parentage, the defining moments of Anna's life, the smear and shame of her past, never to be spoken of again until much, much later when everything would finally unravel.

When he returned he plonked himself down on one knee on the wet tiles next to her. In his hand was a Mr Whippy cone with a chocolate flake, and balanced around the flake was a gold ring with the most exquisite yellow solitaire in the middle and two smaller diamonds either side, twinkling in the summer sun.

'I want you,' he had said, 'I want you both. Will you marry

me, Anna?'

She had bitten the end off of the flake and said yes.

A church wedding had been out of the question on account of Anna's status as an unwed mother. Churches were for blushing virgins and the upstanding men they were betrothed to, not abandoned teenage mothers and their son's class teacher. They had opted for an intimate registry office service. Anna would still wear white; cherry or no bloody cherry, this was still her first wedding.

She had chosen a long-sleeved, empire waisted ivory dress which fell just above the knee. Ringlets swept back from her face in an elegant twist, white t-bar heels and a fist-full of powder blue roses. She was radiant.

Louie, almost seven, was handsome in his miniature powder blue suit and matching blonde ringlets at her side, dimpled cheeks beaming from ear to ear. Grayson, true to form, had opted for an eccentric three piece suit in blue tartan, his hair slicked back with brylcreem into a pompadour style.

Maggie was her bridesmaid and she and the boys their only guests. Having no family of her own left to attend, Anna breathed a quiet sigh of relief when Grayson's mother had written from Aberdeen to say that she wouldn't be coming. She'd made it perfectly clear that she found her youngest son's marriage to a 'fallen woman' most distasteful.

A couple of cousins and an old school friend turned up in kilts, drinking the small pub where they'd booked the reception dry. Louie, Arthur and Teddy had been completely in awe of these exotic men with funny voices who wore skirts. All three decided that they wanted to be Scottish when they grew up, as long as they got their own sgian-dubhs.

They ate a roast lamb dinner with all the trimmings and retired back to Rosendale Road, where the men passed around spliffs and cigars over bottles of whisky in the dining room, and Grayson clumsily serenaded his new bride with an eclectic mix of Rolling Stones and Scottish folk songs. The Scots toasted the newlyweds to high heaven and it was universally agreed that the little wedding had been a shining success.

They set off for their honeymoon by coach the following day, slightly worse for wear. It had been decided that Louie would join them, and they spent the next week on the beaches of Devon eating chips and feeding coins into slot machines. By the time they alighted the train back at Paddington, they were a ready made family.

EIGHT

Widow, 2022.

nd that was it, thinks Anna from her spot on the hallway floor, one leg asleep. *That was it. Once he'd crossed the door of thirty-two, he never left, my lovely Grayson.* She still misses him every day, it never goes away, it still hurts. Not in the physically painful and sucker punch way that missing Louie hurts, but in a different way. A sad and resigned way, a gnawing kind of longing.

So much of this house and her possessions still remind her of him. She's never really changed anything since he went, reminders of him and the life they shared are everywhere. The shelves and pictures he'd put up. The dinner service his mother had sent from Scotland: a wedding gift. The crystal glasses they'd toasted their good fortune with, and later commiserated into.

Sometimes, she still fancies she can hear him tinkling on the baby grand as she walks past the dining room, pipe hanging lazily from one side of his mouth.

It's not been all bad. There have been good times too, she

tells herself, there is happiness mixed in amongst the chaos and despair that is absorbed in the fabric of these walls. She has plenty to be grateful for.

What on earth would he think if he saw me now? Anna wonders.

He'd remonstrate her for the state of this house for starters, never mind the state of her. He'd loved this house, he put his blood, sweat and tears into it. He'd fixed the place up from cellar to attic, indulging Anna's every whim when she got carried away with swatches and fabric samples. And helped her to fill it with even more laughter. And another pair of tiny pattering feet.

She still can't quite get her head around making decisions without him. He had been the grown up in the house, from the minute his boots had claimed their place at the head of the shoe rack, and she had been more than happy to have been relieved of that burden.

Anna has a sudden and primal urge to smell his smell.

She hauls herself up on the banister post and drags her fast asleep leg up the stairs. She heads straight into her bedroom, opening up the fitted wardrobes, the furthest door to the left. This end was his end, hers to the right. Most of his clothes and belongings were flung into bin sacks in a fit of angry despair at some point in the year of utter desolation after his death.

Anna's lost year.

She had surprised herself. Having dealt with all of the loss that had come before his, she hadn't expected to fall quite so comprehensively to pieces. To stay that way for quite so long. But she had. She had been irrational, entirely at sea without her husband by her side.

Now of course, she regrets the savage way in which she threw so much of his life into those sacks, screeching up kerbs to violently hurl them on the doorstep of Scope. Eyes pouring; a mad woman. After months of crying herself to sleep each night pressing half a dozen of his unwashed shirts to her face, she had woken up one morning *angry*. The shirts no longer smelled of him. His smell had gone. He had gone.

He'd left her, just like everyone else.

At the time, the purge had felt cathartic, but now she wishes she had more of him. A good deal of rummaging and wrestling later, she finds what she's looking for: a camel coloured, double-breasted, woollen pea coat. She'd teased him mercilessly every time he'd worn it. He had come downstairs one day in it, sporting a shark-collared shirt underneath and a fedora on his head, feeling quite Mick Jagger. She'd laughed until she'd curled into a ball on the floor, and peed a bit. How odd that out of everything, this is what she'd decided to keep.

She fingers the wool, noticing the frayed cuffs and tiny holes dotted around the lapels where the moths have feasted, deciding that she will indulge herself today, one last time, before she goes.

She removes the coat from the hanger and sits down on the bed with it, inhaling deeply. It smells musty and damp. She watches in the full length mirror as an unkempt old lady cradles a moth eaten coat as though it were a newborn, and weeps.

NINE

Empty, 2022.

With the help of Arthur, Anna has managed to sort through and clear much of the clutter in the hallway, downstairs cloakroom and the under stair cupboards. It had been a mammoth task for such a small square footage, but it has made all the difference to Anna's morale. She has been surprised at how much lighter she feels already, stepping into her entrance hall and no longer having to attempt the assault course of clutter to get to her kitchen.

She has learned a great deal about Arthur in the last week, Arthur the man. Arthur the boy she had known inside out: sweet natured and cripplingly shy. But Arthur the man, he is new, and not what she had expected.

What had once been timid is now quiet confidence. He is still kind. He is a support worker for a homeless charity in town, and much of Anna's excess he has taken into work where the less fortunate can make use of it. He doesn't eat meat, he tells her, he's an environmentalist. He is the most animated she has ever seen him as he tries to explain global warming and climate change to her, which she struggles to follow. He frequently extolls the virtues of green energy and electric vehicles. Anna smiles and nods.

Electric cars, whatever next? she wonders.

He doesn't have a wife, or a girlfriend at the moment, much to his mother's disappointment. There have been women, he tells her, but nothing has stayed the course. He doesn't have much time, he says, between work and his mother. He is in limbo, waiting for her to die.

But he is happy, and Anna is glad. At least somebody is.

'Where are you moving to?' he had asked her, and Anna hadn't the first clue. She has never been great at decisions, let alone big ones. Choosing which items are to be kept and which are to be thrown away has been difficult enough. But after a phone call from the estate agent, she now has a deadline: one week and two days for the house to be transformed from neglected hoarders lair to large Edwardian semi with potential.

Anna is on the landing again, coffee in one hand, bin bags in the other. There are two bedrooms to her left, two to her right and the bathroom straight ahead. Momentarily unable to choose which Pandora's box to lift the lid on first, she eeny meeny miney mo's. Decision made for her, she pushes open the furthest door to the left and pulls another set of curtains open and watches another lost room wake up to the first daylight it has seen in many years.

The walls are a deep mauve. 'Heather' the tin had said. They are a mishmash of lighter and darker patches, where posters of pop stars and heartthrobs had once rotated, spots left paintless by blu tack decades before. There is a deserted bed frame with a peacock rattan headboard and a bare mattress in the middle of the room, which has forgotten what the weight of a body feels like. The room which had once been teeming with makeup, ornaments, clothes discarded and flung onto every available space is now stark and naked.

A walnut dressing table with a huge built in mirror and matching stool stands against the wall closest to the window. A lone ornament, a little deer, stands sentry; a birthday present from Maggie, Anna vaguely recalls. She opens each drawer in turn and finds nothing except for a Rimmel lipstick from the 1980's, a ghoulish ice-pink.

The abandoned bedroom of her daughter somehow feels sadder than the abandoned bedroom of her son.

'Poor Ella.' she says out loud.

TEN

Daughter, 1971.

Ella Jean Carmichael entered the world on the evening of the 5th November, weighing 6lb and 7oz. As crowds clapped and cheered at London's skyline, lit up in a symphony of red, yellow and indigo, Anna lay simultaneously shivering and dripping with sweat in her hospital bed at St Thomas'.

She gazed unseeing, unmoved by the glittering swathes of colour and light dancing across the inky black surface of the Thames below. Behind her, a growing team of doctors and midwives worked furiously to breathe life back into her blue baby girl.

It had been a wrung out and traumatic birth. Anna's waters had broken in dramatic fashion in the middle of Mr Singh's convenience store. She'd had the shock of her life, dropping the contents of her basket all over the floor, as great gushes of amniotic fluid surged down her legs and down the aisle, jersey royals and cans of luncheon meat rolling all about the place.

She had slipped and slithered through the streams of liquid towards the till, trousers soaked and cheeks burning with embarrassment as she tried to explain her predicament to an increasingly irritated Mr Singh. Albeit not a man of many words, at least not many English ones, he was known locally as a very gracious proprietor and Anna was one of his regulars.

'You piss in my shop! You piss in my shop!' he announced in disbelief, volume increasing with each repetition, as he stared wide-eyed at the sodden crotch of Anna's bell bottoms. It wasn't until Mrs Singh appeared from the stock room, an angel with a bindi, that the misapprehension was untangled and Anna was ushered to a seat by the door and her husband alerted.

She'd sat in a daze, heart thumping, a commotion of Punjab going back and forth over her head until the door had chimed at the arrival of a frantic Grayson. He had practically volleyed her into the passenger seat of his red Ford Cortina and whisked her off to the hospital.

The labour had been nothing like the one she'd experienced as a seventeen-year-old with Louie. Both times it had hurt, of course. Anyone who says it doesn't is lying. But Anna hadn't remembered it being this unbearable, the hours seeming to stretch into days, the pain rendering her delirious. She fancied it would be less painful to bite through her own tongue at points.

It was a back labour, the midwife informed her, the baby was back to front so it probably would be a little more tender. She had frantically sucked at the gas and air, teeth clamped, her entire body trembling.

The intensity of the pain had been so all encompassing

that Anna had begun to hallucinate. At first, the ceilings had started to splinter and crack, the walls shuddering around her. She'd blinked furiously, swiping at the sweat streaming into her eyes, looking upwards.

Hovering directly above her bed was her mother, a person whose face she only knew from photographs. She had died as a result of the complications of Anna's own birth, yet here she was, a look of mirth on her face. Anna reached out her hands, so tangible was this vision just out of arm's reach. This apparition had made Anna laugh hysterically. Of course! How had she been so blind? Of course! This had been written on the wall as clear as day. The sheer audacity of them painting the nursery and poring over tiny white booties suddenly became quite hilarious. *I am going to die today*, Anna panted in cold acceptance over and over again through her double vision, *I am going to die today, I'm marching to my own death.*

Twelve hours of grunting and straining later, when Anna was quite sure her heart had already combusted in her chest cavity and she had ground every one of her teeth into a sandy paste, concerned murmurs became shouts of alarm. Equipment beeping, men in white coats appeared brandishing stainless steel torture devices.

They had sliced and diced and heaved at Anna's insides with comedy-sized barbecue tongs until out popped a tiny baby girl, stone cold, a deep shade of mottled indigo with an umbilical cord looped twice around her neck, an angry pulsing noose.

The men in white coats had taken the baby away and the remaining nurses or midwives had mopped Anna's brow, pushing sugary cups of tea under her nose as they'd sat between her shaking legs with their needle and thread and stitched her back together like an inseam pocket.

Grayson had been brought back in then, ashen faced, stroking her hair and whispering things that Anna couldn't quite catch the thread of.

His anguished face was the thing that Anna remembered as a cocktail of drugs were mercifully administered and she and her bruised and throbbing vagina were knocked out cold.

When her eyes next opened, there was daylight. She was breathing, she was a cat, she had used her eighth life. The bloodied bedsheets were gone and cards and flowers had replaced the kidney dish of metal instruments on the table to the right of her. Her husband was at her left hand side, wiping a tear from his eye with his fingers and next to him was a cot holding a small bundle of daisy patterned blankets.

'It's a girl,' he whispered as he kissed her forehead.

'Oh,' she replied.

Anna was discharged the following week with strict instructions to get plenty of rest and not to exert herself, which would have seemed quite ridiculous had she not been in the care of such a forward thinking spouse.

Grayson was every inch the proud husband and doting father, not at all fazed by changing nappies or leaking breasts, very modern for a man of the early seventies. Anna would have floundered without him, she realised later. He kept them all afloat on the stormy seas of the fourth trimester.

It was only when she watched Louie hold his baby sister for the first time in the living room at number thirty-two, his little face full of wonder as he stroked the baby's cheeks and her tiny fingers gripped his, that Anna had finally cried. She had been hit by the dawning realisation that she might never have seen him again, seen him graduate or marry, her beautiful boy.

Nothing in the world was worth that, she thought, spitefully, nothing at all.

Anna hadn't moved from their bed for a fortnight, citing exhaustion and soreness every time her husband gently tried to encourage her downstairs for a meal he had cooked, or for a walk with her children. She had very little interest in the new arrival and had only held her once. She had handed her back as though she were a burning ember and had avoided her ever since. She was dismayed by the sense of detachment she felt, stung by the lack of likeness. This tiny stranger was nothing like her, nothing like Louie. This baby had brown eyes and a shock of black hair. It had nothing of either of them. No dimples, no soft angular nose. Was this actually her baby, she wondered, had there been a mistake? Grayson was the one who made up the powdered milk, did the night feeds, became master of the terry cloth nappy. He sang her to sleep, burped her, carried her around in the nook of his arm and eventually he named her, too. Ella, after his beloved Ella Fitzgerald, the first lady of song, and Jean for her middle name in homage to Anna's dead mother. A beg for clemency from an angry ghost.

The maternity nurse was called in due course, Grayson's concern mounting.

'A touch of the baby blues,' the silly roly-poly woman had told them, 'perfectly normal.'

Anna was quick to agree, and, feeling the pressure, left the cocoon of her bed and joined the household again. She went through the motions, pitched in with Ella's care, robotically changing nappies and feeding her, but the truth sat heavy like a stone in the pit of her stomach: she didn't love this baby. She felt nothing.

The moment she had first clapped eyes on Louie, she had been overwhelmed with pure love, from the top of her head to the tips of her toes. She had known as sure as the sky was blue that they were soulmates. He had slid into the world with ease, had fed from her breast until he could walk, had been at her side every hour of every day, blonde curls nestled into her bosom. He had seemed to return her gaze with just as much love in his eyes as she had in hers from the word go.

But this raven haired baby was different. This baby squawked and screeched, arched her back and lay awkwardly in Anna's arms, stiff as a board. Grayson was the only one who could soothe her. When he returned to work, she wailed for hours and Anna threw her at him and fled up the stairs the moment he walked back through the door each day.

The thing that grated upon Anna the most was the way that Ella infringed upon the precious little time she spent with Louie, before and after school. Should Anna be over-seeing bath time or reading his bedtime story, inevitably the screeching would begin until it became louder and louder, impossible to ignore. Time and time again Anna would roll her eyes and begin the walk towards the Moses basket, tension mounting, jaw taut with irritation.

Eventually, she confided in Maggie. After enduring a morning's bout of particularly fervid screaming, she stomped into Maggie's kitchen and flung the baby into her lap.

'Take her!' she demanded, unwashed hair jutting out at all angles, purple ringed eyes with a crazed look about them, 'before I dump her in a fucking bin in Clapham Common!'

'I'll save you the trouble of an alibi and a fake ransom

demand.' Maggie said wryly, lifting Ella up onto her shoulder and circling her tiny back with the palm of her hand. Ella let out a giant belch and fell asleep instantly.

'I did that! I already did that! I did everything!' lamented Anna in despair, wiping salty tears roughly from her eyes with her knuckles.

Maggie deftly re-swaddled the sleeping Ella and handed her back to Anna.

'You're stressed and tired, that's all. She can tell.'

Anna looked into Ella's sleeping face, tiny lips pursed, still flushed from the melodramatics. 'She hates me.'

'Don't be silly, of course she doesn't. She loves you. You're her mother. Here, calm down, you just need a really good sleep.' Maggie insisted as she poured them both a brandy from her crystal decanter.

'She does, Mags. She does nothing but screech at me all day long, nothing I ever do is right. The thing is, I hate her too.'

Anna knocked back her brandy in one gulp and held her tumbler out for more.

Maggie eyed her friend with caution and took in the pallor of her skin, the livid purple rings around her eyes, her chapped nose and lips. She took the baby back onto her shoulder and led her friend towards the sofa and instructed her to close her eyes. She slept for fourteen hours.

As Ella got older, it became easier. She eventually grew out of being an angry little goblin and turned into a curious toddler, and Anna's resentments began to subside while her tolerance for the cuckoo in her nest began to grow. The chasm between Anna and her daughter dissipated as a routine emerged. Life limped onwards in the Carmichael household, much to Grayson's relief.

Anna enrolled Ella into the local day nursery as soon as she could sit upright, and her life became a whirlwind of school runs and nursery drop offs, dinners and bedtime scuffles. She acknowledged the divide under her roof, the contrast in the feelings she had towards her two children but she left herself no time to dwell on it. What was the point? Nobody would understand. She couldn't force herself to adore Ella, nor could she hold a gun to Ella's head and force her to love her in return. She resolved to always be mindful of treating them fairly; to do the same for both children as far as was possible. She may not take the same pleasure in spending hours reading picture books with her daughter the way she had with her son, but she would do it anyway. It was fair.

The disparity between the siblings grew by the day. Where Louie had hit all his milestones early, Ella did everything frustratingly slowly. By the time Louie had walked and talked, Ella was still a gurgling lump sat around on the floor. Seven year old Louie had an endless supply of patience for his accident prone little sister who courted chaos everywhere she went. Anna felt she was forever on the receiving end of judgmental stares and concerned whispers, always the mother pushing the pram of the toddler with great ugly bruises and scrapes all over her face.

Ella's clumsiness was infuriating.

The main thing that Anna found irritating about Ella was her lack of joy. She was content, sure, but her eyes never really lit up the way Louie's had at the same age. He had gazed in wonderment at the tiniest of things: a wren on the garden wall, a paper bag floating on the breeze, the crunch of a leaf underfoot on a frosty day. Ella was much harder to please, particularly for Anna. She seemed to spend all day saving up every one of her smiles and laughs like golden tickets for her father and brother.

As the years went by, Anna simply stopped trying. Every rejection stung. It had felt like a long series of favours and services that Anna was bestowing upon Ella day to day. From the meals she made to the park trips, hours spent colouring and crafting, sitting on her bedroom floor until her knees ached brushing the tails of her thousand toy ponies... and for what? It wasn't like Anna *wanted* to do these things. These hours spent were Anna's attempts at bonding with her daughter, trying to get to know and understand her, trying to raise a smile here and there. Her efforts were continually met with little more than nonchalance.

Her father and brother would arrive home later and join the tail end of the painting or pony brushing that Anna had been the co-participant in moments prior and be met with unabashed joy. Ella's eyes crinkled in delight as she launched into lengthy monologues about people and places that Anna never seemed to be granted permission to be party to.

'Fuck your silly fucking ponies,' she would seethe under her breath as she left the room, swearing that tomorrow she wouldn't bother trying.

And then one day she didn't: she retreated. It was a moment of acceptance. Knowing that the damage had been done to their relationship in the early weeks and months following Ella's birth, rendering it impossible to repair, Anna simply got on with her life.

Of course, meals were prepared, faces washed, laundry done, school uniforms pressed neatly at the end of beds. To the outside world they were a nice, normal family. It was only inside the walls that the elephant in the room lingered.

The females engaging in a strange dance, sidestepping one another in corridors, polite smiles tweaked and perfected. The males, perplexed by the awkward dynamic, too gutless to confront the issue. And so the years flew by uneventfully, small and large resentments bubbling beneath the surface, slowly becoming a normal part of the fabric of their lives.

ELEVEN

Regret, 2022.

Anna replaces the ceramic deer she has been fingering, a ripple of discomfort at the memories shuddering up her spine.

She'd never really known her only daughter. It's one of her life's great disappointments, and also regrets. She had always viewed Ella as secretive, had never quite been able to reach her, always hovering just out of grasp. Even as a small baby.

Of course, that type of ailment of the mind has all kinds of names these days. Postnatal depression, postpartum psychosis Jenni Murray had called it, something like that. Anna had sat to attention at her kitchen table, ears pricked and back ramrod straight and soaked in every word the day she happened upon that particular special on Women's Hour. There had been lots of call-ins that day, and the presenters had urged each woman to 'ask for help' and called for healthcare professionals to be vigilant in recognizing the signs in new mothers.

There was treatment now, there were pills and counselling.

Not in my day, thought Anna. That ship has sailed. Sailed and sunk, languishing at the bottom of the ocean, a great anemone-covered heap of rust.

But you were the adult, she admonishes herself, it was your responsibility. You were the mother. She has wondered often if things might have played out differently had she been able to connect the pieces of this particular puzzle. It's something she is resigned to never being sure about.

The rest of the room is empty, Ella had packed her belongings and left long ago. A thief in the night, never to return.

All of the furniture can go to the women's refuge Arthur had been telling her about. But she will keep hold of the deer, just in case.

TWELVE

Arthur, 2022.

Arthur arrives the next morning to check on her progress and lend a hand. He is concerned about the strange old lady who rattles around in the house next door to his mother. It's impossible to ignore how alone she is in the world, and he feels a sense of responsibility towards her.

It's his day off today and he's been to see his mother already, glad she is safely ensconced in The Cedars, surrounded by catheters and toothless smiles. Anna's house is a mausoleum in comparison.

He has brought his laptop with him so Anna can begin to have a look at where she might like to move to. But no matter how hard she squints at it, the shapes on the screen are fused and tangled. What is wrong with bloody brochures, something you can hold in your hands? She wonders in irritation.

She has been irritable all morning. She slept terribly, clammy and claustrophobic in her bed, suddenly hyper aware of her unwashed sheets and the cloying smell of damp. The night too still, too silent. Unwanted memories had run riot and she had woken this morning both exhausted and vexed.

'If it was insured, I'd just bloody torch the place,' she mutters, picturing the scene. A lit match through the brass letter box. Flames licking up the heavy drapes. Curls of smoke and ash billowing in great spirals through the sky. The roof caving in and each ghost sprinting for freedom.

She unearths an ancient bottle of whisky from the pantry – sticky with dust – and splashes the dregs into the coffee she is nursing. She knocks it back and plonks herself down at the table.

Arthur laughs.

'It's hard work, a lot of bloody hard work! I'm an old lady!' she chastises him, irked by his good humour. 'I don't need any of these things, I would be perfectly happy to start all over again somewhere else, I don't care where… It's the *guilt*, Arthur. I feel like I'm throwing things away that aren't mine, even though I know nobody is coming back for them.' she rubs her temples. 'It's exhausting.'

Arthur feels a wave of sympathy for the hard-nosed pensioner sat in front of him, a different animal altogether than the Anna Carmichael he knew as a boy. She has been many things, she was the young one, the fun one, the one who didn't mind the mess or the noise. Later on, perhaps she was more uptight, a little less forgiving. And after *it* happened, she sort of disappeared, morphing into the bitter and gnarled old lady who sits in front of him. Life has taken its toll.

'They're only things, Anna. I can help you,' he tells her, gently.

She leads him up the stairs and he notes the unnatural tilt

of them, the upended boards and splintering handrail. It is a far cry from the last time he made this journey, so many years ago. Whoever buys the place will have their work cut out.

She stops on the landing and gestures to her childrens' childhood bedrooms.

'Have a look, see if any of the furniture will be of use to any of your unfortunates.'

Arthur smiles at Anna's political incorrectness and in-stinctively walks straight into the back bedroom, a room in which he spent many hours of his formative years. He is not immune to the shock of the lack of life in here. He blinks, trying to get his bearings.

The bed has been moved into the corner. He is oddly placated to see that the frame is still covered in stickers. It's sitting in the spot where their electric guitars – their pride and joy – and amps used to live right next to Louie's hi-fi system.

Maggie had reluctantly conceded to his constant badgering one Christmas and he'd awoken to a rosewood Fender Stratocaster wrapped in gold ribbon, the most beautiful thing he'd ever seen in his short life. The guitar went with him next door that day and Louie's bedroom officially became teen rocker headquarters.

Louie had a natural aptitude for music, playing his guitar or any instrument he could lay his hands on, spending hours downstairs with his step father on the piano. Music had been a love they had shared throughout his childhood.

Arthur had had to work hard to keep up. As with every-thing in life, he was always a step behind his friend, but he hadn't minded. Louie was an excellent musician, without ever seeming to try. Arthur had been a content and loyal sidekick, it had never made him like Louie any less.

Until it did.

The bureau and chest of drawers – once a dumping ground for homeless, music-related junk – are in the same place, notes Arthur. Both have seen better days, scarred and scratched, but good solid pieces nonetheless. Nothing a good sand and oil wouldn't fix.

'Are you sure?' he asks Anna. 'It's good stuff, this. You could probably make a few hundred quid if you put it on eBay or Marketplace. Mid-century furniture is popular again now, plenty of people would bite your hand off.'

Anna has no idea which bay or market he is talking about. She shakes her head.

'I don't need the money,' she tells him, and she doesn't, not really. Polly from the bank appears to have taken some sort of pity on her, granting her a payment holiday until the house is sold.

In curiosity, she has perused the windows of the estate agents on her way to buy a loaf of bread a few times now. She has seen houses like hers – replicas in layout at least – a mere couple of streets away going for extortionate sums of money. She'd had to ask a passer-by: 'How many zeros is that, dear? Are you *sure*?'

Of course, hers would need considerable modernisations, but still. These kinds of figures were more money than she'd ever dreamed of. More money than she would ever need at almost seventy.

'Well, thank you,' he mumbles, and sits down on the edge of the bed, running a hand through his mousey hair.

Anna sits down next to him. 'It's unnerving, isn't it?' she

ventures. 'I'd never understood that a *room* could be dead, but somehow, it is...'

Arthur is beginning to feel a little peaky.

'Of course, he loved covering everything with his silly stickers and attacking things with his compass. It will cost you some hours in elbow grease before you can pass them on.'

They sit side by side lost in their thoughts for a few moments more, each re-living their own moments within these walls. Then they make their way down the hall to Ella's old bedroom, smaller in size and even more stark.

The heat creeps up the back of Arthur's neck, as if he's doing something he shouldn't be, assaulted by a far more cumbersome and complex set of memories in here.

He'd always known deep in his heart that with Louie, there was nothing he could have done or said. But with Ella, there probably was. He could just never pin down what.

***

Arthur is walking at a brisk pace, he doesn't know where to. He'd made a hasty retreat, wittering ten to the dozen about a mate with a van and having a few bits to do for work. He needs to clear his head. He is struggling to fathom the feelings he is experiencing: the anxiety and the guilt. The capable, solvent, patient Arthur in his middle fifties has been transported back to the anxious teenager he had once been.

He thought he had laid these demons down to rest, but here they are, following him down the high street, breathing heavily down his collar.

He sits down outside a nearby café and hastily orders an

americano, a drink he doesn't even much like. He needs to be alone with these fresh waves of devastation. Letting them take him wherever he needs to go before he can set foot through the yellow door again and put the beds in which they'd once lain into the back of a transit.

He needs to exorcise his conscience one last time, go through it all step by step. He needs to be sure.

Maybe he had always been a little bit jealous of Louie, underneath the surface. It would only have been natural. Of course it has its difficulties, growing up side by side with a child prodigy... So handsome, amiable, unruffled. Everybody loved him.

Especially me, thinks Arthur, we were practically brothers. He was more of a brother to me than Teddy ever was.

They had trodden very different paths, Arthur and Teddy. They had been opposites all of their lives, personality wise. Teddy the dominant, petulant smart alec. Arthur, the docile, people pleasing straggler. The gap widened as they grew. When Teddy had left St Winnifreds at 11, he had gone straight to boarding at Lancing without a backward glance. When Maggie had queried this decision over dinner one evening, Teddy had looked at her over his green beans like she had taken a turd on the centrepiece.

'You don't have to go to Lancing just because your father did, Teds. There are other great schools too, you know. You could take the eleven plus, you're more than smart enough. The grammar school is excellent and only up the road. You could walk it, stay close to your friends. You should have a think about it.'

'Of course I'm smart enough, but why would I bother?' he had retorted arrogantly, 'Plenty of lads in my year are smart enough too, but they couldn't afford a term at Lancing. Why wouldn't I want the best if I have the best as an option?'

Arthur sat there, chewing, listening to his brother quote their father verbatim, having been party to the many monologues they had endured about the world class tutors, the brotherhood, the best days of his life. He inwardly cringed for his mother, and wondered why she bothered. His older brother idolized Walter and hung on his every word, managing to omit his every transgression from his stream of consciousness entirely.

There had been a notable increase in the regularity of said transgressions since Oksana had become the new Mrs Maxwell the year before. Missed parents evenings, birthdays, let downs for pick ups when it was his weekend… they had become so commonplace that he didn't even *have* a weekend anymore, the boys mostly considered that they probably wouldn't be spending the weekend in Holland Park and made other plans which would then be re-jigged at the last minute should their father deign to turn up for them in his Jaguar XJS. There had been only once when Teddy had expressed any anger towards Walter. It had been his school graduation, before he was to start at Lancing. True to form, Walter had assured his son that he wouldn't miss it and he had of course, missed it. Oksana had taken one of her 'funny turns' he had explained to Maggie over the phone. He couldn't possibly leave her.

'She has rather a lot of *funny turns* for an otherwise healthy twenty six year old, doesn't she? I suggest you take her to see a specialist. Get to the bottom of her mysterious ailment before your sons have forgotten your name.' she had responded, and neatly slammed down the receiver.

When he picked them up the following weekend, Teddy had sulked theatrically and stared out of the window, not saying a word.

'Don't be like that, old boy. You know how women can be, especially these feisty eastern Europeans. There is a price to pay for a prize like Oksana, and one has to pick their battles, sometimes.'

The only thing his father ever *picked,* Arthur had thought, was Oksana.

'But I promised Richard Mather he could ride home in your car.' whined Teddy churlishly.

'Well, let's swing by his mothers', see if your pal's available for a milkshake and a cruise, shall we? See if we can't find you chaps some stunning blondes of your own to keep you busy.'

Teddy had smirked, Arthur had winced. Imagine choosing Oksana over his lovely mother. She didn't always look like she had stepped from the pages of a magazine. No, Arthur had seen the dark bags under her eyes like stains, the oily roots when she was overdue her bi-weekly salon visit. He had heard her scream and curse at his father, heard the threats she made in broken English. She always smelled faintly of booze, she never rose from her bed before 11am and she always forced upon them those awful fake kisses on both cheeks leaving their school collars thick with streaks of yellow make-up. Arthur certainly didn't see the appeal. He endured the weekends he did turn up out of politeness and duty. He could never wait to get back to Rosendale Road and give Maggie all the details, the names they had called one another, the stacks of empty bottles next to the bins.

And so off Teddy had gone to Lancing like his father before

him, waving to his mother and brother as though he was accepting an Oscar in the passenger seat of the Jaguar, the cat that got the cream. Walter had made a huge show of the handing over of his engraved pocket watch and leather trunk to his 'son and heir', which Maggie had thought quite insensitive.

They stood on the pavement waving robotically until the car rounded the bend. False smiles are painful, especially extended ones, a matter of stamina.

'Looked a bit of a tosser in that uniform, didn't he?' she whispered, squeezing his shoulders and they had both fallen about laughing. Teddy's departure had lifted the atmosphere in number thirty, they had both relaxed. They didn't bother with the dining room anymore, they ate on their laps in front of the television, Maggie safe in the knowledge that reports of freezer dinners would no longer make their way to Holland Park.

He had come home every other weekend regaling them with tales of Lancing. He was now rubbing shoulders with landed gentry and it quickly became clear that his main motivation for coming home was to boast about it. His friends now had names like Jasper and Sebastian with country piles and legions of hired help. Interestingly, their father became far more accessible on his weekends, keen to take his 'chip off the old block' along with him for a few cheeky ones with 'the old boys'. Even Oksana had become more accommodating, to Teddy at least, having come to understand his loyalty was now firmly seeded north of the river.

When it had been Arthur's graduation the next year, the only thing he had been certain of was that he did not want

80

to become a Lancing boy. His father had been incredulous, throwing around words like 'soft'. He would take the eleven plus like Louie and hope for the best.

He had never been naturally bright, but he was a hard worker. He tried. When he didn't get in, he had been devastated. Maggie had sat cradling him for hours with the rejection clutched to his chest, tears rolling down his cheeks. He hadn't scored high enough. He was clever, but just not quite clever enough. By six percent it turned out. There had never been any question about Louie winning a place.

The only way for Arthur to attend Dulwich College was for him to go in as a boarder and pay the fees. Maggie had fought tooth and nail for Walter to agree to pay.

'If you can pay £6,000 a term for one son at Lancing, you can pay less than half of that for the other at Dulwich College,' she had hissed down the phone at him.

Eventually, she had worn him down and Arthur would start the following term in a blue striped blazer, his best friend at his side.

It was in these blue stripes that they would slowly become men.

I grew into my own skin there, Arthur thinks. He had gone from anxious compliance to forming ideas and opinions during those years. He had emerged from the shadows, still sensitive but now with a quiet confidence, finally at ease with himself. He went back to Rosendale Road every weekend, never to his father's, and Teddy's visits the other way petered down into monthly appearances for Sunday dinners thick with tension. Their allegiances solidified, battle lines had been drawn, minus the battle. It all became very genteel, very British. Arthur would answer the occasional obligatory phone calls from his dad and report any news he felt would please him, and Walter would respond with 'good for you, old boy' and continue to send the cheques. It was a situation that probably brought them all a modicum of relief.

Without the taunts and sneers of his elder brother echoing behind him in the corridors, Arthur had found his place in the world. He and Louie had remained partners in crime, both well liked. Arthur was studious, Louie was the loveable rogue. He never quite got the hang of the tie or punctuality but he always landed on his feet. He could talk himself out of a detention in less than thirty seconds, the rumour went. They did almost everything as a pair. Wherever Louie went, Arthur was too. Louie often loitered around in the dorms after school, keeping Arthur company in the laundry room or in the dining hall.

'Making a nuisance of yourself here again I see, Carlton.' Matron would say, acknowledging his breach of the rules but never quite having the heart to do anything about it.

Arthur would abscond home every few nights also. At first there were rounds of frantic phone calls, a boarder gone missing… and being found at home in his bed. Eventually the calls stopped. If they want to pay for boarding and not actually eat the meals or sleep in the bed, why stop them had been the general consensus, and so it went. Secretly, Maggie had been thrilled at her youngest wanting to stay at home whilst the empty bed at Dulwich College burnt a hole in Walter's pocket.

Their adolescent years had passed easily, nothing beyond the usual mischief that was to be expected at an all boys school. In those days, everything was rather more PG than it is for teenagers now, Arthur thinks. A constant stream of practical jokes, teasing, the smuggling of dirty magazines. The wildest act they had ever partaken in back then was their first experiment with pot, and that had been on home turf in Grayson's study as he tried to extol the virtues of The Dark Side of the Moon. He would play the record on repeat as their heads swam with a heady mix of indica, puberty and psychedelic rock. Anna had popped her head around the door at one point and rolled her eyes. Arthur still doesn't really understand Pink Floyd, that album still reminds him of heart palpitations. The fact that he was getting high with a man who had once been his school teacher hadn't been lost on him. He had concluded that Grayson was very cool indeed, poles apart from his own father. Another area of life that Louie had been lucky in, like a black cat.

Girls had remained a mystery for the most part due to them having such finite contact with the opposite sex. In many ways, it was a blessing. They had been spared the mortification of voices breaking, greasy testosterone pimples, fortuitous erections in the form room. The only knowledge they had of the opposite sex had come courtesy of their mothers, the odd female teacher and Matron, none of which inspired any romantic connotations.

When they were in their fourth year, the headmaster, old Mr Bowen had retired. A much feared but rarely seen ex military man, he was rumoured to have fossilized right there in his oxblood captains chair, maybe even some years before. The younger and more liberal Mr Fitzgerald was brought in, and many of the silly and archaic rules about hair lengths and collars had been relaxed, and slowly but surely, the place was modernized. Huge, menacing oil paintings of the original owners of the turreted manor house turned school, complete with hunting dogs that had loomed over the huge dining tables in the hall were sent to the basement and replaced by much brighter murals. The dawning of this new age brought about another first: socials. Suddenly there were mixers in the calendar. Each term the girls from the corresponding grammar school would arrive on coaches for some kind of dinner or dancing. Everyone had been in uproar, the teaching staff divided. The more conservative members of the faculty felt that Mr Fitzgerald was asking for trouble. The rest felt it a breath of fresh air and a wonderful way for the otherwise cossetted boys to learn how to conduct themselves amongst the fairer sex.

The first of these events had been a painstaking affair. They had been fifteen at the time and entirely out of their depth. A long line of girls had traipsed stiffly into the old hall, skirts around their calves, eyes to the ground. It had taken over an hour for the first inter sex interaction to take place, teachers watching avidly on as though it were some kind of social science experiment.

The one to take the bull by the horns had been Marcus Percival, the star of the rugby team, his meaty torso a perfect triangle. He was the eldest son of a famously crooked investment banker and was every bit as cocksure. After nearly eighty minutes of dithering on both sides of the invisible line on the hall floor, having identified the rose amongst the thorns he clumsily ambled over to her and asked her to dance. The heavily fringed young girl smugly accepted, and the rest of the rugby team had followed suit shortly after. By the time Louie and Arthur had mustered up the guts, the pickings were slim and they ended up with a pair of gangly bespectacled chess aficionados as dance partners for the evening, vowing to get in there earlier next time.

By the third or fourth such event, most of the boys were dab hands, a regular bunch of Casanovas in their ill fitting blazers. Snogs and fumbles in corridors and behind the podium became commonplace and the dorms were rife with tales of the saucier exploits claimed to have taken place. Many boys had gone the route of going steady with one particular girl, the feeling being that this was the quickest route to the ultimate triumph that was losing their virginities. There had even been a virginity sweepstake put together.

Louie had been the first to do it, and he had done it with all of his usual panache. Arthur remembers it like it was yesterday, all of it. The adrenaline high on the night itself and the mayhem that had followed in its wake. The twinkle in Louie's eye that Arthur could never be sure had been there before the act or not. And the gaping hole it had left in Arthur's own heart.

It had been Bonnie Charlesworth, and she had signalled the beginning of the end, like a foghorn on an empty winters' night.

II

Part Two

Louie

THIRTEEN

The dance, 1983.

I t was the end of year party on the final day of term in 1983, the most revered and most formal of all of the socials in the school calendar.

The air had been laced with anticipation, classrooms and corridors echoing with misogynistic jeers and goading, the day long. Louie had stolen into the dorms at the close of the last lesson – a stowaway – to join Arthur and the other boarders in illicit pre-party drinks.

There was Greg, the stereotypical Welsh rugby lad and Tim, a pock-marked Jewish maths genius from Fulham. Louie had swiped various bottles from his parents' drinks cabinet before he left for school that morning and smuggled them into his locker for safe keeping until the final bells rang and they could disappear upstairs to begin preparations.

There were three boys to a room in the latter two year groups which Arthur had found far more palatable than the twelve bed cattle barn he had been in in the years prior.

It still baffled him whenever he walked past an open door

to the younger boys' dorms. How on earth had he gotten a wink of sleep surrounded by eleven other pubescent boys? And the smells, my God, the smells. But somehow he had, and the smaller rooms with their iron bed frames, a single sink in the corner and the fumes of only three bodies melding into the atmosphere, felt like a night at The Ritz.

The boys spent the early evening jostling for stints in the single mirror in the room. Peach fuzz cheeks slapped liberally with Aqua Velva, four heads of shaggy hair swept and sprayed so voraciously that they had to open a window.

Louie dumped his rucksack down on Arthur's bed and emptied its contents whilst the others gathered around to inspect his wares.

'I just grabbed a few from the back while they were having breakfast, so they wouldn't notice,' he said, by way of explanation.

The others eyed the eclectic haul warily. Four bottles of Babycham, a bottle of Artemi dry gin and a half drunk bottle of Bell's. They vaguely understood that whisky was something that dads drank in back rooms at birthday parties, but the other bottles were a mystery.

No matter, contraband was contraband, and the icing on the cake was the pre-rolled joint Louie had managed to light-finger from Grayson's tobacco tin in his desk drawer.

They sat huddled around Arthur's bed, slugging great gulps of the various spirits from smoked coffee glasses with the bottles nestled safely beneath the sheets.

At 6pm they descended the stairs with the hordes of other rowdy boarders. Sticking at the back, Louie and Arthur side stepped through the porter's doors and melted away into the sharp night air. They crouched behind the sports sheds in the quad like outlaws, fumbling with matches and taking hurried drags of the joint.

They could hear the music and the chatter, yellow light spilling from the windows of the great hall, casting long shadows across the lawns. Arthur's lasting memory is of how clear the night sky was. He had never seen quite so many stars.

By the time they joined their peers with glassy, red-rimmed eyes, Culture Club was pumping through the speakers and the party was in full swing. The entire back wall had been taken up by trestle tables laden with enormous bowls of punch and a buffet.

Foil-fringed curtains hung across the walls with the light from the fairy lights overhead bouncing off the mirrored disco ball. Round tables were dotted about the edges of the room as though there had been a wedding, girls decked out in puff-sleeved taffeta, chattering and dancing.

Arthur and Louie milled around laughing hysterically at the slightest thing, greeting friends and acquaintances. Many other parents' drinks cabinets had been raided that night too, the undercurrent heavy with alcohol and testosterone.

The party was getting rowdier by the minute. Shirts were unbuttoned, sleeves rolled up and the dance floor was heaving with sweaty bodies. The punch had been laced with a concoction of whatever contraband spirits still remained.

Marcus Percival, the school's star winger on the rugby team, stood over the punch bowl with his tie wrapped around his head, his booming laugh the only thing that could be heard over the music. He had claimed Lucy Heathcote-Ross as his steady girlfriend in the early rounds of socials. Lucy had straight and silky chestnut brown hair that swished when she walked, huge brown eyes, the kind of hourglass figure that was sexual napalm to a teenage boy and was tipped to be the next head girl. Her father owned casinos in Mayfair and her mother had been a famous socialite back in the 60's, and she knew everything about everyone. She stomped over to him, bottom lip protruding and began to simper.

'Marcuuu-uuus,' she whined in her nasally West London tone. 'I want to *dance.* Everyone is *dancing,* you know how I love the Bee Gees and we're missing it.'

Arthur watched Marcus shuffling awkwardly on the spot.

'I feel like I'm the only girl in the room not dancing.' she pouted, looking up at him pleadingly from beneath her lashes.

'Come on then,' he sighed, grabbing her hand and heading towards the dance floor. She squealed with glee and did an odd half walk, half shimmy.

As she passed Arthur she turned her head, smiling. 'Oh, look after Bonnie, she's new!'

Arthur turned around in confusion and standing only a foot behind him was the most beautiful creature he had ever laid eyes upon. Golden hair cascaded down to her waist and baby blue eyes, huge and twinkling, shone in her perfect, china doll face. She stood, smiling slightly, completely at ease. He was enchanted.

It could have been the booze, it could have been the weed, in later years he would never quite work out where he mustered the confidence from, but he did.

He asked her to dance, and she said yes.

Arthur wasn't a dancer, he considered himself to be far more of a periphery guy. Stand on the fringes and nod your head, tap your feet, maybe a bit of air guitar and lip synching if you were with your mates and it was a *really* good tune.

But as Donna Summer warbled out from the speakers, holding Bonnie by the waist and moving in time with her felt so completely natural. (And he *hated* Donna ruddy Summer. His mother had played the record so much that year he had thought seriously about ripping out his own eardrums with a fishing hook).

The doubts and fears he carried around with him which acted like traffic lights for social situations: red, no definitely don't say that, abort, abort. Amber, give it a few minutes, figure out whether it's appropriate, don't be too eager. Green, it's safe, you can contribute to this exchange and not chew it over for weeks afterwards with knots in your stomach, go ahead. For the first time he could ever recall they melted away, so easy it was with this girl. She was special. He had never felt quite so *alive*. They danced and laughed for more than an hour before there was somehow a telepathic agreement to go and get a drink.

The only option that still remained by this time in the evening was to risk the potent, noxious smelling punch. It looked like an accidental chemical spillage laying there in a crystal bowl, a nuclear shade of green with some suspicious looking chunks floating around on the top.

With uncharacteristic abandon, he spooned the toxic liquid into two paper cups and ventured a non-committal joke about being careful not to stand too close to open flames. She laughed heartily and he glowed.

They found seats at one of the tables, peppered with vol-au-vent debris and half-drunk cups of alcohol, and they talked.

It was a curious thing for Arthur to be so engaged in a conversation with a female. All of the girls he knew – although limited in number – bored him to tears. His mother never stopped harping on about the way things smelt, crumbs in the butter, wet towels. His cousins had their heads permanently hidden behind gossip magazines, wittering incessantly about make-up and shoes. Louie's little sister was sulky and quiet, a little rattish. But this girl, she was a revelation.

She was exquisite to look at. Mesmerising even. Arthur was in a trance as she flicked her hair over her shoulders and raised her eyebrows when she talked. She smelt like wild flowers. Even her accent was exotic.

She had grown up in Switzerland, he learned. Her father had been a diplomat and had died when she was nine of a heart attack. She was a dancer. She and her mother had moved to London when she had won a place at the Royal School of Ballet in Covent Garden when she was twelve.

She'd been very good, winning awards and dancing for the Queen. Until she had a serious knee injury and had had to give up dance completely two years ago. She had thought they would go back to their lives in Geneva until her mother had met her now-husband and had moved the two of them in with him and his three children within the month, swiftly enrolling Bonnie in the grammar school to keep her out of the way like all of his other children.

Arthur was intimidated by this information and suddenly felt very self-conscious about his dancing. Had she been judging him? He was probably crap. He was definitely crap.

His life wasn't exciting like hers. He hadn't really excelled at anything except being nice, which he wasn't sure had much conversational value. He opened up instead about his own broken home, his father's affair, his relationship with his brother. He had never talked this openly with anybody before.

They had just begun to tentatively touch fingers under the tablecloth when Lucy charged over and dragged Bonnie away because: 'the lads are rigging up croquet mallets in the garden darling, it's going to be bloody hilarious!'

He hated vulgar, bolshy Lucy at that moment. He hated himself. He was spineless, a gutless fish. *Why* had he not kissed her? She was perfect, every inch of her was perfect. He didn't think he would ever be able to fall asleep again and not dream of her, her dazzling smile, her eyelashes, her delicate shoulders.

He rubbed the bridge of his nose with his thumb and forefinger, pushed his glasses back into place and swigged the last of his throat searing punch. He needed to find Louie. All the girls swooned and fawned over Louie, he would know what to do.

Arthur gave himself a shake, got up and ambled from group to group in search of his friend. Everyone had seen him somewhere, at some point or another, but Arthur's search was to no avail.

On his way towards the gymnasium where it was said that a few groups had assembled, a strange claustrophobia ascended. The strip lights were too bright, something was buzzing loudly in his ears. He slumped against a wall in the empty corridor for support, frantically unbuttoning his collar which had suddenly become so tight he was struggling to breathe.

He sat for some minutes, head between his knees fighting the dizziness and nausea, until he was nearly knocked sideways by a very drunken Tim and Greg who had been making the same pilgrimage to the gym.

Greg hauled him up over his shoulder and dragged his slumped and sinewy frame up the back stairs into the dorm.

The words faded in and out, but Arthur heard the words 'punch' and 'absinthe' as they tucked him into bed, rolling him on his side with a wastepaper basket directly beneath him. Then the lights went out and Arthur drifted away to blackness.

His last thought before sleep overcame him was that he prayed that nobody told Bonnie what an utter chump he was. Beautiful, beautiful Bonnie.

***

Arthur was jolted awake by the sound of shrieking. His brain tells him *it's a fox in the fields, go back to sleep*.

As he came around, he tuned in to the sound of distant pockets of voices and laughter shuddering up the old water pipes that snaked up the walls and across the ceiling. He heard the sound of glass smashing. And it flooded back to him in waves: the party, the whisky, the joint, the dancing, the punch, Bonnie. Fuck.

His tongue was stuck to the roof of his mouth, feeling like sandpaper, his temples pulsing. He threw his arm onto his bedside table, flailing like a maniac for the glass of water which was usually there and now wasn't, sending the table and its contents flying. He fumbled for the lamp on the other side of his bed and surveyed the debris. The table was on its side, notebooks, pens and coins scattered. He pulled himself up on wobbly elbows and on further inspection, realised that he'd wet himself.

Off came his trousers and underpants, to be hidden at

the bottom of the laundry basket under his wet hockey kit. Propping himself up on the sink he took a few deep breaths before splashing cold water on his face and neck. He scanned the room for signs of his glass but when it wasn't obvious, he bent double and slurped at the running tap.

When his thirst was satiated, he rubbed with his fist at the smears on the mirror. His skin was mottled and patchy. His eyes were rimmed with an angry burgundy, the whites of his eyes covered in red spiderwebs, glasses askew. His hair was stuck to his head and pearls of sweat were pooling at his temples and along his upper lip. He was naked from the waist down and his shirt was stained. He was truly feral.

Before he could stop himself, he vomited forcefully into the sink. Coming out of his nose and mouth at once, he was left gasping for breath. With rattling hands, he skulked back towards his bed. Throwing his hand towel across the still warm patch of urine, he sunk between the sheets and into another fitful sleep.

***

Arthur awakened again to the sound of crockery clattering, the signal for breakfast.

He stretched and studied the landscape. Greg's bed has been slept in, Tim's was made with military precision although that told him nothing. Somebody had cleaned out the sink and opened the windows, and his upended table had been restored to the side of his bed with all of the stray coins, books and papers stacked in a neat little pile on top.

Tim was a stickler for cleanliness and order, sometimes obsessively so. Arthur felt a wave of gratitude for his friend's quirk, which he usually found so irritating, relieved he didn't have to face the clean up himself.

His glass had been cleaned and was standing upside down next to the sink, and his first course of action was to pour and down two pints of water. Wincing at the pounding in his head, he stripped the bed and put the sheets into the laundry basket.

A long shower and clean clothes later he felt almost human, although he still couldn't face brushing his teeth.

He headed downstairs to the mess hall to be greeted by the smell of fried food bringing on another wave of nausea. Greg and Marcus were in a group at the far end table chattering loudly, plates piled high with thick sausages and rashers of bacon. Arthur poured himself a strong cup of tea from the urn and joined them.

'Here he is!' boomed Greg, looking as bright-eyed and bushy-tailed as Arthur had ever seen him. 'Arty boy fell victim to the new punch recipe last night, boys! Sore head?'

'Sore everything.' Arthur mumbled, amidst a round of jibes and back slapping. Conversations continued around him, food wolfed down. Arthur tentatively sipped at his scalding hot tea, lost in his thoughts.

The room erupted suddenly with raucous cheers and a round of applause. It took every morsel of effort left in him to lift his head, to see Louie stood at the foot of the table grinning widely and bowing theatrically. Still in last night's clothes.

He took a place next to Arthur with a huge plate of bacon and toast and started rabidly shovelling it into his mouth.

'He'll need all those extra calories this morning won't you, Carlton?' teased Marcus. Louie smirked and said nothing.

'What happened to you last night?' he asked, turning to Arthur.

'The punch took him!' Greg replied for him. 'Found him passed out in the corridor and embarked upon a rescue mission, didn't we? What are friends for, eh?'

That's it, tell the room. Thanks friend, Arthur thought, feeling like he might start hyperventilating.

'You missed all sorts last night, Arty. Casanova here, busy rolling around in the mud, deflowering young blondes on the football pitch!'

Endless puns about scoring followed from up and down the table with more cheering. Arthur looked over at his friend, who was still grinning and saying very little. There was a tiny twig tangled in amongst his curls, and specks of dried mud down his back.

'Come on, Casanova, details!'

'A gentleman never tells,' Louie replied as he mopped his plate with a slice of toast and leaned backwards into a stretch, his chair on two legs.

'Don't be like that! Did she squeal in Swiss or in English, then?' goaded Marcus. 'Those ballerinas in the circus can get their legs behind their ears!'

'Swiss isn't a language, and those are contortionists,' Louie retorted, whipping Greg with his napkin. 'And she's bloody lovely.'

Arthur felt the walls close in around him and pressed his forehead to the table. 'No,' he whispered to himself, 'please, no.'

FOURTEEN

World's end, 1983.

Arthur's first major hangover lasted at least three days as he recalls it. The car journey home early that afternoon had been excruciating. Maggie picked him up from the front gates, and as he'd climbed shakily into the passenger seat, Louie had bolted out after him, shirt still undone and hair unruly with his backpack slung over his shoulder.

Maggie wound the window down. 'What are you still doing here, Louie?' she chuckled. 'These poor sods can't get rid of you.'

'It was a heavy night, Mags,' he said, leaning his elbow on the roof, smiling his winning smile. 'Can I grab a ride home?'

'Of course you can. Jump in and you can tell me all about it. Oh, to be young again.'

To add insult to injury, Arthur had to get out of the car and pull the passenger seat forward so Judas could impinge upon his journey home. Louie nimbly hopped into the back seat and chattered happily all the way home, every inch the

100

charmer. Mothers loved him as much as daughters: he had them hanging on his every word.

You're doing this on purpose, Arthur thought, seething, are you gonna try and fuck my mum, too?

He stared sullenly out of the window for the entirety of the drive, eyes narrowed, thinking wretched thought upon wretched thought. Every word his friend uttered made his blood boil. He wanted to rip those dimples from his cheeks, tear his throat out like they'd done with that rat's innards in biology.

He was lost in a daydream about smashing Louie's teeth out one by one with a hammer, when his mum pulled him back to reality.

'Why are you so grumpy, Art? Have you been struck down with a terrible case of beer flu?' Maggie was laughing.

He winced in response, and she got the picture. His mother knew him too well to attempt a denial. And he didn't have the energy, in any case. Luckily, she found the novelty of his hangover hilarious and tittered about it all the way home.

'So, any girls?' she said a few minutes later, wiggling her eyebrows.

'*No*,' said Arthur, forcefully.

'What about you, Louie? Nobody catch your eye?' she continued. 'I know how it is at your age, you can tell me…'

Louie was laughing along with her, head lolling between the two front seats.

He's not even wearing his seatbelt, she wouldn't let me do that, Arthur inwardly fumed.

'You would, of course, be the first person I would tell, Mags,' Louie flirted, 'but no, my heart is still there for the taking.'

He laughed, putting his hand on Arthur's shoulder. It

was all Arthur could do not to turn around and bite his treacherous fingers clean off.

Although he was in the car with the two people in his life who knew him best, not a single one of them had any idea what was going through his head. Both parties had put it down to his hangover. It was unthinkable to both his mother and the boy he'd grown up alongside that they would ever fall out. They'd never argued before, not properly.

To everyone else in the car, the boys no longer speaking was completely out of the realms of possibility. But Arthur knew that he would never speak to Louie again, and he would certainly never tell him why.

Arthur took to his bed for the next week, refusing to see Louie or anyone else. Even when his pulsing headache and swirling stomach had abated, his deep misery rendered him bed-bound and it was at this point that Maggie started to worry.

'Maybe he's come down with something?' Maggie whispered to Anna in the kitchen on the eighth day of Arthur's bedding in. 'He's hardly spoken a word since he came home. He won't come downstairs, he won't have the lights on. He *swore* at me when I tried to open his blind yesterday! He's never sworn at me before! It's Teddy who's the obnoxious one, not Arthur. I'm worried, Anna.'

'Oh, he's a teenager, Mags,' Anna waved her hand dismissively, 'it's just a phase. Leave him to it, he'll get bored eventually.'

Anna had been right. He did get bored, eventually, but still he steadfastly avoided Louie. He feigned illness each time Louie knocked for the first week, just for ease. But when that wore thin, he had no choice but to be more direct.

'You feeling better, now? You wanna come for a jam? We're getting fish and chips,' Louie said from the doorway, still wearing the grin which now had Arthur clenching his fists, and whispered, 'I've got some hash as well, for later. Go and grab your stuff, you can crash.'

'I can't be bothered,' Arthur responded robotically.

'What?' Louie laughed, incredulous.

'I said: I can't be bothered,' Arthur repeated, more slowly, more venomously. He shut the door unceremoniously in Louie's face and went back up the stairs, slamming his bedroom door so hard that the windows rattled.

Maggie was eavesdropping from the dining room and could see Louie still stood on the step, scratching his head. He caught her eye through the lace curtains and shrugged in a 'what's up with him?' gesture. Maggie shrugged back and rolled her eyes. He took the steps three at a time and waved as he strode through the gate.

Later, over dinner, Maggie asked, 'What's wrong, Art? Why are you pissed off with Louie? He's your best mate.'

'I'm not pissed off with him,' he replied, spearing a piece of broccoli, 'I just don't like him anymore. Can you leave it, please?'

'You can't just not like him, he's your best friend,' she said quietly as she spooned more mashed potato onto his plate, and that was the end of the matter.

**

Louie didn't come knocking again after that, and Maggie didn't blame him. She and Anna discussed the mysterious tiff at length.

'Do you think Arthur might be a bit...put out?' Anna suggested one evening during one such discussion, over a glass of red on Maggie's back porch.

'Put out? What do you mean?' replied Maggie as she snuffed her cigarette out in the ashtray and lit another.

'I mean... Louie has no idea why Arthur won't see him. He says he hasn't done anything... I thought maybe they'd had some kind of drunken argument at the party but Louie says they didn't. He's mystified, and devastated of course. Do you think Arthur could be...a bit...well, a little jealous, maybe?'

'Jealous of what?' Maggie retorted sharply, accidentally flicking ash all over the table. She knew that yes, there probably were plenty of reasons poor Arthur might be jealous of Louie, but she wasn't going to spare Anna the awkwardness of spelling it out to her if she was going to throw around insinuations like that. Arthur had endured a lifetime of being pipped to every post by Louie and had always taken it with great sportsmanship, it had never been an issue before. He was hardly likely to be suddenly jealous now, was he? Was he?

'Oh, no, probably nothing. No, that won't be it, of course it won't. I just wish he'd tell us all, Mags. Louie keeps saying he can't say sorry when he doesn't know what for, and he's right.'

'I'll talk to him again,' said Maggie, thoughtfully, 'see if I can get anything out of him.'

But she hadn't managed to. Every time she had tried to broach the subject of Louie, he had shut down and spent the hours that followed in a foul mood. She had quickly learnt that whatever it was, it was better left well alone.

As the weeks passed, Arthur had gradually come out of his

depression, much to Maggie's relief.

He began eating again, had been out for kickabouts, trips into town and to the cinema with friends from school every now and again. He still spent the largest portion of his time in his bedroom strumming away on his precious Fender, which he had tasked Maggie with fetching back from next door. But the occasional day of socializing and fresh air was better than nothing.

***

On the other side of the wall, it was a different story. Anna had barely seen hide nor hair of Louie since the summer holidays began. He had been out at all hours. Every night of the week there was some teenager or other throwing a party in a basement in London and Louie was always on the guest list. She would lay awake at night, straining to hear the sound of his key in the lock, him creeping up the stairs. He would rise from his bed and join them for breakfast, play a few games with twelve year old Ella who worshipped the ground he walked on, ruffle her hair and kiss their cheeks and be gone again.

'I much preferred it when he was thick as thieves with Arthur,' she confided to Grayson one night in bed, 'at least we knew where he was. It's never crossed my mind in all these years that Arthur had been such a good influence on him. He's a loose cannon without him.'

Grayson put his book down and put his arm around his wife, noticing the worry lines around her eyes. He kissed her forehead.

'Don't worry, they'll make it up, they're only kids. And him being out all the time, that's normal, I promise, that's just boys. I was like a stray cat at his age.'

'An alley cat, more like.'

'Potato, potato.' he replied, and they both laughed.

FIFTEEN

Wild west, 1983.

Arthur begrudgingly agreed to spend the final week of his summer holidays in Holland Park with his father and brother, who he hadn't seen for nearly two months.

'A change of scene might do you some good,' Maggie had offered as she'd driven him through Clapham Common.

'Yeah, great,' he'd replied morosely.

He was therefore surprised to arrive to great fanfare at Campden Hill. Walter answered the door holding a huge bottle of Veuve Clicquot, his ruddy cheeks and glassy eyes the tell-tale signs that he'd already been at it.

'Both of my sons, under the same roof at last!' he gushed.

Maggie smirked, kissed Arthur's head and shooed him up the front steps.

The size and sterility of the house that he'd last known as a young boy unnerved him these days. It was even more pristine since he and his brother had left, thanks to the maids Oksana insisted their father employ, and the lack of children.

The click-clacking of her silly kitten heels along the marble floor announced her before she was visible. 'Ah, here he is!' she exclaimed, with the same glassy eyes as his father as she lunged for kisses on both cheeks. 'Velcome home, Arter.'

He followed them through to the dining room, heavily draped, and lit by the giant crystal chandelier that hung from the ceiling casting a soft, film star glow over the inhabitants. The huge glass and marble monstrosity of a dining table took centre stage, set as though for an eight course meal, embroidered napkins and silverware everywhere.

Teddy was sat in his usual place with the same flush as the other two, champagne flute clasped between pudgy fingers. He looked much rounder than the last time Arthur had seen him, bordering on overweight.

Must be all of the lamb cutlets and veal he waxes lyrical about every time he comes home, thought Arthur, which Maggie had always taken as a slight on her roast beef.

Arthur wasn't sure where to sit and stood awkwardly until Walter pulled out a chair across from his brother and ushered him down into it, pouring champagne into the glass in front of him.

Once everyone was seated, his father raised his glass. 'To my prodigal son, no, no, to *both* my boys. Here's to a wonderful week under my roof!' he bellowed, sloshing champagne from his flute with his salute.

'Here, here!' Teddy said, sounding far more British than Arthur remembered, causing him to stifle a smirk behind a fake cough.

A young, red-haired and freckled girl in an old fashioned pinny brought out the first course. Arthur would have sniggered at the pretentiousness of it all if he hadn't felt that it would embarrass her.

'Quails eggs, wonderful, my favourite!' declared Teddy, 'Do thank cook for us – exquisite!'

He jammed the little egg into his mouth with a fork so tiny it made his fingers look like large sausages tied with elastic around the knuckles.

Arthur was relieved to find he wasn't expected to contribute much to the conversation other than a nod here and there. Both Walter and Teddy were more than happy to take the lead, talking over one another as they raced to fill Arthur in on the 'simply divine' Michelin starred restaurants they had frequented the past weeks; the happenings at their club; unkind gossip about people he hadn't seen since he was six.

The long-winded, laborious tale about one of the neighbours' wardrobe blunders at Ascot is completely anti-climactic to be on the receiving end of. But the telling left both men guffawing, tears streaming from their eyes.

Arthur steadily sipped at his champagne, enduring the mediocre tales of a world he didn't inhabit with a polite half-smile plastered onto his face. He had stopped eating some time ago and had spent the last two courses pushing pieces of food around his plate. The extravagant meal they'd just consumed could have fed a family of twelve for a fortnight.

Luckily, nobody noticed, the company being far too self-involved to trouble themselves with any matter that didn't directly affect them. And of course they were all rather worse for wear come dessert when a yet another bottle of Veuve was uncorked.

Oksana took her glass and retired upstairs for a bath. Walter passed a carton of cigars around the table. Arthur refused, Teddy accepted and sat there with it between his chubby fingers looking every inch a boy playing dress up.

Walter was a repetitive drunk, and Arthur lost count of the number of times he'd gushed about quite how wonderful it was for them both to be there. Arthur side eyed his brother, expecting Teddy to be more put out than he outwardly seemed to be at the attention being lavished upon someone other than himself.

'Of course boys, it's Saturday tomorrow so the old schedule's rather full. Oksana and I have our swim and massage at the spa and then we have a lunch booked in and a matinee later on. But I'm sure your diaries are much the same of a weekend, my young strapping boys,' Walter said, through a cloud of smoke.

'Oh, yes,' replied Teddy. 'Giles' brother is having a barbecue, he's leaving for Cambridge in September so his parents have arranged a few farewell drinks. I mean, he's majoring in *literature*,' he continued with a look on his face like he'd tasted something sour, 'but still. A fair few of the chaps from school will be there, and of course his sister is at Roedean, so there ought to be a bit of skirt hanging around too. Ought to be a great knee's up, starting at lunch time, finishing whenever.' He turned to face Arthur. 'You should come, Arthur, if you're free. Meet some of the boys.'

Walter beamed. Arthur wasn't sure he'd heard correctly. His brother had never invited him to anything before, anything at all.

For no other reason than a complete lack of plans tomorrow, and a morbid curiosity about all of the sons of Sir-so-and-so he had heard so much about throughout the years, Arthur found himself saying, 'Ok, sure.'

Pleased, Walter and Teddy left their cigars smouldering in

the ashtray and retired to their rooms.

Arthur helped the young red head, all arms and elbows, clear the table, an awkward silence throughout. When she finished he realised he had no idea which room he was supposed to sleep in. So he headed upstairs towards his childhood bedroom which bore no resemblance to its previous incarnation. The walls were now magnolia and a huge sepia print of a half-naked woman hung over a king-size bed which was never his.

His suitcase was at the end of it though, so he must be in the right place.

***

Arthur awoke late the next morning, finding himself alone in the house by the time he'd made it downstairs. The hired help didn't work weekends and the huge house was eerily empty. Walter had left him a note on the kitchen counter, next to which was a silver front door key and a twenty pound note. 'Don't have too much fun!!!!' he had scrawled.

He was surprised to have been entrusted with a key on his first day, and twenty pounds was a lot of money. He was beginning to feel very grown up indeed. Champagne at dinner, cigars, door keys, being left to do as he pleased. It was the polar opposite to life in his own house.

Maggie never let him sleep past 8am, her favourite mantra being: 'you're young, you can sleep when you're dead.'

There was always bacon on the griddle by the time he came downstairs, Maggie warbling tunelessly along to the radio as she buttered slabs of toast. He was very rarely left alone in the house.

Pocketing the key and money, he decided to treat himself to a lengthy bubble bath, filling it to the brim with the most expensive-looking of Oksana's potions which took up every available surface. He even tried the jacuzzi feature, but a very loud and juddery noise unnerved him.

He couldn't stop picturing it exploding, the house flooding. His naked body being found floating in the tepid, overly perfumed water, still sparking.

He switched it off.

He was returning to his bedroom with a towel wrapped around his waist when he heard the front door open and the sound of two voices, only one of which he recognized.

'Arthur, are you ready?' boomed Teddy from downstairs. 'He's probably still bloody asleep.'

Heavy-footed steps came thundering up the stairs and Teddy appeared on the landing.

'You'll need some clothes on, it's not that kind of party, not until after midnight anyway,' Teddy sniggered, 'and anyway, the ladies will run a mile then they see that pigeon chest. Bloody hell, look at the colour of you. They ought to prescribe you some iron.'

Arthur looked down at his pale and slender torso, the odd wisp of hair here and there. Then appraised the gluttonous mound that was straining to escape from between his brother's taut shirt buttons, but didn't say anything.

Teddy followed his gaze, placing a protective hand across his stomach. 'Come on sissy boy, we haven't got all day. We'll miss the food.'

Maybe *you* ought to miss the food, Arthur thought spitefully as his brother turned and clattered back down the stairs.

Minutes later he was ready, his jeans and unbuttoned shirt

not quite in keeping with the brogues, chinos and cricket jumper look that his brother and his friend favoured.

'You'll do,' they told him, and the three of them set off walking.

Brief introductions were provided on the way, Arthur discovering that Teddy's companion was Charles, a Lancing lad, his father was the owner of a hotel chain with branches throughout Europe. Both Teddy and Charles were in the same house at school as Giles, whose brother was having the party.

Giles' father was the much-loved MP for Kensington and Chelsea, revered by everyone in the borough for both his moral standing and approachable manner. Arthur vaguely recognized his name – probably from the newspaper – but he wasn't really up on politics. Maggie reckoned they were all dogs, anyway.

Arthur was beginning to sweat at the thought of what he would talk about with these people who casually hang around the halls at Chequers. Or jet across Europe opening luxury hotels, spending their winters aboard their parents' yachts in Monaco. He had almost finished concocting a convincing excuse to leave when his brother pressed a buzzer on a giant pair of gates. He talked into a box and the gates began to open.

Arthur had never known a person who lived in a house with magical gates.

They were soon walking up the driveway, ensconced by tall trees all the way around. The house was a huge, white-fronted thing, a pillar on either side of the black front door. Funny little trees stood in front of the pillars, cut into strange shapes, rather like poodles' tails.

The door was opened by a severe looking woman, who could be anything from mid-thirties to fifty. With the amount of enhancements she'd obviously had, it was difficult to tell. She had the look of an angry cat, her peroxide blonde hair pulled tightly back into a high chignon, her eyebrows painted on so high up her forehead, she looked permanently startled. She seemed vaguely familiar but Arthur had no idea how.

'Charles, darling, wonderful of you to come. Edward, darling, so glad you could be here.' she said, air-kissing both of their cheeks.

'Thank you, Lena, we wouldn't miss it,' Teddy wheedled. 'This is my younger brother, Arthur. He's in town this week and is keen to meet Giles whilst he's here, I hope that's fine.'

*In town for a week? I live in Dulwich, not Madagasca*r, Arthur muttered inside his head.

Lena ran her feline gaze up and down Arthur, sizing him up like a fat mouse. Seemingly satisfied, the plastic smile returned as she said, 'Of course, how wonderful to meet you, Arthur. Do come through, it's this way.'

They followed her down a long hall, past a staircase and into a large marble kitchen.

It was the stuff Oksana's wettest dreams were made of, Arthur thought.

There was a huge table laden with cards and gifts to one side. Enormous glass doors were open straight ahead, leading out to an expanse of grass.

Various tribes of people lounged in different corners of the space. A group of older men, whom Arthur assumed were the dads, were gathered near one of their number in an apron brandishing an oversize fork over the barbecue.

Then there was a group of beautiful twenty-somethings on

114

picnic blankets in the middle of the lawn, all wearing identical sunglasses and clutching what looked to be sangrias.

Behind the beautiful people, at the end of the garden, was a blue summer house with a group closer to Arthur's age spilling out of it.

Teddy waved greetings to various people as they crossed the lawn, each one appearing genuinely happy to see him. These people liked him. Arthur was so used to his brother's arrival being pre-empted with a: 'he may be a little priggish sometimes, but he's still your brother', and covert eye rolling, that the thought of his brother living a life in which people enjoyed his company left him reeling for a moment.

They arrived at the summer house and Arthur was introduced to 'the gang', which was a conveyor belt of double-barrelled surnames, titles and references to parentage followed by disinterested boys dutifully raising glasses.

More beers were passed round and more Lancing-based anecdotes regurgitated. The group had a never ending supply of in jokes, many rounded off with 'ah, you had to be there' together with a sympathetic look thrown Arthur's way, accompanied by a bottomless pit of shared elitist opinions.

As soon as the opportunity arose, Arthur excused himself and headed towards the drinks table to find something stronger. Something to help smooth the strumming of disquiet deep in his chest. He was a lamb in a lion's lair, precariously close to tripping himself up at any given moment.

He was staring at the line of spirits standing to attention on the table when a voice from behind him said, 'I haven't seen you here before, young man. Are you at school with Giles?'

It was the man in the barbecue apron who appeared much taller up close, at least six foot four. Arthur stared up at him, recognising him at once as the man he had seen in the papers: the beloved MP.

'N…no, my brother Teddy, erm, Edward is though.'

'But you're not at Lancing?'

'No, sir, I'm at Dulwich College,' Arthur replied, and waited for the inevitable look of distaste he had come to expect after the last five variants of the same conversation he'd already had that afternoon.

'A good school.' said the man, nodding, 'Great sports facilities if I remember rightly, and a notorious rugby team. I'm Peter, Giles' father. Pleased to meet you.'

Arthur shook the man's hand shyly. 'Arthur Maxwell.'

'What's your tipple then, Arthur?' he asked, nodding towards the drinks table, 'I'm a scotch man myself if you'd care to join me?'

Arthur had never had scotch but drinking scotch with this man who was probably the closest to a famous person he had ever met appealed to him, so he accepted. They chatted a bit more about school, a little about music, and it was the most pleasant conversation Arthur had had with anybody since he'd arrived.

He was impressed by how interested this man was in him, the effort he made to make him feel welcome. The encounter was all of twenty minutes at best, but by the time the MP left to greet more guests, Arthur was more than a little awestruck by this classically handsome and charismatic man.

He'd always pictured members of parliament as dour old men in three piece suits, but Peter was far more debonair. Almost a little James Bond.

'Ah, he's won your vote then, I see.' said a mousy haired girl in a summer dress.

'I'm not old enough to vote.' Arthur responded, caught red-handed in his hero worship, casting admiring glances towards Peter's retreating back.

'Of course you're not, but still, good to see that his public relations course was worth the money.' she replied, stirring her drink.

'You don't like him?'

'Of course I like him, he's my dad. I just wish he'd have a day off of the patter for once.'

'So he's not really that…you know, that *nice?*' asked Arthur, disappointed.

'He's nice, I mean, in the same way most people are nice, right? But nobody really truly gives a fuck about every stranger's life that they meet, because you can't, can you? Not unless you're trained to, and paid handsomely for it. And therein lies the crux of it: it's all bullshit. It's essentially a popularity contest featuring only rich men. And the one who convinces the most people that he cares about them takes the salary and sits in the big chair, writing out cheques for his chums in the good name of his constituents, pretending he gives a shit about any of their plights. It's so much theatre, so much smoke and mirrors. It's the most egocentric profession there is, I think.'

The girl had the good grace to look as shocked as Arthur was about her outburst, but managed to quickly shake it off and extend her hand. 'I'm Lucinda.'

Arthur liked this strange, cynical girl at once. Whilst her long nose and even longer fingers meant she wasn't particularly attractive, he could tell that there was no hidden agenda. She wasn't going to expect him to laugh along at boorish puns, or pretend he understood anything about either lineage or golf handicaps. There was something faintly amusing about such open scepticism.

'Arthur.' he told her, 'I'm Teddy's brother.'

'Oh Christ, you're not one of the Lancing crowd, are you? You don't *look* like one of them, but perhaps you've come in disguise. You're trying to trick me, standing there without a blazer on a scorching hot day.'

Arthur laughed, and reassured her that no, he wasn't at Lancing and had never fenced or played bowls. Satisfied, she took him off to meet a different crowd, where people were introduced by first names and an interesting fact.

He found he didn't forget a single name this way. It was impossible to forget Christina who could balance four coupe glasses at once on her head (complete with demonstration) or Jonathan who once sneezed in Prince Charles' tuna niçoise. This was a different genre of privileged offspring, he realised.

Their boasting was more refined, less obvious. They debated the merits of Keats over Wordsworth, openly discussed politics. He still wasn't ready to commit to an opinion but he didn't need to; there were so many opinions flying back and forth already that there was more than enough room on the fence he sat upon for the rest of the evening.

The following hours flew past in a haze of debates, alcohol and red meat. He liked these people, and felt flattered when his opinion was sought more than once as the deciding factor at the tail end of a heated difference of opinion. Even more so when his refusal to commit to either way was met with begrudging respect and remarks like: 'keeping your cards close to your chest, eh? Very wise'.

They thought he had cards! They thought he knew things. They assumed he could contribute and had his own ideas, that his reservations were rooted in politeness.

He was an imposter but he was enjoying it. It was nice to feel important.

SIXTEEN

Secrets, 1983.

It was a humid evening. Dusk had rolled over the fenced garden and out across London. Arthur had been so enraptured by this new world of current affairs and clever viewpoints that he hadn't relieved his bladder even once, and he was five bottles of beer deep.

He was waved in the direction of the downstairs cloakroom, weaving his way through pockets of people to find his way back to the glass doored kitchen.

The lights inside were low for ambience related reasons, he assumed. There was nobody inside the kitchen, everyone was outside enjoying the warmth of the evening.

It was only when he was directly crossing her path that she reached his line of vision. At first, it was only the back of her, silhouetted against the lights of the fridge, pulling out a carton of orange juice. Something stirred in him, an uncomfortable déjà vu.

It was when she turned around that the air escaped his lungs and the empty cup he had been holding clattered to the floor, a noise which seemed to bounce off of every white wall too forcibly, much, much too loud.

'Y...you scared me there,' he said, following up with a nervous titter that left his mouth in a far higher pitch than he would have liked. He bent down to pick up his keys and tried to compose himself.

'Oh, sorry,' said Bonnie. 'I didn't mean to. Are you here for the party?'

She was looking off to the side, then fiddled with her drink before looking at the floor, anywhere but meeting his eyes.

Perhaps she was feeling badly about the way things turned out, thought Arthur. Perhaps she was feeling guilty.

Somewhere inside, Arthur had a brief stirring of guilt laden delight at this thought. So frequently had he tortured himself with the idea that the chemistry that night, the feelings, were entirely one-sided, that he'd convinced himself it had all been in his head. That she'd had no idea she had strung him along. She was just being friendly, and ideas of romance had been purely his own. But her visible discomfort seemed to contradict that line of thought. Yes, that must be it.

She looked up into his eyes then, and they both laughed at the ridiculousness of how ill at ease they felt.

'I'm here with my brother,' he told her. 'I didn't know you were here, I haven't seen you outside.'

Arthur was frantically trying to connect the dots, to piece together how the girl he'd tortured himself with thoughts of could be serendipitously standing in this kitchen in Kensington, six weeks later.

'Oh, she didn't make the guest list for this particular soiree, did you, Bonnie?' Giles was stood in the doorway with his arms folded across his chest. 'Or any other party from now until she's dead.'

Another boy was stood behind him, sniggering.

Giles turned to address Arthur, 'You don't have to be polite to her, she's a disgrace. She's not even supposed to be downstairs. Luckily, we won't have to look at her for much longer. Go on Bonnie, off you go, before you find yourself in a patch of grass with your knickers around your ankles again.'

Arthur was struck dumb, standing there with his mouth hanging open, a comatose flounder.

'What was that about?' said Teddy, coming up behind Giles, posing with another silly cigar. His cheeks were blotchy, his eyes glassy again. He really was a terrible looking drunk.

'My wayward step-sister again, trying to sweet talk your brother. He's probably the only one here that doesn't know the depths of her indecency. How embarrassing.'

Arthur had an acute sense that he should have been stepping forward in this moment, to defend her honour. He was very close to doing so, dithering between doing the virtuous thing and doing nothing that might rock the boat. Aware that Bonnie's eyes were on him but refusing to allow his gaze to so much as wander in her direction. He didn't want to cause a scene, not here, in front of all of his clever new friends.

The aggression coming off of Giles was like molten tarmac in a heatwave. The venom in his eyes as shocking as his language.

Arthur comforted himself with the thought that he probably hadn't ingratiated himself into his brother's group as much as he might have and he wasn't at all confident that he was considered above being socked in the mouth should he go against the grain.

And besides, she had slept with his best friend while he lay a desperate heap in a sodden bed. She'd caused him enough embarrassment already.

The moment had escaped, and she turned on her heel to retreat silently down the hall into the darkness.

Arthur felt himself complicit. Maggie would be ashamed of him.

***

It wasn't until the next morning that Arthur was able to get to the real crux of the matter. Walter and Oksana were sat at the dining table, eyes wide on Teddy's excessively embellished version of events, knowing looks passing between them.

'Well, it's not the first scandal that's played out in that house and I dare say it won't be the last. Never trust a politician,' stated Walter. Oksana nodded her head vigorously. 'There was all of that hoo-haa when his first wife left him, rumours of infidelity, an underage girl it was said… Of course there was a big cover up and all parties were paid off handsomely so we're unlikely ever to know the full story. But shit sticks, as they say.'

'I don't see how they're going to cover this one up. You can hardly cover up a pregnancy in this day and age,' Teddy chipped in as he brushed the crumbs that have pooled in his lap onto the floor.

'You'd be surprised, and besides, the girl isn't related to Peter. It wouldn't surprise me if he dropped them like hot potatoes the minute the news breaks, if it ever does, of course. Rumour had it that he only moved them in so quickly to quell the gossip about another one of his indiscretions. He likes them young.'

But Arthur had barely heard, his brain snagging on the word he'd heard seconds before, so everything that came afterwards sounded like echoes underwater.

'She's pregnant? Bonnie is pregnant?'

'That's what Giles told me,' Teddy continued, 'in the strictest of confidence, of course. It's all very hush hush. They're sending her away to some home for unwed mothers next month he says, to nip the problem in the bud. The public story is something to do with rehabilitation for an old dance injury. After that they'll likely send her to board somewhere abroad, in exile as it were, what with the elections coming up next year. I can't see how that will wash, though. If this one stays under the radar it'll be a miracle in public relations.'

'The general public is eighty per-cent idiots, old boy,' replied Walter as he dabbed at his mouth with a napkin.

The ramifications of this news sat like an anvil on Arthur's shoulders. Did Louie know? Did Louie care?

'What about the father?' Arthur said.

'If she knows who it is, she isn't telling. Lucky for him, they're baying for blood. When they find him, he won't have any testicles left.' Teddy poured himself another cup of tea while Arthur watched the floor falling away from him. 'Imagine her besmirching their good name like that, when they gave her and her mother a home. They were up to their eyeballs in debt, bordering on destitution before they met Peter. What a way to repay him! Ghastly.'

'Quite,' agreed Walter. 'The man should have known better than to invest himself in a woman who is desperate, particularly a foreign one. You'd think he'd know an agenda when it stared him in the face.'

The irony of Walter's words wasn't lost on Arthur as Oksana sat across from him brazenly sipping orange juice from one of his mother's crystal glasses.

Arthur excused himself and hid upstairs for the rest of the day, his brain on overdrive. There was, he speculated, the chance that she'd slept with more than one person in the last eight weeks. *If* she's as loose as they said she was…but he concluded that this was unlikely. After all, she was only sixteen. There wasn't *that* much opportunity.

There were so many unanswered questions. The most pressing one being whether or not he should tell Louie. His anger towards his ex-friend was wavering, yet it seemed unfair that he could be completely unaware of the chaos unfolding that he potentially had a leading role in.

But then, maybe it was better he didn't know. Maybe Bonnie would go away, maybe this problem would go away, maybe the cover up would be successful and all of their lives could go on as before.

What if Arthur were to tell him, and he left her alone in her disgrace? But then, what if Arthur were to tell him and he didn't? Was Louie ready to be a father? Was Louie ready to be a husband? Was Louie willing to walk into this blazing inferno of a mess he'd made, and if he was, what of him then? Either way, it wouldn't be good.

Arthur was no closer to any kind of definitive course of action by the time it was time to return to school.

So many futures were hanging in the balance, and he had no idea how far reaching his decision would turn out to be.

SEVENTEEN

After, 1983.

L ouie and Arthur were face to face for the first time in five weeks, in geography. It was the longest period of time they had been absent from one another's lives since they were juniors.

Louie strolled in late, the half-hearted reprimand from Miss Greaves met with an apology and the trademark winning smile. Not quite as winning as usual, Arthur noticed. Today it was marred by an uncharacteristic pair of bags under his eyes. He looked a little drawn, a tiny bit sunken. Was that because he knew?

Arthur struggled to look up from his sweating palms, unable to find the words to broach that kind of conversation with Louie. Not after the way Arthur had treated him in the interim. Explanations would be expected to progress towards that kind of intimacy now, explanations Arthur never thought he would have to make.

He wasn't sure he could. In the cold light of day, with time in-between and the knowledge he now had, what had passed before now seemed trivial. A bit…silly. Juvenile, even.

What on earth would he say? *I'm sorry, Louie, I know we've been best friends for most of our lives but I thought I was in love with Bonnie because I spent a couple of hours with her before you met. And when you slept with her I was devastated and angry at you, even though there was no way you could have known how I felt. And I'd never had any indication that my infatuation had been reciprocated.*

No. No, he could never say it. Just thinking it was excruciating.

By the time the lesson ended, Arthur hadn't heard a word. Louie was the first out of his seat, exiting the classroom without a backwards glance.

The next three periods were subjects they took separately. Arthur spent them doing nothing but ruminate over his imminent first exchange with his oldest friend, working himself up into quite a fluster by the time lunch break came around.

Louie was at the quad, stood in the middle of a group of mutual friends, a roll up clasped between his slender fingers.

'You smoke roll ups now?' was Arthur's unintentionally abrupt opening gambit, but his emotions seemed to have gotten a hold of his vocal chords.

Louie looked down at the cigarette and back up at Arthur through his fringe. 'Yeah, a few weeks now… I smoked that much weed through the holidays that when I ran out I just kind of carried on with the tobacco. It'll stain my teeth, apparently.'

Arthur nodded, his brain malfunctioning: he had nothing to say next.

'You're talking to me again now, are you?' Louie continued.

'Only, I thought you couldn't be bothered.'

Arthur's throat became painful, his eyes prickled with tears. He bit his lip. He would never hear the end of it if he cried right here, right now, surrounded by his classmates. Panic made his heart race, forcing his eyes to look left and right and left again. He hammered his brain to come up with a satisfactory response, but it had turned its back on him. It was punishing him too.

He deserved it.

'I…' he fumbled. But no, that was it. There was nothing else.

Louie took a final drag of his roll up and flicked it across the flagged stone. 'Look, don't worry about it. Whatever I did, I'm sorry…can we just forget about it? Only, things have been a bit shit, mate.'

Louie's gaze was on him, the tears pushing their way to the surface even more forcefully. Arthur trembled visibly trying to hold them back. It was barely believable that the friend he had so unceremoniously and savagely cut all ties with was showing him this kind of mercy.

He swallowed the now boulder-sized lump in his throat which sank with painful slowness down past his collar bone, mumbling, 'I'm sorry too.'

Louie threw one arm around him and the steady thump of his palm on Arthur's back made everything right in the world again. Well, almost everything. They headed towards the canteen together, Arthur still too choked up to speak.

Tentatively, they slipped back into their former roles within the relationship through the rest of the afternoon. By the time the final bell of the day clanged across campus, Arthur still hadn't found an opening in which to broach the delicate subject of Bonnie's pregnancy.

In a way, he was relieved: maybe someone else would tell Louie, relinquishing Arthur gratefully of the role of informer.

***

As it transpired, nobody else did.

Instead, a strange chain of Chinese whispers snaked its way from Chelsea, across the Thames to Dulwich College, and the presented facts became a wildly distorted version of reality.

On Thursday evening they were alone in Arthur's dorm, Arthur propped up on his elbows on the bed. Louie sat on the window ledge with a roll up. Both the smoke and the cold night air blew backwards into the room, and Arthur was beginning to get annoyed. Smoking was strictly prohibited; the Matron had the nostrils of a Pointer and the temper of a Doberman. He was about to make this point when Louie started speaking.

'I liked her, you know,' he said, addressing the star lit sky. 'I really liked her. It feels stupid now after the way it played out, but it was like being struck by lightning or something. I never saw a girl like that before. I thought it could be good, you know? I thought we'd see each other sometime, maybe go to the pictures, or we could go ice skating, something like that…

'She was panicking. The sun was coming up, it was cold and she'd missed the bus back to town with the others…said she would be in trouble. I gave her my jacket, told her I'd call her a taxi. I came inside and everybody was still sleeping so I used the phone in the office. When I came back outside, she'd gone.'

He flicked the roll-up out of the window and ran his hands through his hair before continuing.

'I thought she might get in touch. She knows my name, she knows who my friends are. I went to some parties out west. I saw some people. Thought I might see her. I didn't. Some nights, when I'm high, I think I might've just imagined her.'

When he finished speaking, he looked at Arthur, a film of sadness painted over his face. Here they were again; Arthur being the one with the secret knowledge. The one holding the tin opener for the can of worms he wanted to shove to the back of the cupboard.

Forget about her, he wanted to tell his friend, *she'll only spell trouble. You don't want any part of the drama unfolding in Kensington, it's best that you're kept out of it. There will be other girls.*

'That's shit, mate,' was all he said out loud.

***

On Saturday, Louie and Arthur were on the common with a small group from school. It was another clear and humid day, and what seemed like the entire population of South West London had chosen the same venue to enjoy the end of a glorious Indian summer. The boys lay in the grass, their faces up to the sky, shooting the breeze over bottles of dandelion and burdock and passing around one of Louie's joints.

Everything was exactly as it should be, until a trio of shadows fell over them to tip the balance.

'Oh, *look* who it is!' exclaimed a nasally voice.

Arthur raised himself onto his elbows, squinting to identify the intruders. Lucy, armed with a couple of dress-alike clones, arms heavy with wicker baskets and tartan blankets, were standing over them.

'Fancy seeing *you* here!' she continued, with no surprise in her expression whatsoever, laying down the blankets directly next to them before plonking herself down. The other two girls subserviently sat down on either side of Lucy, unpacking the baskets and offering the food around.

Arthur was torn somewhere between being vexed at the intrusion – something he seemed to feel often when Lucy was around – and relieved that someone had had the foresight to bring consumables. Smoking pot made him ravenous, and the paper plate of pork pies in front of him seemed like a gift from heaven itself.

'This is Polly, and this is Jane,' Lucy was saying, presenting her friends with a flourish. She continued around the group, rattling off names. She got all manner of thrills from introductions, being the one who knew everybody.

Both of her friends shared the same long, straight style of hair and all three of them were wearing the same type of summer dress, differing only in colour and pattern. They were irritating in their symmetry and predictability, sat cross legged, picking at their food and laughing coyly at the right moments within the conversation. Not one of them was a patch on Bonnie, Arthur believed, and he wondered if Louie was thinking the same.

'Heavens alive, that isn't *pot* is it?' Lucy said loudly, waggling her finger at Arthur and making silly tutting noises. 'I might have expected it from this cad over here,' she gestured towards Louie, 'but not *you* Arthur. I thought you were a gentleman!'

'Would you like some, Lucy? He'll save you some for a cream cake.' Louie replied, giving Lucy a salacious wink.

Lucy threw her head back and laughed so loudly that anyone within a half a mile radius looked their way. It echoed around the park like rounds rattling off of an enemy machine gun. She was more jarring than ought to be humanly possible.

'You are a one,' she said, pushing Louie's shoulder with her hand. 'Goodness me. *Imagine*! It may have worked on Bonnie Charlesworth but it'll take more than a little wacky backy to make a dishonest woman of *me*, Louie!'

The group fell silent, as though loud-mouth Lucy had just stuck a pin into a balloon. Polly elbowed her in the ribs, trying to communicate something using a series of eyebrow lifts. She looked like she was having a stroke.

'What?' demanded Lucy, throwing her hands up into the air. 'Are we not allowed to mention her now, or something? For goodness sake, she's not *dead*. What a fuss.'

'Leave it, Lucy,' said Marcus, his brows drawn together.

She bit into the last cheese scone with more aggression than seemed necessary, gave Marcus a dirty look and then gazed out across the park, all good humour evaporated.

The conversation managed to splutter back to life with no further mention of Bonnie, and the afternoon trundled on. The atmosphere lifted and Arthur dared to hope the beginnings of a crisis may have been averted. The picnic was quickly demolished, and the ensuing game of rounders was a hilarious shambles from start to finish.

As dusk fell, all parties busied themselves trotting back and forth between the blankets and the bins disposing of paper plates and plastic cutlery. Louie remained lying on his front, scribbling something onto the back of a crumpled receipt with a biro, ignoring everyone around him.

The group walked home along the pavement together, veering off one by one as they passed the points of their own onward journeys. Eventually only Arthur, Louie and Polly remained, the three who lived the furthest south from the common.

It was starting to get dark and Polly's ears had turned a hot red. She'd remained quiet through most of the day, stealing shy glances here and there at the boys, and venturing very little besides. She wasn't someone at home in a crowd or adept at making small talk. She certainly wasn't someone who would usually be walking home in the dark with two boys she didn't know. Yet the alternative seemed equally unpalatable.

'Would it be alright if we walked you to your gate, Polly?' asked Louie, sensing instinctively the importance of being chivalrous. 'Only, it's quite late now. I wouldn't have you walking out here on your own. You're not far from us, are you? We could walk with you on our way back, maybe, see you to your door?'

Polly was relieved. These were nice boys. She'd heard the rumours of late, of course she had. News of Louie Carlton's dalliances had spread across the schools of south and west London like wildfire, elevated to almost mythical proportions. She looked at him, and she saw it. He was undeniably handsome, and charming, too.

Polly wasn't usually the kind of girl who had thoughts like these, she had yet to find a member of the opposite sex attractive. She was usually far too occupied by grappling with her own social ineptitude for thoughts of that nature to manage to cross the threshold of her nerves. But she could recognise a handsome face when she saw one, a nice pair of blue eyes. Kind eyes. She noted the dimples, the curly hair, the slight swagger to his walk.

It was his confidence that set him apart. The kind of assurance that was an ease, a comfort in one's skin. Not the arrogance she had been expecting.

'Thank you,' she said. 'That would be nice.'

Polly and Louie continued talking about school. He asked her about her friends, about music. He asked all the right things, and she replied accordingly. It was a pitch perfect exchange of polite chatter, with Arthur bringing up the rear, barely able to conceal his boredom.

By the time they reached her gate, something had shifted in her manner. She turned to Louie and thanked him, appearing more at ease than earlier, probably more than she'd ever felt in the presence of near strangers.

She hesitated as she turned to go inside, saying, 'She asked me about you, you know.'

'What did she ask?' Louie replied, streetlights glinting off of his eyes.

'What I'd heard about you. Whether I'd seen you.'

'And what did you say?'

'Yes, and no. I've heard things,' she told him, looking at her feet, wondering if she had overstepped the mark already, by saying the little she had said.

She'd met Louie a number of times at socials and parties. He wouldn't remember her, she didn't begrudge him that. She knew she was forgettable. A wallflower, her mother called her. It didn't help that she was best friends with Lucy, who eclipsed her entirely from peoples' vaguest recollections.

He took her hand and she jolted as though he had stung

her, trying to snatch it away, but he held it firm.

'I need to know,' he whispered, as though addressing a baby bird. 'It's like she has disappeared off the face of the earth. If she doesn't want to talk to me, that's fine. But she should tell me that herself, shouldn't she?'

'She can't,' she replied. 'She's not allowed out. She's not in school anymore. She's home schooled now.'

'But why?'

Go on, thought Arthur, you're at the precipice. Just throw him off the cliff already, so I don't have to.

'Ask your friend,' she said, glaring across at Arthur leant against her garden wall, hands thrust deep into his pockets.

Arthur groaned.

Louie's eyes narrowed as he looked over at Arthur. 'Will you see her?' He returned his gaze to Polly, the gentleness evaporated, overtaken by a sense of urgency.

'Tomorrow. Our parents go to the same church. It's the only place she goes.'

'Will you give her this?' He implored her, proffering the crumpled receipt, ink bleeding into its crevices, a pitiful looking scrap.

Her eyes were fixed on the pavement. The very idea of finding herself with a role in this most unbecoming saga troubled her, but his sincerity had captured her. He was hard to resist, almost as hard as resisting the thrill of suddenly being a part of a story that even Lucy hadn't managed to wedge her way into the heart of.

'I'll try.' she said, snatching the scrap of paper and walking briskly up the steps towards her door.

'Thank you, Polly!' he called after her.

All she offered was an awkward one-armed wave above her

head without turning around before disappearing through her front door.

The boys stood silently looking at one another under the street lamps, a siren wailing somewhere in the distance. Louie pulled a roll up from behind his ear and lit it, inhaling deeply.

Arthur could feel his friends gaze burning through his shirt and the cogs whirring behind his eyes.

'You're gonna tell me everything.' Louie said at last.

And Arthur did.

EIGHTEEN

Bonnie, 1983.

Bonnie sat at her dressing table staring hard into each one of the trio of mirrors atop of it in turn. She was tired. Her hair hung limp, a little oily at the root. Her face was grey, ashen, erring a little closer to being dead than alive.

It had been six days now since she'd seen anything or anyone outside of the house. The beginnings of the pangs of nausea had begun, but she couldn't be sure whether it was pregnancy related or the start of some kind of agoraphobia. She had no experience to draw from, and nobody she could ask.

The walls had come down, both literally and metaphorically. Not even her own mother was on speaking terms with her. They had all turned their backs on her, united in their disgrace.

The only small kindnesses she had been shown in the last month had come from a select few members of the vast household staff. One of the maids in particular seemed to be rooting for her from a distance. Mary, the Irish one, had been leaving plates of ginger biscuits and herbal teas on her bedside table and asked her often about how she was feeling.

She was a caged princess, trapped in her bedroom amongst all of her finery, like in one of the fairy tales her mother used to read to her in Geneva before bed. She'd spent large portions of her day laid up in her four poster bed, daydreaming.

She had played out scenarios in which she had triumphed. In some, her father was back from the dead, abhorred by their treatment of her. He'd whisked her away – back to her old life, the one full of pointe shoes, plié and snow-capped mountains.

In others, she had stolen away into the night, eventually finding herself in a television studio, cameras and microphones pointed towards her as she recounted her devastating story, exposing her family's inhumane treatment of her to a shocked and sympathetic public.

The scenarios she liked best, though, were inevitably the ones where she was rescued by Louie, in every possible manner her mind could come up with. All of them ended happily. And yet, all of them were followed with unbidden dark thoughts.

She had returned home early that morning with her tail between her legs and what she had been confident was a watertight alibi. I'm sorry, I had a few glasses of wine, I know, I know, it was very stupid only it was the first time I've had a drink and I felt pressured by the others. I felt quite sick and Lucy didn't want me in a taxi all by myself so she took me back to her house to sleep it off and she didn't have our phone number to let you know. I'm ever so embarrassed and sorry for worrying you like that, yes, I know it could have been much worse, I know, I'm lucky to have such kind friends.

Only, she hadn't factored in Lucy's vindictiveness. It was foolish to underestimate the power of envy in a tribe of teenage girls.

'Bonnie? Goodness me, no, of course she would have been most welcome to come along with me like the other girls did, but she wanted to stay a little later with a boy she had met. We tried to warn her, Mrs Bennett, he's a bit of a libertine. But she had made her mind up and there was nothing I could do...' Lucy had trilled sweetly down the phone with a smirk.

After all, gorgeous Louie Carlton was far too good for the likes of Bonnie Charlesworth. Who did she think she was? It was plain to see that she had just thrown herself at him like a little blonde strumpet. It had gone against every rule in the book. You don't kiss on the first date, you *certainly* don't do anything else. It was an unwritten rule that any matchmaking within the group was presided over by Lucy personally as the girl with the most experience and social connections. It was a pre-approved, meticulously planned process. You couldn't just go rogue at the first pair of blue eyes that looked your way, whether they were the most beautiful blue eyes in all of London or not, you just couldn't. Lucy had been pining after those particular blue eyes for months and the *process* had been well under way. They were deep into the 'make him jealous' stage until Bonnie had scuppered proceedings with her loose drawers. And then she expected an alibi? How ridiculous.

And so the staying out all night, compounded by the lying and the mention of a drunken tryst thrown into the mix had meant a swift and brutal grounding for the rest of the summer holidays.

And then things had gone even more wrong. She had missed her period. It hadn't been a case of I couldn't be, surely not, am I or aren't I? It had been sore breasts and barely being able to sit at the dinner table without dry heaving. Her mother had put two and two together at once and crisis meetings had commenced in Peter's study. No matter how hard they pushed, no matter how many luxuries they took away and threats they made, Bonnie was resolute in not giving up her lover's name.

Where is he? She wondered for the hundred thousandth time. She had no way to know, nobody to ask even if anyone in the household were to deign to speak to her. Her only miniscule link to the outside world were the few words she was able to exchange with Polly Parker each Sunday in church. Getting blood from a stone would have been easier.

Bonnie sighed and ran the brush through her hair for the final time. She was long past caring about what she looked like, having passed that particular benchmark some weeks ago now.

She can't remember the last time she'd given any thought to mascara or blush. Those were things from *before.*

Before life went so miserably and cataclysmically wrong.

Such luxuries had become irrelevant. They were void and pointless. Her future looked bleaker each day, stretching out before her like the never ending black vacuum of space at the death of the universe.

She continued to stare vacantly at herself until she was summoned by Mary to join the others at the foot of the stairs to begin the weekly pretence of being part of a close-knit, wholesome family, suitably pious and decorous.

She would tow the line, shaking hands with the acquaintances of her step father and smiling politely at snivelling constituents, telling their favourite MP what a beautiful family he had.

She continued to derive great satisfaction from the nervous energy that permeated these events, the Bennetts never fully secure in the knowledge that she wouldn't choose that day to lose it. She could feel it, their uncertainty: would she drop the bomb today? It made her feel powerful, even though in every other sense, she was powerless. She liked them believing she was close to the edge. She wasn't really. She hadn't the inclination. She really just couldn't be bothered anymore – with anything.

The routine of the Sunday service passed by in its usual monotony. The sermon, the handshakes, the malted milks. The banality of it was so all-encompassing that she found herself fixated with counting the lines on her left palm. Just to stop herself from screaming.

She startled when Polly sidled up beside her. Bonnie didn't bother to look up, there was little point in losing concentration.

Relations with Polly had never been easy, even before. She had always been aloof, Bonnie had never managed to work out whether she was cripplingly shy or simply disliked her. She had always felt like she was on the back foot with Polly, you never knew where you were with her, she didn't give much away. This had been magnified beyond all reason in recent weeks. Polly's hackles appeared to go up as soon as she stepped into the room. She felt Polly's mortification at her presence from the other side of the church. Being the only two in their age group, they had found themselves pushed together in brief and stunted conversations after every service. Had Bonnie had the hindsight that Polly's stern and freckled face would be one of the only faces she would see for weeks on end, she might have been more forceful in the beginning in the pursuit of Polly's friendship.

Bonnie could see Polly's flat, functional shoes in her peripheral vision. Polly coughed, moving closer until their shoulders were touching. Bonnie's eyes shifted upwards. Polly was not a toucher under any circumstances. She had an acute aversion to intrusion of her personal space, even on a good day. And there hadn't been many of those since Bonnie became a social pariah. Nobody knew, well, nobody was supposed to. But Bonnie had seen enough nudges and whispers. It was an open secret now, however deeply her parents wanted to thrust their heads into the sand.

'I have something for you,' Polly whispered out of the corner of her mouth, face contorted into a strange gurn.

Bonnie watched her quizzically as Polly fumbled around in her pocket and pressed a shred of paper into her palm. She touched Bonnie on the arm and looked into her eyes, something that nobody had done for more than a month now. Her eyes were sad and her smile was kind. Then she was gone, swallowed up into the throng of do-gooders murmuring 'peace be with you'.

***

Bonnie was back inside her prison. Her church clothes had been re-hung for another week and she was back in her pyjamas. There wasn't much sense in dressing if you'd be neither going anywhere or seeing another living soul. It was a dirty protest of sorts; she knew it bothered her mother to see her unwashed on the rare occasions she ventured up into this room, presumably just routine checks that she was still confined and she was still breathing. It was a small win, and there weren't many of those anymore.

She was laying on her bed, ready to unfold Polly's note. She had seen that it was a receipt, she had read the items listed three times now, but it didn't give any clues. A loaf of bread, a tin of spam, tobacco, carrots, orange juice. She had waited to read the contents, she had teased herself, built up to it. It was the only communication she had had with the outside world, even if it was from miserly Polly Parker. Still, the mystery of what Polly might want to say to her was the most excitement she'd had in a while.

She took her time unfolding the note, flattening out each corner between her fingers and thumb before she began to read it. She read it once, twice and a third time. She pulled it taut to make sure it was real.

I need to see you. Monday, 8pm, Emmeline P. L x

Her vision swayed and swirled, she could feel her blood pulsing. A thousand thoughts rushing into her brain to vie for her attention.

The coarse cipher made perfect sense to her, there was no question that it was from Louie or that he was trying to convey more than the few words he had written.

That night, they had talked about so many things. They talked for hours. The sex was only a fifteen minute interlude, a natural progression. In amongst all of that, wedged

143

somewhere in between the trivial and the consequential had been the part where she had told him that the only exciting thing about her time in Kensington so far had been her chance discovery of Emmeline Pankhurst's grave in Brompton Cemetery. It had been her second term in her new school and she had struggled with the adjustment. She had been part-way through a particularly trying piece of coursework on the suffragettes. Coming across the grave had felt serendipitous, like seeing two crows. She had earned an A in the end for her essay and she had returned to the cemetery later that week to thank Emmeline personally. Her silly story had made Louie smile, and they had joked about planning pilgrimages to other famous graves, a tour of the local notable dead. Knowing that he remembered this, a drop in the ocean of the words they exchanged that night, brought with it the harmony of knowing that she mattered.

She had no idea yet how she would orchestrate her departure but she had over twenty four hours with very little by way of interruption to come up with the how. There was no question as to whether or not she would go.

She walked across the room and opened her wardrobe, removing two boxes from the top shelf. One box housed medals and trophies, brass ballerinas with her name and various dates engraved on their fronts. The larger box housed leotards and tutus, great swathes of tulle and sequined show costumes many sizes too small for her now. She pulled out the navy blazer from the bottom and slipped the note into its inside pocket. She held it up to her face, breathing in the mixture of grass and stale smoke.

She was aware of the breath in her lungs, the sound of the clock ticking on her nightstand. She felt vital. She had allowed herself the first threads of hope.

***

It had been easy, in the end. She had sat at the furthest end of the dining table as the senseless charade of a family meal time commenced. It was something that her stepfather insisted upon, that they washed their hands and faces and sat down to eat. It was ridiculous, really, that she was still expected to join them only to endure an hour of being invisible. To him, the ritual implied some semblance of order, a rule being adhered to irrespective of the household's collective discomfort. She would have preferred to take her meals alone in her bedroom as she did during the week whilst her step siblings were at school. She was sure that everyone else would prefer it too, her presence wasn't any more desirable to them than the rigmarole of it was to her.

Her stepfather sat at the head of the table, her mother directly across from him. Bonnie was seated to her mother's right. Peter junior, the eldest, sat opposite Bonnie to her mother's left. He was the most introverted of the siblings. By and large, he kept his own council, likely due to the differences he had with his father in political persuasions. He exuded quiet calm, was non-confrontational and was the only one Bonnie felt anything remotely close to fondness towards. He barely looked at her, but when he did, it wasn't the same look she got from the other two, laced with disdain and contempt.

Between Peter junior and senior was Giles, the youngest sibling, the one Bonnie probably hated the most although sometimes he ran a tight race with his sister who sat between

Bonnie and her father. Lucinda had always been prickly, she had treated Bonnie like an unfortunate inconvenience since the day they arrived. Her gaze was firmly levelled away from Bonnie at all times, she didn't so much as deign her with a cursory glance. Her brand of punishment was absolute absence of any kind of recognition whatsoever.

Giles, however, was open in his callousness. He was the one who sneered, threw out the jibes and seemed to derive the most pleasure from the situation, referring to it often.

As soon as the food had arrived, Bonnie had stated 'I feel sick.'

'I'm sure we all feel sick, Bonnie.' Giles had smirked, eyes full of mirth. He was itching to continue, she was sure.

'Eat your food, Bonnie.' her mother had muttered with a heavy sigh. It was hard work, after all, walking the fine line between not being complicit in cruelty towards your blood daughter and not upsetting the applecart with the other side, the side who held the purse strings. Lena had lost patience with her daughter's insubordination, feeling that she would make life easier for both of them if she could just act a little more contrite. Relations between herself and her husband had been temperamental enough for the last few months. She had been the one who had borne the brunt of his work and family related frustrations. She had been treading on eggshells for so long she was already exhausted before Bonnie had unleashed this showstopper upon them.

Silver clinked and scratched on china, five closed mouths chewed.

'I'm going to be sick,' she said again, more forcefully, to no one in particular. The only response she got was from her mother in the form of another weary sigh.

She stood and left the table. Nobody looked up. She headed up the stairs, turned out her lights, closed her bedroom door and went back downstairs, quietly letting herself out of the front door.

She was elated as she walked down the dark streets. The night was warm, there were plenty of people around which gave her a cloak of security should someone discover her gone and come after her. They wouldn't want to draw attention to her, to *this*.

She savoured the first freedom she'd tasted in weeks, music and laughter coming from behind garden walls, the warm breeze brushing her cheeks.

The hum of humanity living lives of liberty fell away as she neared the cemetery gates. Her footsteps and the occasional rustle of leaves became the only sounds.

It was some time since she'd passed a street lamp and it took a moment for her eyes to adjust to the darkness. She looked left and right. Shadows loomed all about her and her heart started up a drum beat in her ears when she heard him.

'You came.' he said. She saw the curls of smoke and the orange glow of his lit cigarette before she saw him as he stepped out from behind a crypt.

He held both of her hands and they stood at arms width, looking one another up and down. His hair was longer. He was taller than she remembered, thinner maybe. His fingers felt rough between hers. He was smiling, a dimple cheeked boy with a cigarette held between yellowed teeth.

She nodded and he led her down the path. He veered off to one side, stepping over foliage, to the furthest side of the cemetery and lay his coat down on the grass. They both sat down, neither knowing where to begin.

Panic built up at the back of Bonnie's throat, the weight of expectation. Louie shifted up onto his haunches, cupping his hands to protect the flame from the wind. He lit his third consecutive cigarette and looked down at her, limpid eyed.

He took a drag and turned to her. 'I could marry you? I *would* marry you.'

She looked at him. What kind of husband would he be? He was a boy, she realised. Would he work? What work would he do? He would be a kind husband, that much she could see. He was so unspeakably handsome, so beautiful he was almost feminine.

Maybe they would be fine. She wanted to say 'yes'. She rolled the word around her tongue for a few moments, the consonants beginning at the back of her throat to travel towards the tips of her teeth. She swallowed it.

'But what about your life?' she asked him, hoping she didn't have to expand on this and start throwing around ugly words like 'nappies' and 'money'.

'What about it?' he replied. 'We could start a new one.'

'Where would we live?'

'Where I live now.' He cupped her cheek. 'My mum would never turn us away. She was sixteen when she had me…my dad, he didn't want to know me. She will help us, I know she will.'

'She sounds like a wonderful person.' Bonnie said, knowing her own parents wouldn't for a second let things be that simple.

Not with an election on the horizon.

The words hung in the air like chalk dust. A slither of moon escaped from behind the clouds, breathing life into the cemetery's strange sleeping rhythms. An owl hooted somewhere behind them, the silent grandeur of a descending song of night. Bonnie shivered at the anticipation of the dead all around her as she teetered on the precipice of a new kind of life.

'What do you think?' asked Louie. 'Shall we try it?'

She laughed at him then, thinking of them trying this out. As though they might be in a changing room on Bond Street, pushing their arms into cashmere jumpers to see if the shades suited their complexions.

As though the fate of three lives weren't hanging in the balance.

'Yes, let's try it.'

Then they were both laughing. He brushed the hair from her face and kissed her. His breath sour, the tips of his fingers smelling like burnt wood. But still, he was lovely.

They zig-zagged through the streets with her tucked under his arm, concocting decadent versions of themselves as mother and father. They went back and forth, scene by scene, through their lavish wedding: the songs they would dance to, the food they would serve, adorned with top hat, cravats and tiaras.

And Bonnie's mother would stand with her nose pressed to the window begging for redemption, finally understanding what it meant to be excluded.

Their laughter built to a feverish crescendo, both giddy in their respective relief.

As they turned into her street, he pulled her into him, suddenly serious.

'It will be alright, okay? Just tell them. Tell them what will happen, tell them what we'll do, they can't stop us. And I'll be here, I'll be here at five o'clock tomorrow, okay?'

'Why five o'clock?' she mumbled into his shoulder, anticipating the obstructions, the angry words she would have to endure with that kind of wait.

'I have school until three.' he said to her, as though she'd missed the obvious.

There was a shift then, the sentence a stark reminder of their youth and joint incompetence. She hadn't imagined that he would be going to *school* – not now.

But she was tired. The rollercoaster of their rendezvous – the nerves, the elation – had exhausted her.

The lights were on in her house, they knew she had been gone. She had another battle to steel herself for behind that front door.

'Okay.'

She kissed him quickly and pulled sharply at the gates until they came apart enough for her to squeeze through. She looked back at him and he was walking backwards, eyes still fixed on her.

He blew kisses, doffed an invisible cap, bowing with a jaunty wave of his hand.

She laughed before he stole into the night.

NINETEEN

Ghosts, 1983.

'Good evening, I'm here to see Anna, please.'

Anna sat frozen in the armchair, tremulous. Her senses stood to attention, everything in a heightened state. His voice ran through her like electricity through ground wire.

'What is this about?' she heard her husband asking.

She walked quickly out into the hallway. As she came up behind Grayson, he turned slightly, a questioning look on his face. This is it, Anna thought, this is where it all unravels.

She was standing at the door frame now. Fight or flight. She was ready to go head to head with him this time.

'What do you want?' She demanded. Her voice had gone up an octave, the adrenaline making her shrill. Grayson sensed her distress and placed a firm, reassuring hand on her shoulder. The gesture a signal to the stranger: there are two of us (and one of us is a proper grown up).

'Anna Carlton...' he said. The way he ran his eyes over her in her nightgown felt like a rape.

'Carmichael.'

'My apologies: *Carmichael*. I do hate to inconvenience you at such an hour, and you too, Mr Carmichael. Only, I think we need to talk. May I come in?'

No! No, you fucking can't! Anna was about to shout, when Grayson beat her to it.

'Yes, I think you'd better had, and tell us what on earth this is all about.'

He turned and began walking back towards the living room.

Anna was grateful of his calm authority, his height, the broad shoulders under his dressing gown. She was a doe in headlights. She felt bald, sixteen again. She trotted down the hall after her husband, instinctively wanting to keep him within touching distance. The door clicked shut behind her, his brogues echoing on the tiled floor. But she didn't look back.

Grayson was pouring himself a whiskey from the drinks trolley. Anna hovered behind him, unsure where to put herself.

Peter Bennett reclined into the Eames chair, clasping his hands together. His flick-knife smile and wolfish eyes were cold and withholding and Anna was unable to meet them, however much she willed some bravado to appear.

To all intents and purposes, she had just seen a ghost.

Grayson eased himself down onto the sofa with his whiskey tumbler and Anna dutifully dropped down beside him.

'So, Mr…?' Grayson began.

'Bennett, Peter Bennett. I apologise, how crass of me,' Peter returned, all charm, extending a hand towards Grayson.

Grayson shook it. He was not outwardly ruffled, but Anna

knew her husband. The slight tilt of the head, clench of the jaw. That name wouldn't have gotten past him. He would understand the gravity of this man's presence. The feel of his hand on her knee confirmed this.

'Mr Bennett, how can we help you?' Grayson said.

'It seems we share a little problem, and I was hoping we might manage to come to some kind of solution between us.'

Why is he talking in riddles? Anna wondered.

'If it's the house—' Anna began, a stern sideways look from Grayson silencing her mid-sentence. I will handle this, his eyes were telling her.

'Oh, no. I didn't realise you were still in the dark. That makes things more difficult... It's a rather – *delicate* matter.'

'Spit it out, Peter.' Anna said sharply. She was sure he was enjoying this, dragging out the suspense of whatever bad news he had turned up on their doorstep to administer. Watching her squirm.

The vein on her neck was pulsing. She couldn't wait any longer to be pushed from the cliff he was dangling her over.

'Very well, Anna.' The wolf behind his eyes licked its lips. 'My step-daughter is pregnant,' he said slowly, 'by our son.'

The air had left the room. The world shifted to slow motion. Having delivered his blow, he began to relax backwards into the chair.

And then stopped.

The colour drained from his face.

Anna followed his gaze.

'*Our* son?' Louie asked from the doorway.

153

TWENTY

The father, 1983.

For days, the memory of that night provoked shudders in Anna. A tangle of ugly emotions had tornadoed their way around her living room with a velocity that had surprised every one of them.

His malignant smile through china-white teeth had flaunted his resolute sense of superiority over her. The moment he had popped the cork, any tiny shred of composure she had managed to claw together had vanished. She had gone utterly to pieces, screaming and wailing like a toddler having a tantrum. He had excused himself shortly afterwards, never once looking Louie in the face.

What happened after that point was now difficult for Anna to remember. Tears had run like slipstreams down their faces as confessionals were eked out of both parties, little by little.

Everything between them had blurred, their roles irreparably skewed as the past met the present like a car crash, crushed metal crumpled, glass shattering into a thousand pieces.

154

Grayson had been the only one capable of mitigating the tempest. He had become both comforter and mediator to mother and son. Plucking the facts from their torrents and laying them out to create some semblance of order.

The last time Anna had seen Peter she had been the same age Louie was now: callow and bewildered, floundering in a dark sea of grief.

She had become an orphan less than a year before, her father dying suddenly of cancer. Except it had only been suddenly for Anna. He had known and chosen to omit his prognosis from his only child to save her from worry, but succeeded only in rendering her entirely unprepared.

He had been a simple man, a decent man. A run in with some rogue shrapnel during his service in France had left him with a terse nib where his ear had been and rendered him mostly deaf. He called it his lucky ear: both of his brothers had lost their lives on the front line whilst he had sat out the rest of the war in the medical tent, his gruesome wound more superficial than anyone had realised at the time. He returned from the war to his sweetheart, Annabel, maimed but in one piece. A year later, he married her. Three years of heartbreak and disappointment followed, as they tried to conceive. All Annabel wanted was to be a mother. Finally, in 1949, they had cause to celebrate: a miracle baby to welcome in the new year. By 1950, he was a single father, having lost the love of his life to childbirth. He brought Anna up alone in a mucky old tenement building in Catford.

His melted face and disability rendered him unemployable to most. So, the steadfast loyalty with which he served his eventual employer knew no bounds. And that employer had been Marcus Bennett, heir to a land-owning dynasty that spanned centuries. And that would eventually be handed down to (and sold off by) his son, Peter Bennett.

Anna's father had doffed his chauffeur's cap and polished his boots with military precision for the remainder of his life. When he'd learnt he was to meet his maker, he went to his employer's son and had wept with gratitude when he'd agreed to take his teenage daughter in as a nanny, thanking God for this wonderful family who would repay his decades of devotion to them.

So, Anna lost her father and within a matter of days found herself living and working in Kensington, au pair to two beautiful children. She loved the job, but she detested her mistress, the belligerent snob that Cressida had been.

She was a woman destined never to be happy, one of those people for which nothing would ever be good enough. She would come home from appointments at extortionately priced salons declaring the stylists 'amateurs' and the style 'ghastly'. In restaurants, her food would always be sent back. The chateaubriand had never been cooked quite well enough, it had always been too tough, or too pink. She was a woman who enjoyed the 'I'm so sorry madam's' more than the event itself.

She was eternally unimpressed, a look etched upon her face that told only of life letting her down. Nobody had suffered more than she. And the biggest let down of all had been her husband. Whenever they were in the same room, she looked as though she were chewing something sour.

Anna had felt quite sorry for this poor man who could do nothing to please his wife. She marvelled at the patience he extended to his spouse. That Cressida used the same scathing tone of voice with him as she did with the household staff had generated a kind of kinship between Anna and Peter. An affection that hurtled quickly into liaisons of variable heat.

A sympathetic ear over clandestine liqueurs in his study while the house slept increased to stolen kisses in the laundry room, the heaving clothes pulley hiding them from view. Fingers ran up stockinged thighs, hands inside knickers in the outhouse.

Until eventually the inevitable had happened.

She had been in love with this dashing and debonair man of the world. Her young, fragile heart had worshipped him, as though amazed that it could beat again.

Her eyes rolled back at every touch. But the only thing he worshipped had been her taut, youthful flesh. And her willingness; an enthusiasm not shared by his wife.

And of course, he was a father to his two bright-eyed toddlers (sweet in an overindulged sort of way, whilst they were still innocent enough not to know any better) and another on the way.

Anna spooned mashed food into the mouths of these children. She lathered their small heads and bodies with soap. Built blocks with them, kicked balls and played make believe. All the while her thoughts geared only towards when she could next create a way to be wrapped around their father.

At night, the guilt had been debilitating. But it hadn't stopped her. Peter had been mid-campaign when the inevitable had happened, sperm meeting egg inside a fertile teenage uterus. She had been crestfallen at her own stupidity and what it would mean. For she knew what it would mean. It took her months to tell him which only aggravated the situation further.

'How could you have been so stupid?' he had asked her.

'Do you really think my wife – with child herself - would not have *known?* You don't *go* anywhere, Anna. You have nobody to visit. She isn't some sort of *imbecile!*'

These were the kindest words he had ever uttered in his wife's direction and they stung sixteen year old Anna more than the consequences of their actions.

Her fall from grace had really been the only potential obstacle he had encountered yet between himself and his seat on the local council. The trajectory of his ascent had never been called into question, the nepotistic nature of those circles had ensured that. The council seat was just a formality.

The hush money had been a necessary consequence, a slap on the wrist: he must be more careful.

A bolder, brighter young girl might have cost him far more. He had never given the by-product of these dalliances a second thought; babies were things for wives. Elegant, stockinged debutantes who came equipped with bridal trousseaus and family money. Not for some time irresistible but unfortunate young household help.

He had written her the cheque that had bought her the house and walked out of her life.

TWENTY ONE

Debris, 1983.

With all the closets emptied, skeletons removed and deposited in full view onto the thick pile rug in front of them, mother and son were, somehow, able to reach the kind of understanding that comes about only when souls have been bared and shared epiphanies have been had.

There was a path to be carved here amongst the detritus of Anna's past life and Louie's contentious future. And both parties were determined to wield the scythe. Each had a motive, after all: Louie's to be the father he had never had, to break the chain and to rescue his damsel from her ivory tower. And Anna's to spite Peter for his absence, to be the keeper of another of his secrets and to feel its power in her hands this time.

Grayson was the only one to show any reticence. 'We don't know this girl,' he said. 'There's a lot involved in being a father.'

Neither had listened to him. Of course, he ended up being

right, as he usually was.

***

Negotiations occurred in the weeks that followed over brandies and cigarettes in a booth in an upmarket bar in Chelsea. Grayson was the one tasked with putting forward their case, whether or not he was in complete agreement with it had become irrelevant. It was he who was to organise the transfer of Bonnie and foetus from Kensington to Dulwich.

As expected, he was met with strong opposition.

Grayson found himself inwardly in agreement with almost all of the objections that Peter made. Yes, they were too young. No, they didn't know what they were doing. Yes, it was most unsavoury given the circumstances. Yes, it absolutely had the capacity to go tits up.

Yet what was left unsaid made Grayson resolute in his outward display of unity with his wife and Louie.

It was clear to see that Peter Bennett's half-hearted protes-tations were not being thrown around in lieu of concern for his step-daughter. Grayson would have respected him far more if Peter just came out and said: 'Look, I'm a member of parliament and this matter represents a stain upon my reputation which I can ill afford.'

But of course, he didn't. He kept up the pantomime of concerned step-father which only made Grayson more determined than he might have been to see him squirm.

In the end, beyond a very public abduction, he was left with very little say in the proceedings.

Bonnie was dumped on their doorstep by her mother the very next day, a woman with features so sharp and angular that it seemed as though the world might tear and fall away like a stage backdrop every time she turned her head.

Bonnie stood in the middle of three huge trunks looking up at her mother as Anna opened the door.

'Goodbye, mum,' she said, as the sharp lady tutted and turned on her heel.

Anna ushered Bonnie down the hall and into the kitchen where she busied herself making a pot of coffee.

She stopped half way through, turned and said, 'Bloody hell, you do drink coffee, don't you?' And they both laughed.

'Thank you for allowing me into your home, Mrs Carmichael.'

Anna snorted, leaning down towards the hob to light a cigarette before resting back on the kitchen worktop to take a drag.

'Let's do away with the Mrs Carmichaels for starters. I'm Anna. You're here because we want you here. You and the baby. All of us. I've walked in your shoes, Bonnie, everything you're feeling I have felt. I'm not a wise woman, but this is a subject I know well. You'll always have a home with us.'

And she had meant it.

***

Bonnie had been in residence for three whole days before Maggie had heard the news on Monday morning. She had charged in as the family were eating breakfast and sat herself down at the head of the table.

'What the bloody hell has been happening here if you'll pardon my French?' she demanded, remembering Ella at the far end of the table and sending a wink her way.

161

'Does anyone tell me anything around here anymore? Hello love, I'm Maggie.' she said, throwing a warm smile in Bonnie's direction, who still hadn't made it past the awkward politeness stage yet.

'You're not the only one…' Ella muttered sullenly, as she roughly scraped butter across her toast. She had been quite put out by the sudden appearance of the interloper, even more so by the time it had taken for anybody to offer any kind of explanation. She was in high school now and everybody still treated her like a baby. Louie gave her hair an affectionate ruffle.

'Alright Ella, eat your toast.' Anna said dismissively, plonking a coffee down in front of Maggie.

'And you…' Maggie had continued, waving a finger in Louie's direction before thinking better of it and throwing her hands in the air and turning back to Anna, 'I mean, weren't we only going to watch them run around in tights on stick horses in Robin Hood five minutes ago? What is going on here? It's like I've woken up one morning and landed in a bloody soap opera.'

The two women laughed loudly, Louie grinned, Bonnie blushed and Ella sulked.

Arthur was the next to pop his head around the door.

'Toast, Arts?' Anna said, throwing a charred piece of bread in his direction.

It was surreal for Arthur to see Bonnie sat there in the middle of the table, suddenly ingrained in the familiar every day of his life. It looked wrong, somehow.

'We're gonna miss the bus.' he said to Louie, who snatched up his satchel and roughly kissed his sister's forehead the way he did every morning, leaving a smattering of toast crumbs

162

in her fringe. Anna was next to receive her compulsory peck on the cheek and he started towards the door, remembering at the last minute that there was someone else now to bid his farewells to. He turned back to the table and lifted Bonnie's chin, unselfconsciously pecking her on the lips and whispering, 'Bye, beautiful.' before swooping out of the door.

Ella rolled her eyes.

Grayson was the next to appear in the door frame. 'Time to go, Ells.'

Anna met him with a kiss and a paper sandwich bag, stopping him to readjust his tie. Ella sighed loudly and stomped past him. He shot a look at his wife who curled her lip and shrugged in a gesture that conveyed that her daughter's moods were anyone's guess. She sat down at the table and offered cigarettes around.

'How far along are you then, sweetheart?' asked Maggie.

Bonnie realised that it was she who were being addressed, but didn't quite follow. She was so unused to her pregnancy being a thing that was spoken of outside of the closed doors of studies in hushed and anxious voices that she wasn't familiar at all with the corresponding terminology.

Seeing her confusion, Maggie continued, 'How pregnant are you?'

'I'm not sure…' she began.

'Well, when did the sex happen?'

Bonnie could scarcely believe she was being asked these things by this woman she had met only minutes before, in front of her almost mother-in-law, whom she had met only three days prior. She had never thought herself a prude but she could feel the blush creeping up her neck.

'Behave, Margaret.' chided Anna, flicking her ash straight

onto the table.

'Well, we're all girls here, aren't we? You can't blush at the mention of sex anymore, sweetheart. From now on it's going to be piles, constipation and latex gloves scrambling around in your innards and that's before you even get to being on all fours and screaming bloody murder at the white coats!' Maggie replied triumphantly.

Bonnie swallowed hard. The words coming out of this crass woman's mouth were ugly words, however well she pronounced her vowels. She hadn't given any thought to the ugly words. She had thus far focused on words like bundle, booties and cherub. She suddenly felt quite sick.

'She's right,' Anna conceded, 'We need to think about registering you with a doctor and having a check-up.'

The idea of this brought about a sense of dread in Bonnie. She was not somebody who would find that kind of examination, physical or verbal, in any way comfortable. The most physical contact she had had with adults in any capacity in her life so far had been Madame Bernard forcing her leg above her head to perfect her arabesque and she had found that disquieting enough. The free spiritedness she had felt so alive with since her night with Louie had abandoned her at the very first whispers of stethoscopes and stirrups.

Maggie patted her hand.

'We're old hands, sweetheart, we'll be there every step of the way.' She told her, and Bonnie sat there thinking *I bloody hope not.*

TWENTY TWO

High school honeymoon, 1983.

Bonnie and Louie were enjoying playing grown-ups. Bonnie had been a resident of number thirty-two for a week. She was both charmed and fascinated by the complex micro-climate of relationships that existed inside the walls.

She was beginning to adjust to the rhythms and synchronicities of the house. The times at which various bodies left in the mornings and returned in the evenings. Cues as to the moods that one might provoke in another at certain points of the day. The creak of the third stair from the top. The sound of the rattling sash windows each time a double decker went past.

Ella was surly and a bit of a know it all. She was an interesting specimen, sulking behind her thick dark fringe in the ill-mannered way that pre-teen girls do. She looked nothing like her brother and Bonnie was of the opinion that she definitely drew the short straw in that regard.

Ella had inherited none of Louie's charm or easy manner.

165

She didn't have the dimples or the bright blue eyes. The only discernible trait they shared was the gap between their front teeth, which was endearing on Louie and unfortunate in amongst Ella's other facial features. Ella's eyes were huge dark things, slightly frog-like. Her nose and chin were just a little too long, her skin just a little too pale. It all looked like it had been crammed haphazardly onto her tiny face, each feature braying for attention and none of them really succeeding.

Grayson and Anna were the most unconventional adults Bonnie had ever had experience of. Their liberalism was cool in lots of ways, and shocking in others. Bonnie couldn't imagine her own mother draped around a man in full view, let alone smacking his bum with a tea towel or calling him a tosser. Louie's parents were open in their affection and they laughed together constantly.

It was as if she'd dropped into a parallel universe where so many of the taboos she'd always known had been banished. Anna approached life in what Bonnie characterised as a juvenile sort of way. Forever burning meals, forgetting to buy milk and rifling in Louie's bureau to steal a cigarette. On the occasions that Anna licked chocolate milkshake powder off of a spoon straight from the box for breakfast, Bonnie had to look away.

Anna's lack of boundaries made Bonnie feel uncomfortable, but she was sure Anna hadn't noticed.

Grayson was Bonnie's favourite. There was an aura of calm openness that transcended him, an almost physical sensation when he entered a room. He reminded Bonnie of an ageing Hollywood heart throb, classically handsome with a weathered edge.

Family conversations covered almost every conceivable topic. They talked openly about sex and political persuasions. Differences of opinion weren't pounced upon, nobody demanded evidence over the dinner table if they didn't agree with somebody else.

The only subject that seemed to be off the table was her step-family, who hadn't been mentioned once since she arrived. She supposed that Anna and Grayson assumed it would upset her (it wouldn't, she would have quite enjoyed relaying the martyrdom of her weeks of incarceration), but still, it was rather at odds with the measure of manners otherwise on show.

So far, so good. She spent the majority of her time in Louie's bedroom, which was now her bedroom too.

When Anna had started to protest Louie's manoeuvring of her trunks towards his room, he had grinned and quipped, 'Well, what's the worst that could happen? Oh, wait, *that*.'

'Fair point, lover boy.' she had snorted, shaking her head.

It was much tidier than it had been on her arrival, and it certainly smelled better. She'd enjoyed playing house for the last seven days (albeit on a small scale) but it was still much too teenage-boy-pit for her liking.

Even so, the bedroom had become their kingdom. Each day he got the bus home from school, his newfound punctuality and the care he now took not to be slapped with after school detentions (which had formerly been a routine part of his school day) a testament to his commitment to her.

He referred to her as his bride, greeting her with soft kisses on her knuckles and asking, 'how was your day, dear?'

They spent every minute they were able to holed up in his bed by lamp light. They were getting to know one another intimately, in the manner of a VHS in fast-forward. They never ran out of things to talk about and when they did, there was always the other thing: well, they may as well.

If he was beautiful in daylight hours, he was strikingly so in repose. Bonnie watched him for as long as she could get away with, acknowledging and taking ownership of all the tiny things that nobody else would get to see.

The way he started and jerked when he was falling asleep and the open-mouthed breathing he did afterwards. His night sweat and morning breath. How often he forgot to brush his teeth. The concave of his pasty boy-chest and the trail of baby hair from naval to groin. The mysterious items of jewellery that appeared and then disappeared with alarming frequency, leaving green rings around his fingers and neck and making him look a bit of a dandy.

As the days and weeks passed, what Bonnie felt towards him bordered on obsession. Her world had shrunk. With little else to occupy her, her life had become everything within the four walls.

She found herself irritable when he lent his attention to someone or something else. She was struck with an incurable melancholy when she'd waited all day for him to return and he fell asleep at midnight when there was still so much that they could talk about.

If she could have, she would have double locked the bedroom door and blinkered him like a shire horse facing only in her direction.

The following Friday night, he walked through the door a full hour late and stood at the foot of the stairs leisurely discussing football scores with Grayson for *another* twenty minutes before coming in to greet her.

'Ah, my beautiful bride!' he exclaimed as he swept through the bedroom door with his shirt undone and a roll up hanging from his lower lip. He marched towards the wardrobe and flung open the doors, rifling through her dresses with his nicotine stained fingers.

'Where were you?' she asked him through gritted teeth.

He ignored the question, instead dropping down onto his haunches to face her. 'My lady, get dressed,' he whispered, 'we are going to a party.'

Before she could protest, or even make her affront more obvious, the stringy figure of Arthur sidled in and she was forced to serve up her most gracious smile instead.

'Hello Arthur,' she said, all pearly whites from her spot on the bed.

She was no longer sure what she was angry about. Louie's tardiness? His obliviousness to her? His presumption that she would accompany him to a gathering of their peers knowing that she had been the golden nugget of salacious gossip all summer? Or that he had brought Arthur into their sacred space without giving her any prior notice. She might have washed her face.

'Hello,' he replied, focusing on the wall just above her head.

There was an unbearably intense awkwardness between herself and Arthur. They had disproportionate difficulty meeting one another's eyes.

For her part, she felt judged by him. She probably *had* led him on at the social, the tiniest bit. Only, she hadn't really known anybody, and her so-called friends had dropped her like a hot potato the minute that any boys of interest had made appearances. She remembered how he had looked at her, hanging on her every word. She may have thrown him a swish of hair or fluttered her lashes, once or twice. She might even admit to having enjoyed the attention under interrogation. But it had been harmless. She hadn't promised him a thing. She hadn't any idea that he even knew Louie, let alone spent most of his life trailing around after him like a redundant spare appendage. He had no right to be cross with her for any of that. Plus, he had stood just feet away from her and watched her stepbrother humiliate her in front of all of his friends. And he had been related to one of them! It didn't bear thinking about.

Arthur was cross with her, but his reasons were broader. He couldn't be sure whether she had intentionally led him on or not. The more time that passed between the night in question and today, the more his suspicions grew. But it was more than that, now. Now she was *there*. What should have been an embarrassing memory, a moment in time he might have been able to look back upon with good humour in years to come, had become an inconvenient throbbing thumb which encroached on his day to day life. Louie, who he'd spent most evenings alongside since he was six, was now morally bound to consider this trespasser in any plans they might make. Suddenly, his sidekick couldn't justify a jam, was unavailable most evenings and had 'priorities'. Put flatly, this girl was the most humiliating moment of his life manifested and she was impeding his friendship with Louie.

They were each wondering what justified the others' presence at the forthcoming party.

Grabbing the dress that Louie held out to her, Bonnie insisted that the boys wait downstairs whilst she got ready. Whilst part of her was reluctant to leave the safe haven of the bedroom and face the inevitable stares and whispers, another, larger part, couldn't resist the lure of being an enigma and making a grand entrance on Louie's arm.

The boys sat downstairs in the dining room with Grayson, taking turns on an acoustic guitar whilst he tinkled on the piano. They shared a few beers and a joint was passed around. By the time she walked into the room an hour later, preened to perfection, they were both too high and intensely involved in an argument over chords to notice her presence.

She coughed impatiently at their backs.

'Ooh la la!' Louie exclaimed, swivelling in his seat to face her. 'You look knockout!'

He's wasted, she thought, annoyed.

His eyes were swimming, his words beginning to slur.

Arthur seemed to be faring a little better, he was more upright. But he looked at her in a way that made her feel garish and exposed. She wanted to run back upstairs and change into jeans.

They squeezed into Grayson's Cortina for the short journey to Herne Hill. Bonnie rode up front whilst the boys sniggered in the back seats, referring to people and jokes she wasn't party to.

Anger simmered under the layers of pan stick and rouge. Grayson smiled kindly at her and made small talk here and there.

They alighted outside a stucco fronted house which was identical to the nine other stucco fronted houses in the cul-de-sac. The only thing setting it apart was the helium balloons trailing the path to the door and disco lights turning a closed curtain window from pink to blue to pink again. The street was still and quiet, save for a heavy, unrecognisable bass line, muffled by walls.

Bonnie felt conspicuous in her sequin mini dress and platforms. Her hair was too big, her kohl too intense and her heart was beating too loudly in her ears.

The front door was flung open by Marcus Pervical.

'Louie! Arthur! You bloody made it, you devils!' he boomed, grabbing Louie under one arm and roughly rubbing at his crown with his fist. 'Get in, get in, you're playing catch up now!' he continued, propelling them down the hall.

Bonnie slipped in behind them just before Marcus slammed the door.

The noise and the lights were an assault on the senses, bodies crammed into every inch of the place.

'Louie!' came various cries as they crossed the room in a snake.

Drinks were thrust into Louie's hands at every turn. By the time they'd woven their way into the kitchen, his arms were full. He was pulled into a circle of boys holding shots in the air and chanting like gorillas.

Nobody seemed to have noticed that Bonnie was there. It wasn't exactly the gasp and gawp scenario she'd been expecting.

After half an hour, still nobody had uttered so much as a word to Bonnie. It wasn't as awkward as it could have been, but standing around staring at her boyfriend's back as he chatted animatedly to strangers – her existence seeming to have escaped his consciousness entirely – was not what she had envisioned. Not at all.

She had never been surplus before. She had never been forgettable.

In the absence of anyone offering her a drink, she huffed off to the other end of the kitchen to get one herself. She located a bottle of vodka and some mixers on the kitchen counter and began a tentative ransack of the upper cupboards for a vessel in which to pour them when she was nudged sideways by an arm rifling in a cutlery drawer.

'Oh!' exclaimed a wide-eyed Lucy Heathcote-Ross. 'It's you!'

Bonnie had never seen Lucy lost for words before and she was thrilled.

'Yes,' she said breezily, 'it's me.'

She plucked a large wine glass from the cupboard and took her time pouring the vodka into it while Lucy looked her up and down, mouth agape like a hooked sea trout.

'But I thought you...'

Jennifer and Polly came up behind Lucy and they gawped at Bonnie, en masse.

Bonnie took a sip of the vodka, engaging every muscle in her body in the act of not wincing. Then she turned and busied herself pouring tonic into it, glad now that she'd done her hair and worn her dress.

She knew the politics and hierarchy of these girls: she'd been one of their pack a few months ago.

'Aren't you... *pregnant?*' Lucy tried again, emboldened by her minions.

'Yes,' said Bonnie, as though they were discussing a pair of shoes they had seen in a magazine and not a fact that had purportedly ruined her life. She followed it up with a slight raise of her eyebrows, hoping to convey the '*and?*' she was saying in her head.

Lucy was confused. Expressions travelled across her face like a silent movie until she reached her destination, her lightbulb moment.

'So you're here with Louie?' she leaned in closer, knowing there was only one socially acceptable answer to this question.

'Of course I am,' Bonnie replied, feeling smug and no longer surplus, delighted to be the epicentre of such morbid curiosity. She was more than ready to roll out her tale of unjust hardship turned happy ending, complete with evil step family, heroic rescue and handsome prince. She would make them work for it, though.

'Oh, that's *fab*, hon,' said Lucy with a brittle smile, as though she hadn't been the eye in the storm of malicious rumours that had raged around South London on this very subject for weeks. As though the designs she had openly talked of having on Louie Carlton the night of the social had never passed her lips.

If she was disappointed by Bonnie rising from the dead she had an excellent poker face, presumably honed to perfection in one of her father's casinos.

Jennifer was nodding enthusiastically, breaking into a wide smile now her ring leader had signalled the required response. Polly's smile was tighter but more genuine.

'So you two are an item, now?' Lucy persisted.

'Oh yes, we're going to be married soon.' Bonnie offered a sanguine smile, enjoying every minute of being on the front foot of this exchange.

Lucy's eyes looked like they might pop out of her head.

'*Really?*' she shrieked. '*Louie* is getting *married?* Well, that *is* a turn up for the books! Have you set a date?'

Bonnie was trying not to read between the lines and began to feel like she might have been wrong footed. She was also mildly offended by the connotation that it was shocking that

Louie would be marrying *her*, but not so shocking the other way around.

'Almost. A winter wedding, we think,' said Bonnie, off the cuff. They had been thinking no such thing. No plans had been mentioned since the night at Brompton Cemetery, which had been a source of both worry and ongoing frustration for her. 'How about you and Marcus?'

'Oh, *that*,' Lucy giggled with a dismissive waft of one perfectly manicured hand. 'That was just a little bit of fun, we are just *such* close friends, there was no sense in spoiling things. That was a couple of months back. You should ask Louie about it, actually.'

Jennifer and Polly looked from Lucy to Bonnie, hawk eyes gauging any reaction but none was forthcoming.

Bonnie understood that she was expected to press Lucy further on this but her mulishness prevented her from doing so. Having spent the previous months in social exile, tonight's comeback performance of cool aloofness had taken on more momentum than any truths which might be garnered here. If she could convince Lucy that she was fully recovered from her social leprosy, she would have convinced everyone.

Electricity would surge through telephone wires tomorrow as the lines were lit up across the borough with Lucy as the chief operator.

Instead, Bonnie settled for a smile. 'I'm glad you're happy.' She excused herself and walked back out towards the hall, her back as straight as gravity would allow. She pinched past a heavy petting situation at the foot of the stairs and headed up in hopes of finding a bathroom, or any lockable door she might be able to hyperventilate behind in peace.

The party hadn't spilled all the way up the stairs yet and

to her great relief she didn't see another person between the stairs and the bathroom. She locked the door behind her and slumped down onto the side of the bathtub. She inhaled deeply, breathing out slowly through pursed lips, the way Madame Bernard had taught her as an aid to expel pre-performance jitters. She only had time to notice how much her hands were shaking before there was a knock at the door.

'Just a second!' she called, propelling herself towards the mirror and fumbling with toilet roll to dab at the pearls of sweat gathered on her upper lip.

'Bonnie? Bonnie, it's me!' a voice whispered.

Bonnie opened the bathroom door to the singular figure of Polly Parker who had mutinously left her captain's side.

'Are you alright?' asked Polly, still whispering. Her eyes were wide with concern, falling down to Bonnie's empty glass which she snatched and filled with cold water. 'Here, drink this.'

Bonnie did as she was told and perched back on to the bathtub. Polly sat down alongside her. When the glass was empty she returned it to Polly.

'Are you sure you should be...' Polly nodded towards the glass. 'Only...' Polly's words trailed away, she was not brave enough to finish even a mildly confrontational sentence. 'I haven't seen you in church. I was worried, I gave you the note, and, you know...' Polly was also not brave enough for awkward silences.

'Thank you for the note, Polly,' Bonnie said, turning to look at Polly with the sudden realisation that this timid and peculiar girl had been the unlikely vector of her passage from damned to living. 'He asked me to meet him... He asked me to marry him, he came and collected me the next day. He took me out of that house, Polly, that house, I can't even begin to tell you...'

Polly nodded as though she knew, but she didn't. All she knew was that Bonnie's family were valued and respected members of the parish and the community. Bonnie's abrupt disappearance had been unnerving at first but Polly had assumed that her absence from Sunday services had been another layer of Bonnie's rebellion. The broad view was that Bonnie was spoiled, vindictive and out of control. Polly preferred a more diluted version in which Bonnie was confused, a lost soul.

'None of it would have happened if it hadn't been for you, Polly,' Bonnie told her. Polly's eyebrows shot up at this. 'Now me and Louie can be together, a proper couple with a proper baby.'

Polly patted Bonnie's hand in place of any words she might have attempted to club together. The right thing to say would be 'don't worry about it, it was nothing, I'm so happy for you.' But she couldn't. Polly had principles, even if she wasn't always in possession of the courage to vocalise them.

Polly was dubious of this happy ending and she was uncomfortable to be the recipient of gratitude on behalf of it. A girl like Polly, with her faith, her pimples and her Velcro-strap shoes, was less prone to fantasy or hysteria than girls like Bonnie. She was able to look at a love story with a healthy dose of scepticism.

She had watched Bonnie during those weeks, silent and downtrodden in the pews. And in those very same weeks she had seen Louie. In basements and corridors, slurring and swaying, swapping money for powders and pills. Swapping saliva with a blonde, swapping a blonde for a brunette.

It was difficult for her with this data she had gathered to put it side by side and come up with any variant in which the resulting scenario could be described as a happy ending.

***

Louie was standing half in, half out of the front door with a bottle of Merlot in one hand and a joint in the other. To his left, hunched against the door frame with his hands in his pockets, was Arthur. To his right, leaning on his shoulder and saying something only millimetres from his earlobe, was Lucy Heathcote-Ross.

Arthur was the only one who noticed Bonnie and Polly descend the last few stairs. He nudged Louie in warning. Louie held the joint out to Arthur without tearing his eyes away from Lucy's.

Bonnie caught the end of Lucy's sentence, '...could have told me yourself, though.'

When Arthur coughed and said, 'Alright, Bonnie?' Lucy's head whipped round. Louie was slower off the mark. There were a silent few seconds where the girls engaged in a crossfire of loaded stares. Lucy didn't remove her hand from Louie's shoulder but stood there proprietorially, an amused smile playing across her lips.

'Oh, hi girls,' she said in her loud West London hoot. 'Louie's just been filling me in on your great escape, Bonnie! Goodness me, how scandalous! Haven't you just been through it! And Polly, where have you been hiding?' she added, a little more sharply.

Polly looked down, fiddling with the clasp of her bag.

Lucy squeezed Louie's shoulder, telling them all, 'We'll

catch up with you again later, darlings! There are so many people I need to catch up with here, if I don't start the rounds now, I'll never leave!'

She laughed her ugly laugh and sashayed past them, hooking Polly's arm as she passed and dragging her along.

Louie blinked slowly and stupidly, a grin spreading out across his face. 'My bride!' he rasped, holding the Merlot out to salute her and stumbling slightly as he did so.

'Can we go home, soon?' she asked him, wincing at the smell of stale wine and pot on his breath.

He laughed loudly as though she'd just told the best joke he'd ever heard.

'Home? It's only—' he waved his wrist around and squinted at it, bringing it closer to his face and then further away again. This was funny, too. 'What time is it, Art?' he asked his friend, throwing his arm clumsily over him, sending red wine cascading down his shirt.

Arthur steadied the bottle and checked his own watch. 'Ten thirty.'

'*Ten thirty!*'

Louie took a triumphant swig from the bottle, some of which dribbled back out of the corner of his mouth and down his chin.

'I'm tired,' said Bonnie, who was suddenly feeling very tired. She wanted to retreat, to return to Louie's bedroom and barricade herself away from any uncomfortable truths that might find their way into her ears. Truths it was better not to know.

'Don't worry, babe, I know just the thing, if my guy's got any left…wait right there, don't move,' he said, thrusting the remainder of his joint at her as he stumbled past and back into the disco lights.

'He's wasted,' she stated.

Arthur sighed, scuffing his foot before giving a, 'Yeah.'

'I really want to go home,' she told him, 'I don't feel good.'

Arthur shrugged and looked at his shoes. This wasn't his problem to deal with, surely? What did she want him to do? He looked up, intent on searching for Louie, but saw she was crying.

She was a beautiful crier, he thought, like a porcelain doll.

His heart fluttered as he looked about behind her, trying to locate somebody who might be able to comfort her, or at least somebody who might have more experience with pregnant teenage girls in tears, but the hallway was empty.

He watched her flinch as the sound of a loud crash resounded across the music, followed by loud jeers and the unmistakable sound of Lucy's machine gun laughter.

'Do you need some fresh air?' he asked, and she nodded.

He grabbed a coat from a peg next to the door and folded it around her shoulders as they stepped out. He closed the door behind them and they walked across the front lawn to their right. There was a wooden bench pushed up against the wall dividing this house from the one next door, damp with night time. They sat side by side looking out onto the quiet street.

'I shouldn't have come,' she said into the silence. 'Is he always like that?'

Arthur smiled, not in an unkind way. 'Yeah,' he said, taking a drag on the joint. 'Yeah, he is. Did you not know that?'

'Know what?' she asked.

He shrugged. Louie's hedonism was no secret, anyone who knew him would agree. He was surprised that this aspect of his friend was so unexpected for her. He would have been no different on the night of the social.

He was the life and soul of every party, a party could hardly be called a party within a five mile radius if he wasn't on the guest list. His aptitude and tolerance for alcohol and occasional dabbles in other bits and pieces was essentially his by-line. Arthur wasn't sure what she'd thought she was buying, but she could hardly return it now.

Her eyes shone in the moonlight like coins in a wishing well and he let out a breath. She had fallen into their lives like a beautiful silk scarf that looked and felt more exquisite than anything they'd ever seen, but was ultimately ill-fitting and inappropriate.

'He'll be fine,' he said, wanting to placate her. 'He's just… being Louie.'

'He looked like he was about to pass out.'

Arthur laughed at this. 'Oh, he won't. He looks like he will, but he won't. He'll still be going at the same speed when the sun comes up. His stamina is famous. Don't worry about him, he'll be fine. He'll wake up tomorrow morning as fresh as a daisy with a smile on his face. It's one of life's great mysteries.'

'But what about the next night, and the one after that? What about when there's a baby?' she asked, her eyes searching his.

Arthur swallowed. He wasn't sure what she was looking for from him. This was bigger than him, he didn't have the answers.

He was seventeen, he was a virgin. He had absolutely nothing to draw from, no experience even remotely relative. It wasn't as though they were in their forties. It wasn't as though Louie woke up in the morning trembling until he managed to locate an errant can of cider.

It was just a bit of fun.

He had no crystal ball to call upon to dole out advice or reassurances about the future. If he was really honest, he had no idea how this would all play out at all. He couldn't hedge any bets on his friend's capacity to change, it really was nothing to do with him.

It was typical that he would be the one sat outside in the cold, expected to find answers to these questions whilst the perpetrator was inside exercising his joie de vivre.

'Sorry Arthur,' she spoke into his thoughts, 'I'm just scared.'

She lay her head on his shoulder. An unlikely truce had been called. He closed his eyes and allowed himself to imagine, just for a moment, that it had been him who lay nose to nose with her on the school field that night. That he was the one who would live out his life in such proximity to her.

He held her hand and they sat there, quietly.

We are all in trouble here, he thought, *each one of us.*

TWENTY THREE

Fireworks, 1983.

The Carmichaels and the Maxwells were gathered in the garden at number thirty-two to celebrate Ella's thirteenth birthday.

Between them, Anna and Maggie had laid out a rather eclectic buffet on the kitchen counters. Sticky sausages met a side of baked salmon. A paper plate of monster munch tucked up adjacent to an artisan cheese board. A hotch-potch of culinary delights.

Grayson's contribution was the crate of fireworks he drove back from a stall at Peckham market on the same date every year, taking great pains to detonate in a crowd-pleasing manner.

To him, to triumph at this birthday tradition was tantamount to the success of the gathering, and therefore tantamount to Ella's happiness. Back and forth he would run, to the end of the garden and back with his trusty red safety lighter, lighting fuses and scarpering back to the patio to gauge the levels of crowd satisfaction from the ooh's and ahh's.

Ella, however, found fireworks cumbersome by now. Every birthday that had been and gone had been choreographed around them. It was just one of the crosses she had to bear, sharing her birthday with this silly holiday, celebrating a silly man failing at an even sillier plot. Why couldn't she go to the cinema, or go ice skating like everyone else? It wasn't fair.

Ella had started at the local comprehensive last year and had invited two of her new friends, Suzy and Helen, for her first ever birthday sleepover. The hierarchy amongst the fresh faced second years was still in the very early stages of development and as such, in Ella's young mind, it was imperative that she impress them.

And the two girls were impressed, mightily impressed. Not with the big house, not with the curious hybrid party food, not with Ella's young parents who knew their Dylan from their Young, no. The single entity which both were so enamoured by was sitting at the head of the garden table with barbecue sauce dripping down his chin, knocking back his baby sister's birthday champagne like there might not be a tomorrow. Oblivious that he had become an object of obsession for these two quiet girls teetering on the edge of their journey into womanhood.

Once everyone had cleared an acceptable amount of food from their paper plates, it was cake time. Grayson entered the garden with a huge chocolate gateau adorned with strawberries and candles. A noisy, out of tune rendition of 'Happy Birthday' commenced while Ella cringed. He plopped the cake in front of her as the hip hip hooray's died out.

'Make a wish!' he said to her, and she did.

'Come on then sis, what did you wish for?' demanded

Louie.

'You can't ask her that! It won't come true!' said Anna, refilling everyone's glasses.

'Nonsense! Superstitious tripe. I just want to know what my baby sister's most divine wish is, what's wrong with that?' he asked, winking at Ella.

Ella, who would never in a million years own up to what she had wished for, quickly sided with her mother, an occurrence rare enough to raise eyebrows.

'It's bad luck,' she said. 'I'm not telling.'

'Aw, no fun.'

Grayson began to slice the cake, roughly plonking slabs on napkins at every place at the table, skipping the part where the manners he had been brought up with dictated that he first enquire as to whether each guest would like a piece of cake, and then serve up accordingly in his haste.

'He hasn't even remembered the cream,' Anna whispered to Maggie, 'he won't be able to think of anything else until he's lit the damn fireworks, bloody pyromaniac.'

At this point, Bonnie arrived at the table. She had spent most of the day asleep, managing to forfeit lending any kind of helping hand in the preparations whatsoever and it hadn't gone unnoticed.

This would be one of the first times that the family had quietly noticed that she wasn't 'one of them'.

Carmichaels loved a shindig from start to finish: the planning, the preparation, the execution. Food, booze and party spirit was an intrinsic part of the lives they led. It glued them together.

It didn't have to be a birthday, they were quite happy to capitalise on each and every religious holiday despite their collective atheism. Bank holidays, all personal and professional achievements, *sunny* days. Anything could be turned into an impromptu celebration, and why not? There hadn't been very much to celebrate in Grayson or Anna's early lives. Grayson grew up in the arse end of nowhere with a couple of stiff and joyless Scots and Anna's father had worked frantically every day of his life until the day he'd died.

It had been an unspoken agreement between them from the word go that they would squeeze every drop of joy from life that they could. Between them they had cultivated a life for their offspring that was everything they had never been blessed with themselves. An open door policy, the importance of hospitality, the necessity of chatter and laughter.

Yet this propensity for having a good time had resonated far more with the first child than the second, so far.

There were no seats left at the table and Bonnie stood awkwardly as Louie made a long and drawn out attempt to shake the last drops of champagne from the empty bottle. Arthur stood to offer her his seat and she smiled gratefully.

As Grayson passed the last piece of cake her way, Bonnie stopped him.

'Oh, no, not for me, thank you.'

'It's *cake!*' exclaimed Anna.

'It looks lovely but I'm not feeling great,' said Bonnie.

Anna and Maggie shared 'the look'.

'Morning sickness already, you must be having a girl!' declared Maggie.

Suzy and Helen stared openly at Bonnie, who surely must be *far* too young to be having a *baby*. Helen had a sister who was sixteen and she wasn't even allowed to the pictures on her own yet.

186

Bonnie's jaw tightened at becoming the unwitting headline act yet again.

'Nah, it's a boy,' said Louie, with the clumsy confidence of a boy who'd finished off both his own slice of cake and the one that Bonnie had refused, and was now lighting the joint he had tucked behind his ear at the table.

'Do you have to?' Bonnie hissed.

'Have to what?' he asked, exhaling into her face.

'Smoke that stuff! It bloody stinks, I hate it. I'm growing a baby here and you're blowing toxic fumes all over me, twenty-four hours a day!'

Bonnie wasn't sure she could stomach another night of him traipsing up and down the stairs for snacks that he would consume noisily in bed as she tried to sleep. He dropped crumbs everywhere before he passed out next to her and snored like a train.

The hand holding, back rubs and whispering sweet nothings had been a fleeting thing. The reality of sharing a sleeping space with Louie had been a rude awakening, and he was only one getting any sleep during the dark hours.

She usually dropped off out of sheer exhaustion as dawn was breaking, only to be awoken again by Louie thumping around the room searching for rogue socks and unfinished homework. It surprised her that more murders of snoring husbands hadn't been committed by spouses in the twilight hours. By now she considered it to be a perfectly understandable and legitimate excuse for an execution in cold blood.

He laughed and made a show of leaning his chair back and blowing the next toke out behind her. 'Chill out, Bon.'

'She's right, not at the table please, we have guests,' said Grayson, in an effort to distract them into a ceasefire, having noticed the hard set of Bonnie's jaw.

'You don't mind, do ya, girls? A bit of smoke's not gonna kill anyone.' He smiled impishly at his two-girl fan club who gazed adoringly back at him, vehemently shaking their heads. 'See?'

He was triumphant, having equally made his point and thrown a spotlight on the implication that his girlfriend was up tight and prickly. He threw his palms into the air, joint between his teeth and waved his hand in a mocking flag waving gesture.

'C'mon Arthur, what the lady wants, the lady gets!' he said, ever the parent pleaser, and pulled Arthur down to the shed at the bottom of the garden. They stopped and leant against it, passing the joint between them.

After a few moments, Louie leaned in, conspiratorially, 'So I've treated us,' he whispered. 'Feast your eyes…'

Two tiny, round tablets were retrieved from his trouser pocket. Arthur leant in closely to inspect them. They were both imprinted with the shape of a dove.

'What are they?' he asked.

'A little something to enjoy the fireworks with,' replied Louie, tapping the side of his nose. 'I had them with Essex Dave at that party his sister's mate had, and it was just like… the music, the lights, the *feeling*… Trust me, they're bomb. You'll love it.'

'Is this likely to end in my mum tucking me into bed in the recovery position and shaking me awake every half hour to check for signs of life?' Arthur asked cautiously, casting his mind back to the last time Louie had turned up with goods by way of Essex Dave, an oddball if Arthur had ever seen one.

He was a skinhead, a skeletal man with skin like a lizard

and a gold tooth who whipped around on his clapped out yellow moped. Selling drugs to school kids and hanging around afterwards, outstaying his welcome, as though he had nowhere else to go.

Louie laughed and clapped him on the shoulder, not answering his question. Instead, he stuck out his tongue and placed one of the pills onto it, wiggling his eyebrows as he dry swallowed.

He held the other pill out on his index finger, giving Arthur a look with the kind of intensity only boys of a certain age will understand: a look that spoke of peer pressure, conveying a dare.

Arthur rolled his eyes and followed suit before they both headed back up the path towards the gathering.

'Right! Fireworks! Let's get this show on the road, it's bloody Baltic.' Anna was saying, blowing into her cupped hands.

Anna and Maggie passed around sparklers and hot cups of mulled wine as Grayson busied himself at the bottom of the garden. All bodies huddled together against the cold on the patio to watch the display.

Nobody was more mesmerized than Arthur. For the first fifteen minutes, he stood amongst his kin folk and dutifully made the right noises at the right intervals. But at some point, his heart began to beat a little quicker and he could no longer feel the cold.

The lights got brighter, sharper, the colours more electric. He was flooded with heat and an intense gratitude for this time and place, the colours, the beauty in his world.

He gripped Louie's arm and Louie grinned, nodding in encouragement, passing him a second cup of the mulled wine.

Arthur gulped at it like a Bedouin coming upon a watering hole after three days of mirage. The night was alive, the fireworks dancing above them like spirits telling them that life was great, life was perfect – and Arthur believed them.

He'd never felt so indestructible before.

When the last bang sounded out, everybody clapped, neighbours wolf whistled and Grayson did a graceful bow in the middle of the garden, smiling from ear to ear.

Ella and her friends retired upstairs to her bedroom. Grayson had spent hours constructing a huge den out of old sheets and string lights, with mattresses and sleeping bags on the floor underneath. Ella had been mortified at the concept, insisting that dens were for *children* and they weren't *children* anymore. She had u-turned on this stance immediately upon seeing the projector he had borrowed from school and rigged up to play films cinema-size on her bedroom wall, pronouncing it the coolest thing she had ever seen.

Everybody else gathered around the kitchen table and more wine was poured, cigarettes were lit, a record was put on.

Arthur was tingling. He looked around the table at his loved ones from one person to the next and he could feel their vibrations like electric pulses. He felt so connected to them that he wanted to touch them.

And there was nobody he wanted to touch more than Bonnie. Once his gaze had landed on her, it refused to take off again. He could feel every part of her from across the table with every intake of breath. Her eyelashes, her finger nails, her long slender neck. He was captivated, despite the crossed arms and face like thunder, shooting daggers at Louie as he jerked around the kitchen with his arms in the air, completely out of keeping with the mellow tones of psychedelic rock exiting the speakers. Her anger was beautiful, like a wild horse in a storm.

Everyone else was oblivious to her incandescent rage, too half cut to consider questioning Louie's amped up movements or his jaw, jutted out like a typewriter at the end of its margin. When his flapping arms knocked a glass to the floor, they whooped and laughed like children.

I'm surrounded by infantile half-wits, thought Bonnie, incensed. *No wonder he is the way he is, with these people as his examples.*

She glanced across at Arthur, dismayed by his lopsided stare and the strange glaze to his eyes, the weird way he kept running his tongue over his top lip.

'I'm going to bed,' she spat, standing up abruptly and pushing the table out, disgusted in a way she could neither describe or fully understand.

'Night babe!' called Louie, throwing himself towards her. She pushed him away and stalked towards the door, both hands balled into fists. The last thing she did before she disappeared through the door was to return Arthur's stare.

The unmistakable look of disappointment bored deep into his soul.

He was instantly chastised and listened forlorn to the beat of her footsteps retreating up the stairs. This was the second time he had witnessed her walking out of a room in pain and the most terrible hopelessness washed over him, so intensely that he followed it with his fingers as it ran down from his crown over his face, down his neck, his shoulders, down, right down until it reached the tips of his toes.

The sadness was all encompassing.

Arthur put his head in his hands and Louie was at his side in an instant, whispering, 'Come on, we're off.'

TWENTY FOUR

Dawning, 1983.

T he bus journey passed by in a haze of lights and sounds. They alighted on Blackheath High Street and crossed over the road. Louie strode purposefully onto the common with Arthur trailing blindly behind.

This kind of inebriation was a different animal all together. It wasn't the merry and clumsy enthusiasm of alcohol nor the slow burn of a joint. It was an amalgam of heightened sensations, ethereal and rushing and anxious. Arthur must be diligent in sticking close to his flighty friend.

They crossed the common and turned into a quiet road of houses not dissimilar to where they lived: towering Georgian terraces and mature greenery stretching as far as the eye could see. Arthur was panting loudly now, his heaving breaths echoing out into the cold night air, leaving trails of mist.

Louie turned into one of the terraces, surrounded by wrought iron railings. He banged at the brass knocker, a roaring lion's head. They stood with their hands inside their pockets and waited, listening to the muffled sound of voices and indistinguishable music floating up from a grated basement window below them. When nobody answered, Louie pushed the door open and disappeared into the dark hallway, Arthur hot on his heels.

Louie followed the noise, Arthur followed Louie. The music became clearer as they descended the staircase. Flashing technicolour lit up the darkness, smoke spiralling towards them.

The party was in full swing and it took a few moments for Arthur's senses to regulate. The room was concrete floored, white-walled and empty, save for some turned over crates shelving a huge sound system.

Sweaty bodies threw themselves back and forth, none of them acknowledging the boys' arrival. Louie and Arthur made for an adjoining room where the atmosphere was less severe. The music had lost its ear-splitting volume and the lighting was dimmed. There were utility units lining two of the walls and patches of damp running opposite.

A group held court in the middle of the room and Arthur didn't know any of them. Louie was received with the usual reverie: hugs, kisses, high fives. Arthur was introduced to the circle and although it was still too loud to hear any names clearly, the expressions were welcoming and Arthur was instantly at ease. He was handed a plastic cup of peach schnapps and received his own selection of high fives and back slaps.

The night ambled on infinitely, blurring and morphing into this and that, carrying Arthur with it. The tablet with the dove inscription showed no sign of wearing off and Arthur was in a trance, carried away on various tangents by the lights and sounds.

The music pulsed through him as though it were his own blood. He laughed loudly and uninhibitedly at peoples' jokes, unselfconsciously throwing his arms around strangers and complimenting them on their eyes, their smell, their teeth. It was as though he had been unleashed, shed his insecurities like the diaphanous dead skin of a serpent.

Suddenly, he *understood* things; things, all things and no things. Nebulous concepts became crystal clear to him in his euphoria and for the first time in his life, he was invincible.

Sooner or later he ended up outside smoking cigarettes with a pixie-faced redhead who was deeply knotted into a sad story about her traumatic childhood. As she chain smoked, tears streamed down her face and Arthur struggled to fight the primal urge to touch her hair.

'Come on, Mandy, let's get you inside,' came a voice, and two silhouettes escorted her indoors. A third stood next to Arthur, lighting up.

'Catholic girls' school, predatory priest, devout and dis-believing parents. A terrible business, just as predictable as it is outrageous, re-lived and dissected each and every time alcohol is consumed. I probably sound terribly hard faced. I think I've become slightly immune to the tale now, truth be told.'

Arthur beamed, carried away on the unbridled joy that seeing a face he recognised had brought. The girl from the party with the clever friends. Lucinda Bennett. Sister of Giles Bennett.

Lucinda laughed. 'Not masquerading as a Lancing toff tonight, then?' she continued with a smirk.

'Nah, I'm an accidental addition, my mate dragged me

along. I don't even know whose party it is, but it's fucking fantastic.' he enthused.

'The fellow on the decks, Greg, his parents go off to Malta every few weeks and their lovely home becomes a free for all. Well, the basement does, anything ground level and above is strictly prohibited. He's become quite the prolific host of late,' she told him. 'Lucky for us. Nobody else is stupid enough to lumber themselves with the kind of clean up job he'll have in the morning. Motivated purely by the lure of kudos, of course.

'Popularity is an intoxicating affair altogether if it hasn't been attainable before... All of these beautiful people de-camping in his home, telling him he's marvellous. All because he's provided an occasional space for them to vomit and fornicate all over. I mean, look at him... his acne is so unsightly that before these parties, he was fondly referred to as Pimple. We only learnt his Christian name at the third or fourth bash. How else would he fill his house with so many girls?'

'Are you always this cynical?' Arthur laughed.

She threw her hands up. 'Once a politician's offspring, always a politician's offspring. In any case, all of poor Pimple's hopes of becoming the town Adonis have been thwarted by your curly-haired friend. I've lost count of the number of friends and acquaintances he's swept from their feet the last few weeks. He's become quite a face.'

'Louie?' he asked, stung at not being included. 'He comes here?'

'Oh yes, he comes here. Drinks all the booze, takes all the drugs, fucks all the girls and disappears into the night. He ought to be careful, he's going to turn himself into a none too salubrious urban myth.'

It took Arthur a moment to take this in. This was the first he had heard of this. His friend, who he had shared each and every detail of his life with since he was a boy, had neglected to mention these parties he'd been frequenting, the girls he'd been fondling as Arthur sat at home alone, rueing the loss of him to his new girlfriend, assuming she had been the one monopolising his time. But no, it seemed that Bonnie and Arthur had both been left behind.

Louie had been leading a double life.

'A girl from our upper sixth bore the brunt a fortnight ago. Will admit only to third base, but who knows? He disappeared shortly afterwards and she's taken to her bed ever since. She's probably still there now. It isn't like she wasn't warned, it was an almost exact replica of his performance last month with Angela Jones who's in the same *form* as her.' Lucinda rolled her eyes. Something told Arthur that Louie's magnetic charms would be benign against Lucinda Bennett.

The comedown trickled over him like a thick treacle. His heart, his shoulders, his stomach; everything sank at once. The void that appeared within his being was enormous and devastating. His head fell into his hands. The rain felt like one hundred tiny fingers tap-tapping at him. Life was conspiring against him and he was powerless. He was adrift.

Had it not been enough for Louie, to snatch a girl like Bonnie, to implant her with his seed that marked her forever as his? Arthur had gone through the motions of losing her to him, then losing him to her. Now he was being inexplicably ejected from Louie's life. He had become disposable; another person to take liberties with and run rings around.

'Are you alright?' asked Lucinda. 'You've gone very pale. You haven't taken anything, have you?'

Arthur mumbled incoherently and a horn beeped close by. Lucinda looked towards the noise and back to Arthur.

'That's my cab,' she said. 'Do you want me to get somebody before I go?'

'Can I have a lift? I need to go home.'

She hesitated.

'Alright, but if you puke, you pay.'

She linked his arm and he leant his weight on her until they were safely in the car.

'What time is it?' Arthur asked, in a daze.

'Oh, it's only ten-thirty,' she told him, 'but my brothers are on their way and if anyone knows how to murder a party, it's them.'

A sense of unease gripped Arthur but his brain was too dry to join the dots. So he closed his eyes instead, trying to lose himself in the sensations of cold sweat trickling down his back, his shirt sticking to the plastic seat and the feel of Lucinda's long, bony fingers in his vice like grip.

***

Bonnie sat at the bay window and watched the fireworks going off in all directions across the horizon. The house was dark and quiet. Anna and Grayson were warm in their bed, sleeping the sleep of the intoxicated. She hadn't heard a sound from Ella's room for half an hour or more.

She often sat like this of a night. The view from Louie's bedroom was majestic. There was something soothing about the rooftops of London after nightfall, sprawling out as far as the eye could see. The world seemed endless, things felt possible. She could pretend she was simply immersed in the view, not waiting for the clang of the gate or the scraping of a key unsteadily in a lock.

She had become a mere spectator, waiting stagnant for something to happen which might move her this way or that.

The footsteps she heard next weren't familiar, the gate that opened below her wasn't theirs. She watched Arthur cross the pavement, his gait heavy, bypassing his front door and heading around the side of the house into the back.

She treaded as softly as she could across the landing and down the stairs into the kitchen. She was gentle as she opened and closed the kitchen door. She walked across the damp grass and through the gap in the fence, into the Maxwells' garden. Arthur was sat on their porch step, smoking a cigarette and staring straight ahead.

'Where is he?' she asked him.

'Blackheath.'

'Who with?'

'I don't know.'

She sat down beside him and gasped at the temperature of the stone step. Their thighs were touching. She was shivering, he was perspiring inside his jacket. He was both exhausted and alert. He rubbed at his eyes and his jaw, bringing his fingers into a steeple across his lips in an attempt at gaining some clarity, but nothing was forthcoming.

'I think it's me,' she whispered. 'I think I'm driving him away. I don't know how to not be angry. I spend so much time wondering and willing him home. And by the time he does come home, I'm so irate that I spend the whole of it trying to restrain myself from ripping out his eyes.'

'I don't think it's you,' he said, quietly. Before tonight, he had. She had been the ideal scapegoat, the girl who'd scorned him and trapped his friend. But not now. Louie wasn't trapped at all. That night on the playing field, she'd only done the same as the ones who came after; the bedridden upper sixth girls nursing injured pride and the Angela Jones's. All unwitting, all naive in lust.

The unfortunate thing for Bonnie had been the order of things. Being the first, the one that lit the fuse under a boy already doused in gunpowder, was almost an inevitable way to wind up disappointed. She'd given Louie an introduction to the power of wanting and being wanted.

He was never going to stop at the first.

Perhaps he'd never expected to see her again, despite what he'd said. Perhaps it was all hot air, a show piece, an elaborate pantomime to distance himself from the sins of his father. Or, perhaps he was well intentioned.

The result was the same: a beautiful girl with a full womb, cold and alone in a garden on a winters' night.

Except for me, Arthur thought, *except for me. I'm here.*

'Then why does he go? What is wrong with me? And why am I still here?'

Arthur leant towards her and kissed her trembling lips, the taste of her salty tears both a question and an answer. He let himself pretend, for a moment, that they had just spent the evening talking and dancing in the great school hall and that this was the beautiful culmination of all of the things that were exchanged. But, when he opened his eyes, she was still the tear stained girl in a nightgown who slept in his best friend's bed.

He ran his fingertips down her cheek and she smiled the

saddest smile he'd ever known.

'I'm sorry, Arthur. I wish things had been different.'

He watched her walk away for the third and final time.

He would never see her again.

***

Another tear stained face stood behind the curtain of her father's study, watching the faith breaking embrace of two shadows below.

As their lips had collided, all that she knew that was right and good in the world had been thrown into question. She sat amongst the rubble of what had once been the shaky foundations of her trust in humanity.

Never again would she trust a single soul. Nobody was true. Not mothers, who only had enough love for one child at a time. Not fathers, who were so weak that their love was conducted in conciliatory gestures, never quite bold enough to break cowardice and upset the status quo by calling out the unjust. Not brothers, who replaced the objects of their affection at whim, perpetually dancing a deceptive tango of lavishing affection and snatching it away again.

And most definitely not wishes. Never again in her life would she indulge in anything as fanciful as a wish, especially not one sent longingly up into the sky over a cake and some candles. Wishes were the greatest ploys of all, deceptive in their optimism.

A dog? Don't be silly, Ella, you couldn't even keep your cactus alive, anyone capable of killing a bloody succulent certainly isn't responsible enough for a pet. Dance lessons? Impossible. You know that Louie has piano lessons on

Tuesdays and you know that his grade seven is coming up and how important it is, how selfish. And besides, you're ever so heavy footed.

A first kiss with the boy you have been in love with all of your life? The boy who read you stories, held your hand crossing roads, squeezed your fingers under the table and whispered kind words each time your mother slighted you? No, that kiss isn't for you, Ella. And in case that wasn't clear enough, a belated birthday gift: a front row seat as he shares said kiss with someone else and betrays the trust of all of those that love him.

As she stepped out onto the landing, Bonnie was climbing the stairs.

'I saw you.' she told her.

Ella returned to her bed with her eyes wide open to an ugly, ugly world.

***

As the house woke up the next morning, Louie's bed was empty. One inhabitant was still missing in action, a stray. The other had folded belongings and pride back into monographed suitcases and departed into the shadows of the night.

Discovery of this desertion was delayed on account of the hangover-induced malaise and presence of two extra twelve-year-olds who required feeding and delivering home in one piece.

By the time all of this was done it was lunch time. The missing parties, presumed to be one-part hungover and one-part lazy were finally sought out. Anna poked her head around the door, rolling her eyes at the carnage. She flicked on the light switch, coughing loudly. When that wasn't met with any movement, she pulled the duvet back and finally understood that no one was beneath it.

Back in the kitchen, she rubbed her temples, looking to her husband. 'Did Bonnie and Louie go out this morning?'

'How would I know?' he replied. 'Probably.'

Neither Grayson nor Ella, beside him, looked up from the crossword they were being beaten by on the kitchen table.

Anna bit her lip. 'Well, should we worry?' she asked in a way that deferred the decision of concern to her husband, the way she usually did with anything distantly related to responsibility.

'I doubt it. They probably went for a walk or something.'

'Hmm… they must have gone early. We were up and about by eight.'

'I suppose it's unusual,' he said in his monotone half-listening voice.

The clock ticked loudly on the wall and Anna tapped her fingers on the table, unsure whether to fret or take herself back to bed.

Grayson sighed and looked up. 'Would you like me to run down to the common and check?'

'Yes, yes maybe.'

Ella was the next to emit a loud sigh. 'There's no point. Bonnie's gone and Louie never came home.'

'*Gone?* What do you mean, *gone?* Gone where?' gasped Anna, joining Grayson in levelling Ella with an alarmed stare.

'Gone *wherever*, I don't know, *gone!* She left last night. I heard her dragging her bags down the stairs.'

'What the bloody hell do you mean she *left?* Are you telling the truth? Why the bloody hell wouldn't you *say* something?

What is *wrong* with you?' Anna was shouting now, pacing back and forth, both aghast and furious, trying to make sense of these events and the delay at becoming aware of them.

Grayson shot her a look and said softly to Ella, 'Why didn't you tell us, Ell?'

'Because I don't fucking *care!*'

Her chair landed on its back with a clatter as she exited the room and stomped up the stairs. The slam of her bedroom door vibrated around the house and then all was quiet once more except the clock, tick-tick-ticking as Anna and Grayson stared at one another.

Grayson climbed the stairs two at a time and flung open the wardrobe doors. Bonnie's side was empty, as were the drawers. All traces of her had been removed.

Anna was biting at her cuticles when Grayson returned to the kitchen. 'All her stuff is gone.'

'Shit.'

They sat silently for a few moments more.

'We should probably call her parents,' said Grayson.

'But she might come back?' Anna offered weakly, racked with the dread of initiating any further contact with that family and being forced to admit to their negligence.

'No.' her husband replied decisively. 'I'm going to call them.'

TWENTY FIVE

An unravelling, 1983.

Louie left the house on Bonfire night and returned three days later with two black eyes and a broken nose.

He cut a horrific sight, stood there in the doorway with one eye closed shut and the other a distended purple mess, caked in dirt and dried blood. It was Ella who opened the door to him and she nearly passed out on the spot. He was barely recognisable.

The drama of Bonnie's silent departure had expended so much of Grayson and Anna's energy that they hadn't given too much thought to wayward Louie's whereabouts. It wasn't unheard of for him to be gone for a couple of days at a time at whichever friend's house, without any word.

That's just boys, Anna told herself, over and over again.

Their main concern was how they would break the news that Bonnie had gone without a trace to Louie, and how he might react. It had taken until the morning of the third day for them to become concerned, knocking on next door and grilling Arthur for any information he might have.

'He was having a great time when I left.' he had shrugged.

'He'll be out chasing pretty girls and ale, you know what he's like. I wouldn't worry,' Maggie added.

So Anna hadn't. She had gone home and made the decision that if he hadn't returned by lights out tonight then she would ring around his friends in the morning and seek him out. It was disrespectful, after all, to go four days without so much as a courtesy call and she didn't like having to lie to Matron on his behalf.

So by the time he sauntered in, a bloody mess and still half cut, she was more angry than worried.

She managed to chivvy him through to the living room where he mumbled incoherently and swiftly fell asleep. He didn't stir for the next twelve hours – even as she washed his wounds with a sponge soaked in TCP.

'Jesus Christ, Grayson,' she said later that evening, her hands still trembling.

'I know,' he said, 'I know. Ella was in pieces.'

'Who the hell could have done that to him? Should we not be taking him up to the hospital? To the *police?*'

'I think it's mainly superficial. That nose looks a mess, though. We'll take him in the morning to be sure. But tonight I think the best thing he can do is to sleep off whatever he's on.'

Anna looked up sharply. 'Oh, so it's his fault, is it?'

'I didn't say that.'

'Then what *are* you saying? He's drunk, or he's high, and he brought it on himself?'

'I didn't say that, either.'

'Well you're insinuating it! Come on, speak up. If you've

got an opinion please do enlighten me.'

Grayson sighed. 'He's not a child anymore.'

'So what?' she hissed, standing abruptly and slapping her palms down onto the table, primed for warfare. 'He's not a kid anymore, he's had a drink so he probably deserved to be beaten half to death? Is that what you're trying to say?'

'No, that isn't what I'm saying. Please don't put words into my mouth,' he said, pressing a weary hand to his brow. 'But I do think we need to iron out these… these situations. We can't keep making excuses for him. It's time for him to take some responsibility. He disappears for days at a time. He impregnates a young girl, brings her home and drops her like a hot potato as soon as anything sounds more exciting. Now he comes home beaten to a pulp and scares his sister half to death. What's next? He's going to send us to an early grave.'

'He's not *violent*! He's never been violent!' she shouted, incensed. She could scarcely believe the words coming out of her husband's mouth. 'He's set upon by some thugs and it's his fault because he likes to have a good time? All teenage boys like to have a good time!'

'A good time is one thing, Anna. I don't know any other teenage boys who can polish off a full bottle of red and still be standing upright asking what's next, do you? How many other teenage boys do you know? Does Maggie sit around for days at a time wondering where Arthur is? Does Arthur—'

'Arthur's different!'

'How, Anna? *How* is he different?' Grayson stood to meet her eye to eye across the table.

She threw her hands into the air and started to pace. 'He's *wet!* Arthur is *wet!* He's a people-pleaser! He doesn't have the same spirit that Louie has!'

'Fat lot of good that *spirit* is doing him, eh?' he replied, nodding his head towards the living room door. 'No Anna, the difference is this: Arthur knows when to stop; Arthur respects his family; Arthur has limits, boundaries.'

'Arthur has a silver fucking spoon!'

Grayson fell back into the chair and rubbed at his temples. This wasn't an argument he was ever going to win or a point he was ever going to be able to make. His wife was a smart and reasonable woman, until it came to her son.

'Do you really believe that Louie has suffered, Anna, because his father didn't want him? Has his life really been so bad that his circumstances can excuse his attitude? Has he really been affected, handicapped by a man like Peter Bennett not being in his life?' his tone was slow and quiet now, almost defeated.

Anna's eyes darted left and right, fumbling for the right answer – any answer – that would exonerate her son from these allegations, these smears of his character.

'Yes!' she said, eyes ablaze. 'Of course it's affected him! Of course it has! What must it feel like, to not even be acknowledged by a parent?'

'Did I not do enough?'

The question sucked the wind from her sails, the subject matter so delicate that even in her agitated state she knew she must find a way to quell her rage. Stop herself saying things that she would regret. She sank back down into the chair opposite Grayson and the tears spilled over.

'Of course you did. But it isn't the same.'

'So it's not been good enough? I have loved him like he was my own since the day I married you.'

'You saw how determined he was with Bonnie, how he

wanted to atone for his father's sins and be there for his baby, come what may.'

'And where is Bonnie now, Anna?'

Anna felt the frustration build again and began to grind her teeth. 'Fuck knows! *We* weren't good enough for Princess Bonnie, obviously! It was plain to see from the moment she walked through the door, you could see it all over her bloody face, *"Toto, I don't think we're in fucking Chelsea anymore!"*'

'No, Anna. We were perfectly good enough. But Louie wasn't.' Grayson leant forwards, the hand reaching for Anna trembling. 'Would *you* have stayed on the promise of marriage from someone who disappeared in a poof of smoke every few days, only to reappear in a progressively worse state each time? If you were vulnerable, would you rely on that person? Is that really him righting his father's wrongs, trying to do the right thing for his child, or is that just Louie doing what Louie wants?'

Adrenaline surged. She wanted to throw herself at him, sink her teeth into him and lock her jaw. Her anger was so powerful she was sure he wouldn't manage to shake her off without losing a blooded slab of shank.

'There's a problem here, and we need to address it. We need to deal with *him*,' Grayson said. 'I love him as much as you do, Anna, but it doesn't blind me.'

Her sweeping arm, propelled with white hot fury, sent plates and glasses spinning and crashing to the kitchen tiles.

She leant across the table, looking Grayson in the eye. 'No, you fucking don't.' she hissed through her teeth.

She stormed from the room, so consumed by her visceral pain that she didn't notice the jagged chunks of smashed stoneware slicing into the soles of her feet. Bloody footprints followed her out into the hall and up the stairs.

***

Upstairs, Anna sat in bed cradling a bottle of chardonnay, swigging from the bottle until she swigged herself to sleep.

Downstairs, Grayson kept sentry, creeping into the living room to check on Louie every thirty minutes until he was beaten by the weight of his eyelids as he sat at the kitchen table.

An hour later, Louie arose, pilfered the drinks cabinet and slammed the door behind him.

Nobody stirred.

TWENTY SIX

Switzerland, 1983.

The Carmichaels limped towards Christmas seething like rats in a sack, fractious and divided, each turned with tunnelled vision towards the respective axes they were grinding.

Louie was becoming more erratic by the day. As though he'd gone out to a string of parties and left his soul at one of them, the very core of him had been lost. The sparkle in his eyes had been replaced with something duller and more calculating.

He had become wrathful and secretive, and each family member walked the precarious tightrope of his volatility whenever he was in residence, which was less and less. He offered up no explanation for his comings and goings, the family left in limbo for periods of time that increased in length and frequency.

Grayson and Ella had seemingly become united in some kind of coalition against Louie's lifestyle choices. Father and daughter talked in hushed tones behind Ella's bedroom door, which had become the unofficial enemy lines.

Numerous tactics had been trialled with little success, while Anna watched on as her husband veered clumsily between good cop and bad cop. A dichotomy of heart to hearts and attempts at the hard line of zero tolerance.

Anna, in turn, felt slighted and suspicious of what she perceived to be their plotting, the guilty silences that descended every time she walked into a room serving only to aggravate her further. She was in lioness mode, and must protect her cub from the knives being sharpened behind his back, regardless of his behaviour.

The frustration was blinding and all encompassing, her stubbornness isolating her. Maggie was her only port in this storm, her quiet wisdom the only thing that was even marginally able to pierce through her defences.

'Of course he's angry!' she ranted in Maggie's kitchen. 'She just bloody stole away into the night without a word! With his child in her belly! No explanation, no nothing! How could she do that? She's *evil*!'

'Has he not spoken to her yet?' Maggie asked gently.

'No! God knows he's tried! Grayson has been called over to Kensington countless times to go and pick him up from their front gates, they won't even let him inside, never mind grace the poor boy with a face-to-face conversation! He's *broken* Mags, he's *broken*. And to top it off, it seems like everyone else is out to get him too!'

Louie had turned up, in various states of intoxication, over twelve times to the Bennett's white stone villa. To the Bennett's, he was simply a nuisance; a threat to their reputation and their place in the world. To Anna, he was a boy drowning in devastation, Bonnie's fingernails hooked like cat claws into his schoolboy prey-heart.

The procedure played out each time in the same way: Louie arriving at the magic gates on the back end of some party or other, pendulum swinging between despairing sobs and screams of rage. The phone ringing at number thirty-two to inform the Carmichaels that if he wasn't removed immediately, they would have him forcibly removed (how and by whom they never specified).

Grayson would then jump into his Cortina, tight jawed, speeding back to Kensington to cajole his step son into the car. Anna would greet them on the kerb as they arrived home and throw her arms around him.

They'd turn their backs on Grayson who was now surplus to requirements, walking into the house together, a unit. She to administer whatever comfort was required, be it wiping his tears and holding him tightly as sobs wracked through his body, or sitting at the sofa and nodding furiously at his jumbled rants, affirming his feelings and taking on some of his anger as her own.

One day, the phone rang when Grayson was at work.

'Hello?'

'Anna, it's me.' said Peter Bennett, 'He's here again.'

'No he isn't. He's at school.'

'Anna, he's here.' There was a muffled shuffling of the phone being moved away and Anna heard her son's manic voice crackle through the static of an intercom. 'This has got to stop, Anna. It's bordering on harassment. Lena wants to go to the police.

'Obviously, the matter is far more... *delicate* than she is aware of. None of us want or need that kind of exposure. But if this carries on, she says she will report him with or without my blessing… She's very threatened by him, and—'

'*Threatened?!* He's a bloody school boy, don't be so bloody ridiculous. Instead of wasting police time, why don't you try treating him like a bloody human being? All he wants is to talk to her!'

'It's not that simple.' he said.

'Of course it is!' she snapped, 'He's hardly turning up to protest high rise plans on the green belt! She just pissed off, Peter, without a trace! And he deserves an explanation.' She twisted the phone wire tightly around her fingers.

'She isn't *here*, Anna.' he sighed.

'Oh, really? Then where is she?'

'She's in Switzerland, with an aunt. She left a fortnight ago. I've told him, but he doesn't believe me. I can hardly throw open the doors and let him search the place, can I? You need to come and get him.'

'In *Switzerland?*' she shouted. 'In fucking *Switzerland?* She's got his bloody baby in her stomach! What sort of people *are* you?'

'She hasn't… there *is* no baby, Anna. She had a termination.'

The quiet matter-of-fact delivery of this statement made Anna's blood run cold, the heaviness of the words sinking down into her stomach like a stone.

After a few moments of silence, he continued, 'She was resolute. She wouldn't speak to him, she couldn't have a baby. She wanted to go home. My hands were tied. It's a frightful mess, I agree, but we can only draw a line under this if we work together here. Come and get him, Anna. Take him home.'

'Does he know?'

'No, he doesn't know.'

'Then *tell* him. You bring him home and *you* tell him. It'll be the only thing you've done for him in his entire life.'

She slammed down the phone and when it rang again, she yanked it from the hook and left it to dangle. She sat on the bottom step with her head between her knees, paralysed by fear of the future.

She was still there over an hour later when a horn beeped outside. She opened the door and saw Louie, wild haired and empty-eyed, stumble out of Peter's Porsche and fall into a heap on the pavement. She ran towards him as Peter clambered out of the driver's side and they each hooked one of Louie's arms over their shoulders and dragged him into the house, depositing him on his bed. Anna pulled the curtains closed, the door to and they headed back down the stairs.

Anna turned into the living room and poured herself a whiskey which she threw back in one, comforted by the heat travelling down her throat.

'Did you tell him?' she demanded.

Peter stood, rubbing at his brow bones with his fingers. 'Yes, I told him.' he said.

'And?'

'And nothing.'

'Well, what did he say?'

'He didn't say anything, Anna. Not a word.'

He sank down onto the sofa and sighed. He was looking drawn, she noticed, a little older, a little less sure. Perhaps even slightly remorseful. She handed him a whiskey which he swallowed gratefully.

'I'm sorry, Anna. I'm sorry for everything... for all of it. Seeing his pain like this, it's been... it's been...'

Anna watched him coldly, saying nothing. His apology

215

wasn't the edifying experience she had always expected it would be. Not whilst her son was laid upstairs comatose, another heart torn in two at the hands of the Bennetts.

'It was excruciating, the whole thing. Sitting in such proximity to him and having to look him in the eye, the man who abandoned him. I expect it was exactly the punishment you anticipated it would be. The ugly truth of it is that I had never pictured him as a person, as skin and bone, living a life with my blood running through his veins... I never considered that our paths would cross at all, let alone like this. I'm sorry, Anna. I'm sorry to you and I'm sorry to him. I could have... I could have been better.'

'Yes, you could have been.'

He nodded and pulled himself up from the sofa. He handed her the tumbler and ran a hand through his hair. 'I'm just—'

'Oh, just piss off, Peter.' she sighed. She wasn't interested in an epiphany that was sixteen years too late, that she was able to derive no joy from.

He nodded and slunk out of the room, down the hall and into his car. Back to his life, the one which he had cultivated with great care and precision. The one in which he held all the cards, only needing to pretend to bother about the problems of the proletariat.

Anna returned to Louie's bedroom and perched on the bed, looking down at her son. His skin was blotchy and the salty trajectories of the tears he had shed ran down each of his cheeks. The faint shadow of his bruises could still be seen, patches of skin with yellowed undertones. The bridge of his nose startlingly crooked. His lips were cracked and he was snoring softly, oblivious to his mother's fingers combing through his lank and matted curls. She gazed down at him as her thoughts eddied and swirled.

She felt his pain viscerally, as though it was her own.

She laid down beside him, tucking her knees behind his and burrowing in until her face was in his hair and she could feel the steady thump of his heart and the spindles of his spine. She breathed him in, her mind racing from one thing to the next.

She pictured him in Peter Bennett's car, receiving another slice of information which would ravage the course of his future so swiftly and brutally. She pictured Peter looking at his son properly for the first time, searching his face for any likeness and wondered if he found any. Angles, contours, the particular shade of an iris are not things you can give or take by choice. There are no certainties in the sticky business of inheritance and this man ought to know better than to try and claim a dainty nose or an angular jaw sixteen years later.

'You're better than him, and you're better than her.' she whispered into his hair.

She reached around his waist to take his hand, a hand that was heavier and coarser than the last time she'd held it. She ran fingers over dirty nails and softly brushed circles into his palm.

'One day, this will all be a distant memory. You're so young, Louie, life can be anything you want it to be – anything at all. There are so many more girls for you to love and reasons for you to wake up in the morning.'

He moaned in his sleep and threw his arms up over his head. As she slipped out of the bed, he rolled to lie flat on his back with his mouth hanging open. She looked down at him with so much love pressing at the cavity of her chest that she felt she might burst.

She tucked him in and left the room.

TWENTY SEVEN

Jingle bells, 1983.

Every Christmas morning since Arthur could remember had begun the same way: he would be woken up by the sound of Christmas carols on his mother's radio floating up the stairs, accompanied by her intermittent off-key caterwauling and the smell of toast under the grill.

On Christmas morning 1983, Arthur didn't wake up to the sound of singing, nor could he smell any toast. What had woken him up had in fact been the angry slam of his front door and the string of expletives tumbling like rapid fire out of Anna's mouth as she charged up the hall.

He crept down the stairs and tentatively peered around the kitchen door. She was slumped at the kitchen table mid-rant, a cigarette between two fingers shedding ash all around her as she gesticulated wildly.

'*Have* Christmas!' she shouted, '*Have* fucking Christmas! Surely we could just *have* a coffee, or *have* breakfast, at least give him until 10am before we just go ahead and *have Christmas* without him!'

Maggie threw an apologetic look his way as he made his way around their angry neighbour and sat down at an empty spot at the table. The one his mother lovingly set for him every year with a cracker, a card embossed with his name framed by holly and a gold rimmed plate from her special occasion dinner set was covered in a layer of errant cigarette ash.

Anna stubbed the cigarette out directly onto the plate and lit another one without coming up for air.

'It's not like Ella's sat there chomping at the bit to see if Father Christmas has been. She's thirteen for Christ's sake – not three! What's the issue with waiting a few hours? It's like he doesn't want him there!'

'Merry Christmas, Anna,' said Arthur quietly, already accustomed to the ranting and raving that seemed to go hand in hand with the spontaneous combustion of a happy marriage.

'Merry fucking Christmas, Arts, merry fucking Christmas…' she muttered.

'No Louie?'

'He'll be back, you know what he's like, he'll have lost track of time…' She looked up at him, her eyes darting back and forth across his face, silently begging for his reassurance.

He nodded and a pathetic look of relief washed across her face. She leaned forward, elbows on the table. 'Did he say which party he was at?' she asked, a little frantic again.

Maggie put a coffee down in front of each of them and slid in next to him.

'Er, no, he didn't…' replied Arthur, not wanting to say the wrong thing and get Louie into trouble.

'Did he say who he was going with?' she probed.

'Uh, no, he has a few different sets of friends I don't know that well, er…' He looked worriedly at his mother, who squeezed his arm.

'I'm sure he won't be long, Anna.' Maggie said. 'Hang tight, he'll be walking in any minute.'

Anna sighed deeply. 'He better bloody had do. Christ, I'd better get back, I don't want Scrooge senior and Scrooge apprentice opening the door with faces like slapped arses when he does finally show up, he'll turn on his bloody heel.'

She stubbed out her cigarette next to the other butt and stomped off down the hall.

'Dinner will be ready at four if you're not here before, okay?' Maggie called after her.

'Ye-es!' Anna called back in the manner of a teenager who had been nagged to tidy her bedroom for the tenth time in a row, not a woman whose friend was serving her entire a family a three course meal in a few hours' time.

The door slammed loudly again behind her.

Maggie raised her eyebrows up to the heavens and tipped Anna's discarded coffee into the sink. She exchanged a worried glance with Arthur before he headed upstairs for a shower and she started to peel potatoes.

***

The Maxwell residence exuded festive cheer as the doorbell chimed at exactly 4pm. The table was set, the dinner service, place mats, crackers and centre piece in situ. Lights twinkled on the tree as Elvis Presley warbled from the speakers.

Maggie was in the kitchen manoeuvring expertly from steaming pan to steaming pan, pink face glistening and tea towel draped over her shoulder.

Arthur went to answer the door. Of the three Carmichaels standing on the step, only one was smiling. It didn't quite reach his eyes.

'Happy Christmas, Arthur.' said Grayson, shaking his hand. Ella stood next to him, eyes to the ground, wishing it would swallow her up. Anna brought up the rear, openly scowling, a bottle of wine in each hand.

'Happy Christmas,' Arthur replied nervously.

The Carmichaels trooped down the hall and into the kitchen and Anna thrust the bottles at him.

'I couldn't remember if she said red or white.' she muttered as she shuffled past, her breath already heavy with the stench of wine.

Grayson kissed Maggie's cheek. 'Smells amazing, doesn't it Ella?'

'Yes.' said Ella, smiling shyly as Maggie gave her a kiss and a squeeze. She stole a quick glance in Arthur's direction before returning her eyes to the floor.

The two of them went past the table and through to the living area. Anna stayed behind and leant against the kitchen counter, lighting another cigarette.

'No sign yet?' asked Maggie from behind a rush of steam as she opened the oven doors and gave the roast potatoes another prod.

'Nope. But he'll be here. He won't miss it, I know he won't.' said Anna, looking far less sure than she sounded.

The tension was palpable as they eventually sat around the table, the empty seat with Louie's name place like a beacon, taunting them. Maggie dragged out the serving of drinks and small talk for as long as she could until eventually, after a short silence, Grayson nodded towards the prawn cocktails lined up and beginning to sweat on the kitchen counter.

'So, shall we start?' he asked with a false smile.

'Let's wait.' Anna chimed in quickly, 'Let's have another glass of wine.'

'The food is ready. We should start.' Grayson replied, smile never breaking.

'I want to wait,' said Anna, jaw clenched so tight the muscles showed under her translucent skin, turning to look at him with the threat of melodrama in her eyes.

Grayson turned to look back at her and replied coolly, 'We've already waited. Dinner was ready at four, like we knew it would be, *all* of us. We've been here for an hour now. *That* food,' he pointed towards the kitchen with his fork, 'has been sitting on *that* counter since we arrived. *That* food, that Maggie has kindly cooked for us, is ready. And we're ready. And we thank you, Maggie, for your generous hospitality and your patience with what is already enough tardiness.'

Just as Arthur was poising himself for Anna's battle cry, every head whipped towards the door as the doorbell chimed out. Anna was the first out of her seat. She re-entered the room with a predictably worse for wear Louie on her arm. His shirt was stained and lopsided, the buttons in the wrong holes and he smelled like a labour club carpet.

He plonked himself down in the empty place, between Maggie at the head of the table and his sister. He hooked Ella's neck roughly with his elbow, pulling her towards him.

'Merry Christmas, kiddo.' he whispered, looking around the table at each person in turn, grinning widely. He pulled a roll up from behind his ear. 'Sorry I'm late.'

'Well, you're here now.' said Anna, her face wearing a look

of triumph.

'I hope you're hungry.' smiled Maggie, getting up and heading back towards the kitchen.

'Don't smoke at the table please, Louie. We're guests.' Grayson added tersely.

Anna rolled her eyes and lit her own cigarette, then passed the lighter to Louie. A vein throbbed furiously in Grayson's neck as Maggie walked around the table serving prawn cocktails in sparkling glasses.

The meal passed slowly with sotto voiced pockets of polite conversation going back and forth over the table. To everyone's great relief, Louie cleared his plate and laid the charm on thickly, flattering Maggie's cooking at every opportunity, instinctively foreseeing and swerving the ambush should he stumble.

By the time the Christmas pudding had been smothered with an ignited ladle of brandy, the table exhaled in the collective relief of almost being at the finish line without a fracas.

Grayson wiped the sides of his mouth with his napkin, a paper crown sitting jauntily across his forehead. 'Thank you Maggie, that was delicious.'

'Hear, hear,' concurred Anna. 'You bloody smashed it, as usual.'

The table erupted in murmurs of agreement and Maggie sat at the head of the table waving away their compliments. 'Oh, stop…' she said, and when they did, 'Keep going!'

When all the food was devoured, Anna helped Maggie with the dishes and the teenagers gathered around the Commodore 64 Arthur had received for Christmas, taking turns at controlling a pixel man escaping with his gold.

The evening was pleasant, if not rather fraught. Each one of them watched Louie from the corner of an eye as he unwittingly walked the tightrope between peacetime and warfare. Would he stay, or would he go? Would he pass out in silence with a gut full of rum or would he beat his fists on the ground in tyranny?

The festive cheer hung by a thread, entirely at his mercy.

The unofficial yuletide armistice remained mostly intact until Louie headed through the kitchen and towards the back door, where he lit a spliff as Maggie and Anna stood side by side washing and drying the dishes.

Anna's eyes met Maggie's with a questioning look on her face. She knew it was uncouth for her son to be blowing great clouds of smoke out into the night as someone's guest on Christmas day. Compounded by his lateness, it was perhaps even rude. Six months ago, she might have collared him for it, but today… the tides were so volatile, the boat already so waterlogged that she daren't rock it.

As her closest friend, Maggie understood this without the necessity of words. She relayed her support with a smile and a shake of her head and Anna beamed back in relief.

Moments later, Grayson walked in, stopping in his tracks, eyes boring into Louie's back. Louie turned around, leaning back onto the doorframe and smiling lopsidedly at him. He blew a perfect trio of smoke rings back into the kitchen before shutting his eyes for the rest of the exhale, an act of defiant effrontery, swan-like in its graceful execution.

Anna was frozen mid-wipe, tea towel in hand as her husband's gaze slowly turned towards her and narrowed as he contemplated her complicity. She was on a knife edge waiting for him to erupt, not even daring to breathe. But he didn't. He fixed her with a look and small shake of the head that communicated the gravest disappointment, signalling a tear in their relationship that might never be mended.

Her cheeks burned furiously and her eyes filled with tears as he turned to address only Maggie, thanking her again and excusing himself to go and call his mother.

Anna pressed her thumb and forefinger into her eyes and exhaled loudly. 'Shit.' she whispered.

Louie flicked the stub out onto the patio and kissed his mother gently on the cheek.

'Don't worry about him,' he smirked, eyes alight with mischief, 'You'll always be *my* number one.'

She smiled and shut her eyes as he breezed past. When she opened them, Maggie had her arms folded.

'Don't let him walk all over you.'

'I'm not... it's just... ah, I don't know Mags, it's not as though I don't know he's behaving badly or can't see when he's being provocative... but he's still a kid, a confused kid and he needs someone on his side. Nobody else is.'

'But why does there have to be sides? He *is* a kid, you're right, and he's running rings around you.' Maggie replied, 'You can discipline him, or at least call him out when he's in the wrong without turning your back on him. All you're doing is sending him the message that this is all fine, when it's quite clearly not.'

'There are sides though, Mags. Grayson's supposed to be the adult and he's walking around giving Louie the silent treatment, making him feel as though he's a stranger in his own home. I mean *that*, just then... When did Grayson become so disapproving? Is he not the same husband who rolls a fat one before bed each night? It's like he's taken against him so completely that there's no in between, just his way or the highway… do as I say but not as I do…'

Maggie poured her another glass of wine.

'It's such a mess,' Anna continued, taking a long sip, 'we can't even have a conversation without everything coming back to Louie. Grayson's become the bull and Louie's become the red rag. He works late every night, he sleeps in his study. I'm only trying to protect my son. I feel like I can't win.'

'Anna,' Maggie said more directly, 'you've been more than happy for Grayson to behave like Louie's father for the last twelve years. To love him, to nurture him, to provide for him. You can't deny him the right, as a father, to punish him now because you're scared it will upset the apple cart. He's either his father or he isn't, it's not something you can accept during the good times and snatch away at the first signs of conflict. No marriage could withstand that. Your children are your children, for better or worse. I don't think Grayson's problem is Louie. I think it's you.'

'I never said that, I-'

'You have to find a way to tackle this *together*. Or you're going to end up tackling it alone.' finished Maggie, returning to the dishes.

***

Teddy arrived at midday on boxing day with a couple of intricately wrapped and ribboned boxes tucked under his arms. Maggie fussed as she trotted back and forth from the kitchen, serving the second multi-course dinner in as many days.

Arthur was bemused and saddened by the displays of extravagance she put so much blood, sweat and tears into each time his brother was in residence. Teddy rarely appreciated it. If he did, he never commented and she visibly deflated as the hours rolled by.

Arthur couldn't understand why his mother felt she had so much to prove. As though her husband left her because her culinary skills were under par, or her floors didn't shine brightly enough. He found it sad that she still cared so much and wished that she didn't.

Teddy relayed the tedium of the carol service at the Royal Albert Hall and afternoon tea at Claridge's with Oksana's mother, the thinly cloaked boasting serving no purpose except to make his mother feel inferior.

'So what's been happening on Rosendale Road, then?' he asked in a tone of voice that said he was asking out of duty, not interest.

'Oh, just the usual,' Maggie replied, almost apologetically, 'We did the rounds in the morning and then the Carmichael's came over for Christmas dinner.'

'All of them? Did the prodigal son return, then?'

Arthur and Maggie stared at one another in a confused silence.

Eventually, Maggie asked, 'What do you mean?'

'Oh, I wasn't sure whether the fuzz had caught up with him in the end after the debacle on Christmas Eve. He really is starting to become a running joke, isn't he?'

'What debacle?' Arthur asked quietly.

'You don't know?' exclaimed Teddy, in a voice much louder than necessary, scarcely able to disguise his glee at being the bearer of the gossip, 'He was at one of the Roedean girl's Christmas soirees, you know: mulled wine, canapes, charades, grandparents, that type of thing. He turned up in a diabolical state, stumbling and slurring, shirt torn, stinking like some sort of street urchin… I really have no idea why he's invited to these things anyway, you'd think people would know better by now.'

'Yes, well, there have been a few issues lately, Anna and Grayson are beside themselves trying to address his alcohol intake…' began Maggie, tapering off when she realised she had no hope of eliciting any empathy from the round, smug face that sat across the table.

'Alcohol? And the rest! That's the least of their worries,' he sniggered, 'In any case, some of them took pity on him and cleaned him up, fed him and tried to get a bit of water down him. When he excused himself to go to the lavatory and didn't come back they became worried and sent the poor girl's father to check on him. He only went and found him passed out in the hall, with one of his daughter's diamond necklaces stuffed into his pocket! Needless to say, all hell broke loose. He was chased from the property and I assume the police were called. He never managed to make away with anything, but if he hadn't been caught red handed, who knows?'

Maggie's hand flew up to her mouth.

'Louie's not a thief.' Arthur said firmly.

'There must have been some misunderstanding—' added Maggie.

'Don't be so naive, mother, it's hardly his first trainwreck. Golden boy has been garnering quite a reputation for some time now. From guestlist to blacklist. I couldn't count on my fingers the number of people who can't wait to get their hands on him right now.' he smirked.

'He might be a lot of things, but he's not a thief,' insisted Arthur, 'We've known him since we were knee high, he's never stolen a penny!'

'With the kind of habits he's developed, who's to know the depths he's capable of sinking to? It's not as though he invites you as his plus one anymore anyway, is it? I don't know why you bother. In any case, don't shoot the messenger.'

Who was this person that they were discussing, so far removed from the Louie he had sprung from a sapling beside? And at what point did he just decide to embark on this new life, with these new friends they've never heard of? Where did this great distance between them come from?

Arthur was both gobsmacked and stung by these revelations. He counted the minutes until his brother's taxi arrived to take him back to Kensington.

'I'm going to have to talk to Anna.' said Maggie when they had waved him off.

'Don't, not yet. I'll go and talk to him, find out what's happened. He wouldn't steal, mum.'

'He wouldn't, would he?'

'No, he wouldn't. I'll go over later.'

***

As it turned out, Arthur didn't need to go over later. Louie tapped on the back door as they sat down to a cheese on toast dinner. Neither of them could face a proper meal after their enormous lunch. As they turned their heads towards him, he let himself in and joined them at the table looking far brighter than he had yesterday.

'Hello, love,' smiled Maggie warmly, 'Cheese on toast?'

'No thanks, Mags, I'm watching my figure,' he laughed. He turned to Arthur. 'Do you fancy a walk? A Christmas stroll, admire the lights and all that?'

Arthur knew that the stroll was a poorly disguised circuit around the block so he could have a joint away from the disapproving eyes of his stepfather. Maggie looked at Arthur, eyebrows wiggling not so discreetly.

'Yeah, alright.' agreed Arthur, taking his empty plate across to the sink.

'I'll do that,' said Maggie, snatching the dish, 'You go and get your coat. Are you going to be warm enough, Louie?' she asked, eyeing his thin sports jacket.

'I'll be fine, Mags,' he said, kissing her cheek with a grin.

They stepped out into the evening. Louie lit the joint on the front steps and walked briskly down onto the pavement, Arthur falling into line alongside him.

'So...' began Arthur, 'Everything alright?'

'Yeah, well, you know... Grayson wants me hung, drawn and quartered, but aside from that...'

'Only, you didn't look so great yesterday...'

'Aw, thanks mate!' Louie laughed, punching him on the shoulder and passing him the joint. Arthur took a drag. He wished he were self-assured enough to broach the subject head on. *No cajones*, his father's voice echoed in his head. 'Just a monster hangover, fresh as a daisy after a decent sleep.'

'Is that all?'

'Of course that's all. What do you mean?'

Louie stopped in his tracks, his smile turning into a questioning frown as he waited for Arthur to answer.

'You're just... you're drinking a lot... I'm worried about you...' Arthur fumbled.

231

Louie laughed and threw an arm over his shoulders. 'It's Christmas! Everyone's drinking a lot. I'm fine. Anyway, come on, we're late.'

'Late?'

'For the party.'

Arthur's stomach sank into his shoes as he contemplated his friend. He was dressed in the tracksuit bottoms he'd been lounging around in all day. He hadn't expected to actually *see* anyone this evening. The last thing Arthur expected to be doing on what ought to be a lazy boxing day evening mastering his new computer game was to be chaperoning his wayward best friend in his lounge wear. But he could hardly let him go and wreak havoc alone after what he had learned today over lunch, he clearly needed his back watching.

'But first, mate,' Louie grinned at Arthur, 'we need to go pick up a couple of things.'

***

After a twenty-minute trudge through the quiet streets, the boys arrived outside what looked to be a decidedly dodgy pub. Two of the windows had been boarded up, the rest were murky with heavy half nets hanging behind them. Weeds were growing out of the frame of two on the upper storey. There was no signage save for a peeling board announcing 'Woolton's Tavern' above the door.

The interior was in even worse shape. Smoke hung in the air in a suffocating mist. A tired looking woman stood behind the bar with a peroxide crown and two missing teeth. She seemed to know what each of the even less salubrious looking punters wanted without them having to ask. Grubby and stained velvet booths hugged the walls, pock-marked with gaffa-tape repairs. The rest of the tables were covered in deep scratches surrounded by mismatched chairs and stools.

A sign hung on the wall next to the door to the gentleman's lavatories on which was scribbled 'DRUG USE WON'T BE TOLERATED'.

Louie sauntered through, nodding at the drinkers with the type of confidence only borne from familiarity. He walked past the powerless jukebox and up towards a raised area that housed a pool table which had also seen better days.

A group of men who looked to be roughly in their late twenties stood around the pool table, the youngest of all of the clientele by quite a stretch, save for a group of three girls perched on stools behind them who must be the same age as Louie and Arthur underneath the thick layers of make-up.

The men nodded in acknowledgement of Louie without moving their eyes from the game. One of them leant his cue against the wall and beckoned to Louie, who followed him into the gents. Arthur stood there lamely until one of the girls waved him over to their table. He sat awkwardly on to the empty stool as they all slurped on their straws and eyed him with curiosity.

'You a friend of Louie, then?' one of them asked with the kind of London twang that didn't hail from somewhere like Dulwich. Her eyes were coated in thick blackness and her cheeks the brightest fuschia, going all the way up to her temples, like a caricature who had been crayoned in by the hasty fingers of a school child. Her hair was huge, her heels huger and her bare, bandy legs were on display all the way up to the top of her thigh where a neon tube dress began, ending at her bust and leaving absolutely nothing to the imagination.

In a different time and place she could be a real beauty, Arthur thought. A bit of modesty and giving her face a good scrub would be all it would take.

'Y-yes…' he gulped, 'I'm Arthur.'

'Nice to meet you, Arfur. I'm Charlene.' she beamed, holding out a hand of tiny fingers adorned with gold medallions bigger than her knuckles and chipped green nail varnish, 'And this is Sharon and Trish.'

The other two girls smiled and turned their attention back to their beaus, whichever ones they were. They all looked the same to Arthur, each of them sharing the same floppy haircut and wearing variations of the same Fred Perry polo shirt.

'So er… how do you know Louie?' he asked, struggling to find any other common ground on which he might base a conversation.

Charlene giggled. 'Oh, I actually met him at a party over in Herne Hill a few weeks back and we got chatting… ' She leaned towards him and lowered her voice, 'He's just gorgeous, ain't he? And so posh! One thing led to another and, well… don't say anything in front of Mike,' she continued, nodding towards the cluster of football hooligans, 'I told him we went to school together. Louie wanted more gear and Mike's the only one I knows would 'ave it.'

'I see…' said Arthur, lost for words at yet another fine line his friend was walking. He glanced over at the pool table again and his heart began to beat a little faster. The tattoos, the scarred knuckles, and the hard faces had become even more intimidating now he knew the type of fire Louie was playing with.

'Has he really not got a girlfriend?' Charlene whispered.

They both turned around as Mike emerged through the swing door of the toilet, a misty-eyed Louie following in his wake. Mike returned to the pool table and Louie sat down at the table.

'Hey girls, all looking beautiful tonight,' he said, voice slow and slurred. Charlene beamed as the other two rolled their eyes and tutted. 'Anyone for a drink?'

They all shook their heads bar Charlene, who chirped, 'Voddy and coke, please. I'll help you carry them.'

They went off towards the bar together, leaving Arthur with Sharon and Trish, unsure whether he was supposed to attempt any small talk or not. He was even more mystified as to how reedy, baby-faced Louie was getting served by the hard-nosed woman on the bar who had clearly been around the block a few times and would know a teenager when she saw one.

The pair returned, Louie carrying a circular tray full of drinks, Charlene staring doe-eyed up at him and giggling loudly. A few scowls were thrown in their direction as the pool game continued wordlessly.

As Charlene doled the drinks out, Sharon moaned, 'I wish they'd bloody hurry up, the party'll be over at this rate. All that money I spent on this perm, a month's wages, wasted.'

The girls launched into a lengthy back and forth about the cost of perms and the meagre pay packets they received for their various Saturday jobs which they lambasted as slave labour. They went around the table annihilating their bosses, competing for the title of shittiest job and then moved on to the sacrifices of the perm, the easiest Woolworths to nick eyeliner from and the merits of Simon Le Bon vs George Michael (which became rather heated.)

The drinks were mostly just melted ice by the time they crashed to the floor as Louie's head fell forward and he lay passed out, face down in the centre of the table.

'Shit!' Arthur cried, leaping up as the girls screamed. A confused babble of voices and movement followed. Louie lay slumped across the table, blood and booze dripping from his hair.

'Shit!' muttered Arthur again as he rushed around the table and tried to pull Louie upright. His eyes rolled back as his head lolled backwards onto the velvet booth. Blood trickled from his brow bone where a shard of glass the size of a fingernail was wedged. Arthur shook him, then gently slapped him on the cheek. 'Louie!' he hissed. '*Louie!*'

'Oi!' shouted a stocky, grey haired man in a grubby vest from the end of the bar, 'Get him out of here *now*! What have I fuckin' told you, Mike? No overdoses on my fuckin' premises. They're kids for Christ's sake! Out, *NOW!*'

'An overdose?' exclaimed Arthur, cradling his friend, eyes wide with panic.

'Fucks sake!' muttered the men around the pool table, throwing their cues against the wall.

'I told you he couldn't fuckin' handle that gear,' one of them said to Mike as they both moved towards the lifeless Louie and hoiked him up onto their shoulders. His feet dragged on the stained and threadbare carpet as they walked him outside and dumped him in a heap next to an industrial sized bin.

Arthur was on his knees, shaking like a leaf as he tried to find his friend's pulse. Charlene wobbled over after him, doing her best to swerve the potholes in the pavement. She crouched down and tenderly stroked Louie's face.

'What the hell has he taken?' asked Arthur, ashen faced. 'I

need to call an ambulance!'

She looked worriedly towards the curb where the pool players and her friends were clambering into a couple of clapped out Fiestas.

'Get a fucking move on, Charl!' commanded Dave from the driver's seat.

She rooted around in Louie's pocket as Arthur looked on, dumbstruck, and pulled out a roll of tin foil which she examined, then exhaled in relief.

'He'll be okay.' she told Arthur, 'He's not smoked much. Just get him home and keep an eye on him. When he comes to, he'll be throwing his guts up for a couple of hours. Plenty of water and plenty of sleep.'

She started to stand up and Arthur snatched hold of her arm and pulled her back onto her haunches. 'Are you sure? How do you know?'

'I just know,' she said with a decisive nod. 'He'll be okay. Ask him to call me, will you, when he comes round?'

And then she was gone. Arthur sat in the darkness of the alley clutching his friend, paralyzed with fear. Eventually he mustered up enough courage to run to the pay phone on the corner, his entire body trembling as he called home to request an urgent extraction from Peckham.

As Grayson's Cortina mounted the kerb, Louie sat bolt upright and vomited into Arthur's lap.

TWENTY EIGHT

Auld Lang Syne, 1983.

I n the interim of Boxing Day and New Year's Eve, there was radio silence from Louie. Crisis talks had reached a crescendo next door, Arthur's mother told him, with options like inpatient rehab facilities becoming strong possibilities. Therefore, it came as no surprise when Grayson arrived in their kitchen to impart the news that Louie would be leaving for one such facility in a fortnight's time.

'It might seem extreme,' said Grayson, head bowed at the kitchen table, 'and it's costing us money we scarcely have, but we don't feel like we have a choice. Things have happened that I can't even…'

Grayson shook his head, unable to continue. He suddenly looked far older than his forty years.

'It doesn't,' replied Arthur, still shellshocked from his experience in Peckham, 'it doesn't feel extreme.'

'It's the right thing for him,' soothed Maggie, 'you know we all love him.'

Grayson cried openly, a spectacle which made Arthur uncomfortable. He had never seen such a display of emotion in a grown man and he wanted to look away, but couldn't. Grayson reached his hands across the kitchen table and took Arthur's within them.

'Thank you, Arthur,' he said, looking Arthur straight in the eyes, 'For being the one true friend he has. Louie is lucky to have someone like you in his life.'

Arthur welled up too at this point, which everyone assumed was in the intensity of the moment. *If I'm the best he's got, what hope does he have?* Arthur wondered, the kiss on his porch step running through his consciousness in vivid technicolour.

***

On New Year's eve, Louie was at their front door looking better than he had in months. His colour had returned, the whites of his eyes restored to frame the twinkling baby blue iris'. Even his walk was different; lighter, somehow.

'Hello, mate.' he smiled sheepishly from the door step, 'Can I come in?'

'Course!' Arthur beamed.

They walked through to the kitchen. Maggie dropped her tea towel immediately and rushed over, enveloping Louie in a tight hug and kissing the crown of his newly clean curls.

'Hello, stranger,' she smiled, 'You're looking fantastic. Tea, coffee?'

'Thanks Mags,' he smiled. 'I just wanted to apologise, mate, for the Woolton... I must have scared you half to death and, well, for the last few months really. I just lost it for a while there, you know...'

'Don't worry about it.' cut in Arthur, needing no more explanation. His friend was back, and that was enough.

'Only I'm going away for a bit, as you know… and I just wanted to… to let you know that I appreciate you, mate, and sort of, I dunno, make sure you knew I was sorry before I went…'

'We're so proud of you, Louie.' said Maggie, coming around to hug him again.

'Thanks.' he replied quietly.

Maggie put two cups of tea onto the table and said, 'I'll leave you both to it.'

'When do you leave?' asked Arthur, sipping his tea.

'Thursday after next.'

'How long for?'

'I'm not sure. Months, at least. They'll know more when I'm there and I've had some assessments, they said.'

'Right…' said Arthur, imagining padded cells and circles of crying men.

'That's why I'm being let off my leash tonight. For one night only, my final hurrah. On best behaviour, of course.'

Arthur's heart sank, knowing immediately that whatever it was, it was a terrible idea. There was no possible circumstance in which it was safe for his friend to be hurrahing at all, not after what he had witnessed less than a week ago. However much sleep he'd had, however many showers, however much honesty he'd practiced and however much insight he now believed he had, Louie was far too fragile to be put in temptation's way.

'Where are you going?' he asked.

'*We*. Where are *we* going.'

'No—' Arthur started.

'Lucy's having a New Year's Eve bash at one of her father's casinos in Mayfair. Black tie, no expenses spared. Everyone will be there. Including her parents. I'm on a strict curfew, and I can promise you my behaviour will be pristine.'

'I'm not going.' said Arthur with a wince.

'Well, you have to. Only, I can only go if you do. And what I really need, more than anything, to be able to do this… to be able to face what I know lies ahead, is to say a proper farewell to all of my best friends. And it wouldn't mean anything, anything at all, if you weren't by my side, like you always have been.'

Arthur felt himself begin to thaw, ever so slightly. Louie was as sincere as he'd ever seen him. He would recognise a trick if he saw one, especially from Louie Carlton. Wouldn't he?

'Please, Arthur.'

Against his better judgement, Arthur took a deep breath and said, 'Alright then.'

***

The West End of London on New Year's Eve is a dazzling sight, and 1983 was no exception. Bodies came and went in every direction, spontaneous bursts of singing and laughter flying from the mouths of strangers. Small crowds gathered in clusters on the pavements, over which hung never ending strings of twinkling lights, the air heady with promise.

The two young boys in their dapper black suits weaving through the masses could scarcely believe their luck at being in amongst it. They watched in quiet awe as glittering young women tottered out of black cabs, music of every variety spilled out of the doors of cocktail bars and slick haired men with shiny watches lit cigars and toasted good fortunes.

If they had gaped in wonder outside of the casino, the inside was even more impressive. Softly lit with enormous crystal chandeliers hung majestically over plush blood red carpets, the teenagers were spellbound by their first glimpses into the nightlife of London's elite. There were beautiful people everywhere. Slender legs perched on velvet stools, the swish of shiny hair and glossed red smiles as cocktail glasses clinked and croupiers spun wheels, expertly flicking cards with a flourish.

They were led across the main floor to a roped off area, presided over by an enormous man in an impeccable black dinner suit who unclipped the rope and gestured them through to a smaller side room, reserved for guests of Miss Lucy. A mahogany half-moon shaped bar ran down one wall with highly polished teenagers scattered around it, the low hum of polite chatter ricocheting off the ornate gold cornicing.

Lucy was upon them instantly, kissing both of Arthur's cheeks before moving on to Louie, whose kisses she lingered over a little longer than necessary.

'Don't you two scrub up well? You *are* a sight for sore eyes!' she enthused, standing with her hands on her hips expectantly, waiting for a compliment in exchange.

Her beauty was obvious that night, even to Arthur who couldn't usually see beyond the red mist of irritation that went hand in hand with her presence. The sweetheart neckline and thigh length split of her gown did more than subtly hint at the curves of her torso and the tone of her tanned legs. Her hair was swept up on top of her head, presumably to show off the coin sized diamonds which hung in her ears and draped around her neck.

She oozed money, as did their surroundings. Arthur couldn't help but think of little Charlene from Peckham, ensconced in the grubby booth at Woolton's and had to stifle a laugh.

'You too, Luce.' smiled Louie, lowering his eyes and kissing her hand.

'Thanks for having us. Nice place.' added Arthur, still not quite willing to acknowledge her get up.

'It's wonderful, isn't it? It was Daddy's first site, so it's his true love really, his pride and joy. Now he has another four, of course, but he proposed to Mama here so it holds a special place in his heart. He'll be through shortly, I'm sure, he just had a little business to attend to first.' she said, waving towards the rope as more voices came up behind them, 'Sorry, I'd better get back to doling out the greetings, but please, grab yourselves a drink. The cocktails are world famous.'

'I'm on my best behaviour, Luce.' said Louie with his trademark impish grin, 'No drinks for me.'

'Oh.' she replied, a look of disappointment flickering across her face fleetingly. 'We'll catch up later, yes?'

She swept past them with a coy smile to accost the next set of newcomers. They moved forwards towards the bar and delivered their own set of greetings to the growing array of school friends, acquaintances and strangers filling the room.

People were drinking in a different way tonight. Not for oblivion this time, as though they could sense the decorum required in an establishment like this one, and the night passed pleasantly enough.

Arthur hadn't let a drop of alcohol pass his lips, a nod

towards his best friend's sobriety. That, and feeling like he should lead by example. What good was he as a chaperone, half cut?

'Have a cocktail,' Louie encouraged, 'Just because I'm shackled to cloudy lemonade doesn't mean you have to be. Go on, enjoy yourself. I'll behave, I already promised.'

Arthur only hesitated for a nanosecond before smiling sheepishly and heading towards the bar, leaving Louie in the relatively safe hands of Marcus and co. He waited at the bar an extortionate amount of time, watching pretty girls flutter both eyelashes and five pound notes at the lone barman and being served in order of the best looking.

At exactly the moment his impatience was about to get the better of him, the barman came towards him with a smile and asked, 'What can I get you?'

As he started to speak, a voice directly to his left pipped him to the post and ordered a Bacardi and coke. He swivelled around in fury to be met with a dazzling and apologetic smile.

'Make that two, please!' she called after the barman. 'Sorry! I hope you like Bacardi. You might be waiting a while again if you don't.'

Arthur couldn't help but be swept away by her mischievous brown eyes and good humour.

'I'm Imogen.' she said, holding out her hand.

'Arthur,' he replied, taking it.

'Bacardi, then?' she asked, raising her eyebrows.

'Thank you.' he smiled, having no idea what Bacardi was but deciding on impulse that he would like it.

Three Bacardi's later, they were sat at the small outdoor terrace at the arse end of Imogen's life story to date. Imogen's time on this earth was surprising in its banality, even when told through plump lips and bewitching chocolate coloured eyes.

She was the archetypal Chelsea girl. The only tales she had to tell began and ended on Sloane Street with Daddy's credit card. They were the kind of tales that would only ever extend to European trips and charity balls with a tactically chosen husband of the future's credit card.

By the end of it, even her generous cleavage was boring, not to mention her chain smoking.

'Goodness me!' she exclaimed, finally noticing the glaze over Arthur's eyes, 'I've been rambling, haven't I? How rude of me, now tell me about *you*. What is it your parents do, again? Did you say you board?'

I said I *am* bored, he wanted to quip, but didn't.

He was at the crossroads that blighted so many teenage boy's nights out; he'd served so much time already pretending to listen intently to her painstaking self-analysis (and pretending that he, too, found it fascinating) that he may well be better hedging his bets and staying put for the duration, seeing if he might get a fumble out of it before the night's end, or at least a kiss. *Or* he could throw in the towel and see if he might double up elsewhere.

It was risky, of course: the evening was getting later, people had already begun to couple off. A kiss at midnight hung in the balance but, somehow, her perfectly plump and flirtatious lips had progressively lost their allure as they chuntered onwards, churning out smoke and bullshit.

He politely extracted himself from her attentions and headed towards the gents, which held far more appeal. Marble urinals for one, and a man in a waistcoat handing out lemon scented hand towels.

He was enjoying watching his urine run down the marble as Marcus appeared on his left, unzipped and started pissing like a racehorse.

'So,' he smirked, 'Imogen Braithwaite, eh?'

'Do you know her?' asked Arthur, finding the thunderous sound of Marcus hosing down the marble off-putting and zipping back up.

'Not really, met her a few times. Great boobs, but notoriously frigid, apparently.'

Arthur nodded. Typical.

'You never know, the chime of the bells and the old Maxwell charm might just be the golden ticket to nipplesville!' he added crassly, nudging him with one elbow and tucking himself back in with the other hand. 'The possibilities must seem endless now Casanova's not going to be there turning all the heads!'

'Is he with you?' asked Arthur guiltily, realising for the first time he had neglected his chaperoning duties at the first flutter of eyelashes in his direction.

'Nah, he was, til the hostess smuggled him away around the back somewhere,' Marcus sniggered. 'Gets her off my back, doesn't it? Once she's got you in her sights she's a woman possessed.'

'I'd better stage an intervention.' said Arthur, shuddering at the thought of ever being in Lucy's sights.

They headed back towards the bar, scanning left and right. It was far busier now than when he first accompanied Imogen outside. There were boys in black tie everywhere, like an upper class game of *Where's Wally*.

Arthur did a full circuit of the room, enquiring after Louie each time he recognised a face, but nobody had seen him.

There's no cause for alarm, they reassured him. After all, Louie's Houdini acts at parties were nothing new. But Arthur knew better. He wasn't supposed to let him out of his sight.

He had known this was a bad idea.

He left the private bar and headed into the main room of the casino which was far livelier than when they'd made their entrance only hours before. The glamour was melting, somehow: the suave, suited men sweated at blackjack tables, faces pitted with anxiety. The shiny, pristine women were red cheeked and raucous. Things were beginning to unravel.

Arthur bobbed and weaved through the sea of bodies, becoming increasingly frantic. He checked the toilets, the cloakrooms, the corridors and then turned back on himself. His palms were sweating now, his heart beginning to palpitate. He needed fresh air.

He stumbled towards the fire exit and pushed open the heavy door. He found himself in a concrete stairwell, blinking at the harshness of the white strip lights hanging overhead. The one door ahead of him was marked 'Staff Only' and when he tried it, it was locked.

He started up the stairs, the sound of his footsteps bouncing off the cold concrete and echoing up the walls. He looked up at the never ending steps circling above him, fading into darkness and turned around to head back down. As he passed the door again, he heard a noise. He stopped dead, frozen to the spot and strained to hear. He edged closer to the door on his tiptoes and pressed his ear against it. He heard it again: the sound of a girl crying.

When he tapped at the door again, the crying stopped. He knocked again and was met by only silence. He hesitated before turning around. It could be nothing, entirely unrelated but he couldn't shake the feeling that it was *something*. Just as he was about to walk away, he heard a sniffle and charged at the door, banging at it with his fists.

'Louie?' he bellowed, 'Louie, is that you? LOUIE!'

He pounded at the door until it clicked open. Lucy stood in front of him with a quivering bottom lip, her eyes puffy and her face stained black with streams of mascara.

'He's not here,' she said as she started to sob again.

Arthur pushed past her into the room, scanning it in the manner of a navy seal. Desk, bookshelves, filing cabinets, metal safe. He checked behind the door. No Louie.

'Where is he?' he demanded, 'Marcus said he was with you.'

'He *was* with me,' she said, dabbing at her face with a square of sodden tissue, making even more of a mess, 'Then he just *disappeared.*'

'What do you mean, disappeared? He can't just disappear, he's not David Copperfield. Where did he go?'

Her shoulders racked and heaved with ugly sobs. He grabbed her by the shoulders and guided her back into the tiny room, depositing her on the corner of the desk and leaning his face closer to hers.

'Lucy,' he said slowly, 'This is important. Where did he go?'

'He left.'

'Left where?'

'How would I know?' she retorted crossly, blowing her nose.

'Come on Lucy, this could be serious. You were the last to see him. Give me a clue, would you?' he pleaded, throwing his hands in the air and beginning to pace. Typical Lucy, the first to come forward with illicit bits of scandal and hearsay, yet utterly useless in the gathering of any kind of information of consequence.

'Alright, *Arthur*, since you asked so nicely,' she puffed, 'We were talking. Things got a little… heated. He said he was going away, I got upset… and he left.'

'Left where? You're not making any bloody sense!' Arthur shouted in frustration, immediately regretting raising his voice as the sobs heightened in their decibels. He took a deep breath. 'Lucy, I'm sorry, I shouldn't shout, okay? …okay?'

She nodded.

'I need to find Louie, it's very important, he's very fragile right now and I wasn't supposed to let him out of my sight. So please, I'll ask you again, talk me through it. Where did he go? Where do you *think* he might have gone?'

'He brushed me off, if you must know, and I got a little upset. We've shared a few… intimate times over the last few months, and I had stupidly thought it was leading somewhere. Well, it wasn't. And then, to add insult to injury, he suddenly became all distracted and just walked off in the middle of our argument. He just *walked away*, Arthur! It was beyond rude, it was downright disrespectful. When I went to go after him, he didn't even look at me, just kept staring at the door. He said something about speaking to his dad, and off he went, without so much as a look in my direction! He couldn't give a *damn* about me!' she threw her hand onto her heart and stared sorrowfully ahead, a picture perfect performance in melodrama.

'The front door?'

'*Yes*, the front bloody door. Thanks so much for caring, Arthur!' she snapped.

'I have a feeling you'll be just fine, Lucy.' he muttered.

He took a couple of strides towards the door and then

jumped back at a series of loud bangs and shouts of 'Happy New Year!' which emanated from the other side of the fire door. The cheers seemed to go on forever before the bagpipes started up. Both of them stared at the floor as a chorus of Auld Lang Syne rang out.

'Oh, fucking marvellous!' muttered Lucy, stomping past him.

He looked across at the phone on the desk and made a snap decision. He didn't want to unnecessarily worry anyone, and he would have loved nothing more than to find Louie loitering outside somewhere finding utopia in the arms of another long haired girl... but he had a feeling, deep down in his gut, that something was wrong here and should he leave this room without picking up the receiver he would only be delaying the inevitable.

He sat down at the desk and dialled his house phone, the only number he knew by heart. He chewed his fingernails as it rang out. *Shit.* His mum would be next door, or in the garden with Anna, dancing around on the patio. He tried again. On his third attempt, just as he was about to give up, a small voice answered, 'Hello?'

'Mum?' he shouted down the line, static crackling.

'It's Ella.'

'Ella! Ella! Is Mum there? Or your mum? Or your dad?'

'They're dancing on the kitchen table.' she said, nonplussed.

'Can you get them down? I need to speak to someone.'

'I can try.' she sighed. 'But I doubt it.'

'Ella, it's urgent. It's Louie.'

He heard her sharp intake of breath over the whoops and cheers behind her. 'Is he okay? What's happened?' she demanded.

'I can't find him, Ella, he's walked out of the party. I don't know where he is. Can you get one of them to come down here?'

'We're on our way. Stay there.' she told him authoritatively before hanging up.

Arthur waited by the phone for a further five minutes in case one of the adults called back, and when nobody did, he left the office and pushed back through the fire door into the casino. He wove his way through the pulsating thrum of revellers and out through the front doors, manned by two suited bruisers with earpieces.

'Alright?' asked one of them, eyebrow raised.

'Waiting for my dad.' he told him, leaning back against the wall to catch his breath. Satisfied, the man nodded and went back to the business of admitting the wealthy and scaring off the riff-raff.

What felt like hours later, Grayson's Cortina screeched around the corner and pulled up on the double yellows directly outside the front doors.

'You can't park there!' protested one of the doormen.

'It's an emergency!' shouted Grayson, pelting past them into the casino. They shared a surprised look and trailed inside after him.

Arthur stood on the kerb, bewildered, as Ella climbed out of the passenger side and walked around the car to shut the door on the drivers' side that Grayson had left hanging open. She leant against the car and produced a pack of Marlboros from the pocket of her velvet shift dress and held them out to Arthur. He took one, still in a daze.

'They shouldn't have let him come. It was stupid.' she stated.

Arthur stared at her, wondering where these insights had come from and when she started smoking.

'He was never going to just *have a nice time*, then go home, was he? When has he ever done that? This whole thing was just setting him up to fail.'

'Yeah, maybe.' replied Arthur quietly, feeling chastised by the thirteen year old.

They finished their cigarettes in silence and then she walked back around the car and opened the door. She pulled the front seat forward and gestured at him to get in.

He hesitated. 'I'd better go and find your dad.' he said. She shrugged and climbed in as he ran back through the front door in search of Grayson.

They exited an hour later, escorted to the door by exasperated members of staff who had been very accommodating in allowing them to search even the broom cupboards for a boy who had clearly buggered off into town to some party or other.

A call to the police proved equally fruitless, eliciting much the same response. He is sixteen, they were told, and male: almost an adult and very low risk. He had to have been missing more than twenty-four hours to be considered a missing person and besides, it's New Year's Eve and he's probably snuck off to a party. Even after hearing his backstory, they weren't convinced, but promised to send out a description through the radios and keep an eye out for him, stressing that it was a very busy night for law enforcement and that they should call back in twenty-four hours if he still hadn't turned up.

The three of them stayed out until the early hours, scouring the streets and establishments of central London looking for a needle in a haystack, never destined to find it.

They returned home defeated. Ella and Arthur fell to sleep exhausted on either end of the sofa while Grayson waited at the kitchen table, biting his nails to the quick.

Staring at a phone that would never ring.

III

Part Three

Ella

TWENTY NINE

Full circle, 2022.

Anna is in the study, sitting in Grayson's battered leather desk chair. The arms are scuffed and cracked; the thing is so past it that it whelps a creaky protest each time she readjusts herself. She's only seven stone – she checked last night after unearthing a pair of ancient scales in the back bathroom – this chair is an accident waiting to happen.

The room is small and originally had been dubbed as the fourth bedroom, though it was impossible to get much beyond a double bed in here. But although the space is small, the task is mighty.

Grayson was a meticulous record keeper. He processed all of their accounts, bills, fines and bank statements in here and filed them away for safekeeping into the abyss of his filing cabinets which take up one wall. He'd built a shelving system into the other two walls, heavy with hardbacks and files which sit nose to nose. His huge ornate antique writing desk, which had been his father's and grandfather's before his, sits in front of the window.

The room is unknown territory to Anna. She has never had cause to spend time in here besides the dropping off of hot beverages, the occasional snack and her one-time cameo as a sexy secretary clad in stockings, suspenders and some old reading glasses she'd found in a bedside drawer.

It baffles her, this amount of paperwork. She supposes there are some things of importance here; the deeds to the house, her children's birth certificates. That she will likely have to sit here for hours fossicking through utility bills from 1969 to locate these things means it isn't a task she will relish. She is not somebody who finds cleaning or sorting of any kind therapeutic.

'For Christ's sake, Grayson,' she grumbles, 'you bloody hoarder.'

She is half way through the first filing cabinet when she finds them. She is on the floor, swimming in a sea of tax returns spanning the last half a century feeling rather put out. The dust is playing hell with her sinuses, she already has two paper cuts and she has sworn extensively at her dead husband throughout. She opens the folder she is holding labelled '1983 Tax Return' and three small bits of paper waft innocently to the floor.

Anna painfully bends down to retrieve the three bits of paper. They are cheques. Signed: P Bennett. Sifting back through the clandestine file, the accompanying correspondence is brief and on headed parliamentary paper. A testament to his absolute confidence that their family had been successfully silenced.

Arrogant prick, Anna thinks.

Please find enclosed provision for Ms Charlesworth, as discussed.

The cheques are for the paltry sum of one hundred pounds, seemingly posted out each month. Anna has to laugh at the miserliness of it on top of the audacity. She also notices that not one of the cheques had ever been cashed and for that she feels a rush of affection for her proud and upstanding husband, the one she had been loudly cursing moments ago.

That's a good man, she thinks, *that's a man with real scruples.*

Not the narcissist who signed these cheques. She wants to spit on them and the insult they represent even after all this time. But she won't. These are evidence for three things: that Peter Bennett was a bad man, a fraud void of principles. That Grayson Carmichael was intrinsically a good and moral man who took care of his family, no matter the personal cost. And thirdly, that Anna had done one thing right: she had chosen the right man. The second chance the universe had gifted her had paid dividends.

Grayson had shown her unquestioning devotion and loyalty throughout their marriage. He had loved her completely, of that she had been sure. But she had never been more sure than that night when Peter had finally come knocking. She had never expected Grayson to stand shoulder to shoulder with her like that. He had done so much for her already, but that night, he had single-handedly exorcised the demons of her past. He had gripped them by the collar and sent them on their way.

CHAPTER THIRTY

The living, 2022.

Arthur is in his mother's kitchen, absentmindedly leafing through a week old copy of the Evening Standard over his morning coffee. He hasn't slept well. He hasn't slept well in weeks.

His thoughts have been as disobedient as his sleep has been broken. Difficult memories are forcing their way to the surface one after another, day after day, like scenes from a static home video tape. He is having difficulty concentrating on the here and now, especially at night, lying in his bed, when the lines between past and present become obscured and distorted. Night after night, his body jolts back into consciousness every time he drifts off, sure he's heard their voices right there with him in the room.

It is entirely possible that he could be going mad. He's seen it enough times at work; the frantic look those losing their minds have in their eyes. So he checks his reflection often to make sure.

His main worry is the conundrum of at which point one

might lose their ability to recognise their own madness. If this is, in fact, a mental health crisis, not just a delayed onset of some malady of guilt.

Still, he doubts the reliability of his own accounts of the past. After all, everyone has their own versions of things, things which shift in shape through the passage of time.

Side by side with these ghosts of the past, he is plagued with thoughts of death and the question of his own mortality. His own mother has been on death's door for months now, they keep telling him. He's been so preoccupied with keeping up the 'dutiful son', complete with 'cheerful smile and stiff upper lip' act, that he hasn't ever stopped for a minute to consider the implications of the loss of his mother and what it might really mean. It would make an orphan of him for starters. Walter had died some years back now, cirrhosis of the liver in the end. A horrible way to go, even for a man in his mid-seventies who had pickled himself in drink for decades.

'I've seen plenty of life, old boy, there's no sense in denying oneself small pleasures at my age,' he would say like a mantra every time he poured another scotch, as though the words themselves might absolve him of the responsibility of the reality of his diagnosis. But that's alcoholism, Arthur supposes; the denial, the downplay. Oksana had gone a decade before, back to the homeland arm in arm with an old beau she had reconnected with online, leaving him a bitter old cuckold. Not that he hadn't been a drinker long before that, he had just been one you could ignore; one less prone to falling or pissing himself. When she had gone, he dropped the pretence and became maudlin and repetitive, an old soak stuck in a loop of his own regrets.

His mother is old, yes, and sick, certainly. Her heart is failing her but she has lived past two sets of prognosis of 'only weeks', now. The mind is a powerful thing and Maggie's mind is fighting fit. Arthur is sure it is that which has carried her this far. She'll go when she decides she's ready, Arthur has no doubt about that. For now, she's sent the afterlife packing.

She has always been his anchor in life, the one who doled out the advice and the comfort. The idea of her not being on the end of a phone anymore fills him with unspeakable dread.

Who would he call, then? Teddy emigrated to Oregon not long after finishing university, to marry Veronica, an ugly American heir to the acres upon acres of vineyards that had made her father a millionaire. He'd replaced the affectatious braces and waistcoats he favoured in London with the ridiculous cowboy hats and vintage smoking pipes of the American mid-west.

There is no other family, bar a couple of cousins he long ago lost contact with. No girlfriends, nobody has been significant, nothing has stuck. He doesn't have many friends. He lost contact with his school friends shortly after he left. There is nobody. Nobody else loves him, everyone who might have done once is gone.

In many ways, he is just as lonely as Anna Carmichael, he has just worn it differently.

He gives himself a shake and tips the tepid end of his coffee into the sink. He had long ago made a pact with himself that the only thing he would bring to Maggie's door would be positivity. He uses the drive to The Cedars to try and regain some of this; he can't face his dying mother with a face like a slapped arse.

He needs to talk to his mother, to try to explain how he has been feeling, to try and make sense of some of the memories that have resurfaced. They are gauzy and he isn't sure how much of it might be poetic license, the reality of events taking on shifting shapes within a fertile and traumatized teenage mind in order to assuage his culpability.

Of course, it had been a traumatic time for Maggie, too. They haven't spoken of any of these events in decades; he has no way to know what kind of reception he will get. He would hate to upset her. But the burning desire to see if she can corroborate his account of things has overcome him and there is an urgency to it. If she does die like the professionals keep saying she will, she won't be there to ask for much longer.

He parks up, greets staff, and makes his way to his mother's room. He has followed this routine for so long now that the process has become automatic.

Maggie is sitting in the armchair by her window with a blanket on her lap and her glasses on the end of her nose. Her hair is piled up on top of her head, which he kisses before he sits opposite her. She puts her book down and removes the glasses which hang on a chain around her neck.

'Well, now,' she says, 'You look like the walking dead. You haven't slept. I do hope it's woman trouble. I'm excellent at breaking down the barriers of the female psyche.'

He smiles, feeling a rush of affection for his mother and her ability to read him so succinctly, an ability she has always had. There are still no flies on her. He shakes his head, unsure how to initiate the conversation he wants to have.

'Then what?' she persists. 'Come on, spit it out whilst we're still both of this earth.'

He smiles, marvelling again at her accuracy. 'It's Louie. Well, it's all of them. I've been helping Anna to clear the house and it's just... it's brought some things back. Things I haven't thought about for years, memories I'm not sure are even my own.'

'Mmm, I could see this coming. Have you talked to Anna about any of it?'

'No, no, goodness no!' The idea is ridiculous to him, badgering an old woman for details of the run up to her son's demise which are quite possibly fantasy or irrelevant.

'Perhaps you should,' she tells him. 'I'm not the person to ask, Arthur. If I'm right, and I think I am, the things you're wondering about are things that I most probably wasn't party to. Of course, I caught the basic gist of things, I understood everyone's thoughts and feelings in the aftermath. But that was the measure of it. I didn't bear witness to the dynamics of things before it happened. They didn't define my life the way they did with the two of you. It was awful, of course it was, but the loss wasn't mine.'

'I'm just not sure I can—'

'Talk to her.' Maggie cuts in. 'Talk to her. Do you honestly think that these things aren't keeping her awake at night too, packing up whatever is left of their things? Of course they are. It's high time she had the full picture, the woman has driven herself quite mad in the absence of it.'

Arthur nods. She's right, again. There are a few beats of silence, each of them in quiet contemplation.

'And while you're at it,' Maggie continues, leaning towards him and placing her hand on his knee, 'bring her in to see me. I have a few things I would like to say to her too, before

I cop it. She doesn't have to spend the rest of her days alone, the stubborn old mule...'

Arthur hates the casual manner in which his mother refers to her own death, the way she is so blasé about it. She does it more and more these days, as though she knows something that he doesn't. It unnerves him.

Nicola brings a pot of tea and a tray of pastries and they return to easier topics of conversation, like the aesthetic consequences of Teddy's American diet and how his wife's pinched expression might hint at her struggle to pass a bowel movement.

They laugh until their faces hurt.

***

Later that afternoon, Arthur arrives on Anna's doorstep armed with a transit van, a pair of helping hands and a fresh outlook. The helping hands belong to Bernie, a young colleague from the charity who has the physique of a swimmer and smokes like a chimney. Between them they heave, haul and manoeuvre furniture down stairs and around corners, sweating and swearing profusely.

When the van is packed full, to the point at which it couldn't possibly take any more weight, they drive it off to a storage facility in Vauxhall where four volunteers help them unload it a darn sight faster than they had loaded it.

Bernie takes the van and Arthur hops on the 436 bus towards home, stopping en route to pick up a Chinese take away and a bottle of red. He is back on Anna's door step by 7.30pm and together they pile their plates high with chow mein.

'Good heavens,' she says, rolling herself back into the sofa and letting out a belch. 'That's the most I've eaten in years.'

'Good for you, it's a celebration,' laughs Arthur. 'It's been a big day!'

Number thirty-two feels cavernous now, with so much of its innards removed. All that's left are the basics, a skeleton of fundamentals that a person might require to live, like the kettle, and an eclectic collection of items that Anna has decided she cannot bear to part with.

Arthur has booked a company who will arrive first thing in the morning and do what they call a deep clean. Anna isn't sure what is meant by this. How deep is deep? She had thought the cost extortionate when she was perfectly capable of running a hoover and a mop around herself, but Arthur had insisted that it was necessary and so she had trusted his better judgement.

The estate agent will arrive at midday to do the photographs and her house will officially be for sale.

There has been such build up, so many hours of labour have gone into getting to this point, that Anna's mixed emotions are overridden by excitement. She can scarcely imagine the kind of freedom she will feel when the house is sold, when the money is in her bank account and she is at liberty to go wherever she likes and do whatever she pleases. Never, since her childhood, has she moved about the world without the excess weight of baggage.

'I couldn't have done any of it without you, you know that. Thank you, Arthur Maxwell, from the bottom of my heart.' she says, eyes shining. 'You truly don't know what it will mean for me to leave this all behind. It's been a rod for my own back, this house, it should never have taken me as long as it did.'

Arthur swigs back his Merlot and leans towards her.

'You're more than welcome. Besides, my mother would have had a fit if I hadn't been here to provide daily progress reports. It's been... it's been a bit of a journey for me too, Anna. Being here, seeing all their things...'

She nods.

'I'm revisiting memories I didn't know I had,' he says, looking at the wall behind her. 'I feel like there are dots I'm supposed to connect somewhere, but I can't find them. It's all so long ago, one thing melts into another and... Sorry, this probably sounds silly.' he says, losing his nerve.

'No,' she says. 'it's not silly. I have relived every moment of 1983 so thoroughly that sometimes I'm surprised at the date at the top of my morning paper.'

She is playing it down. She isn't ready to own up to the amount of times she has stood agog at the television, wondering who that man is and where Maggie Thatcher has gone. Or found herself thinking 'it really is such a shame about poor John Lennon.'

At her age, people would suspect dementia, Alzheimer's, the shrinking of the brain. But Anna knows that she is perfectly compos mentis. It's grief, and the whirlpool of confusion that it brings with it. It's a trick of the brain, it's a survival instinct: if one small area of grey matter can convince its neighbours that it's still the 1980's, maybe the rest will follow and Anna could be blessed with blissful ignorance. Her life a loop of a year where nothing bad had happened yet, forever more.

'That's what all of this has been for, Arthur. Because it isn't 1983 anymore. I've been wrapping myself in nostalgia as though it's a cashmere blanket and where has it got me? I've spent forty years trying to put one over on myself, wishing my life away until the moment that my brain finally fails me and I become so detached from reality that I might believe my own fibs.

'As the years have gone by, the fewer people there have been left to challenge my account of my children and of myself. So I've gotten away with sitting stagnant with only the memories that bring me comfort. The ones I have cherry picked.'

Anna's words have provoked Arthur's own epiphany. It strikes him that the courage it has taken for Anna to untangle herself from this house, pack away her belongings and wave them off to pastures new is remarkable.

And what of the memories? Which are the right memories to cling on to? The ones that cast the people you have lost in the best possible light to the detriment of the bigger, darker picture?

Arthur's struggle, he is realising, has been futile. He has been fighting tooth and nail to keep the ugly parts at bay. It has sapped him of his energy and filled him with self-doubt.

'I keep remembering the shit bits, Anna. The times when he acted like a dick and I wanted to slap him. And it makes me feel like a bad person.'

Anna smiles and reaches across to place her hand on his, a mountain range of blue veins.

'The shit bits don't make you a bad person, quite the opposite. They are a privilege, a testament to the depths of a friendship you shared. To know someone so completely can be equal amounts blessing and curse. There's no sense in shying away from the truth if you can stomach it, not when it quite clearly costs so much to do so. Me, I've never been able to stomach it, not now and not forty years ago. Perhaps if I had, things might have been different. But I'll never know. So for me, the painful parts, they're better off buried.'

This was where the natural close in the conversation was, and with that, he thought, the end of Arthur's quest. But Anna Carmichael has always enjoyed foreplay, the dangle of the carrot.

'I like to think that there isn't much that can shock me any-more, well, I had thought so anyway until you appeared on my doorstep again, not only a tree hugger but a communist to boot!' she says with a cackle. 'But I suspect that Louie's life, the one he lived outside of this house, may well be too gritty for me to manage. For me, it's time to close the door on the past and learn how to sleep at night again. There's no use in me raking over old sores, not at my age, what good could it do? But *you*, you're still a youngster. If you want the truth, I think it's up there.' She waves a bent finger, gesturing above them.

Arthur closes his eyes. 'With the angels.' he says under his breath.

Anna's eyebrows shoot up. 'In the bloody attic, soft arse!'

***

Against Arthur's better judgement, they have made light work of the Merlot and he is half way up an extremely temperamental ladder. Every step elicits a louder creak than the one before. Anna stands on the landing at the bottom, gesticulating up towards the loft hatch as if in some great hurry, oblivious to Arthur's peril.

'You'll probably have to give it a bit of a thump,' she tells him with a smirk. 'It's been a while. Oh, and be on alert for rodents.'

'*Rodents?*' he gasps.

'Well, who knows? I wouldn't hear them, would I?'

'You're enjoying this.' he says over her sniggers, watching her shoulders shake with laughter. This is the most fun she's had in ages.

The ladder teeters precariously as he reaches the top and he takes a sharp intake of breath. The hatch is in the middle of the landing. The fall wouldn't be ideal in either direction, but the right hand side would probably kill him, or at least paralyze him. By the third rung he was past the height of the banister and he really doesn't fancy a tumble down two sets of stairs.

'Stop being such a Jessie,' she continues, smacking the bottom of the ladder in delight. 'Grayson would have been up and down thrice in the time it's taken you to crawl this ladder. Men, nowadays. Not so nimble, not so quick.'

He does indeed need to give the hatch a thump, and there's another thing he wouldn't mind thumping as well, truth be told. This is a relatively manly task for Arthur, who has never been much of a ladder type man. He's never owned a pair of overalls or been the ecstatic recipient of a combi drill for Christmas. To be fair, the probability of him being handy had been slim. Walter had been a man who had felt himself to be in an entirely different class than those who partook in manual labour. He paid a young Pole to whitewash his walls twice a year.

As the hatch falls open over his head, a thick clump of spiders web falls down onto his face and he is emasculated further as a shriek of shock escapes.

'Piss! Shit!' he shouts, scraping at his face, pulling away a cluster that looks like it's fallen out of his vacuum cleaner.

Anna is having a party at floor level. She is bent double and gasping for breath in between violent torrents of laughter.

Doing his best to ignore her, he pulls himself up through the hatch and reaches for the torch in his back pocket. There isn't enough height between the boards and the ceiling for him to stand up, so he remains on all fours and attempts to get his bearings.

There are a dozen boxes to the far end of the space, with various unboarded areas in between, only yellow tufts of insulation and plaster between himself and the lower storey. He crawls forward tentatively, dubious of the joists ability to take his weight. He manages to skirt around the boardless patches and withstand the creepy crawly related anxiety that threatens long enough to make it to the first box. Curiosity takes over at this point.

'Well?' demands the little voice below him.

Well, indeed, Arthur thinks, *you can wonder*.

The first couple of boxes contain old toys, stale dollies which stare at him grotesquely with half of their faces rubbed away. Another is full of the dusty pieces of scalextric which himself and Louie had spent hours constructing and racing. He hopes that can come home with him.

It is the three boxes behind that he is looking for. He pulls out the cardboard edges and recoils in shock to see a full colour school photo of Louie, the last one he would ever have taken. On the back, somebody has written Dulwich College, 1983.

He is exactly as Arthur remembers him, the twinkle in his eye projecting outward with an otherworldly intensity beyond the faded portrait. Underneath the photo there is a bundle of other photos, letters and notebooks. Next up is Louie's record and tape collection and the third, smaller box is a box of Ella: the threadbare stuffed rabbit she dragged behind her everywhere she went as a child, some school books and drawings. This is the treasure he has been sent up here to find.

***

All Arthur's attempts of sleep are fitful that night, thwarted by seeing his best friend's face again after so long. It has thrown him so far off kilter that in the early hours, he's given up and returned to the kitchen table, re-opening the boxes he had carried home with him earlier.

The photo is placed on the table and he studies it for what feels like hours. Louie stares back at him, face awash with mischief. The colour is a little off and the edges are curling, but the contours of his face and the laughter in his eyes is a haunting kind of déjà vu.

'You bloody idiot,' he tells it. 'What were you doing, you bloody idiot? You threw it all away.'

He is startled to register the silent tears streaming down his cheeks and wipes his eyes roughly on his sleeve. The clock on the wall tells him it's 3.35am.

He admits defeat and returns to his bed. The twilight hours are no time to be poring over photos from the past, the world seems far more futile at this time, far more hollow.

***

He has called in on Anna first thing, suspecting he may need to extract her from her bed before the cleaners arrived (he had). He hadn't fancied watching her trail around after the two ladies, interrogating them as to the mechanics of the steam cleaner all day, so he had left them to it.

He is back at his kitchen table, ready to tackle the boxes. When a pep talk in the bathroom mirror had failed to elicit any more enthusiasm, he had nipped in to work in Maggie's fiesta under the premise of picking up some paperwork from his office behind the soup kitchen at exactly mid day, hoping to bump into a particular client of his, Irish Jimmy Nesbit. Jimmy had lived on the streets long before Arthur started at the charity fifteen years ago. He is so blackened nowadays he could almost pass for a chimney sweep. He has one tooth left at the top and two at the bottom. Every smile takes on the look of a jagged skyline. Below all the dirt, longer serving colleagues tell Arthur that he has the colourings of a cartoon leprechaun: alabaster skin smattered with freckles and the dirt-coated dreadlocks on his head are purported to be the colour of a perfect tangerine. He sleeps under a disused railway bridge in Wandsworth and sits at the entrance to the station every morning, appealing to commuters with tragic tales of misfortune, a family 'back home' amongst the bogs and the bracken of County Clare, and his sad green eyes. He can usually be found around the corner in the off license by 11am, exchanging the grubby shrapnel he has collected from his morning shift for a bottle of Smirnoff which he refers to only as his 'medicine'. He makes his way around to the soup kitchen every day like clockwork, with the bottle up his frayed sleeve to receive his daily meal. His whereabouts after that are varied and unknown; he has been spotted in any number of boroughs over the years, but his sleeping spot and his morning routine have remained the same.

Via Irish Jimmy, Arthur is able to procure some medicine of his own. Being slipped an eighth of hash by a tramp with half a bottle of Smirnoff down his gullet is no easy trick. He has to remind Jimmy (who insists on calling him 'Boss') numerous times that this is a sackable offense. It is probably the most illicit thing that Arthur has ever done, despite him paying wildly over the odds as a charitable gesture. By the time the transaction is complete, Jimmy is collapsed at the roadside belting out lines of Molly Malone and Arthur's nerves are shot to smithereens.

He stops at a petrol station on his way home and buys tobacco, Rizla, a six pack of lager and a microwave lasagne.

Louie's photograph is propped up against the five remaining bottles of beer in silent observation as Arthur attempts to roll a joint for the first time in twenty years. It is a lost skill, an artform which requires considerable dexterity. Arthur is all fingers and thumbs.

'I know,' he tells the photo as though it were mocking him. 'It's been twenty years, I'm past it now, mate. Lucky for you, you don't have to worry about disguising man tits or a receding hairline.'

He struggles to light the result at the gas hob. It's a flimsy, amateur thing, a five year old's origami project. After twenty minutes of rolling and un-rolling, he concedes that it is the best he can do and forges ahead with it.

Whatever it looks like and however many times he has to re-light it, its innards are the same. The sensation comes quickly: a slight drowsiness, a slower beat of the heart. The idea is this: to catapult himself back into seventeen year old

Arthur's state of mind, to authenticate proceedings and pay homage to a lost friend. A hazy salute.

He doesn't trust his middle age constitution and thinks better of it, leaving it sitting limp in an ashtray for a while. He reaches blindly over the top of the box, unearthing the stack of photos bound together with string, an eerie montage of past Carltons turned Carmichaels in chronological order. He flicks through them feeling like an unwelcome voyeur, his senses heightened: a frighteningly young, thin Anna, clutching a small pink bundle to her chest. It could have been the flash, but something tells Arthur it's not; she looks bewildered, terrified even. Toddler Louie, cherub faced, sat on a blanket eating raspberries in a garden somewhere followed by four or five more shots, identical but for inter changing food stuffs and backdrops. There are no more of young Anna and Louie together. There had been nobody to take one and so Louie is solo in all of his early years shots. The beginning of Anna's re-entering the frames signals the Maxwells' arrival into her life, and Arthur smiles at the gawkiness of his childhood self, the precociousness of his brother and the vibrancy of his mother. Various birthday parties and park trips follow, even an odd day at the beach, these two women and the trio of children. Enter Grayson, dashing in a tartan suit with a white clad Anna on his arm, smiles wide with pride and optimism outside Chelsea town hall. In the next few, Ella's arrival are chronicled. Grayson proudly cradling an angry purple baby with a shock of jet black hair, Louie in his school uniform with said baby in his lap, socks to his knees and missing teeth. There are school concerts, paper-mache Halloween costumes and eventually, they are the teenagers they would become.

The photograph in his hands causes him to inhale sharply. After a few moments, he realises that he is still holding his breath. His teenage face stares back at him from his mother's hallway, where he stands awkwardly next to movie-star handsome Louie, both clad in full dinner suits. He shakes his head, squeezes his eyes shut and takes another look at the photo, running his eyes over every centimetre of it incase he has missed something.

The smiles grind to a halt at this point. Arthur finishes his beer and pops open another one. This is the point of no return, the point where he leaps into the quagmire of his past. However much he wants to turn away and return them to the box, he knows he must keep going, like a dilettante sleuth. There could be clues, if he looks carefully enough, whatever suffering it might cause him. Of course, there were clues everywhere, plenty of conjecture but the burning question is this: what was Louie *doing* that night, and where had he gone?

THIRTY ONE

The reaper, 2022.

Anna is awoken by the shrill sound of the landline ringing in her hallway. She is out of bed with her heart hammering so hard she can hear it in her ears. Phone calls before a certain hour of the day never bring good news, she has enough experience of that kind of thing.

She snatches up the receiver with an intake of breath.

'Hello?' she says, steeling herself.

'It's me, Anna, it's Arthur. Sorry to call so early.'

'It's your mother, isn't it?' she replies. 'Do we have time? Shall I get dressed?'

She doesn't give thought to whether her words are presumptive, that there would be any question as to the appropriateness of her presence after such a long leave of absence. She and Maggie are still family, after all. They have become entwined together in triumphs, tragedies and losses spanning fifty years. She has lost her once, to the home. She won't stand idle and lose her for the final time without saying the things she ought to. She is confronting her demons these days, after all.

Arthur is momentarily taken aback by Anna's oracle-like assessment of the situation, before he says, 'Yes, she's taken a bad turn. They don't think she will make it through the day. I've been here all night. She's been asking to see you.'

She hears him choke on his words.

'Of course she has.' she says matter-of-factly. She glances at the clock on the wall, an angry crack running through its face. 'I'll be there in forty minutes.'

She puts the phone down and springs into action. There is a taxi number scrawled on the corner of the calendar on her telephone table, the firm she had used three years prior to travel to and from a root canal. She's in luck, they're still in business and Tariq will be with her in fifteen minutes.

There are things to be done. She dresses, washes her face and brushes her teeth. She won't grace her best friend's death bed with onion breath. She begins to run a brush through her hair and then thinks better of it.

She grabs a satchel from a peg in the hall and begins to throw things into it. She scours the book shelves in the dining room until she finds what she's looking for: the photo albums. They are caked with dust. For years Anna has eyed them warily every time she walked past. She used to pore through them until her eyes were raw, torturing herself with their faces during happier times, searching for clues. But memories don't fill empty rooms.

She is waiting on the curb when Tariq pulls up outside, seven minutes late, muttering apologies and lamenting the terrible traffic on the Westway. Anna isn't listening. She is impressed at her own composure and the anticipation has brought with it a kind of serenity.

She has never yet had the opportunity to choose the last words that someone she loves will hear, every other time she has been blindsided and found lacking. She comes into this moment with the wisdom of years on her side and is grateful that she might be given the opportunity to thank her friend for all of the good she brought into her life. To send her onwards to wherever it is that they all go with words of love ringing in her ears.

She is just about to jump into the cab when somebody calls her name. She looks about her to identify the source with her squirreled eyes.

The estate agent boy is upon her in moments.

'Mrs Carmichael!' he exclaims breathlessly, having sprinted from his parking space. 'Are you going somewhere?'

'As a matter of fact I am,' she replies brusquely, moving to open the car door. She hasn't time to wonder what he might want, she hasn't a moment to spare.

'But… but the viewings. I have a couple from Herne Hill arriving in ten minutes! A barrister and his wife, cash buyers, looking for a project…'

His coat flaps in the wind as he stands there.

Bloody old ladies, he thinks irritably. He's put on his best suit, polished his shoes and spent an extra ten minutes on his hair. He needs this commission. He'll never be able to pay off Tony at the pool hall without it and if he doesn't come up with something soon, his dad will find out and he'll get a good hiding to boot.

Anna looks from the cab, to the boy and back to the cab again.

'Here!' she says, digging around in her bag and flinging her house keys at him. 'You don't need your hand holding, do

279

you? I'm late for my best friend's death.'

***

She arrives at The Cedars and is taken through to Maggie's room by Nicola, in her tunic and neon pink rubber clogs.

She stops by the door and says, 'She's been in and out of sleep all day. Her pulse is weakening, but she's had a few moments of lucidity. He hasn't even torn himself away for a toilet break yet.' She nods towards Arthur who sits with his back to them at Maggie's bedside, gripping her hand as though the pressure applied might somehow force some life back into his mother.

Anna enters the room and notes the smell, stale and sterile all at once, a mixture of death and bleach. Her friend looks diminished, a tiny thing tucked underneath the sheets, the barely perceptible rise and fall of her chest the only clue she's still with them. Her face looks sunken, all of the colour in it has moved on to pastures new and she is already beginning to take on some of the waxy pallor of a corpse.

Arthur looks up as Nicola pulls up another chair next to his for Anna. She looks down at him, exhausted and bewildered and sees the boy he had been.

'Thanks for coming,' he rasps. 'She hasn't woken again since the early hours.'

'Go and take five minutes, get some coffees, splash some water on your face or something... I'll be right here.'

He looks uncertainly at his mother whose hand he hasn't put down since he arrived yesterday afternoon, who he doesn't trust not to die as soon as his back is turned. He nods, his knees crack as he stands. 'Back in five.' he tells her.

Anna shuffles over into his chair and takes the mantel, reaching across for Maggie's cold hand.

'Well,' she starts. 'Here we are Mags, just the two of us.'

She squeezes the cold hand and studies it inside her own. Two sets of bent and weathered digits, age-spotted and translucent. Two sets of thin and brittle nails, two bulging networks of veins.

'We've had some laughs, haven't we? And some tears too, of course. You've been the most wonderful friend to me. Of all the people who have come and gone in my life, you have been the one who lasted it out. In for a penny, in for a pound, you used to say. You are so bloody loved Mags, but you already know that.

'The thing is, the one thing I've learnt is that this, all of this, is a journey. Time is sacred. We don't get it back. Every minute we're given is a gift. From the minute we're born the clock is ticking and you're heading towards your destination. Some people are lucky, some people aren't. Nothing is for keeps, however hard that might be to bear. You'd think I'd have some wisdom by now to offer you, some small bit of insight into death but I'm sorry Mags, I don't. I don't know where you're going. I don't know what it looks like. I don't know what happens next. If it's reincarnation, come and find me. If you return as a ghost, give me a sign, hey? I'd love the company.'

Arthur places a mug of coffee silently onto the table beside her.

'I've summoned that bloody husband of mine more times than I can count, but the old sod isn't half as reliable in death as he was alive. I even came home from Camden market with a Ouija board once and they're a load of old tripe, let me tell you.' A laugh breaks through her tears, an empty sound. 'It's a maddening thing, being the last one standing, wondering where everybody is. Are they up in the clouds somewhere, having a jolly good knees up? Are they roaming around my house, leaving me clues that I'm too senile to notice? Or are they just thin air now, a pile of splintered bones inside an expensive box a few feet under ground? Out of all of them, you're the one I can count on. If there's a way, any way at all that you can ease my mind before I join you, find it. And for my part, I'll be here, keeping an eye on Arthur and making sure he doesn't let any unsuitable maidens ransack the family jewels.'

Arthur snorts out a laugh behind her and she turns to him and smiles. She turns back to her friend and finishes, 'Goodbye, Mags. Thank you for blessing my life with your friendship.'

She leans over and kisses Maggie's cheek, then holds her old friends weathered hand against her lips for a heartbeat. She can almost feel her own heart cracking in two. She then moves aside to give Arthur his place back at Maggie's bedside.

They sit side by side listening to the rain drops bounce off the window panes, one or the other of them intermittently breaking the silence with a memory to share.

As the sun retreats behind the horizon and the world is cast in gold hues, a nurse comes in, checks for a pulse and doesn't find one. Maggie is gone.

THIRTY TWO

A viewing, 2022.

Back at the house, the final viewing is wrapping up. The viewer, a single woman that Daniel estimates to be in her late thirties, had been almost an hour late. He'd been locking up just as she'd sauntered up the path without a care in the world, with no thought to those who had homes to go to, or pub quizzes to partake in.

At first glance, he hadn't been at all sure that she wasn't a chancer. She ought to be too young to have the means to buy a gaff like this, but in Daniel's line of work, you see all sorts. Maybe her folks had croaked it and left her wadded. Maybe she was some kind of lawyer, or in finance, something like that. She looked the type, with her angular nose and harsh haircut. She hadn't bothered with make-up he noticed, nor had she laughed at any of his best lines. She was a miserable sort all together.

'Well, that's it then,' he says, standing in the middle of the kitchen, where they had begun. 'If you've any questions, fire away.'

'Who lives here?' she asks.

'Oh,' he replies, not expecting that kind of question. 'A lovely elderly lady who has called this her home since just after the war. She's widowed and is finding the maintenance difficult to keep on top of, as you can see with the wear and tear. She wants to relocate to somewhere smaller and leave her beloved home in a safe pair of hands.'

He falls back onto his heels, pleased with himself. He prides himself on his ability to think on the spot, to ham things up a bit, to ice the cake a little, as it were. He could hardly tell her Mrs Carmichael was a grubby, angry old bat who referred to her beloved home as a shit pit and that she couldn't wait to see the back of the place.

'Mmm,' says the woman, running a finger down the work top. 'And where will she go?'

How the hell would I know? He thinks, *and why would I care? I'm meant to be meeting Tina from accounts at the Fox and Grapes in fifteen minutes, I haven't even got time for a wash behind the ears now.*

'Umm, somewhere smaller. A bungalow, most likely.' He makes a show of looking at his watch, hoping she'll get the hint.

'I might take another look round,' she says.

As soon as she leaves the room, he groans. She isn't going to put an offer in, he could tell in the first five minutes, you can always tell. The ones who do display palpable excitement. He could watch them mentally arranging their furniture in each room. Oftentimes, they started throwing around ideas about colour schemes and other such things. Daniel lives for these moments, when he can stand there in mock-awe and ask them if they're interior designers, only, he hadn't thought of that shade himself but now he's picturing it, it would look amazing.

By the time she's finished he's in a foul mood. He hates time wasters, especially when he has somewhere else to be. He sees her to the door with his best false smile, in such a hurry that he doesn't notice the small ceramic deer that she is slipping into her pocket.

He runs back up the stairs and treats himself to a gentleman's wash in the avocado sink, drying his balls on Anna's hand towel before he lets himself out. He is on a promise, after all.

THIRTY THREE

A farewell, 2022.

nna returns home that evening to her dark and empty house. She pours herself a robust measure of whiskey and sinks onto her sofa. Maggie's death had been anti-climactic, in a way. All of her other loved ones had gone out with such a bang that the whiplash had rendered her catatonic. Tonight, she felt a strange sense of peace. It felt natural, somehow, to die in your sleep at a ripe old age with your child at your bedside.

A graceful departure.

It's the most any of us can wish for really, thinks Anna.

No flashing lights or invasive medical procedures, no gut wrenching screams. It had been serene in that room, just the three of them.

'Maggie! Maggie Maxwell!' she calls out into the near-empty room. 'Show yourself! If you can hear me, give me a sign!'

She waits for a few moments, eyes darting about the room. She isn't sure what she is hoping for. An apparition, perhaps.

The ceiling to start shaking. Cupboards flying open and doors falling off their hinges. She laughs and holds up her glass.

'Cheers to you, Margaret Maxwell, a magnificent friend and a crap ghost! Far too busy gassing with the previously departed to bother turning up here.'

She smiles to herself and swallows her whiskey in one. She returns to the drinks trolley and pours another, running her spindly fingers along the tarnished metal.

She allows herself to wallow for a while, to reminisce about the people she has loved who have gone before her. Maggie's death has brought about an extraordinary sense of peace in Anna. Wherever she is, truly she knows that she will be holding the fort for her.

***

Anna and Arthur silently watch South London slide past the windows of the hearse in slow motion. The air is clear and crisp, the sun is high in the sky, and surrounds them with the twinkles and winks of the dew and frost that cling to the morning.

'Are you sure I look alright?' Anna asks him for the fourth time. The last funeral she had attended had been her husband's. She can't even remember what she'd worn, not that she would fit it now. Today, she'd resorted to doing what she had always done should an important occasion arise and turned up at number thirty to raid Maggie's wardrobe, coming away with a black trouser suit and a small feathered hat.

'Only, it looked very Jackie-O on the hanger, but on me it

looks more… Barbara Windsor.' she says, fiddling with the hat.

Arthur smiles. 'You look fine.'

'Are you sure?' she twitters. 'I hope nobody recognises it, bloody hell, I've pilfered the wardrobe of my dead best friend for her own funeral.'

Arthur belly laughs at this, glad for the distraction of the odd comings and goings of Anna's stream of thoughts which lift him momentarily from his desolation. The lingering emptiness he has felt since his mother had taken her last breath.

It hadn't been like this with his father. Of course it had been sad, and of course he walks past certain brands of port in the supermarket or hears a song on the radio which reminds him of his father and has to stop and take a moment. But now he is walking around permanently feeling like something is missing. Or that he's forgotten something.

It's unnerving. He wants to ask Anna if it will always feel this way now, but he is too afraid of the answer.

'Are you sure the feathers aren't too much?' she continues. 'I don't want everyone standing there whispering, "look at her in that feathered hat, who does she think she is"…'

'I think their minds will probably be geared more towards mourning my mother to be honest, Anna.' he says, face turned towards the window.

Anna's face crumples. 'Oh Arthur, I'm so sorry, I didn't mean to—'

He leans towards her. 'That was for the ladders,' he whispers with a smirk.

'Bloody hell!' she gasps, thumping him on the thigh as hard as her brittle old-lady bones will allow. 'That was bloody wicked, Arthur Maxwell, bloody wicked!'

The crematorium is packed to capacity. Maggie has touched lives of all ages, some Arthur recognises, some he doesn't, but he appreciates their presence either way.

Nicola and her colleagues have brought a large and slightly rowdy gang from The Cedars. There are wives of Walter's colleagues, a group of ladies she had been in the tennis club with, the parents of his school friends who are still here amongst the sea of faces.

Maggie had asked for only two things for her funeral via a note handed to him by Nicola amongst all of her other papers: white lilies, and for it 'not to drag on until people are bored'. Arthur has honoured this and the service is short and sweet, over and done with in less than an hour. The vicar read a short eulogy based on a hastily written list of qualities and achievements Arthur had managed to club together, followed by a poem chosen by Anna and one hymn.

As her coffin disappears behind the velvet curtains and Judy Garland sings about rainbows, Arthur feels a sharp nudge in his side. He looks down at Anna staring up at him, whose wrinkled face appears childlike underneath the mass of white hair and the feathers. She is whispering something he can't make out.

'What?' he whispers back, leaning down towards her.

'Promise you'll come to mine?' she asks, nodding towards the curtains.

'As long as the buffet's good,' he whispers back, and she smiles.

He has done Maggie proud, Anna thinks, watching him greet strangers and friends with grace in his perfectly pressed suit and shiny shoes.

He spends the rest of the day smiling sadly and humouring the never ending crowd of pensioners keen to share their Maggie-related anecdotes, and fending off questions of the whereabouts of his elder brother.

'He was unable to get a flight, one of his daughters is unwell,' he lies, when in actuality, Teddy probably just couldn't be arsed. It's not quite as devastating a blow, he surmises, when you only phone half a dozen times a year. That isn't much to miss.

He touches arms, shakes hands, re-fills beverages and thanks people for coming. He is every inch the picture perfect son, gentle and patient, a testament to the deceased.

At last, Anna allows her mind to drift back to the time and place she'd been putting all of her effort into not remembering these past weeks. The final weeks, so long ago now, and the naïve and yellow-bellied way she had excused his behaviour. Convincing herself that it was normal, a phase, his way of dealing with the stress of the situation, a bit of a blowout.

Her unwavering belief that it would work itself out and her cold, hard horror when it hadn't.

THIRTY FOUR

New Years' Day, 1984.

It was a knock on the door, in the end.

Two police officers, one male, one female, hats held to their chests, asking if they might come in. And once they were, asking everybody to sit down.

They were sorry to have to impart the tragic news of the discovery of a body by a cleaner in the early hours, found face down on the tiled floors of a toilet cubicle in a backstreet Irish bar in Soho. Laid in a pool of his own vomit, a needle trumpeting from his vein, irises lost, heart no longer beating.

In later years, Anna would come to remember very little of the symphony of devastation that day. Nor would she ever be able to accurately recount the despair, the confusion, or the sedatives as she retreated into the comparative safety of silence and alcohol.

The only thing she can remember with any clarity is her immediate response.

'No,' she said, with such cool confidence that it cut through the moment like a knife. 'It's not Louie.'

'Obviously,' said the male officer gently, taken aback, 'there will need to be a formal identification before we can confirm anything, but… I'm sorry, Mrs Carmichael, we have reason to believe that it is Louie.'

'What reason?' snapped Anna aggressively, folding her arms tightly.

'Well, he, uh… the body fits his description exactly, Mrs Carmichael… a teenager, five feet ten, slim build, blonde curly hair, blue eyes, dinner suit…'

'It doesn't sound that specific to me, officer. That could be plenty of people.'

'There was, um, nobody else fitting that description or even marginally within the same age range reported missing last night.'

'There are plenty of missing people without families looking for them. This is bloody ridiculous.'

Grayson moved towards her slowly, putting a protective arm around her.

'Anna…' he whispered, as Maggie, Arthur and Ella shed silent tears behind shaking hands in the hallway.

'What?' she snapped, swivelling around and snatching her coat from the peg. She threw it over her shoulder and marched past the gobsmacked police officers.

'Got some time to kill, have you?' she shouted as she exited the front door. 'This what we pay our bloody taxes for, is it? Fucking useless!'

'Mrs Carmichael, if you could just—'

'Just *what?* Do you want your John Doe identifying or what? Let's get to it, I'll go and ogle at some young boy's body, you can scratch Louie from your list and start doing your job properly, and I can get back here and wait for my son to get his arse home. Not such a stretch, is it?'

She walked to the car without looking back.

The police officers looked at one another and shared an almost imperceptible shrug before following her out of the house and down the path towards their waiting car.

'Shit.' whispered Grayson, running trembling fingers through his hair as he started to move towards them. He hesitated at the door and turned to look at white-faced Ella standing beside his neighbours. He turned to Maggie. 'Can you—'

'Of course,' she said, pulling Ella in towards her. '*Go.*'

Grayson nodded and the front door clicked shut behind him.

***

The real agony is in the waiting. How does one even begin to sit around and wait for that kind of news? What Anna had done with her angry words and absolute faith was to weave the most tenuous thread of hope inside the onlookers. Whilst their rational minds understood the odds, their hearts now dared to hope that against all common sense, the boy lying on the slab in the mortuary was someone else's son, brother and friend.

Ella didn't utter a word for the duration. She stared resolutely ahead, ashen faced, rocking back and forth on the sofa whilst Maggie squeezed at her hand and intermittently suggested a sweet cup of tea.

Arthur was also mute at the other end of the sofa. The only thoughts he was able to gather were of the last words Louie ever uttered to him, the promises of best behaviour and the false sense of security they had lured him into. He knew, somehow, from somewhere deep inside of him, somewhere beyond the knots in his stomach and his rapid, shallow breaths, that he would never see his best friend again. He could *feel* the lack of him in the world.

He would spend the next two decades, at least, agonising over his decision to walk to the bar. To become distracted by a pair of 34D's. To spend so long tolerating the life story of a girl whose name he could already no longer recall as events unfolded that could never be reversed.

He would be so busy grappling with guilt and blame that he wouldn't quite manage to sit his exams, or make it to university, or partake in any activity that might once have brought him joy.

This moment in time would haunt and stunt him in equal measure, its effects rippling outward on the lake of his life, reaching far and wide, changing everything that could have been into things which became unattainable and unrecognisable.

What would I have done differently, he asked himself, if I had any inkling that Louie's life had been a time card with one last punch hole?

***

In Southwark mortuary, Anna stared through a pane of glass at the unmoving body of her eldest child. He was almost ethereal, an exceptionally beautiful young boy deep in a sleep from which he would never wake up. His closed eyes looked to her as though they may flutter open at any moment. His curls softly grazed his temples, sweeping down inside of his shirt collar.

He looked peaceful. That was the only difference in him. The chaos had gone.

Anna's forehead fell against the glass, her heavy exhale misting over, tears dropping in rivulets down her nose. Her shuddering body collapsed forward, her palms pressed against the glass.

Grayson wiped his eyes and nose with his shirt sleeve and nodded at the waiting police officers. He stepped forward to take his wife in his arms, stroking her hair and whispering, 'I'm here. It's okay.' Over and over.

When her violent shaking subsided, she took a step back and looked about her as though seeing the world anew. She turned back towards Grayson, animal-eyed.

'You should have fucking found him!' she screamed, shoving him with a force neither of them knew she had. *'You didn't look hard enough!'*

As both officers stepped towards the couple to intervene, she turned sharply and stormed out of the room and back out into the world.

Grayson held his head in his hands. 'I'm sorry,' he said softly, 'I'd better go after my wife.'

THIRTY FIVE

Jingle bells, 2022.

Arthur wakes up on Christmas morning alone in his childhood bed. He could move into the master bedroom, he supposes, but he hasn't. He doesn't want to tempt fate. He really has no idea where he stands with the house. She had alluded to a will a few times, but never specified what was in it. For all he knows, she could have bequeathed it to Battersea Dogs Home for a laugh. He wouldn't put it past her.

The festive period is the worst time of year to lose somebody you love. Not only does it put a dampener on things, making every Christmas song sound try-hard and tinny and making every bauble and string of tinsel look gaudy and pointless, but the timing itself is just unfortunate.

For a start, everything closes. It's as though the world stops. Everybody is busy. The few casual friends he has who might have accompanied him on sorrow drowning missions to the pub are otherwise engaged in turkey dinners and other such festivities.

I haven't sent a single card, he realises.

He opens his curtains. Trees and fairy lights are twinkling in each bay window as far as his eye can see. Some residents have gone even further, their frontages lit up like fairgrounds, adorning their lawns with reindeers, sleighs and blow-up Santas. He tuts at the thought of the energy these silly attempts at one-upmanship must use.

For the first time since the Maxwells claimed it, Christmas has skipped number thirty. He hadn't thought to buy a tree or bring down the string lights and baubles. It had sort of crept up on him.

He glances across at next door's yard, reliable in its absence of Christmas cheer. Numbers thirty and thirty-two cut a sad little pair in the middle of the street.

He showers, dresses, eats a few rounds of toast and flicks between channels. When he's had his fill of Charles Dickens acted out by the muppets, he throws caution to the wind and heads for the front door, tucking the hamper he never got to give his mother under his arm.

Anna takes an age to answer the door.

'Merry Christmas!' he says from the doorstep.

'Is it? Already? Bloody hell.' she says, shaking her head and waving him inside. They walk down the hall to the kitchen.

'Is that for me?' she asks, eyeing the hamper. She can't remember the last time she got a Christmas present.

'It is, now.' he laughs. 'I thought we could crack it open and have a champagne, cracker and piccalilli fest. If you're not busy, that is.'

Anna is delighted. 'First it's Christmas, now champagne and piccalilli, how exciting! She never used to save me any of the truffles, evil witch.' she says, rooting around in the

297

cupboards for the champagne flutes that she definitely had at some point in the 90's. 'I threatened to break in and pinch them once. Over my dead body, she said. Well, exactly. Who's laughing now?'

'Did you really not know it was Christmas?' he asks, amused.

'Well, I knew it was *soon*. I just didn't realise it was, you know, today.' she says, shrugging. She wipes the dust out of a pair of old wine glasses with a stained tea towel as Arthur pops the cork and pours.

'To Maggie,' she declares, holding her glass aloft. As Arthur's glass meets hers, she adds, 'And to finally getting my hands on her truffles, over her dead body!'

***

The sun is receding behind the skyline and the day has been filled with laughter. This is the first Christmas that Anna has enjoyed in years. The hamper has been picked dry, as has the drinks trolley. They have spent the last three hours engaged in an intense battle of rummy across the kitchen table. On the cusp of being beaten for the fourth consecutive time, Anna throws her cards on the table and folds her arms.

'My eyes are tired. I'm old. You're cheating.' she whines as he sniggers.

Both are warm, stomachs full and festively woozy and they settle into an easy silence. Anna's eyes wander to the empty seats at her table, her mind drifting back to the last time they were all occupied. She fixes her gaze on Arthur as the years melt away.

'It's strange, isn't it, that we should be the last ones standing.'

she says.

Arthur nods. 'Do you ever stop missing them?'

'No,' she says, 'No, you don't. There does come a point where you can wake up in the morning and they're not your very first thought, though. Some days I can get to lunch time or even dinner time before I remember. At some point you learn to accept death and see it for what it is, just another part of the great primordial soup of our lives... and after that, you just learn to live with it. It's always with you but you can focus on other things, live your life and it becomes part of the background.'

'I thought I knew all about grief, the five stages and all of that... I'm surrounded by grief at work, I've seen what it can do to people and I know the theory inside out. I thought I had prepared myself, heaven knows I've had enough time. But I had forgotten the physical feeling of loss. The heaviness in my chest, the churning of my stomach... It sounds stupid, but I hadn't factored it in, and now it's here... the memory of the *feeling*. It feels like I've lost everyone I love all over again.' Arthur wipes his eyes and an apologetic laugh escapes. 'Sorry...'

Anna hobbles around the table and puts an arm around him, bending his neck at an awkward angle and resting his head on her absent bosom. Even though her jumper is itchy and smells of damp, the physical proximity of another human is so soothing that Arthur wants to cling to her like a child. Eventually she pulls away. She pulls out the chair next to him and sits down, her knobbly little knees resting between his thighs.

'Any advice I could offer you would be useless, Arthur. I can hardly sit here and claim to have mastered the art of living with loss, can I?' she laughs. 'More like it's mastered me. It's consumed me. The pain, the anger, the questions. I didn't have time for anything else. And then suddenly, life had passed me by. It took a couple of bank urchins to force me back into the land of the living. What a waste of a life, don't you think? So I suppose, whatever you do, find a way through it. Like you did last time.'

They both look up at the picture on the wall and Arthur exhales loudly, sitting heavily on the kitchen chair like a deflated balloon.

'I still miss him, too.' he says.

'Oh, I know. He took so much of us both with him. I tell him off for it every day as I make my breakfast.'

Arthur laughs and doesn't doubt her for a minute. She heaves herself up and busies herself locating a pair of tumblers into which she pours the final drops of whiskey.

'A nightcap is in order, I think, and then it's time for bed. This is the hardest I've partied since the eighties.'

She hands him the meagre shot of whiskey and as he knocks it back, she tells him, 'You were a good son, Arthur. You were loyal and dutiful and everything a mother could wish for. She was so proud of you, and she knew you loved her which is really the most important thing, to a mother. It's difficult, being a mother to a boy. You love them so fiercely, but always, in the back of your mind, you are waiting to lose them… usually, to friends, girlfriends, then wives… The best you can hope for is to still be considered every so often. And you gave her so much more than that.'

'Thank you, Anna.' he says, tearing up all over again.

She pats his shoulder absentmindedly and continues, 'Not like mine. That's one of the reasons I get so cross. Not a thought for his mother. Or anyone else for that matter.'

'We were so young, though, Anna,' he says, defending his friend automatically, 'I don't think I really understood the concept of empathy until I was well into my thirties. We're not as quick off the mark, us boys.'

'Bollocks to that. You've always been a good boy. But of course I've considered it. That, and every other excuse I can possibly find for him. And if that's the case, then I'm still angry. Angry at the world, for never giving either of us a chance to find out what or who he could have been.' she says, waving her arms crossly towards the window and then folding them.

Arthur pulls himself up and envelopes her in a hug, her small pinched face resting in his armpit. As he takes hold of her shoulders he is alarmed by her lightness and by how much of her frame is made up of woolly jumper rather than actual flesh.

'I think he would have been just great, Anna. Thanks for a lovely Christmas.' he gives her a tender peck on her head and sees himself out.

Anna sits down, knotted fingers twisting around frayed sleeves, sunken eyes fixed once again on the portrait. 'Yes…' she whispers, 'Yes, he would…'

THIRTY SIX

The will, 2023.

Arthur is sitting at the kitchen table a few days after the dawn of the New Year, the yellowed polaroid of himself and Louie, shoulders back and chests puffed out, peacocking in full dinner dress in his mother's hallway, between his thumb and forefinger.

He chuckles at his seventeen-year-old self. How debonair he remembered feeling and the disparity between that and the gangly bespectacled nerd in the photograph. That young man had never understood why he was always the one to be bypassed by the fairer sex on their orbit towards his friend. The answer is glaringly obvious. Even within the fuzzy confines of a forty-odd-year-old polaroid, Louie is a classic heartthrob. Had he made it to the 1990's, Arthur was sure he would have made it into some boyband or another, hung up on teenage girls bedroom walls the world over.

This is the last photo in the pile. The last photo of his best friend alive. He has spent the strange interlude that is the Christmas holidays more or less alone, pottering around his mother's house waiting for the world to wake up from their turkey coma's and get back into motion.

He has leafed through every photo and scrap of paper within these boxes twice over. All that he has learned is that their collective teenage lyrics had most certainly not been the ground breaking future number one hits they had believed them to be as they were penned, and that his friend had certainly not gone to an early grave without seeing a pair of boobs or ten.

The celebrations of the New Year had passed in the same fashion it has done since 1983: a few strong sedatives and a very early night. He has never been quite brave enough to dip his toe in the water and see if he might be able to enjoy himself.

The few ex-girlfriends he has had have found the ritual both perturbing and peculiar. If he'd ever found a way to confide in them, they may have been sympathetic. But he's never been able to cross the boundary of uttering Louie's name to anyone who hadn't already known him. Even the thought of such a conversation is painful.

And now, on the third day of January, the postman's face is the only human contact he has had since he left Anna in her kitchen on Christmas night, unless you count the robotic grunts of the teenager employed in the twenty four hour garage up the road as he hands over the change, which Arthur doesn't.

'Lovely day, ain't it?' says the postie, with a somewhat manic grin. 'Happy new year to ya. Oh, this one's wantin' signin' for.'

He hands over a brown envelope as Arthur attempts to scrawl a signature onto the hand held screen with the funny plastic stick attached to it. The end result is a series of strange lines that look nothing like a signature. *I could have been anyone really*, thinks Arthur. He hands the machine back to the postman, who lingers on the step.

'Looks important.' he remarks, nodding towards the envelope.

'Hmm, yeah.' says Arthur, examining it.

'Cheerio, then.'

'Yeah, thanks.'

Arthur closes the door, his eyes never leaving the letter. He knows exactly what it will regard, even before he sees the logo of the small firm of solicitors who represent his mother. Having been her power of attorney for the best part of two years, he's more than familiar with Mr Greaves, both of the sons who work alongside him and the three cheerful secretaries in their employment.

He sits back down at the kitchen table and tears the envelope open, running his eyes quickly over the contents as he always does before he reads anything properly.

Whilst the content of the letter isn't unexpected, the method of delivery comes as somewhat of a surprise. He had been expecting some kind of a summons, an appointment with a sympathetic Mr Greaves senior at which he might sit before a mahogany desk, in a room crammed with leather bound legal tomes and antique desk lamps, where he might be read the final wishes of his mother in regards to her vast estate. Instead, he has an A4 typed document which tells him, pretty plainly, how much she's left and who to. Mr Greaves has, at least, signed underneath his name with actual ink, the only personal touch whatsoever.

He reads it three times, just to be sure. His mother has

never been somebody he could accuse of being predictable, but he hadn't expected her to be quite so bold in death. She certainly hadn't been worried about apple carts.

She has left almost everything to him. The house, its contents, the car, a not unsubstantial number of shares and a rather hefty amount in a savings account are all to go to him. She has left nothing for his brother, and Arthur has no idea if he will have to be the one to impart this awkward piece of information or whether he will already have been informed. This on its own is enough to potentially cause some considerable discord.

'He's got his wife's money, and plenty of it,' he can still hear her saying.

The last paragraph, however, is the one that would wreak havoc: a sterling silver necklace, a painting entitled 'The Dunes' and £25,000 to be left to Ella Johannssen (nee Carmichael).

***

At 2pm he is perched on a kitchen stool with his laptop open, making mechanical ding-a-ling noises as it tries to connect him to his brother in Oregon. His timing is deliberate: it will be roughly 8pm on the other side of the pond, by which point his brother has usually finished his evening meal and is most of the way through a bottle of his own Pinot.

Merry and amenable, that's what Arthur is hoping for.

'Howdy, bro!' quips the pixelated face of his brother, the toggled strings of his silly hat meeting just below his beetroot coloured jowls.

'Hi there, Teddy.' smiles Arthur, whose accent always

becomes that bit more clipped and quintessentially British when responding to his brother's affectatious Americanisms.

'How's it hangin' in old Blighty?' he continues as though he's a true Oregon native, not a public schoolboy with a British lineage spanning back to the 1600s.

'Not bad, thank you, not bad. Listen Teds, I won't beat about the bush. I'm calling about mum's will.' says Arthur, bracing himself.

'Oh yeah? What calamities has the old girl bestowed upon us, then?' he drawls, puffing at his cigar.

'Well…' starts Arthur, with a cough, 'She hasn't really… the thing is…'

'Spit it out, brother.'

Arthur takes a deep breath. 'She's left everything to me.'

'Oh…' says Teddy, rubbing at his chins, 'Ouch.'

'Yeah…'

'So, like…*everything?*'

'Yeah, everything.' he lies, 'So, are you… are you going to contest it?'

'Hmmm…' Teddy considers it, continuing to stroke his chins. 'Nah. No sense in gettin' greedy, I'm already a millionaire,' he adds, boastfully. 'Say, has she still got that paintin' in the hall, by that Francis… that Francis whats-his-fella?'

'Bacon. Francis Bacon.'

'Yeah, that's it. The weird one.'

'Yeah, it's here.' says Arthur, screen jerking and WIFI glitching as he wobbles out into the hall and tries to focus the tiny lens on it.

'That's gotta be worth a few bucks now, right? Veronica loves that shit, British artists or whatever. How's about you

FedEx that over as a good will gesture and we'll forget about the rest? I'll just say there was nothing left after the home or somethin'.'

Arthur hadn't expected to be engaged in some kind of long distance bartering with his elder brother over his mother's Last Will and Testament. One of them sat in his mother's terrace and the other sat in his ranch-style mansion surrounded by the three acres of vineyard to his name. Nor had he been expecting the insinuation of Veronica's displeasure over it.

'Sure.' says Arthur. He won't tell him that he's always found the painting a little sinister anyway, or that the artist was actually Irish.

'Okay, great. Do you need me to sign anything?'

'Nope. Just er, don't take me to court, basically.' Arthur nervously titters.

'You got it!' he booms, 'Alright, better run, I'm holdin' up a seriously tense game of poker, here. Catch you soon, buddy, God bless!'

Arthur waves and the screen goes blank.

***

Later that evening, Arthur sits alone in the kitchen, pondering his future over a fancy bottle of Pinot he picked up at Bargain Booze, his brother's rival brand.

He has unhooked the Bacon painting and set it down against the fireplace so he can have one last evening looking at it before he takes it down to the post office tomorrow. He studies it closely and decides that, nope, he still hates it. A victory all round.

He still can't really believe that she has left him so much. The entire house was so unexpected, never mind the money, too.

He had been anticipating the clearance and orchestrating a sale in order to wire his brother's share to him. Perhaps using the money on an upgrade to his small one bed in Vauxhall which he spends very little time in anyway, but now…

Well, now he could *stay* here, if he wanted to. He could live here. Sure, it's a big old place to potter around in by himself, but who knows what the future could hold? It's high time he was optimistic. He knows first-hand that it's a perfect house to raise a family in, should he ever find himself in the position of having one. He knows and likes the area.

And with a mortgage free house and all of that money in his bank, he wouldn't have to continue to work, although he knows he will. His job is important to him. Helping those in need, it has always been more of a vocation for him. His small way of paying it forward. The times he's walked past former clients in the street and they've stopped to say hello, and told him about their new lives: their jobs, their homes, their futures.

It has given him more than just pride, or job satisfaction. It has gone a small way towards easing his conscience and dousing the flames of regret that have engulfed his life since the one time he didn't get it right.

But just having the option, that freedom of choice is liberating enough.

As he's pondering all of this, he makes his way back through to the hall and opens the under stair cupboard. He fights his way through his mother's excessive collection of outerwear towards the small safe at the back and taps in his birth date.

He reaches around in the darkness, pulling items out one by one until he finds what he is looking for: a jewellery box and a small square canvas wrapped in parcel paper. He carries them back through to the living room.

First, he opens up the jewellery box. Inside is a small, thin silver chain, most unlike anything he can imagine his mother wearing. On the end of it dangles a tiny white crescent moon shaped pendant with a black dot inside. He turns the cheap velvet box around in his fingers, perplexed as to why his mother would choose to leave this to somebody over any of her vast Van Cleef or Tiffany collection. He shakes his head and wonders what to make of it as he moves towards the parcel.

He carefully and methodically undoes the coarse string that binds it and unfolds the paper. The painting is small and prosaic, but for an unshakable feeling of deja vu it brings about for him. He pushes his glasses back from where they are perched on the end of his nose and moves closer to the painting, trying to connect it with the bells of recognition that are ringing in the back of his consciousness somewhere, but he just can't quite recall… he's probably seen it hung up somewhere in the house, that must be it.

It can't be worth anything, beyond slight sentimental value. He likes to think he is up on his art, but the artist isn't somebody he has heard of. The painting itself is unremarkable: a pretty bog standard British beach landscape.

The exclusion of Anna and the inclusion of Ella is what is really perplexing. He had understood that they were close, Ella and his mother. He had often come home to find her at his kitchen table with Maggie wiping away her tears. She had been closer to Maggie than her own mother, Arthur knew that. But she had walked out of their lives over thirty years ago, without as much as a whisper ever since.

Sure, his mother had a soft spot for the girl, but it still made no sense.

As he leans forward to prop the seascape up next to the other defector, a sheaf of papers fall out from behind the frame and scatter across the wooden floorboards.

Arthur picks up the closest one, and as he reads the words in copperplate hand, postmarked from Devon, some of the pieces begin to slot into place.

THIRTY SEVEN

Grief, 1985.

I n the summer of 1985, a year and a half after the death of Louie, the Carmichael household was still crawling firmly through the trenches of grief and chaos. Grayson had died of a heart attack in April at the wheel of his beloved Cortina, on his way home from one of the after school clubs he so enthusiastically signed up to preside over after Louie's death.

The Carmichaels' marriage had never recovered from the rift that began during Louie's fall from grace, and catapulted into a full blown estrangement after his death. Anna had been unreachable and desperate, accusations and pent-up rage pouring out of her during the venomous tirades she directed at her husband. Finding someone to blame had felt far easier than shouldering any responsibility herself on top of her crippling grief, or looking in the direction of the lost soul of her son.

Grayson had retreated from her, too, and consequently from his daughter, as he avoided their home. So difficult had it become to be in the same vicinity as his wife, whose wrath could be unleashed unexpectedly at any moment. He spent as many hours as he possibly could on school business, becoming the most committed employee St Winnifreds had ever known. Subsequently, his rise up the ranks during this period had been meteoric and at the time of his death, he had been a much loved headmaster, due to be named on the board of governors the following term.

He left behind a fifteen year old daughter, pitiful in confusion and emotional neglect, and an outraged wife still very much lost in the quagmire of loss and regret.

Ella had taken to arriving on the doorstep of number thirty after school each day in search of a friendly face and a full stomach. This quickly morphed into sleeping in the spare room a few days a week, the times when her mother was particularly tumultuous.

Anna had taken to drinking upon waking, and was usually in a terrible state by late morning. She drank, she wept, she shouted, she smashed things, she slept and she drank some more. She quite forgot she had a daughter during those few months and her volatility had become frightening.

By June, having given her dear friend quite enough time to work through the emotions that engulfed her and return to the land of the living on behalf of her remaining child, it became apparent that no such return was imminent and it was time for an intervention.

Maggie bowled in, packed suitcases and bundled the two remaining Carmichaels into the back of her brand new Volvo estate and sped down the M3 towards Devon. She had rented a little cottage on the sea front in Woolacombe for the entire month, where she had hoped that she might perhaps be able to coerce her friend out of the rawness of grief and back into the present. The remoteness, the sea air and the salty waves of the Atlantic might set the scene for the kickstarting of the healing that mother and daughter so desperately needed.

It was a gruelling month for all three women. At points, Maggie had been all but abandoned by any shred of optimism. However, by the time they returned to London, somehow, some way, Anna's broken heart was finally taking baby steps towards salvation.

The wreckage of her daughter's had been shattered beyond redemption.

THIRTY EIGHT

The seaside, 1985.

The cottage was a perfect Cornish postcard cliche. It sat at the point that the grass verges met the sand, whitewashed, delicate white window frames with sky blue shutters, quaint little window boxes sprouting spring bulbs and a matching sky blue front door. White wooden decking ran the entire length of the house, upon which sat wrought iron garden furniture and surfboard racks.

The interior matched the stereotype exactly: country cottage meets bohemian beach retreat. Three small bedrooms and two bathrooms ran off the large open living space. White walls and furnishings smattered with nods to the nautical; a ship in a bottle here, a dining set made of repurposed driftwood there, a macrame hammock in the corner and so on.

'Lovely.' Maggie announced like an army major, dropping their cases on the floor, eyes roving the space as her diminished cadets shuffled up behind her. 'Now then, girls. We're going to do some laughing. We're going to do some crying.

We're going to do some talking, some soul searching and probably some shouting. We might even need to throw things at some point, and that's okay. Ideally, this won't be indoors, but if it is, a hefty surcharge is the least of our worries. Now, let's unload the car, settle in and I'll whip us up some lunch.'

Her enthusiasm had wavered somewhat when lunch was ready, upon finding Anna sat on her bed, jittery fingers struggling with the screw top of one of the litre bottles of vodka she had smuggled in her rucksack. But this was sink or swim, and Margaret Maxwell was made of sterner stuff than that.

A pattern emerged in that first week that went some way to painting a picture of life behind the closed doors of number thirty-two.

There had been a role reversal of sorts. Anna had become the objective teenager, fingers permanently curled around the neck of a bottle as she went through the motions of self-pity, rage, blame and mirth on repeat, unable to acknowledge any other human being within her orbit, or at least any living ones.

Ella had become almost matronly in her disapproving glances and scowls of disgust, but was too timid to step over the line of looks into the realms of words. Her default mode was impenetrable silence, her face set like stone, willing to share neither thought nor feeling.

She was bordering on vacancy in both mind and body. She was pitifully thin, her collar bone jutting grotesquely outward, which was no wonder: Maggie watched her as she spent most of their mealtimes scraping knife and fork together, engrossed in the pantomime of cutting every morsel of food into thousands of tiny pieces and pushing them about her plate, only miniscule amounts ever reaching her lips. It was an excruciating thing to watch.

For Maggie, it quickly became a juggling act: to spend an hour with Ella alone, trying to coax words from her sealed lips, meant later having to retrieve her mother from a heap on the floor, prising an empty bottle from her grasp as she kicked and whined like a petulant toddler. And so the plates were spun.

By the middle of the second week, the atmosphere was beginning to thaw. Anna's aggressive outbursts were slowly diminishing and her defences were beginning to fall away.

Maggie had insisted upon them stretching their legs each day, aiming to get each of them out of the house for as long as she could, her faith in the healing powers of nature never wavering.

So far, she had had to go between mother and daughter working in shifts, trying to cater for the very different needs of the two broken hearts she had tasked herself with mending. However, as time went on, the occasions they did find themselves sitting around a table as a three were becoming less and less volatile.

Maggie was already feeling rather pleased with herself. Although the assignment had been a demanding one and she had fallen into bed every night exhausted and emotionally wrung out, her plan was working.

The fresh air, the exercise, the unspoilt scenery, the change of routine, or perhaps a combination of all of them together, was bringing about an epiphany in Anna, Maggie could feel it.

She had seen the way her friend had begun to observe her daughter with a strange look on her face, considering her words before letting them escape. She had also noted the way her fingers now hesitated when she reached for the bottle, sometimes snatching her hand away before it could pour.

On one of their daily walks, they stopped to sit down on the verge of Potters Hill, looking down to where the long grass met the dunes as salty winds whistled through their hair. They let their eyes run across the beach, mostly deserted but for the odd dog walker in the distance.

'Beautiful, isn't it?' remarked Maggie.

Anna nodded and bit her bottom lip. 'Thank you, Mags.' she said, still staring straight ahead, elbows resting on her knees.

Maggie turned towards her and smiled. 'Don't be silly.'

'You won't leave me, will you?'

Maggie reached out and took her hand. 'Of course I won't.'

They sat quietly together, hand in hand, watching as the sun slowly descended into the sea, the sky awash with the golds and pinks of a proper summer sunset. When it had been swallowed up entirely, Anna stood abruptly, a woman who had made a silent decision.

'I need to sleep, Mags. I haven't slept properly, not since...' she began, furiously blinking back the threatening tears.

'Yes.' Maggie nodded, pulling herself up. 'A good sleep is exactly what we need.'

Maggie took off her coat, wrapped it around Anna's shoulders and led her back towards the beach house. When they arrived, she walked her into her bedroom, took off her shoes and tucked the duvet around her tightly, like a sickly child. She turned out the light and crept away from the door on her tiptoes.

She threw herself back onto the huge sofa and exhaled

deeply, feeling the euphoria of victory running through her body.

Ella glanced up from her book and eyed her quizzically. 'What?'

Maggie smiled and leant her head over the back of the sofa. 'I think your mum is starting to come around.'

'What makes you think that?' replied Ella dubiously.

'She hasn't had a drink today.'

***

Anna was still out for the count when they woke up the next morning, having slept for fourteen hours already. When Ella emerged from her bedroom, there was a full breakfast spread waiting for her.

'Good morning!' beamed Maggie, gesturing towards the table, 'Dig in. I wandered into the village and found the loveliest little bakery. I never have been able to resist the smell of freshly cooked pastry.'

Ella walked around the table and began to nibble on a still warm pain au chocolat, oozing from the centre.

'She dead?' she asked through a mouth full of pastry, nodding towards Anna's bedroom door.

'She's tired. It will do her good.' said Maggie, placing a cup of tea down in front of her.

Before they arrived here, Maggie had thought she knew all there was to know about the Carmichaels, but both of them had surprised her. She had understood Anna's volatility and her stubborn tunnel vision, but she had rarely experienced the ferocity of it first hand and she had certainly underestimated its frequency.

But whilst the temper tantrums and bloody-mindedness could be an uphill battle, Anna's feelings read like a book. There was no need for guessing. Ella, however, was a different kettle of fish. She was so closed that Maggie had realised that in actuality, she knew very little about the teenager besides where she went to school and how many sugars she took in her tea.

She had always just been *a good girl.* The type of girl who would be referred to as 'never any trouble' by everyone except her mother, who had always been convinced that she was some kind of enemy insurgent.

'Do you fancy a bit of pampering today, Ella?' asked Maggie, the cogs whirring as she took a closer look at the mousy strands of hair that hung limply around Ella's thin face and her bitten and chapped fingers.

'Like what?'

'I saw a little salon when I was up in the village and thought it looked good. Maybe a manicure, pedicure, a little trim? Whatever we fancy, really. I know *I* could do with it.'

Ella had never been inside a proper salon. Anna had always cut her split ends at the kitchen table with minimal fuss. A salon wasn't something that Ella had ever had the inclination to enquire about; she had never been particularly interested in clothes or make-up the way her school friends were, forever fussing over the beauty pages they had torn out of their Jackie magazines in the form room and obsessing over a different boy each week. Ella's heart had belonged to only one boy for as far back as she could remember and he was unlikely to ever look twice at her. She doubted a bit of mascara would make much difference, except to make her feel gauche and silly.

Sensing her uncertainty, Maggie added, 'It'll be fun. We can make a day of it, check out the shops and have some lunch.'

'What about Mum?'

'I think,' said Maggie, sweeping stray flakes of pastry from the table and gathering up their empty plates, 'that what your mum needs is a lot of sleep and a bit of alone time.'

'Alright then.' Ella shrugged.

***

When they arrived at Curl Up and Dye, it was empty besides a lone pensioner sat underneath a hooded dryer on the back wall. A bored looking girl with one of the biggest perms Maggie had ever laid eyes on sat at a small reception desk flicking through a magazine. 'Morning, have you got an appointment?' she asked.

'No, we haven't, we're here on holiday.' said Maggie, peering over her shoulder at the empty seats and tired decor. It was a world away from the chicness of Johan's place in Chelsea, he'd have a fit if he caught wind of this! Ella stood behind her, wrinkling her nose at the smell of ammonia.

'I see.' said the girl, sighing. 'Let me see if we can fit you in.'

Maggie looked around again, incredulous.

'Carol!' the girl shouted.

The woman who appeared from a door behind the back-wash basins looked more like a Dolly Parton impersonator than a Carol. Her peroxide blonde bouffant was larger than her little head and her make-up was as heavy as any that had graced a West End stage. She was all cerise pinks and enormous flapping eyelashes. Underneath her apron, she wore a silk shirt with tasselled arms which tapped against each other as she walked towards them in white cowboy boots, a huge smile plastered across her face.

'Welcome, ladies!' she beamed. 'I'm Carol, thanks for coming by. What can I help you with?'

Maggie took Carol in, a larger than life woman of no more than five feet, and decided that even letting her loose on her locks for a blow dry might prove to be a fatal mistake. But they were here now. She cleared her throat and smiled in return.

'We were hoping you might be able to fit us in today, just a wash and blow for me, perhaps a manicure if you've anyone doing nails?' she said, casting her eyes back over the salon and deducting that the probability of their being a dedicated nail girl was slim.

'Absolutely!' Carol chirped. 'I just need to finish Mrs Pearson's set, and then I can be right with you. Tammy here is our resident nail girl, she'll do you a fabulous set. Please, take a seat.'

She gestured to one of the chairs with a smile so huge it might crack her maquillage. Tammy, still leafing through her magazine, let out a low sigh.

'And you, little darling?' Carol asked Ella, kindly.

'Um, I'm not sure...' mumbled Ella, looking at her feet.

'Perhaps she'll have the same as me?' suggested Maggie, coming to her rescue. 'If you decide you fancy a trim or a little re-style, you can just say the word.'

'Alrighty!' smiled Carol, ushering Ella towards the chair next to Maggie. 'What beautiful hair you have, sweetheart, and so much of it! You're going to look sensational, I can't wait to get started. What a treat!' she continued, running her fingers through it. 'I'll be with you shortly, ladies!'

She trotted off, humming happily, towards Mrs Pearson who was fast asleep under the hood dryer. Maggie watched Ella's face through the mirror as an expression of surprise morphed into a flicker of pride, and decided that she liked this woman immensely.

'What do you think?' Maggie whispered, 'A little re-style? Or just a wash and blow dry?'

Ella studied her reflection in the mirror, feeling the disparity between her own lacklustre and the vibrant colours and excessive heights of the two women they had just met. 'A re-style, maybe, I think?' she suggested tentatively.

Carol waved off a very happy purple-rinsed Mrs Pearson and stood behind their chairs. 'How about I get started on your wash whilst the little lady decides what she might like?'

'She's thinking about a little re-style.' Maggie grinned.

'*Fabulous!*' she exclaimed with unconcealed glee, clapping her hands together. She handed Ella a small stack of magazines. 'I was hoping you'd say that! Have a look through these whilst we're washing, see if anything catches your eye! If you're not sure, Tammy can help you whilst she does your nails!'

Tammy wheeled a little stool over and opened a bag full of nail varnishes and files. 'You want a colour?' she asked. She noticed the magazines on Ella's lap and her interest piqued. 'You having a cut?'

Ella nodded.

'Can I do it?' she asked. Sensing Ella's reluctance, she added, 'I'm fully qualified in a couple of months. Nearly finished my City and Guilds. I know all the most trendy styles.'

'Oh… alright, then.'

When Maggie returned with a turban towel on her head,

Ella and Tammy were deep in conversation, hunched over one of the magazines. They had become best friends in twenty minutes.

'Trust me! You're gonna look unreal!'

'Tammy's going to do my hair.' Ella told her, as Carol came up behind them.

'Is she…' Maggie started, looking questioningly at Carol as she unwound the towel.

'Oh yes!' she smiled, 'My Tammy has such a flair for cutting, all of her tutors say so. She's been helping me in here since she was knee high, haven't you, Tams? She's got hairdressing in her blood, this one, she'll be taking over a few of my regulars soon. *Stunning* singing voice as well, right set of pipes on her! Voice of an angel, her music teacher told me once. That's just a bit of fate at work, I says to her, cos I named her after Tammy Wynette!'

***

Almost four hours later, Maggie paid up and they walked out of the salon. Maggie couldn't deny that the transformation suited Ella. The sharp fringe, the feathering and the volume were far more in keeping with her age and had done wonders in softening her sharp features. Ella was thrilled, staring at her reflection in every shop window they walked past in disbelief.

'Reckon Mum'll like it?' she asked, a shadow of anxiety crossing her face.

'Course she will! You look fab.'

'But what if she doesn't?'

'Well, it's your hair, not hers. But she will, I promise.'

'I bet she doesn't. She might hate it.' said Ella, stopping dead on the pavement, eyes filling with tears as her new-found confidence evaporated.

'Oh, Ella.' said Maggie, rummaging in her bag for a tissue. 'She'll love it. I know she will. She loves Madonna, doesn't she, and it's *very* Madonna.'

'But not on me.' she sniffed, 'She hates me.'

Maggie plonked down onto the closest bench and pulled Ella down into a huge hug. 'Your mum loves you.' she said firmly, wiping at the tears with her thumb. 'I know she may not be great at showing it sometimes, especially not right now. But she does. I've known her since before you were born, so I should know.'

Ella wiped her nose onto her sleeve, looking unconvinced.

'Listen,' continued Maggie, 'It's been a really tough time for both of you, but it won't always be like this. Your mum needs a bit of sense knocking into her from time to time, I admit, and that's what I'm here to do. Things won't ever be normal again, not normal as you've known it, you'll always miss them, both of them. But you'll be alright, your mum and you, you'll look after each other. You're a team now, Ella, and you can help each other through this. She's grieving, and all that pain can make you say and do silly things sometimes. But don't ever doubt that she loves you. You're the person she loves most in the world.'

'She said that?'

'Of course she did.' said Maggie, planting a kiss on her forehead and realising that no, she'd never said those words. For the briefest of moments, a niggle of worry began to creep in. Maggie swiftly swotted the thoughts away like a fly. *Of course it's true,* Maggie told herself, *of course she loves her daughter.*

***

They picked up three huge portions of fish and chips and made their way back to the house. When they arrived, there had been another transformation. Anna was sitting on the porch with a cigarette, fresh from a shower. Her wet hair glistened in the sun and she was wearing a clean strappy summer dress. She stood up as they walked down the path, the cigarette between her fingers, staring at Ella.

'Wow!' she said, 'Your hair... you look... you look *beautiful*, Ella, like a pop star. It really suits you. Nails too!' she said, grabbing Ella's pearly pink fingernails and holding them up to the light.

Ella's face broke into a bashful smile.

'*And* chips!' she said, eyeing the newspaper parcels, 'I hope you got enough for four.'

'Four?' exclaimed Maggie.

***

Arthur sat at the table, morose as his mother and Anna stared at him expectantly and Ella stared at her chips, the only plate that was still full.

'So?' prompted Maggie, 'What happened? Have you and Jen had an argument?'

'*No.*' he replied sullenly, inadvertently telling everyone that yes, they obviously had had a fight.

'What happened?' she persisted. 'You haven't been being moody again, have you? He can be so grumpy.' she said to

Anna.

'Just leave it, mum. My head's banging.' he said irritably.

'Okay, okay, I'm only trying to help,' she said, throwing her hands up in surrender, 'We know a thing or two about women, believe it or not. But as everything's fine, you don't *need* our help…'

'I'm going for a lie down.' he said, walking outside.

Maggie turned and watched him go. When she was satisfied that he was out of earshot, she leaned forward and announced, 'Love's young dream is turning out to be love's young nightmare!'

'What's happened?' asked Anna, pinching chips from Ella's plate and smothering them in ketchup.

'Oh, God knows, he never gives me any details, the bloody spoilsport. But he's come home three times in the last fortnight looking all exhausted and bereft, slamming doors and whatnot. Stomping around muttering "why do I bother."'

'Smells like trouble!' said Anna, warming up her speech extolling the evil and manipulative tendencies of teenage girls, the subject being something of a specialty of hers in those days.

'Mmm,' said Maggie, 'I think it's pretty normal. First love and all that, all those hormones and things. She's got him wrapped around her little finger, poor sod. She seems nice enough, very polite whenever she's been over… pretty little thing. Doubt it'll last though, he's not very good with the old amateur dramatics.'

'Long way for him to come, all the way to Devon. Can't be looking too good.' remarked Anna.

'Mmm, if I know Arthur, I'd guess the writing's on the wall.' agreed Maggie.

Ella gazed into space feigning disinterest, her heart dancing.

***

Arthur stomped down the beach with his hands pushed into his pockets and his brow furrowed, cursing his very existence. He was so deep inside his own self-pity that he almost failed to stop when a couple of children careered past him towards the sea, their cries of happiness reverberating through his skull like ping pong balls.

Why did everything have to turn to *shit?* And why did he always have to be so *weak?*

He'd been avoiding his mother for a fortnight now, too scared to come clean about being kicked off of his college course. Not that he'd been particularly enthusiastic about enrolling in the first place, but an A-level drop out didn't have very many options. Nobody saw the trauma of a tragic bereavement, just a lack of staying power or commitment.

He was sick of living with the anxiety of yet even more failure, coiled up like a viper in the pit of his stomach, ready to pounce at any moment: in the college canteen, in the corner shop, in his girlfriend's bed at her parents' house.

It was excruciatingly embarrassing, the tell-tale prickling sensation coming up his neck, the sweat trickling down his temples, the burn of his lungs struggling for breath, the sheer terror of it. And the awkward, pitying looks afterwards, especially from Jennifer. Jen didn't understand, how could she?

'You're hard work, Arthur. I never feel like you really appreciate me. You're always so quiet, I can never tell what you're thinking. It makes me feel very insecure. I felt like I *had* to go for a drink with Mike from work, just to know what it *feels* like to be wanted again.' she had explained last night.

Of course he appreciated her! Of course he wanted her! He worshipped her. But there I go again, he thought, ruining everything. It's hardly her fault that his tongue lays fat in his mouth like a snail, slow and stunted when she persistently questions his feelings for her. Of course she hated the way he clammed up when she cried, and how he had to walk away. She deserved more than that.

So, no college, no friends, no girlfriend, his future sliding down the toilet like a proverbial piece of turd. And then, to add insult to injury, he went and clipped his car and smashed a wing mirror clean off in his panic to get to Devon, running to his mum again like the wet lettuce Jen had so often accused him of being. It was bound to be karma, the universe's way of punishing him for being so pathetic.

He wished badly that he had someone to confide in, someone who could help him find a solution to the endless problems that kept hurtling towards him before they overwhelmed him completely.

He pined for Louie, needing to hear his voice more than anything at all. If he were here, Arthur knew he would have found a way to laugh at his situation already, and they would be busy concocting some kind of scheme between them to talk their way out of trouble. He wouldn't be sitting here on the beach, crying like a baby.

***

Later that afternoon, as Arthur approached the beach house, a piercing scream rang out from the open door. He began to run.

The scene that greeted him was like something from a horror movie: the white wood floors were covered in large pools of blood, his mother and Ella's bare feet slipping and sliding around in it like an oil slick as they flapped around in panic. Anna was on her knees next to the kitchen counter, blood pumping out of her forearm with alarming force. Maggie dropped down next to her and wrapped a tea towel tightly around it. The white square of cloth turned immediately crimson, and Ella handed her a second.

'What's happened?' asked Arthur, surveying the chaos of broken glass and gore all around him.

'I feel dizzy...' Anna mumbled, her head beginning to loll to one side, her skin shockingly pale.

He whipped his head towards the door, hearing the sound of a siren approaching.

'Go out and flag them down,' barked Maggie, 'the last thing we need is them going past us, that road's a buggar for turning around on.'

Arthur headed out of the door, around the back of the house and up the verge, on to the rugged and potholed road, which was more of a dirt track. As the siren became louder, he ran into the middle of the road and started waving his arms up and down. The ambulance approached and came to a stop at the side of the road. Two paramedics climbed out.

'D-down here,' stammered Arthur, 'She's bleeding.'

He took them down to the house and showed them in, then stepped outside and stood next to the door with his back against the whitewashed wall, gulping for breath.

'Oh dear,' he heard one of the paramedics say calmly in his jolly west country accent, 'That looks nasty. Better get you up to the hospital and see about some stitches, eh?'

A few minutes later, the two of them heaved a stumbling Anna up the path with Maggie in their wake.

'Keep an eye on Ella,' she instructed on her way past, 'There's some picky bits in the fridge. I'll phone from the hospital when I know what's happening.'

Ella stepped out of the house looking as bewildered as he was, her t-shirt and cheek splattered with blood. He blew out a slow breath through his lips and pulled a pack of cigarettes from his back pocket. Lighting one, he offered it to Ella, who took it with a shaking hand.

'What happened?'

'My mum,' she said, puffing furiously on the cigarette, 'Drinking again. She dropped the wine bottle and then slipped over on top of it. She had a big chunk of the glass stuck in her arm and she yanked it out and started screaming blue murder.'

'Looked like a bloody murder when I walked in, Christ.' he said, shaking his head.

'Some of it's just wine.'

'Never a dull moment with you lot, is it?' he said, and she shrugged. 'Is there a shop anywhere near?'

'Yeah, but shouldn't we try to clean up?' she asked, looking back through the open door.

'Yeah, we will. But I need a beer first. And we probably need some paper towels or something. We can ask at the till what they recommend for a crime scene clean up.'

'I can't go in.' she said, looking down at her bloodied clothes. It had gotten into every crease of her knees, between her toes, crusted into the ends of her new hair.

'Yeah, maybe not. You can wait in the car.'

Arthur couldn't help but laugh at the absurdity of it all, and soon they were both bent double. Arthur wiped a tear from his eye and shook his head again in disbelief.

***

After a can of lager each on the beach for Dutch courage, they headed inside and got down onto all fours, soaking paper towel after paper towel with blood or wine. Neither of them could tell the difference. Three packs later, they ran out and resorted to the fluffy white bath towels which Arthur threw into a bin bag whilst Ella mopped and wiped down cupboard doors. An hour and a half later, they surveyed their handiwork. Aside from a few pink-tinged floor boards, the place was as good as new.

'A job well done,' said Arthur, 'Shower and then we'll raid the fridge? You can go first.'

He cracked open another can and sat back on a wrought iron chair, eyes closed, allowing himself to enjoy the warmth of the evening sun on his face and the sound of the seagulls last calls. It had taken a real life blood bath to distract him from his woes, but somehow he felt all the better for it.

Ella emerged from the bathroom wrapped in a towel just as the phone started to ring. Arthur rushed in to answer it and almost bumped into her.

'Sorry.' he said, quickly looking away from the curve of her breast and back towards the phone. A crimson blush crept up her neck and she hurried into her designated bedroom.

'Hello? Yeah, yeah, we're fine. We've cleaned up. No

worries. No, not eaten yet. Yeah, course, she's fine. I'll make us something. Anna alright? Oh, is she? Oh right, how long for? Yeah, yeah, that's fine, you stay there. We'll be fine, I'll stay the night. See you in the morning.'

Ella heard every word as she held her breath, her ear pressed hard against the back of the door, heart soaring.

***

Both freshly showered, they carried more beers and a bowl of crisps out into the evening. Arthur lit the citronella then sat down, taking handfuls of crisps and crunching them loudly as the candlelight flickered across the contours of his face. Ella sat opposite him, arms wrapped around her knees, sipping her beer and stealing glances at him as often as she could. She marvelled at her good fortune, mesmerised by the bobbing up and down of his Adam's apple and the freckles dappled across his nose.

'To us,' he said, tapping his Carlsberg against hers, 'and our bright futures in the crime scene clean up business.'

'I don't think I fancy it, I'm not much good with gore.' she said, wrinkling her nose.

'You were great today, a real pro. Anyway, I need you, I can't do it alone and I'm running out of career options.' he said, the three empty cans on the table already giving him word vomit.

'I thought you were gonna become a big detective.'

'Yeah, well, I don't think it's for me. I don't think I've got it in me.' he replied, tapping his fingers against the bottom of his can.

She turned to him in surprise. 'What do you mean? Of

course you have.'

Arthur turned towards her and laughed, the combination of wide eyed surprise and new feather cut, left to air dry and splaying out around her face at all angles, giving her the distinct look of a baby owl stunned by a farmer's torch beam.

'Nah,' he said, swigging his beer and shrugging. 'I'm not smart enough. You have to be really smart.'

Ella was perplexed by this. She had always thought, from the first time she had heard Maggie mention the criminology course at the kitchen table, that Arthur would make a perfect detective. To her, he was already that kind of hero. Clever, kind, fair.

'You *are* smart enough.' she said, frowning. 'You're the smartest person I know. You're brilliant.'

Arthur stared at her, taken aback by the fierce conviction with which she said the words. She wasn't joking. Nobody had ever told him he was brilliant before.

'You're just being nice. But, thanks.'

'I'm not.' she said quietly.

For a few minutes, neither of them spoke, both looking upwards. The night hung above them like a satin sheet, the blackest of black, dotted with stars that twinkled like rhinestones stitched into the atmosphere. The wind whistled through the tufts of sand reed behind them, the waves gently lapped at the shore in front. Arthur remembered the last time he saw a sky like this, huddled behind the quad with Louie when they were still school boys, believing the world lay at their feet.

'Do you miss him?'

'Louie? Or my dad?'

'Well, both of them.' he replied, shocked at his own

clumsiness.

After a few moments, she said, 'Of course. I miss them both. I still get a little surprised sometimes, that they haven't walked through the door at dinner time, or there isn't a place set for them at the table. It's weird. But then, some things I don't miss. In some ways it's easier now.'

Arthur's brow furrowed in confusion and he looked over at her again, waiting for her to continue. 'Easier?'

'Well, yeah. At least we know where Louie is now. Before, we were always waiting, wondering. And there were so many secrets, and all the arguments… It was always Louie this, Louie that.'

She had surprised him again with this small bit of insight. He had spent most of his life growing up in the shadow of Louie's brilliance and charisma, but had never considered that Ella had suffered in the same way. If never quite matching his milestones and achievements in her formative years hadn't been difficult enough to navigate, she was even more overlooked as he went about his fall from grace. She had always just been a nondescript girl, a background character; the type of girl who would be referred to as 'never any trouble'. Just like him.

He nodded and lit them both another cigarette. As she reached across and took it between her slender fingers, he watched her mouth as she talked: the gap between her front teeth, the fullness of her lips which he had never noticed before.

'I miss my dad. Watching her bully him, tell him it was his fault over and over again was hard, but watching him just *take* it was even worse. He used to tiptoe around her, like she was some sort of tiny, fragile child who didn't know what she was saying. She *did* know. He went to his grave believing that she blamed him, and I think that's what's still eating her up now. No wonder his heart stopped. Well, I'm not gonna be the one who sits there and tells her what she wants to hear just to make her feel better. No way.'

'It wasn't his fault, though. Not in the slightest.'

'No, of course it wasn't. He believed her, though. He spent his life protecting her from the things Louie did, glossing them over and shouldering all the worry so she didn't have to. I think he always wondered whether, if he had done anything differently, there might have been another outcome. There wouldn't have been, though.'

'What makes you say that?'

'Because Louie did what Louie wanted. He didn't listen to anyone if they weren't saying things he wanted to hear.'

Arthur let the words soak in, and as he did so, he felt the lifting of a weight on his conscience. They were all members of the 'if only' club, in one way or another, left to wonder whether they could have been the ones who made a difference. He had spent countless hours already, re-living and unpicking the last few months of Louie's life and his bit-part in it.

He watched her closely, the way her long limbs curled and folded around one another. The way she smoked, her slender neck stretched back as the wisps curled upwards with each exhale, into the stratosphere. With her straight back and sharp joints, she was almost regal. Her sureness of her thoughts and feelings were disarming, particularly in regards to such a complex subject matter. He envied her that. She didn't seem, outwardly, to suffer the same confusions and weaknesses as him. In his inebriation, she suddenly felt quite mysterious, as though he had met her anew. He was hyper aware of her every movement, and a longing for her to keep talking and reveal more about herself to him.

'What about you?' he asked, his eyes never leaving her. 'What do you want to do?'

'For a job?'

He nodded.

'I don't know yet. I'm really good at maths and the sciences. I like history and geography, too. I do pretty well at school and I actually enjoy it. Don't tell anyone.' she smirked. 'But there isn't a particular career path that screams out to me. I'll see what my exam results are like, I guess, and choose the subjects I do the best at.'

'You want to go to uni?'

'Of course! Preferably one as far away as possible!' she laughed, and he laughed along with her, although he was alarmed to find that he wanted to tell her 'no, stay here.'

He tipped the can into the sky, letting the last warm splashes of beer trickle down his throat before lining it up on the table amongst the rest of the empty ones and cracking open another. He took a few gulps, coughed and ventured, 'So... do you have a boyfriend?'

She turned sharply towards him, cheeks aflame. *'No.'*

'Why not?' he continued casually. 'You must have them lining up for you at school.'

Ella snorted. 'Oh yeah, I'm really hot property.'

'What, so there's nobody? Nobody you like?' she bit her top lip nervously as he persisted. 'There is! There is someone! Who is he?'

'No one you'd know.' she said quietly.

'Try me!' he laughed, even though she was right; he couldn't think of a single soul he would know who attended St Thomas', let alone any sixteen year olds. For a reason he couldn't yet comprehend, he felt like a dog with a bone. He wanted to hear the answer, meaningless or not.

She shot him a look and countered, 'How's it going with Jennifer?'

'Oh… she broke up with me, met someone else. She's pretty dynamic, you know, knows what she wants and I'm just… I wasn't really good enough for her.' he said, wincing at the words he has thought so often being said aloud.

She frowned again. 'That's not true. It's the other way round. She's an idiot.'

They stared at one another, hearts thumping and stomachs fluttering. Arthur was the first to look away, retreating from the intensity of the moment, subconsciously tightening his grip so hard that the aluminium can began to crunch and buckle.

'You're perfect.' she said, her stare never wavering, a lightbulb hurrying the moth to die.

He moved towards her slowly, not daring to look at her until their faces were inches apart. The kiss, when it came, was an explosion, their two halves colliding: a lifetime of waiting and longing meeting a self-esteem crushed and grasping blindly for validation.

THIRTY NINE

Ella, 2023.

Ella sits at her kitchen table, hands shaking as she reads the contents of the brown envelope for the fourth time. She had come straight in from the station and scarcely had time to make herself a cup of tea before she sat down to tackle the pile of post left for her on the kitchen table. She has always been a stickler for being on top of her paperwork, a trait she inherited from her beloved father.

She feels as though she has been punched in the stomach. She had toyed with the idea of visiting Maggie whilst she was in London viewing her mother's house. It had been, after all, a short note from Maggie that had informed her of the house sale in the first place, but she had ultimately chickened out of a face to face visit. It was far easier to hide behind her yearly correspondence, conscience salved by the small act of letting the woman she remembers so fondly know that she is still alive and well, at least. She had said nothing of any illness in any of her return letters, but then, Ella supposes, she was very late in life. Perhaps there hadn't been any ailments. Perhaps it had just been one of those things, just bad timing. But still; now she'll never have the chance to stand in front of Maggie as an adult and thank her for all she has done for her, keeping her confidence at the forefront of all of it. That that door is now closed to her and yet another one of the dwindling number of people she has loved in her life has now exited, disappeared into time and space…

It's harrowing.

Ella sips at the tepid tea, trying to visualise the painting she has hankered after for so many years. She hasn't explicitly asked Maggie for anything beyond secrecy since the day she left London, apart from that painting. On three occasions, she had offered Maggie money for it. Once, she told her to name her price. On four more occasions she had just pleaded, outright. She knows by now that Maggie had more than an inkling as to its significance to Ella, but she had always rebuffed her and insisted that she wanted to keep hold of it.

Ella can see, now, why that might have been: she couldn't bank on Ella returning for any amount of money. But she knew without a shadow of a doubt that she would return for the painting.

FORTY

Three croissants, 1985.

Ella woke to the sound of the ebb and flow of the morning tide on a summer's day. Golden hues breezed through the curtains, dappled light danced across the white walls. She closed her eyes and stretched, her heart fluttering as she tried to recall every minute detail of the best night of her life.

It was beyond comprehension, a euphoria like this. It was beyond her wildest dreams: the softness of his skin, the curve of his spine, the gentleness with which he touched her. She had loved him from afar for so long, she had sometimes worried that in the extremely unlikely event that life would bestow this most unthinkable of gifts upon her, she might be underwhelmed. But no. She had been right. He really *was* perfect.

She was glad she had waited. Most of her friends had lost their virginities to boyfriend's that had lasted only weeks in all manner of romance slaying locations: absent parents' bedrooms at parties, the backseats of cars, the park. All rather unceremonious, pointless save for the trash talking opportunities it gave them between lessons. This had been different. This had been everything she'd ever wished for. Well, almost everything. The only minor disappointment had been having to wake up alone this morning, but he was right, she supposed: she wasn't anymore ready for an interrogation from their mothers than he was, should they return early.

She allowed herself another few minutes to bask in the wonderment of the day and then threw on a huge t-shirt and poked her head around the bedroom door.

'Good morning!' Maggie said brightly, leaning against the kitchen counter with a steaming mug between her hands. 'Sleep well?'

Ella nodded, trying desperately to stifle the blush she felt creeping up towards the tips of her ears.

'We got back at the crack of dawn,' she continued, rolling her eyes. 'Your mum fell asleep as soon as her head hit the hay, but I had no such luck. I've been sitting here attempting to read a book since six. Do you fancy nipping into the village with me? Have a peep into some of the shops before they get busy? We could bring some breakfast back.'

Ella looked towards Maggie's closed bedroom door, trying to picture him sleeping. She briefly considered a shower, but no; she wasn't ready to wash him off her, not yet.

***

Ella traipsed around the village in Maggie's wake as she zipped from shop to shop with lightning speed, a woman possessed. She hadn't left a single one without purchasing. By the time they reached the end of the small, cobbled main street, she was laden with carrier bags and had a gift for just about anyone you could think of. Handmade jewellery, a blown glass vase, locally produced cheeses… the list went on.

The bakery was the last shop in the row, and Ella's relief at finally making it there was short lived as Maggie's eyes fell upon the small gallery attached to it.

'Oh, look! Let's nip in for a look, shall we?' said Maggie, slipping through the door without waiting for an answer with the same enthusiasm she had ten shops ago.

Ella followed her in. They were the only customers. A small elderly man with a moustache sat behind the counter. 'Please do let me know if I can be of any assistance.' he smiled.

'Thank you!' said Maggie, smiling back at him as she hesitated at a small set of landscapes.

'Beautiful, aren't they? So detailed for such small pieces. The artist is a local man, so they're one offs.' he said.

'What do you think, Ella?' asked Maggie, pulling her closer. She pointed to the one in the middle depicting fishing boats in a bay. 'I love this one! What a lovely thing to have as a keepsake for this trip.'

Ella was immediately drawn to a smaller painting underneath it. They appeared to be in a series, but for Ella, the others paled in comparison. The painting was of, quite literally, the beach they were staying on, from a point of view that couldn't be very far from the house itself at all. The long grass, the incline down to the sand, the curve of the bay going out into the distance. She recognised it instantly, the same view she looked out at last night.

'I like this one.' she said, lightly running a finger over the acrylic. 'It's amazing.'

Maggie watched her. 'Excuse me, how much is this?' she

called to the man, tottering over to the desk and pointing at the painting.

Ella didn't hear the reply, she could scarcely tear her eyes away. After some discussion, the man came up behind her and smiled kindly as he unhooked the painting and took it back towards the counter.

'You're buying it?' she asked Maggie.

'Yes,' she said. 'You seem so taken with it, I'm buying it for your birthday. You're only sweet sixteen once. But you can't have it before, mind!'

Ella was lost for words. 'Thank you…' she gasped, overwhelmed. 'But it's too much, it must be…'

'You're worth it, you silly sausage.' smiled Maggie, pecking her on the cheek as she walked past with the wrapped up painting under her arm and stepped back outside into the sunlight.

***

'I fancy those croissants again,' said Maggie as they entered the bakery. 'I'm going to be twenty stone by the time I leave here, I can't get enough! Same for you?'

'Yes, please.' replied Ella, who was suddenly ravenous.

Maggie strutted up to the counter. 'Three almond croissants again, please,' she said to a lady in a paper hat. 'You can't get rid of me at the moment!' and the lady laughed.

'Three?' said Ella.

'Yes?' replied Maggie over her shoulder as she dug around in her purse for the correct change.

'Does Arthur not like croissants?'

'Oh, Arthur's gone,' she said breezily. 'Left early this

morning. You just missed him, actually. God only knows how she got the number, but Jennifer rang.'

Nausea rose in Ella's throat, the white heat of acid climbing up her oesophagus.

Maggie tutted. 'So it looks like it's back on again, until *next* time, that is. I can't keep up anymore. Honestly, running back to London with his tail between his legs as soon as she clicks her fingers rather than spend a week on the beach with us fine specimens!'

Ella rushed out onto the pavement where she fell onto her knees retching, heaving up acrid bile onto the stone slabs as her nose and eyes streamed. *Of course*, she scalded herself, *you fool*.

***

Arthur's head was pounding as he hurtled back down the M3 towards London. He knew he shouldn't be driving, not in this state. The anxiety was crippling enough by itself, his clammy palms gripping the steering wheel for dear life as his heart palpitated and sweat ran down his forehead and into his eyes. He was probably still over the limit, too.

His thoughts tumbled around his brain sharply as he veered from one lane into another. *Fucking hell,* he thought, *what the hell have you done? She's not even sixteen! And Jennifer! Will she be able to tell? Oh God, oh God, she'll know.*

Somehow, he made it home without interception and managed to shop shaking under a shower so hot it felt like razorblades beating down on his back. Once he had scrubbed himself raw, he doused himself in aftershave and hopped back into his car. He stopped at the petrol station on the way to

Jennifer's and picked up a bunch of wilted roses.

FORTY ONE

Fireworks, 1985.

On the eve of Ella's sixteenth birthday, Maggie and Anna sat at the kitchen table at number thirty, their nightly ritual of the sharing of a bottle of wine restored to its former glory after their return from Devon.

'I don't know what her problem is, Mags, she's driving me to distraction,' said Anna huffily, arms crossed. 'I've picked myself back up, dusted myself off, I've scaled back the drinking and painted on a smile. I try to take an interest, try for a bit of involvement in her life and she just freezes me out. She just stomps around, poe-faced and silent.'

'It's her age. And you've got to remember, Anna, she's grieving too. She's so young to have lost a brother and a father so quickly. It must be very confusing.'

'I know, I know,' said Anna, flapping her hands around in exasperation. 'But she should *talk* to me. I know I've not been perfect, but I'm still her mum. I thought time was supposed to be a healer? If anything, she's getting worse. Refuses to even do anything for her birthday. Doesn't want a party, doesn't want any friends round, doesn't want a cake. She doesn't even want a present, she says. What teenager doesn't want a *present*?'

'You have got her one though, haven't you?' asked Maggie, eyes narrowing.

'Of course I have! I got her a voucher.'

'A *voucher*? You can't get your only daughter a *voucher* for her *sixteenth!*'

'Why not?' demanded Anna.

'It's a special birthday, a sweet sixteen! She's becoming a woman. A charm bracelet, a necklace, something sentimental that she will always keep, to remember the day! God, you can be useless.'

'But I have no idea what she likes,' whined Anna. 'She barely says a word to me! She doesn't show any interest in *anything!* Besides, whatever I get her will be wrong, I guarantee it.'

'I'm not letting her come home tomorrow to open a bloody voucher. I'll march you down to the high street myself if I have to.' said Maggie indignantly, aghast at Anna's thoughtlessness. Poor little Ella, she thought, if I was her I'd be bloody miserable, too.

'Alright, alright, we'll go first thing.' said Anna, rolling her eyes as she lit a cigarette. 'You can help me choose something, you probably know her better than me. Louie was never this difficult.' she added tersely.

'Maybe not with birthday presents, no. But Ella's never given you a scrap of trouble. She's been through so much, the past few years, and she deserves something nice from you.'

'Ella's trouble in a different way. She's secretive, Maggie, she's like living with a stranger and being pretty sure they hate your guts, but never being brave enough to ask outright.

347

She'd never give me a straight answer, anyway. Louie was never like this. I always knew where I was with him, how he felt. For all his faults, I always knew he loved me. I don't think Ella ever did, when I think back.'

'Of course she did! Give the girl a break. And stop bloody comparing them! Two children are rarely alike, I mean, look at my two? Where would I be if I compared Teddy and Arthur? It's not fair to pick holes in her the way you do.'

Anna nodded, duly castigated.

**

Ella returned from school on her sixteenth birthday to an empty house. She flung her school bag onto the floor and was just about to slip off her boots when she noticed a post-it note stuck to the mirror in the hallway.

Birthday tea next door x

She sighed and peeled it away from the glass, scrunching it up in her fist. She wanted nothing more than to curl up in bed with her headphones on and be left alone, but, as usual, she had no such luck.

She peered disappointedly at her reflection. Her large eyes looked even larger now she lined them so heavily with thick black pencil, the same black as her chipped nail varnish. Her group of friends were going through their punk phase, and Ella had found it suited her acute morbidity perfectly. She listened to The Sex Pistols and The Clash cassettes biblically, feeling every beat pulse through her body as if their anarchy were her own.

'You look *scary*,' her mum always told her. 'Like it's Halloween.'

'*Boo!*' she replied, rolling her eyes as Anna stood there blinking.

She slammed the door behind her and trudged down the path, not bothering to change out of her school uniform. Hopefully, this could be over and done with quickly. She let herself in, her heavy boots stomping down the hallway signalling her arrival.

'*Surprise!*' shouted Anna and Maggie, jumping up from their seats at the table and waving their arms around like a couple of cabaret performers. There were boxes of Chinese food from her favourite takeaway laid out on the table, a birthday banner slung overhead and a couple of helium balloons tied to the back of one of the empty chairs.

Maggie pulled her in for a bear hug. 'Happy birthday, sweet girl.'

'We got you Chinese! Your favourite!' said Anna, pleased with herself.

'I can see that. Thank you.' she said, sitting down whilst Maggie brought plates and cutlery. Both women exhausted themselves in their attempts to engage the birthday girl, chattering incessantly, sharing anecdotes from Ella's childhood, trying to raise a laugh.

When their plates were empty, all of their heads turned towards the kitchen door as they heard footfall coming up the hallway towards them. Arthur stepped through the door.

'Mum, we just—' he said, stopping in his tracks as he took in the banner, the balloons and the company. His face paled.

'Hello, love!' said Maggie, brightly. 'Come to wish Ella a happy birthday? How lovely. You've missed the food, I'm afraid, but you're right on time for the cake.'

Another set of footsteps followed him up the hall, and a head of long auburn hair came up behind him. The girl stood at his side and took his hand.

'Hiya.'

'Oh, hi, Jen,' said Maggie in surprise, before she recovered herself. 'Come on in, pull up a seat.'

'Oh no,' said Arthur, deathly white, 'We won't disturb you.'

'Nonsense. It's lovely of you both to drop in.' said Maggie, standing up and ushering them towards the table.

'Yes, *lovely*.' said Ella, her eyes boring into Arthur's skull.

He sat down awkwardly next to Anna who poured him a glass of wine. 'One for you, Jennifer?'

'Oh, no thanks,' said the plain girl, sitting down delicately in the chair next to Ella. 'I'm driving.'

Ella turned her death stare towards the girl, taking in every detail: her waist length red hair, her middle parting, her pale, make-up free face. She was surprised by how nondescript her nemesis was, in her pale yellow sweater and jeans. She couldn't decide whether it was better or worse that she wasn't some sort of bombshell. Jennifer felt Ella's eyes on her and turned towards her, smiling shyly. 'Happy birthday.' she said. Ella ignored her.

'Right!' said Maggie, with a little too much jolly. 'Cake!'

She headed off towards the stove, fiddling with candles as the others sat at the table, entrenched in a painful silence.

'So,' said a bemused Anna, sipping at her wine. 'Jennifer, what is it you do, then?'

'I'm studying medicine,' Jennifer replied, hands folded in her lap. 'I'm in my first year.'

Anna let out a low whistle. 'Rather you than me!' she

snorted, 'Injections, sick people, bed pans… not for me!'

Jennifer blinked, unsure what to respond to such an unusual reaction about her choice of profession.

'Jen's dad's a doctor, and her grandad was too.' said Arthur, trying to rescue his girlfriend.

'Original.' said Ella, deadpan. Jennifer's mouth dropped open, like a little guppy fish. Arthur stared at his hands.

'Haaaappy birthday to yooooou!' boomed Maggie as she walked towards them with a candle covered chocolate cake, gesturing for them all to join in. Arthur's voice was no more than a whisper.

'Hip hip, hurray! Make a wish, Ells!' Maggie cheered, plonking the cake down in front of her.

I wish I could shove Jennifer's head into this cake and the candles would set her hair on fire, thought Ella.

As Maggie doled out thick slabs of chocolate cake, Anna rustled around under the table and produced a card and a small square box. She came around the table and, in an un-characteristic display of affection, wrapped her arms clunkily around Ella's shoulders and kissed her cheek, depositing the box on the table in front of her. She returned to her seat and raised her eyebrows expectantly. 'Open it, then!'

Ella picked up the box and turned it around in her fingers, slowly unpicking the Sellotape, peeling back the paper so that it became a perfect, unblemished square. She popped open the small, emerald green jewellery box and held it in her palm. Inside, two sterling silver necklaces lay side by side on the velvet pad, the pendant on one side shaped to fit the pendant on the other.

'So, what do you think?' demanded Anna. 'It's yin and yang. You keep one half, and then you give the other half to someone you love, and they wear their half. Like a friendship thing.'

'Thank you. It's great.' said Ella quietly, feeling slightly overcome at the unexpected gift. She had never received anything so lovely before. She snapped the box shut and opened the envelope, as the expectant smile Anna wore turned into a look of slight disappointment.

'A voucher, as well?' Ella asked in surprise. 'For Woolworths…?'

'Well, yes,' blustered Anna. 'Just a little something extra. You can buy some more of your shouty music, or some posters or whatever.'

'Oh, right, okay… thanks…'

Maggie smirked at Anna from across the table, who duly ignored her and stuck her nose in the air. Maggie handed Ella a wrapped package of her own.

'You already know what's in it, but I wrapped it anyway.' she smiled.

Ella unwrapped the package which revealed the painting, newly framed. She quickly looked away from the beachscape, the reminder of that day burning at her retinas.

She opened the card on top, which read: *To lovely Ella, may all your wishes in life come true. Happy birthday.*

Ella's eyes filled with tears as everybody looked on. She leaped at Maggie and hugged her fiercely.

'Thank you so much, Mags,' she whispered.

'You're welcome, sweetheart.' smiled Maggie, tenderly brushing her hair from her eyes and planting a kiss on her forehead. Anna watched on with her arms folded, mightily put out.

Ella sat quietly, waiting patiently for an opportunity to

escape back into her bedroom as the conversation went back and forth across the table, her thoughts drifting from this to that as she attempted to block out the sound of Jennifer's simpering voice behind her.

'Beautiful cake, Mrs Maxwell, so moist! Did you bake it yourself?' she crooned. 'You simply can't beat a home bake, I'd love the recipe.'

'So, Jennifer, how is the course coming along? Are you enjoying it?' Maggie enquired politely.

'Oh yes, it's hard work, of course, but having been around clinics my whole life and having that extra bit of understanding has proved to be such an advantage,' she smiled, pleased to be back within her conversational comfort zone. 'I start my placement in the new year, which is exciting.'

'Oh, fabulous, lots to look forward to, then.'

'Absolutely. I was thrilled to get onto the surgery ward in St Peter's, it will be something I can really get my teeth into.'

'St Peter's, I haven't heard of that one.' said Anna.

'Oh, it's out in Surrey, so I'll be relocating there for the year in January. It makes far more sense than commuting each day. That was the purpose of our visit, actually...' she said, as she looked towards Arthur who cringed and gave only the slightest shake of his head before she continued. 'Arthur is going to come along, too. We've found the most beautiful little flat in Chertsey, overlooking the park and a stone's throw from the hospital, so I'll be able to walk each day.'

'Oh?' replied Maggie, rather more sharply than she had intended, and turned towards Arthur. 'What about work?'

Arthur cleared his throat. 'Well, um, I can just commute, until I can find something more local.'

'But I thought you *liked* Mr Hailwood? I thought there were talks about some extra training and a promotion?' she said incredulously.

Arthur had left the house whistling happily each morning since he'd begun his job at the YMCA, an assistant to one of the senior youth workers. The role had brought about such a change in his demeanour as he regaled her with stories of injustice and small victories for the team with such passion.

'There are loads of other jobs, mum,' he said quietly.

'It's not much of a career, is it?' said Jennifer brightly. 'Besides, when I finish my training, Arthur will be able to take some time and decide what he *really* wants to do.'

Maggie sat, her eyes roving between her son and his girlfriend. 'Isn't that another four years?'

'Oh, at least!' laughed Jennifer, unperturbed. 'It could be double that if I want to specialise, but we'll cross that bridge when we come to it, and I could be sent even further afield on my training later on. There's no sense in us living apart all that time. Especially not now!'

Maggie watched on in astonishment as Jennifer beamed and extended her hand over the table, brandishing a small, oval solitaire on a white gold band on her ring finger.

'That's what we came here to tell you, Mum, but...' mumbled Arthur, wishing the ground would swallow him up at the crassness of his engagement announcement eclipsing Ella's birthday celebration.

There were a few minutes of stunned silence before a bewildered Maggie, to her credit, said simply, 'Well, congratulations, both of you.'

Jennifer beamed, completely unaware of the downturn in the atmosphere.

'Yes, congratulations,' repeated Anna, holding her glass out. 'Cheers to you both.'

'Congratulations.' said Ella, into her lap. 'I've got some homework to do, thanks for a lovely birthday.'

'Homework on your birthday?!' shrieked Anna. Sensing her daughter's discomfort, she added, 'Alright then, I won't be long.'

Ella gathered up her gifts and thanked Maggie again before making a hasty retreat. She only allowed the tears to fall when she was back within the safety of her bedroom.

**

Later that evening, when her tears had finally wrung dry, Ella crept down the dark hallway and through to the kitchen, relieved to find she was still home alone.

She leaned down to light a cigarette on the stove then opened the back door, stepping out into the night. The shock of frozen air was a comforting sensation as it assaulted the heat of her cheeks. She sat down on the doorstep and looked down the garden towards the shed, picturing her brother standing there, grinning madly. Fireworks were still crackling in the distance and she thought of her father and his trusty safety lighter, the way he always took ownership of bonfire night and her birthday as though the effort he made would translate exactly into her own happiness. She squeezed her eyes shut.

She heard the open and close of the back door of number thirty, the screeching of chairs being pulled across the paving stones and her mother and Maggie's voices drifting over the top of the fence.

'It's not that I don't like her,' Maggie was saying. 'I just don't like the idea of him sacrificing so many years of his life for her when she could turn around at any moment and drop him like a hot potato! It's not as though she hasn't done it before, *more* than once.'

'If you want my advice, step in while you can. Look what happened to my poor Louie after that evil little witch got her claws into him,' replied Anna.

'Mmm,' said Maggie, marvelling at Anna's ability to turn any subject matter around to Louie. 'After Teddy ran off with the American dictator, I always assumed Arthur would stay close by, meet a nice local girl. Selfish, really. Parenting, eh? It's a bloody thankless task.'

'Amen to that! My beautiful Louie, snatched from us in his prime with so much going for him. Leaving me stuck with sour puss in there.'

'Don't be awful.'

Anna sighed. 'I know I sound awful. I probably *am* awful. But have I always been this bad? Have I been a terrible parent, Mags? I know I was a terrible wife, but I had always thought I was a good mother... except now, I'm not so sure. When I look at what I'm left with, I can't help but feel... I mean, look at tonight. That beautiful necklace, the painting, her favourite food, and still the sour face. Louie was just so full of life. Nothing makes Ella happy. It just doesn't seem fair.'

'What doesn't?'

'That the one who loved life so much is gone, and the one that doesn't...'

Ella didn't wait to hear the rest of the conversation, or even the rest of the sentence.

The sensation, when it arrived, was an odd one: she could

almost hear the crack of a whip as something deep inside her snapped, shearing her into two pieces yet somehow also closing the earthquake-like fissure she had been carrying around in the pit of her stomach for so long.

A strange sort of peace settled on her as she flicked her cigarette across the lawn before padding back up the steps and into the house. It was the kind of serenity that appeared after a decision had been made after many years of agonising over it, having finally received tangible confirmation that her choice would bring about no regrets.

She emptied her school holdall and swept the contents under her bed. She peered out of her bedroom window to next door's garden below. When she was satisfied that her mother was still deep in the throes of conversation, she walked to the far end of the room and opened the door that was referred to as her wardrobe, but was more of an incidental cupboard. It was oddly shaped and backed onto the boiler cupboard, the advantage of which was a toasty warm school uniform every morning she had remembered to hang it up.

She leaned in and forced all of the hangers to one side, reaching her arm around to the back. There was a collapsed panel in the bottom corner which, when dislodged, opened out into a small concave in the brickwork. It had probably only housed spiders until it had been discovered by her brother a few years ago, but after that, it had become a hiding place for all manner of things for the pair of them.

She thought back to the night, two weeks before Louie's last Christmas, when she had awoken to the scraping sound of the panel being moved. She had sat up in bed, rubbing at her eyes as they'd adjusted. As the room came in to focus, the saw the back of her brother's head, his arm reached deep into her wardrobe.

'Sorry, did I scare you?' he had whispered.

'No.' she'd whispered back.

He'd propped the panel upright and closed the door, tiptoed towards her and perched on the end of her bed. He lay her back down and leaned in closely, brushing the hair from her face. His breath had been hot on her cheek, reeking of acrid alcohol and cigarettes as he had whispered, 'It's really important that you don't go into the nook. And don't breathe a word to Mum and Dad, okay?'

'When have I ever?'

'I know, I know,' he replied, stroking her cheek. 'But it's extra important this time, alright?' seeing her worried expression, he added, 'Don't worry, it's nothing... bad. It's just money. But it's a *lot* of money. I'll come back and grab it when Christmas is over and I can find somewhere safer for it.'

'Money? What money?' she hissed, sitting up in alarm. 'You're not selling—'

'No, no, of course not. Somebody gave it to me. I just need to keep it out of sight. There'll be more soon, too, a lot more. And when there is, I'll buy you whatever your heart desires, anything at all. But you've gotta keep this little secret for me, okay?'

'Who gave it to you?'

'My dad.'

'Dad?' she whispered in confusion.

'No, Ells. *My* dad.'

'Why is he giving you money?'

He fixed his gaze on his fingers gripping hers and frowned.

358

'So that nobody finds out I exist.'

'What do you mean?'

'It's complicated. Will you do this for me, little sis? Please?' he asked, holding out his pinky finger. She'd extended her own to solemnly perform a pinky-shake. Then he'd kissed the tip of her nose and whispered, 'Thank you. I love you Ells, sleep tight.'

She had of course slid her hands in behind the panel as soon as the coast had been clear. The small hole was packed with thick wads of notes tied with elastic bands. She had no idea how much it must amount to, but she had certainly never seen that much money before.

She had done as he asked and left it where it was, never uttering a word about its existence to a single soul, even after watching his coffin be lowered into the earth less than a fortnight later and knowing beyond all doubt that he was never coming back for it.

She had borrowed from it on occasion, peeling the odd note from the top here and there when she was desperate for a certain cassette or item of make-up. But, somehow, she had instinctively known that it must be left intact for a time when she might really need it. And she knew, then, that the time was now.

She pushed down all of the wads into the bottom of the rucksack and spent the next hour carefully selecting favourite items of clothing and folding them tightly, so that she might make the best use of the small amount of space left. She pulled photos of her dad and her brother from frames on her shelves and tucked them into the front pocket. When there wasn't an inch more space, she zipped up the bag and pushed it underneath the bed, too.

After she had scribbled a note under her lamp she turned it off and climbed into her bed, still fully clothed.

Her mother poked her head around the door and whispered "night," half an hour later. She heard the sound of the taps in the bathroom, the pull of the chain, the flick of the light switch, the footsteps down the hall and the creak of a bedroom door. She waited another forty minutes, just to be safe before she climbed back out of bed.

She tiptoed across to the door, taking one last look at the room she had slept in every night since the day she was born. She hesitated only at the painting of Woolacombe, propped up on her dressing table. Holding it up to the moonlight, she ran her fingers over it for the second time. Memories of that night forced their way behind her eyes as she fought back even more tears. She tucked the painting under her arm and silently exited the room.

As she descended the stairs, every tiny creak sounded like a wrecking ball. It was hard to believe that her mother wasn't woken by the thunderous beat of her heart.

She unlatched the door, closed it silently behind her and walked down the path, away from a life she knew she would never return to reclaim.

**

The next morning, Maggie shuffled towards the door in her slippers and dressing gown and picked up the pile of post on the mat. A small sellotaped square immediately caught her eye, not for its lack of an envelope but for its lack of address.

Puzzled, she tore it open. There was a piece of writing paper, folded down into a tiny square. As she unfolded it, something fell down onto the tiles by her feet. She ran her eyes over the note.

To Mags,

   I'm leaving. For good. I want you to know that I'm safe and I'll post you another letter soon. Please tell my mum not to look for me. I never want to speak to her again. Love, Ella

Maggie gasped and sank down on her haunches, feeling around on the floor in the dim morning light. She lifted up the white half of the necklace, the yang, and let it dangle between her fingers.

She stepped towards the door and unlatched it, opening it widely and peering down her tiled path. She rose up onto her tiptoes, hoping to catch a glimpse of Ella retreating down the pavement, clinging to the hope that maybe, just maybe, she might be early enough to stop her. But the street was still quiet, the sun only just beginning to rise, clouds drifting across the November sky like slow balloons.

As she turned to close the door, she saw the newly framed canvas propped up at the side of her porch.

'Oh, Ella.' she whispered sadly.

FORTY TWO

A return, 2023.

Arthur has spent the week pottering about his mother's house, trying to action the same plan he had put in place for Anna mere months before. He has found, however, that when the possessions hold memories pertaining to your own life, the process of elimination is far more complex, which makes him admire Anna all the more.

The irony of the strange friendship they have forged has not been lost on him. She is as much of a comfort as she is a nuisance, juxtaposition is the very epicentre of the woman's being. For a person set to be downsizing imminently, she has invested an awfully large amount of time in following him around and unpacking boxes, wittering, 'You can't get rid of *this*! She *loved* this! Well, *I'll* take it, then.' and hobbling off down the hall with some trinket or other tucked under her arm (he can't wait to find out what use she plans to make of the taxidermy owl or the VHS player that isn't any more salvageable than it was in 1991).

He has found himself feeling rather bereft at her departure now there is a time frame. She had arrived earlier in the week on another magpie mission and informed him, deadpan, 'It's sold. I'm rich. I'll send you a postcard from my yacht in Monaco, when I'm taking a breather from my harem of strapping young gold diggers.'

The space, not as his mother's but as *his,* has begun to make sense for him. He has given a lot of thought to the parts of the house he will keep as is, and the ones he will update, but for some reason he still feels nervous. He knows his mother would approve, she would be thrilled he had decided to stay put altogether. His reticence to any change is born of a fear of the undoable. Sure, he could extend the kitchen, rip out the dated country style fittings and replace them with chrome, install some skylights and underfloor heating. But what if he woke up one morning and felt the urge to sit in his *mum's* kitchen?

As the doorbell chimes, he wanders leisurely towards the door in his slippers, wondering if he'd accidentally left it on the latch. The postman has already been, and his only social visitor is Anna, who isn't prone to the courtesy of knocking first.

He pulls it open and smiles reflexively at the lady standing on his front step. 'Good morning,' he chirps, before the penny drops and all of the colour drains from his face.

'Hi Arthur,' says Ella, 'Can I come in?'

***

'God, sorry,' says Arthur as they sit at the kitchen table over a cup of coffee, 'I feel like I've seen a ghost.'

Ella laughs. 'You must have been expecting me a *little* bit, though?'

Arthur rubs at his chin, taken aback by the slight and unfamiliar twang of her accent, wishing he'd had the foresight to shave the unruly mass of salt and pepper stubble.

'Well, I don't know,' he says thoughtfully. 'I wasn't even sure if you were still alive. The will came as a bit of a shock to the system, but I had no idea whether you would still be around to claim it, or even if you'd want to…'

'I don't want the money,' she says quickly. 'I've come for the painting.'

'Well, the money's yours. She wanted you to have it.'

Ella nods. 'But I don't need it.'

'That's not really the issue, though…' he says lamely.

He looks at her then, properly, deducing from her cashmere jumper and sharp haircut that no, she probably doesn't need the money. He had never given much thought to what she might look like as an adult, all of his energy in that regard had been expended on Louie. As it turns out, she's certainly aged much better than he has. She's still slim, but then, he can't imagine a parallel universe in which she wouldn't be. Her eyes are lightly lined, she's taller and her hair is darker. She still has the gap in her teeth. The biggest difference, really, is the confidence with which she carries herself. It's the kind of confidence that turns a lanky person into a tall person, an awkward person into a direct one. That she can sit opposite him, with her shoulders back and look him in the eye as she speaks to him after disappearing without a trace over three decades before is a feat in itself.

He stands up and walks out of the kitchen to retrieve the painting, holding it out towards her as he re-enters. Her eyes light up as he hands it over, her hand flying to her mouth. He watches as she holds it, a look of pure wonder spreading across her face as her eyes move slowly from one side of the canvas to the other.

'Thank you,' she breathes, hugging it towards her chest. 'I'm so sorry about your mum. She was a truly special woman.'

Arthur nods. 'Truth be told, I was pretty astonished to find out that you'd been in touch all this time. She kept your confidence. She never breathed a word. Not even to your mum.'

'Well, I asked her not to. You were lucky to have her,' she says, glancing at the wall to her left that connects to next door. 'We all were.'

She tucks the painting into a tote bag on the floor and stands abruptly. 'Well, I need to be going, I've an appointment to get to, a work thing. Thanks so much for this, Arthur. It means the world to me.'

Arthur is struck dumb, watching her back as she walks through the kitchen door. *No,* he thinks, *this isn't right. You can't let her just leave again.*

He scrambles to his feet and down the hallway after her.

'Ella!' he cries. She turns around and looks at him. 'Could we meet again, do you think? I have so many unanswered questions. I know you don't owe me anything, but…'

'Okay.' she says easily. 'When?'

'Well, any time. When does your appointment finish? Christ, I don't even know whether to ask you how long you're here for, or if you live in London…'

She laughs. 'I'll meet you on the common tomorrow morning?'

'I'll be there,' he says. 'What time?'

'10am, by the bandstand.' she tells him, stepping out of the door and pulling it closed behind her.

Arthur collapses on the sofa and rakes his hands through his hair, trying to get a handle on the hundreds of questions careering through his brain. How had she just reappeared after all that time, drank a coffee at his kitchen table and still he knows *nothing* about her? Where has she been? Why did she go? Why is she the only person besides him that is named in his mother's will? And *what* does she know that he doesn't?

As Ella walks along the pavement, she finds herself equally troubled. How much should she tell him? There wasn't a wedding ring, she couldn't see any evidence of children. But then, that was his mother's house. He probably doesn't even live there. Plenty of people wear slippers indoors. She needs some answers herself, she needs to be sure before she flings open the lid of Pandora's box.

***

At 10.15am, Arthur has worked himself into a terrible state. He arrived at the bandstand at a courteous 9.50 and sat on the bench opposite. The first five minutes had been fine. The sun on his face, the pleasant breeze, the distraction of the succession of joggers and dog walkers had managed to calm the erratic beating of his heart into a steady thump, exactly as he'd hoped. But as each minute ticked by, the anxiety had crept back in and woven its way around his chest. By five past, his lungs were in a vice like grip, his shirt collar had begun to feel tight and sweat trickled from his temples. By ten past, his mouth felt as though someone had filled it with a fist full of sand. And by quarter past, he feels as though he might fall forwards and vomit onto the cycle path at any moment, convinced he is in the throes of some kind of manic episode brought about by stress.

At exactly 10.19, she strolls into view with a beret perched on her head, staring intently at her phone as she makes her way towards him. She only bothers to look up from the screen at the very last moment, clearly not having suffered the same attack of nerves as he has. She sees him and lifts a hand towards him in greeting, a small smile curling up onto her lips. She stands there for a moment until he realises that she isn't coming any closer. He jumps up and walks towards her, almost falling over his own feet.

'Hi,' he says, afluster.

'Hi.' she replies, bemused. 'Shall we walk?'

Arthur nods and they set off down the path, towards the fishpond.

'So…' she says. 'You have questions. I don't know if I'll be able to answer them, but I'll do my best.'

Arthur has been awake most of the night in a frenzied turmoil over the questions he wants to ask. He had finally narrowed them down into a list of only the most vital as the sun had started to come up, and then had set about putting them into order of importance. His instinct is that he is going to be left short changed after this exchange, so he had wanted to arrive as prepared as he could possibly be. But all of this has escaped him, the revision flying out of his ears and floating away on the breeze as soon as his opportunity stands in front of him.

'Where have you been?' he asks, an apologetic look on his face. He worries that she will be disappointed by this most obvious of questions, but, the others having taken leave of him, he is hoping it will provide the opener he needs should they decide to reappear.

'Devon. I've been in Devon. What about you, Arthur, where have you been?' she replies, simultaneously providing an answer and deflecting the question.

'Here,' he splutters, understanding at once that he will lose in this kind of verbal sparring if that's the route she's choosing to take. 'I've been here. In London.'

She smiles and nods. She had expected that. They meander around the duck pond for a few minutes before she turns and sits down on a bench, her eyes never leaving a couple of toddlers noisily throwing thick chunks of bread into the water. 'Do you have any children, Arthur?' she asks.

'No.' he says.

'Did you want any?' she asks, turning to look at him. Her directness would be disarming in a casual conversation. In this situation it feels like a crucifixion.

'I don't know. The opportunity never really...' he says, meeting her gaze for a moment before his courage deserts him once more and he focuses on his hands instead. 'I always thought I would have liked them, but no, it just never happened. It wasn't meant to be.'

She looks out across the ripples on the water again, giving nothing away. 'And Jennifer, is she happy with that?'

'Jennifer?' he exclaims sharply. She looks back at him, eyes narrowed. He shakes his head and a nervous laugh escapes. 'I haven't seen Jennifer for thirty years. We broke up pretty swiftly after I moved out to Surrey. She married the senior surgeon six months later.'

'Sorry to hear that.' she smirks.

'No, you're not,' he says, beginning to ease into her company a little. 'Look, I'm sorry about all that. I'm sure that you couldn't care less, you probably barely even remember, I'm not saying that... well, I'm trying to say that I'm not delusional enough to think that that, erm, that night had any special significance to you, or anything like that, but...'

He winces, struggling to find delicate enough words that will convey what he wants to say without causing offence, embarrassing her or making himself look like an egomaniac. He bites his lip and she nods, willing him to continue.

'I'm sorry... about... about what happened between us in Devon, and all of that stuff afterwards, you know, it was cowardly, so I just want to apologise without making it awkward but I've definitely made a hash of it already so I'll stop.'

She smiles, having survived the clumsy apology unruffled. 'Sorry about leaving the morning after without explanation, sorry about hijacking my birthday with your engagement announcement, or sorry it happened in the first place?'

Arthur takes a deep breath, his knee bouncing up and down involuntarily. He presses his palm firmly onto his thigh but it continues to jerk in disobedience. 'Bloody hell. Yes. No. Well, not sorry for it *happening*, of course not, that would be... That would be...'

She throws her head back and laughs and he finds the relief of that sound a welcome tonic to his mortification. He leans forwards and his elbows sink onto his knees, his head in his hands. 'Bloody hell...' he mutters.

'I was in love with you, Arthur,' she tells him softly, 'All of my life.'

'With *me*?' he gasps in astonishment. She laughs again.

'You really didn't know?'

'Absolutely *not*. God, no. My own girlfriend didn't even love me. Why didn't you say anything?' he asks, knowing that the question is stupid before it has finished escaping his mouth. Neither of them need to spell it out. He hadn't known because he hadn't paid any attention to her. It is a humbling thing, to find out you are the catalyst to the devastation of a young heart. There is nothing flattering about it, only the searing regret of countless missed opportunities in which he could have at least shown her some compassion, if nothing else.

'Would it have made any difference?'

'Of course it would. I can't sit here and say we'd have run off into the sunset together. I was a very mixed up young lad, I made some terrible decisions in my life, truth be known, but… please tell me that wasn't why you left?'

'No,' she says firmly, 'It wasn't.'

'Then why did you?'

'Because it was better than staying,' she answers carefully. 'There have been a lot of secrets, Arthur, twisted by time, by death and by life, too.'

'Right.' he says, sensing that they are on the periphery of something irrevocable. He is ready to hear this, he realises, whatever she has to say. His life has been marred by his inability to pull his head from the sand and find the courage to face his truths head on. If he had a part to play, he is ready to know. If he is accountable for any of this, then so be it. The lives of the Maxwells and the Carmichaels have been entangled since 1966, each of their paths shaped by the other's existence. Now, there are only three of them left. Out of the three, he is the one with the least answers. It is time now, to bring the far flung repercussions of the succession of tragedies to a close, however damning the verdict might be. All he can ask for is the truth, after which he can pray for absolution.

'I want to know,' he says. 'I want to know what made you go.'

'That part's easy. But if I tell you that, I'll have to tell you why I didn't come back.'

'I want to know.' he says again, taking hold of her hand.

She takes a deep breath. 'Okay.'

FORTY THREE

Secrets, 1986.

Ella peered nervously out of the window as commuters hurried past, almost jumping out of the plastic seat as the tray met the table top. Maggie slid into the seat opposite her and took a tight grip of her twitching hands.

'I'm so glad you've come, sweetheart. We've been going out of our minds.'

Ella looked away. 'I'm not coming back, Mags,' she said as the tears escaped. 'That's what I came to tell you.'

'I understand how you must be feeling, Ella, but— '

'No you don't,' she snapped, her tongue as whip-sharp as her mother's. She looked towards the wall, blinking furiously. 'I heard her,' she said more evenly. 'She wishes it had been me.'

'Oh, no, sweetheart, she doesn't, she's been worrying herself sick about you…'

'She does.' Ella said firmly. 'And I've always known it. If I stay, we'll kill one another. She has no idea who my brother really was, Maggie, none of you do. Because my dad protected her from that, and got to live the last years of his life in misery as a result. She wants to believe that he was who she thought he was, that this was all some terrible tragedy that was everybody's fault except his. She would rather be old and alone with the memory of her precious baby blue than face the real world. But I can't live my life like that, Maggie. I want to be free. I want to be happy.'

Maggie sighed at the bleakness of the truth in Ella's words, and changed tack.

'Okay, sweetheart. But how will you get by? You're only sixteen, so young to be out in the world alone. I worry about you every day.'

'You don't need to worry about me,' replied Ella, softening and squeezing Maggie's hand. 'I've got some money. I'll be fine for a while, until I decide what to do.'

Ella watched Maggie's brows furrow, a look of pity etched across her face.

'It's £20,000, Maggie.' she said, defiant as Maggie's jaw dropped.

'Where on earth…' she gasped, eyes wide.

'Louie. Louie left it for me.'

'*Louie?*' she gasped, even more alarmed. 'But how did he…'

'Blackmail. He was blackmailing Peter Bennett.'

'Oh my God,' breathed Maggie, unable to take it in. Anna would be devastated.

'My mum won't believe it. She'd tell you I was a liar, or worse. But I'm not. I'm going to make a new life, Mags, away from all of the blame and the anger… and I'm going to be happy.'

Maggie nodded slowly, still lost for words.

'There's something else, Mags.'

'What, Ella? What else?' she whispered, the coldness of dread creeping up her spine until the tension in her neck built to what she thought surely must be bone snapping proportions.

'I'm pregnant. And my baby won't be born in the shadow of my brother's secrets, my mother's misplaced logic or the tragedy of my father's misery. This is a fresh start. And if you do anything to stop me, you'll never hear a word from me again. You'll never know whether I'm dead or alive.'

FORTY FOUR

An exit, 1986-87.

Ella left London with an unshakeable resolve. Even the six hour stop over at Victoria coach station amongst the drifters and misfits that made up the underbelly of south London during the twilight hours wasn't enough to deter her. She leant against the station wall and watched people come and go in fascination. These nocturnal folk were a different type altogether. It seemed that everyone was escaping something.

The exhilaration deserted her somewhere during the seven hour trip and morphed into the unique kind of exhaustion that comes after an emotional trauma and twenty four hours on high alert. The more distance she put between herself and her problems, the more her stomach churned and her courage fell away. By the time she stepped down from the coach in Devon, not even the sharp whip of the salty wind or the piercing azure sky could break the heavy fog of doubt that had overridden her every thought. She felt cold to the bone. Every nerve ending in her body screamed at her to run straight to the phone box across the street and call home.

What home? She repeated to herself, over and over, until the message finally got through.

She wiped the tears from her eyes with the sleeve of her school sweatshirt and trudged along the high street, adrift. The weight of her rucksack dragged her backwards, absent of the adrenaline that had coursed through her body the night before.

Many of the shops were still shuttered, leaving most of the street looking eerily deserted compared to the last time she had been here. She headed towards Curl Up and Dye, one of the few that looked to be open, in search of a friendly face.

The front desk was unmanned. Tammy was nowhere to be seen and there wasn't a customer in sight. Ella had almost accepted the possibility of an apocalypse by the time Carol shimmied through from the back.

'Oh, my goodness! Hello, sweetheart!' she smiled, coming around to the other side of the counter and taking in the smudged mascara and the school uniform. 'Hmm... something tells me you aren't here for a trim. You look frozen! Come and have a cup of tea.'

Ella's body was flooded with relief and the tears fell instantly.

'Oh, no! Oh, dear!' Carol exclaimed, fussing around the counter to locate a tissue. She flipped the sign on the door to 'closed' and ushered Ella down onto one of the salon chairs, saying gently, 'I'm going to go and put the kettle on, and then you can tell me all about it. A problem shared is a problem halved.'

And Ella did.

Three cups of sugary tea and a pack of custard creams later,

Carol sat back heavily in the chair opposite her and sighed, the only person Ella had ever confided in. She tapped her long cerise talons against the faux leather arm rest as she pondered the tangled web of problems that had been laid before her.

'Well, little lady, you have me quite speechless which is a miracle in itself, I can tell you!' she laughed. 'So you're *sure* you're not going back?'

She threw both hands up as Ella shot her a sullen look and continued, 'Only, you're so young to be out here all by yourself. This is a nice place and all, full of kind folk, but still... I have to ask...'

'I'm sure.'

'Okay.' she said, taking a deep breath. 'Well in that case, your immediate problem is somewhere to stay. You said you had some money?'

Ella nodded.

'Alright, well you only have a couple of options. Most of the B&B's and holiday rentals are closed for the winter, which is why so many shops are closed up now, too. We're a seasonal place here, and most things open back up again in spring time, ready for summer. There are a couple of hotels that *do* stay open all year round, but they don't come cheap. The proprietor is a lovely lady though, a friend of mine, and I'm sure she'll be able to work something out for you. Why don't I call her?'

'Yes please.' said Ella, her voice almost a whisper. She could think of nothing sweeter than a quiet room and a clean set of sheets and knew she would pay whatever it cost, at least for one night.

'Alright, then. I'll give her a call now and then I'll take you over there.' said Carol, disappearing into the back room once more.

She peeked back through the crack in the door at the forlorn figure of the gaunt runaway and curled the phone wire around her finger. She wondered if she was doing the right thing in facilitating her plans. Of course, teenage girls were prone to exaggerations and dramatics. Her mother couldn't be *that* bad, could she? And everyone has had their heart broken, the first time *always* feels like the end of the world. But losing a dad and a brother so close together... sure, what harm could a few days recuperation in the Devonian air do her?

With a few days to gather her thoughts, she'd be sure to call her mother. And if Carol was sure about anything in this life, it was that Tessa Johanssen was exactly the right person to help with the healing of a broken young soul. Where would she herself have been without having known her kindnesses personally? Certainly not standing there in her own salon, that was for sure.

With a decisive nod to herself, she picked up the receiver.

***

Ella would look back upon the day she walked into the hair salon as the first bit of fortuity she had been blessed with in her life. That she had chosen that salon, that it had been empty, that it had been Carol who had received her instead of Tammy, that Carol had thought of Tess Johanssen...

Without all of those factors combined, her life could have unfolded in a remarkably different way. Later on, she would like to think of it as a special instance of serendipity, where everything had aligned so perfectly that it could not be pure chance. It was proof, she was sure, that her brother and father had been by her side, pulling a few strings from wherever they were to nudge her in the right direction.

Tess, it turned out, had been exactly the right person she needed in her life at that point in time. A widow of thirty years, she was beloved within the small community of Woolacombe for her eccentricities as much as her philanthropy.

She was certainly well-versed in young waifs and strays; many a resident of the small village would refer to her as their saviour. She took a special interest in Ella's plight, having been no stranger to grief herself, and felt herself perfectly placed to guide her new protege back to happiness.

After Tess' husband had died, leaving her a hefty life insurance package, she'd surprised herself with how financially savvy she naturally was. She'd started by buying a handful of neglected properties, renovating them and splitting them up into rentals. Spurred on by a succession of similar projects, she'd purchased a far bigger property and renovated it into a hotel.

Ella found herself with an immediate golden ticket into a basement room and gainful employment as a waitress in the hotel restaurant, which was busy all year round, despite the season. As her pregnancy became obvious to Tess, she was moved into a far more comfortable maisonette a short walk from the hotel, and a far less strenuous position on reception.

What Tess had ultimately done for Ella had been so much more than just wages and lodgings. She had recognised something in Ella that reminded her of herself, and fell into the role of surrogate mother so naturally that many hotel guests left believing the two were flesh and blood.

Although Ella was perceived as cold and closed by the younger staff members, Tess had no such qualms about her reserved nature. In fact, she appreciated her disinterest in inane chatter and gossip.

Tess filled the great, gaping hole in Ella's life. Weekends and evenings that had begun with only her own voice echoing off of the walls of her maisonette for company became gossiping under blankets in front of the log burner. Learning the intricacies of cultivating organic vegetables, standing side by side in Tess's beloved greenhouse with dirt encrusted fingernails. And the importance of balancing ledgers and VAT.

Tess was kind, patient and passionate about things that Ella had never had cause to consider before: why shouldn't wealth be distributed evenly? Why couldn't two men love one another without prejudice? Why should being an unwed mother be a disadvantage?

Ella pushed a son out into the sterile strip lights of a hospital room in the March of 1987, devoid of fuss or fanfare. She received three visitors: Tess, Carol and Tammy.

'Aren't you a dark horse then?' the latter had whispered with a nudge. 'Must have been the haircut.'

'Oh, he's just absolutely perfect.' cooed a smitten Carol, who hadn't put him down since she'd arrived.

'And what are we to call him?' asked Tess.

'Grayson.' replied Ella. 'After my dad.'

She could never be sure whether the clouds parting to let the most exquisite beam of golden light through the window onto the lino floor had been a beam of approval from another world, or simply the delirious after effects of the gas and air.

She returned, with two-day-old Grayson nestled into the

crook of her arm, to the ground floor maisonette and thanked her lucky stars for the first time she could remember.

She spent the first few weeks in a haze of utter disbelief that she could ever have had any kind of hand in producing something so perfect. She spent hours gazing down at his pink cheeks and tiny round nose, his miniature fingers and the rise and fall of his little chest in awe. She spent her time embroiled in a dichotomy of equal parts bliss and crippling anxiety over things that *could* happen. Her thoughts strayed back to her own mother and the parallels of her teenage motherhood more often than she would have liked.

With Tess as both her mentor and cheerleader, Ella found a harmony in life she had never known before. She was capable of so much more than she had ever realised. She was able to be many things at once: a devoted parent to a thriving young son, a sole breadwinner and a student, too.

When she had first enrolled onto her business course, she had been unable to quieten the chorus of doubts that ricocheted around her mind, despite Tess's steadfast confidence in her. As time went on, she learnt to trust her abilities.

At her graduation ceremony with Tess and Grayson clapping her all the way up to the stage as she shook the chancellor's hand, she had never known pride like it. The achievement shifted something monumental in her. For the first time, happiness went from being an abstract concept, forever slightly out of reach, to something tangible and attainable. Something that she could choose. Something that she was able to control.

She felt vindicated in that moment. She had made the right choices. This was her family now, and her belief in them and herself was absolute.

Shortly after, she changed their names by deed poll and they became Ella and Grayson Johanssen. An act designed as much to sever all remaining ties to the neglected and unsure teenager who'd arrived there, as to demonstrate her love and loyalty to the lady who had made her happiness possible.

***

Three years later, the hotel proprietor asked her newly graduated front of house to join her for a spot of afternoon tea on the veranda in the middle of one of her shifts.

'Must be important,' her fellow receptionist, Rachel, commented as she took over the small line of guests waiting patiently at the desk.

Ella's heels clipped the parquet floors as she strode through the restaurant, stopping every now and again to exchange niceties with the more regular customers before she stepped through the glass doors and out into the gardens.

The hotel sat at the top of an incline. Almost an acre of perfectly manicured lawn rolled downwards towards a lake at the bottom, framed by thickets of unspoilt woodland. It was a view she could never tire of.

Tessa sat at the furthest table from the entrance on the far right hand corner of the veranda. She was looking out towards the lake with the summer breeze lifting tendrils of her white hair this way and that as Ella approached, the table already set with a brimming cake stand and a steaming pot of earl grey. She smiled and rose to hug Ella, showing far less reserve than was usual during working hours.

After the tea was poured, she got straight down to business.

'I have a proposition for you, Ella. Well, a couple, actually.'

Ella nodded.

'The first thing I would like you to consider is a promotion. You're qualified now. And more importantly than that, I trust you. As I'm sure you've come to realise by now, I began coaching you in every aspect of the business some years ago. You understand my standards and preferences. I want you to step up as the general manager.'

'But what about—'

'Stefano is going back to Italy. He handed his notice in four months ago, and agreed to stay on until after you graduated. He is in absolute agreement that you are the perfect choice for the position. But,' she continued, wiping a blob of clotted cream from her lower lip, 'and there *is* a but... I want you to invest in the business. You still have the capital you arrived here with, and I don't want you to take this position unless you truly see this hotel and indeed this place as your future.

'For a £20,000 investment into the Park Royal, you will receive a 25% share in the business and the deeds to the caretakers cottage, which, just to be clear, equates to the ownership of the property which has no mortgage on it. I have thought long and hard about my offer, and I understand that what you'll need to put in is every penny that you have – your safety net—'

Ella felt that some kind of acknowledgement was required, but all she could do was continue to stare, shutting her mouth, that she'd just realised was hanging open, with a snap.

'So I have tried to bring a different kind of safety net into my side of the bargain. I have also unashamedly aimed to make this offer one that you would be foolish to refuse. But, of course, I want you to think long and hard about it. Take as long as you need.'

Ella nodded, slowly, trying to take it all in.

'Well, not too long, actually. Stefano's flight is in a fortnight.'

They both laughed.

'You know I'm not a fool. I'm not going anywhere. Thank you, Tess.' said Ella.

'Just as I'd hoped,' smiled Tess, reclining into her chair. She waved over a young waiter who uncorked a bottle of champagne and filled their glasses. 'To another new beginning.'

Their glasses clinked and both women looked out to the lake, contemplating this new found future. The surface of the lake gleamed with promise, the foxgloves lilted in the breeze and the starlings chirped a chorus of congratulations, their surroundings exuding prosperity.

'Well, one more cake and then you'd better go and put Stefano out of his misery. He's been champing at the bit to get you enrolled onto his crash course in general management before he packs his cases.'

FORTY FIVE

Grown ups, 2023.

'Wow.' Arthur breathes. His exhale is so heavy that it almost casts a shadow as it meets London's dusk, the sun dipping deep into the horizon and leaving behind it a sudden chill.

He was so rapt on Ella's unexpected soliloquy that he hadn't noticed the jubilant school children and leisurely meanderers make way for the hurried scuttles of the commuters, eyes glued to phones and chins tucked tightly into expensive, high collared coats.

Ella rubs her hands together and blows into them, her fingernails beginning to take on a grey hue.

'You're cold.' he states. 'We should walk.'

They exit the park and walk quickly, without a destination in mind. Arthur peppers her with small curiosities that come to him every few steps pertaining to the story he has just heard. Ella obligingly answers and somewhere between the park and home, the icy chasm of years gone by begins to thaw and an easiness begins to preside.

Emboldened by the slight curl of her lips and the way it is now in synchronicity with her eyes, he asks, 'So… are you going to visit your mum?'

Her face hardens instantly. Arthur curses himself at his bullishness, having known that he should be treating Ella and this entire matter as delicately as the wafer thin china heirloom that it really was.

'I am.' she replies to his surprise. 'But I need to see my brother first.'

Arthur sucks his teeth. It has been a shameful amount of time since he has been in any proximity to Louie's grave. It was never a place he visited as religiously as he ought to have done. The cold slab of stone was an ugly thing, the marble too shiny and sharp looking at first, littered in bouquets and envelopes filled with regret, signed by names he didn't recognise. It had never felt right.

The letters etched so heavily into the stone: his best friend's name, the date his life began, the date it ended, pronouncing him a beloved brother and son… Even its placement in the graveyard felt wrong, so far away from the footpath, indistinguishable from all of the other beloved brothers and sons.

It didn't feel like Louie. It had nothing of Louie about it. On later visits, the tufts of overgrown grass around its edges, the dry stemmed rotting bouquets and the angry flapping sound their cellophane wraps made whenever the wind picked up only made it even more chill inducing.

Truth be told, he hated the place.

'Will you come with me?' she asks.

'If you really need me to.' he says honestly. 'It's not… my favourite place.'

'Nor mine. But I need to go.'

'Alright.'

***

The following day, Ella is already down on her haunches in front of Louie's grave when Arthur walks through the gates. Her eyes are fixed on the stone and as he approaches, Arthur watches her chin move up and down as she conducts a conversation that will only ever be one way. She turns as he nears, the midday sun casting a golden filter across the high points of her face. She smiles widely.

'You caught me!' she says, putting a shielding hand above her eyes. 'Making small talk with the dead guy.'

'We all do it.' he smiles back.

'Do you? I was just asking him to haunt you... a few bangs in the night, footsteps on the stairs, an apparition or two at the end of your bed.'

'Please don't, mate,' he implores the grave. 'We both know my nerves couldn't take it.'

Ella throws her head back and laughs.

'Imagine.' she grins as she pulls herself up to full height and turns back towards the grave. 'I didn't bring any flowers. I never see the point. I mean, look at them all.' she says, waving her hand at the row of lovingly tended graves. 'It's like a bloody popularity contest.'

'It's emotional fly tipping. All that plastic.'

She laughs again. 'I don't buy into all the final resting place stuff, really. I understand its purpose. The ceremony of it. The idea that the funeral is some kind of bridge to closure. People finding solace in visiting the site of the bones decaying in a box with a stone to mark their spot, but… nah, it's not for me. I don't feel any connection to him here.'

'Me either,' Arthur agrees. 'But then, what? Do you think he's just gone?'

'Who knows? Nah, I like to think he's somewhere out there causing mischief… but I don't dwell on it, what's the point? I'll see a robin, or a feather, or a song will come on and I'll think oh, hey Louie, or oh, hey dad… I've been known to thank them on occasion for any particularly good turns of fortune… but I haven't let it define me. Looking back, that was a large part of what leaving was all about, I think: not letting the things I didn't have define my life.'

Arthur nods, his thoughts turning to Anna, who most definitely had let death define and consume her. 'You did the right thing.'

'Do you think I was selfish?'

He cocks his head to the side. 'That's a loaded question. Why does it matter what I think?'

'It doesn't, I'm just interested. Go on, I'm a big girl… was I a selfish witch, leaving my mother to be eaten alive by her grief and regret?'

Arthur pushes his hands deeper into his pockets as the wind picks up and whistles through the undergrowth, blades of grass whipping at his ankles before stopping as suddenly as it started. He stands awkwardly as everything stills, as though the sky, the trees, the grass and the faceless army of deceased are waiting for his answer with baited breath.

He is struck again by that feeling that some people call imposter syndrome. The unease you get as an unqualified bystander being called to action when you're unable or un-willing to get involved. It has been an unwanted companion of his all of his life, one he could always count on at pivotal moments: his dad leaving his mother, the police's arrival at the Carmichael's door, the funerals, Ella's departure.

He would like to have had more to offer in all of those situations. If they had been tests, he had failed miserably. There certainly isn't any kind of honour roll for fence sitting.

'Maybe.' he finally says. 'It's complicated, isn't it? Might your mother have benefitted from your support? Perhaps, but I'm inclined to believe that you wouldn't have seen any of the fruit from that bounty for a long time and at what cost it would have been to you and your own life? I think that you probably did the right thing for yourself, and who's to know if any of it could have been any different?'

'Is she angry with me?' she asks with a delicate tilt of her head.

Will anything happen to me if I fib a little on consecrated ground, he wonders, peering downward at the toes of his trainers and rocking forward on to them as though to test for sturdiness.

He is aching to offer some reassurance, fantasies of himself single-handedly laying the building blocks for a happy ending flitting across his consciousness like butterflies rejoicing the breaking of spring. He pictures their first embrace, wet cheeked and warm, some purpose restored back into each of their lives...

Ella coughs. 'Earth to Arthur.'

'I don't know. I don't think so.' he replies honestly, knowing that if there is one person in his life who never ceases to surprise him, it's the old lady next door.

'I'm nervous.' she admits. 'I never meant to leave it this long.'

***

Ella kicks off her boots and throws herself onto the bed, rubbing at her temples. Her head is throbbing, unwanted thoughts coming thick and fast, the pain behind her eyes warning her of an impending migraine. She places both hands on her stomach and shifts her focus to her inhale and exhale, slowing it down until she can no longer feel the enter or release.

This is one of the many coping mechanisms she has honed and added to her arsenal over the years, having not escaped London as entirely unscathed as she outwardly displays. A few minutes later, her heart has steadied and she tentatively lifts her lids, taking in her surroundings.

One of the downsides to working in the hotel trade is that you're rarely ever able to truly relax and enjoy staying in another establishment. Your professional opinion is constantly casting out aspersions, your fingertips unconsciously roaming over surfaces in search of dust. It becomes an exercise in observation, comparison and more often than not, disappointment.

It also means that all about you are irritating distractions. Ella has far more important thoughts to organise than a slightly crookedly hung frame or the thread count of a pillow case, but these are the things which are vying for her attention as she desperately tries to focus.

She is almost beside herself at the thought of being face to face with her mother after so long, with no idea of the reception she might get. Will she still be angry? Or worse, perhaps she will be completely indifferent? How will she have fared in the passage of years? Is she well? Has she been happy? Arthur hadn't given much away in either direction, although Ella would like to think that he would have issued some kind of warning if there were any immediate health concerns.

She sighs.

It's no use speculating about what *might* happen, she reminds herself, bringing herself back to the present by pinching at the skin between her thumb and forefinger.

She walks over to the window and places her elbows on the ledge. She watches the evening settle across London's skyline, rooftops and chimneys stretching out as far as the eye can see, the buildings seeming to be crammed together ever more tightly with each passing mile.

It's difficult for her to imagine it ever having been familiar.

It is such a sharp contrast to the views from her own bedroom windows. The lapping of the waves and the chatter of the gulls replaced with the dull hum of never ending traffic jams and footfall on the pavements below. Even in the dead of night, it's never really quiet here, the darkness is never truly dark. Even with the dense smog blocking any star or moonlight there might have been.

She casts her mind back across the years, plucking out the memories which are more favourable: her father cursing the shears as he haphazardly hacked at the vines growing up the outhouse wall. Anna looking on in a sundress with her head thrown back in laughter, radiating a piercing beauty of such force that no man would dare to deny her a thing. And later, in the living room, cradling a glass of rioja in the Eames chair as she watched her beloved boys at the piano, serenading her in a drunken duet as she laughed indulgently and sang along in short bursts.

She had always been charged with a rampant energy. Unstable and fatal and completely mesmerising. She'd passed it onto her son silently and seamlessly but it had skipped her daughter altogether, as though it knew she was a bad seed before the rest of them realised.

The uncomfortable truth of the matter for Ella is that whilst there are plenty of memories of happier times to choose from – *true* happy times – in the years when her parents love was unabashed and laughter was abundant, the only role she had ever played was that of an onlooker.

Never had she been at the centre of the laughter. Never had she been the source of the proud smiles. What would she be now? Graciously received as better than nobody by a lonely old lady? Or scalded and sent away for returning like a bad penny?

The mountain suddenly seems too treacherous to climb again, the very thought is overwhelming. The tiny details and 'what if's' threaten to consume her confidence all together.

I am a strong and capable woman, she tells herself, *I am in control, I am in control.*

She returns to the bed and sinks down onto the mattress, closing her eyes and breathing deeply, waiting for the tension to unfurl as experience tells her it will.

She can still picture every detail of her brother's face clearly: the exact shade of his iris, the contours and dimples, the curve of his gap toothed smile. Even his mannerisms.

She has spent a lot of years and a lot of money on various forms of therapy being angry at him and the burden of the secrets he had entrusted her, and ultimately weighed her down with for the rest of her life. A person can be lots of things. They can be a beloved brother and son. They can be charismatic, beautiful and affectionate. They can be funny and kind. They can also be selfish, calculating and manipulative. Impulsive. Reckless.

Humans are multi-faceted by their very nature, their traits and characteristics layered one over the other like the skin of an onion.

It is time to peel her brother's particular onion, and with it, her own. It is a time for truth, and it is time to say sorry.

FORTY SIX

The knock, 2023.

The rain beats down heavily onto the pavement as Ella stands before number thirty and thirty-two, looking between them. The dim glow of lit bulbs tell her that both occupants are in residence.

She begins a slow walk through the wrought iron gate towards the yellow door of number thirty-two, which is looking much more welcoming after its recent paint job. She knocks and waits, never letting her focus leave the brass knocker just above eye level, willing the door to be answered before her courage dissipates and her body takes flight.

A few minutes later, the rattle of chains announces that there is no turning back. The door swings open and Anna, a good few inches shorter than Ella remembers her, peers out suspiciously. Her face is lined and crumpled, like something long forgotten in the bottom of a coat pocket.

'Yes?' she asks as her cataracts adjust to the overcast afternoon.

Ella swallows and removes her hat.

'Mum,' she begins quietly, 'it's me.'

'Sorry? Speak up.' says Anna, brow furrowed in confusion as she pulls her stained cardigan more tightly around her torso.

Ella is quiet for a moment as her brain catches up, her heart beating furiously. It is difficult to believe that this small lady in front of her is really her mother, the same one she left here so long ago. Ella is shocked by how old she looks. So forgotten. She can't help but picture Tessa, who must have been around the same age, give or take a few years, but seemed so much younger somehow. The lady in front of her seems to have none of Tessa's vitality, or indeed, any of her own. The years appear to have sucked the youth from her by way of brute force. Ella doesn't remember her being so small.

'It's me. It's *Ella.*' she repeats more loudly than she had intended. She steps back reflexively, as though anticipating the back of a hand, raindrops running down her face.

Anna leans out further, blinking furiously. 'Why didn't you say so? Come on then, inside with you, you're drenched.'

Ella steps into the hall, water pooling on the tiles at her feet. She takes off her coat and stands lamely in the doorway as her mother's eyes roam up and down her.

'Good God,' Anna announces, bringing a shaking hand up to cover her mouth, 'It *is* you. Let's have a drink, shall we? A nice Irish coffee, I think, I'm not sure a bog standard one will suffice in the face of a resurrection...' she twitters as she shuffles off down the hall and through the kitchen door.

Ella hangs her sodden coat over a radiator emitting no heat and follows Anna through, staring at the back of her as she boils the kettle and opens and closes cupboards.

Ella's eyes stray across the room as she silently takes a place at the kitchen table, the same one she once ate her breakfast at every morning. Everything is the same, yet everything is different. The walls, the carpets, the features and fittings are all exactly as she remembers them, if only a little rougher around the edges. There is lots missing, too. Ella wishes she'd returned sooner so that she might understand whether the emptiness that permeates the place is a result of the sold sign thrust into the barren flower bed out front or a result of her mother being the last man standing.

Anna places a mug, a cafetiere and a half empty bottle of bourbon in front of her. She sits across from her and pours herself a splash of coffee, followed by a rather large measure of whiskey.

'Sorry,' she says, 'No milk. I had meant to go to the shops, but the weather...'

'Black's fine.'

Anna nods and knocks back the liquid as an awkward silence descends, neither woman knowing how or where to begin. Ella looks from the whiskey to her mother and then back down at the table, struggling to push the echoes of old traumas from the forefront of her thoughts. Anna follows Ella's gaze.

Anna's face crumples as she finally gives her body permission to do what it needs to. The tears overflow and trickle silently down her cheeks as she wrings her hands on the table top.

'I'm sorry.' she says shakily, meeting Ella's eyes, 'I've never been the best at apologies, Ella, but I'm so, so bloody sorry. For being a crap mother. I was pretty crap to begin with, really, and then... well, you know. The drinking. I should

396

have been better. I'm sorry.'

Ella breathes in sharply as her own tears begin to fall in return, scarcely able to believe the relief that she feels after the unexpected apology. She had never realised how much she had always needed to hear those words.

'I'm sorry, too,' Ella replies through her tears.

'For leaving?'

'Yes.'

Anna shakes her head furiously and pulls a frayed tissue from up her sleeve, swiping at her nose. 'You shouldn't be. I don't blame you for leaving. I wouldn't have wanted to be here, either. I was selfish, Ella… probably still am, truth be told, but if you'll give me the chance, I'd love nothing more than to try to do better.'

Ella reaches across the table and squeezes her mother's hands in her own, savouring the warmth of them, feeling an immense gratitude that she is still alive, still here, that they have been given another chance.

'Why are you back?' Anna continues tentatively, 'I don't want to assume a reunion if that isn't what this is. I wouldn't blame you… I'm not dying, and you don't need to feel sorry for me, or guilty, or any of that nonsense.'

'Maggie left me a painting. And now I'm here… I want to move on, Mum.'

'Really?' Anna blinks, 'Are you sure?'

'I'm sure, Mum.'

Anna beams, wet faced. 'Well, well that's just… Thank you. Thank you.'

She rises from the table and walks around towards the kitchen counter, retrieving a box of tissues and placing it on to the table in front of them.

'Just look at you,' she says as she stands over her, shaking her head in disbelief, 'A woman. I've tried to picture who you might have become so many times, I don't know why I feel so shocked, but I do.'

Ella wipes her eyes as Anna sits back down.

'I can't wait to hear about your life. I so hope it's been a happy one,' she tells her sincerely. 'Do I have any grandchildren?'

'Yes, you do.'

FORTY SEVEN

A new tide, 2023.

'Psst. We're here.' Arthur hisses at Anna, comatose in the passenger seat, as he parks up outside the Park Royal.

The size of the hotel is the first surprise. He can't help but suspect that Ella had intentionally played it down. When she had told them she had inherited a guest house, the words had alluded to something far smaller. Arthur had pictured a kitsch seaside bed and breakfast perhaps, not the stately home sized manor that he is now staring up at, complete with porters at the door and an enormous water fountain to the front. The driveway had seemed to go on forever. He wouldn't be surprised if he had crossed the borders to another county, the time it had taken them to get from the road to the car park.

He watches as Ella emerges from inside, walking through the door, shoulders back, laughing along with the two porters in their tailcoats. She unselfconsciously scans the rows of cars until her eyes land upon his. Her smile grows wider and she waves.

'She's here,' he says at the snoring pensioner to his left, 'Come on. Wake up.'

Eventually, he has no choice but to pinch her.

'Ow!' she says, rubbing her arm. 'No need for that.'

'The next step was a thump.'

'I was only resting my eyes. No need to be so vicious. Are we here?'

'Yep.' he replies, nodding towards Ella.

Anna lets out a low whistle as she takes in the size and grandeur of her surroundings. 'Wow. Landed on our feet here, haven't we?'

'*We?* I'm just here for a holiday. *You've* landed on your feet.' he corrects her.

'We'll see,' she smirks, 'I've seen how you look at her. Exactly the way she used to look at you when you were teenagers. A regular middle-aged Romeo, you are.'

Arthur rolls his eyes as he climbs out of the car, giving a mock sigh in Anna's direction. She merely smirks again, and he is a little perturbed to see her wink. He allows himself a small snort before closing the door on her.

They have become close during these last few months. Her lack of forward planning on the sale of her house had resulted in her becoming an unexpected lodger at number thirty, turning up one morning and telling him in her most feeble voice, 'Oh, they're moving in next Thursday. It had quite slipped my mind and now it appears to have crept up on me… it's a terrible business, this old age, I get ever so confused. And now I'll have nowhere to go. Not yet, anyway. So needs must, you'll have to put me up. I've an awful lot of cases, though, Arthur, I hope you're stronger than you look.'

Having Anna in residence has been rather a lot like being landed with an unwanted stray cat in decline. For all of her bravado and grand plans, which flitted from sun-drenched tropical retirement communities, to embarking upon various degrees at the open university, to a cottage in the Cotswolds ("It's never too late to chase a dream, Arthur."), as the months went by it became abundantly clear that she was going nowhere quickly.

Indeed, the very act of discussing any of these plans was so taxing for her that after each one, she had to go for a lie down. Without her afternoon nap, she was really rather unpleasant.

But their enforced proximity haa resulted in an attachment they both clearly needed but neither one had ever been able to articulate. He's grown fond of her, and all of her little ways.

He walks around to the boot to begin emptying the jenga of cases he's miraculously managed to squeeze into the small space. He looks up as Ella approaches, flanked by the two porters. She flings her arms around him and nestles her head into his shoulder blade.

'You're here.' she whispers in wonder, breathing him in.

'I am.' he whispers back.

'I can't believe it.'

'Me either.'

She steps back and they watch each other shyly, each one a ball of nervous energy and anticipation.

Almost six months have gone by since their first reunion. At first, the phone calls largely revolved around Anna and her various ailments and predicaments pertaining to the house sale.

As the weeks went by and the voices crackling down the

lines became more familiar, the conversations extended until eventually, phone calls for Anna and phone calls for Arthur became separate things. It was easier down a phone, without a pair of eyes locked on them, to brave the odd flirtatious remark and feign a cool indifference which neither of them truly possessed.

One night, Ella had been sat in the back office with the door to reception ajar, phone perched in the crook of her neck as she rifled through a barely legible 'to do' list her night porter had left her before going home with a stomach complaint.

'If any of these are wake up calls or airport runs, there's going to be a mutiny in here in the morning…' she muttered.

Arthur listened, bemused, from the comfort of his mother's chesterfield, wrapped up in his favourite fleece dressing gown.

'I've not even had chance to go and check on the bathroom installation or turn on the heating at the flat and Gray gets in at 8am! To a cold, empty flat which may or may not have a functioning bathroom… honestly, I'm too old for all this.' she sighed.

'First world problems, eh?' Arthur laughed. 'The worst that can happen is that he'll be forced into a free room in a five star hotel for a few days. Will he see his dad whilst he's back?' he enquired. Ella snorted and the line went silent.

'Sorry,' he added quickly. 'I'm being intrusive. I was just wondering, you know, if you had any help. It must have been hard bringing up a child by yourself.'

'It wasn't,' she said. 'I've been very lucky.'

'I know, I just mean, with no family. Grandparents and stuff.'

'We had Tessa.' she replied tartly, before adding more softly,

'She was amazing, Arthur. I wish you could have met her. So much of what Grayson is, of what we both are, is because of her. I don't know what we'd be without her.'

'I wish I could have, too.' he said, trying to picture the woman who became Ella's family whilst her real mother sat alone at home.

'When she died, it really felt like the end of the world, even more so than with my dad and Louie, because then it was like… oh, shit. I'm the adult, that's me, now. There's nobody left to consult or defer to. There's nobody else's wisdom to pilfer. It was scary.'

'I felt the same when my mum went,' he told her. 'I still do, really. But at least I don't have anyone seeking my guidance, well, only your mother.'

Ella laughed. 'I reckon she's harder labour than *my* dependant.'

'You might be right,' he agreed. 'She's dangerous now she's mastered the laptop. When I came down today, she was seconds away from buying a bloody narrow boat. She was filling in her payment details. She got the right hump when I told her what a terrible idea it was. Not even the waste tank put her off. She hasn't spoken to me all afternoon.'

When she finally stopped laughing, she wiped the tears from her eyes and said, 'Poor Grayson. He's going to have no idea what's hit him when they meet.'

'Ah, he'll love her. Nothing like an eccentric grandparent to broaden your horizons. Does he have any others?'

'No,' she said quietly, 'He never met them.'

'Ah, that's a shame. It'll be a new experience for him, then. I'm sure you don't need to worry.'

'It is a shame. He had a lovely grandmother. I was very

403

close to her, once.'

'You didn't stay in touch?'

'I couldn't.'

'Can I ask why?' he asked, his heart beginning to race, although he wasn't sure why.

'Because I wasn't in touch with his father.'

'Did it end badly?'

'You could say that. Abruptly, more like.'

'Did he treat you badly?'

'Yes and no.'

'And Grayson?'

'He never knew Grayson.' she said, holding her breath.

'He didn't want him?'

'He never knew *about* Grayson. We were very young. I didn't want to put him in that position. He had a career and a life. A partner.'

'Oh, Ella,' Arthur said sadly. 'He was half of his responsibility. He might have surprised you.'

'What would you have done, Arthur, if a girl you'd had a one night stand with turned up on your doorstep with a baby when you were a teenager?'

'Gosh,' he replied, rubbing his temples, trying to picture his teenage self. Not brave, probably not altogether capable enough to have been any kind of role model or provider, but equally incapable of turning his back on that kind of responsibility. He would have tried, he knew for certain. He would have been more terrified of not trying than trying. 'I wasn't exactly solid and dependable breadwinning material, but I'd have done my best. I think most men would.'

'Then I wish I had.'

With all of their cases safely delivered to their respective rooms, Anna and Arthur trudge down the grand staircase together towards the atrium.

'Fancy, isn't it?' she stage whispers. 'I'm going to have to go shopping.'

Arthur looks down at the over-washed and rather off-white shirt she wears and the corduroy slacks hanging from her bowed legs, bunched up at the waist where a leather belt has become the only obstacle between the room and her drawers. She's the quintessential mad old lady that a proprietor's resident parent ought to be. She gives the place some character.

They reach the atrium as various waiters pile the table high with silverware and napkins, pristine in both appearance and movement. Ella arrives, listening intently to the bearded man wheeling a silver trolley laden with cakes and sandwiches towards them.

'Ah, that was quick,' she says, before adding, 'How are your rooms?'

'Bit dated, slightly fusty. Four out of ten. Could probably have done with a bigger bed.' Anna replies facetiously, having sailed on boats that were smaller than the bed in her room.

'I'd pass on your comments, but I've heard the owner is a grumpy cow. Wouldn't want you out on your ear now, would we?' Ella replies with a snigger.

Both women sink down into chairs opposite one another and simultaneously rest their elbows on the table, fingers intertwined beneath their chins. There is far more likeness between them than Arthur had remembered. He sits down between them and nobody speaks as waiters noiselessly glide around one another and platters appear in the middle of the table.

'Quite a spread,' Anna remarks, eyes wide on the chocolate eclairs. 'If I didn't know any better I'd think you were trying to give me diabetes and bump me off. You're not in arrears or anything, are you?'

'If I ever am, you'll be the first port of call. I hear you're very well-versed in them.'

'I have no idea what you're talking about.' Anna chuckles. 'So where's my grandson? I can hardly be expected to dazzle an introduction high on refined sugars with a lap full of crumbs. Not at my age.'

'Incoming.' Ella replies, nodding her head towards the double doors as a young, tattooed and heavily pierced man in harem pants strides towards them, his smile widening with every step. He leans down and plants a kiss onto Ella's forehead as he reaches the table.

Ella squeezes her eyes shut and inhales sharply, waiting for the missile to land. A few moments later she realises there has been no explosion and all eyes watch her expectantly.

'Gray!' she says, leaping from her chair and presenting him to the table in an unusually high pitched voice. 'This is Anna...'

'Your grandma.' Anna adds, pressing her hand to her heart self-importantly.

'... and... and Arthur.'

Grayson beams and sits down next to Anna, pulling his chair in closer as they study one another. He reaches out and takes both her hands.

'I've always wanted a Grandma.' he tells her, his effortless charm an echo of someone they once knew.

Arthur watches on, clocking his dimples and the curls he has pulled back into a bobble. He is more than a whisper of his late uncle, but there's something more than that. Something even more familiar, somehow, that Arthur can't quite put his finger on.

'I can't tell you I've always wanted a grandson. I mean, nobody sits there and thinks to themselves, 'Oh, I can't wait to be old enough to be a granny.' But now I've got one, I'm pretty thrilled about it. And look at all of your fancy nose rings. We're going to have such fun!'

Arthur watches over his teacup as they fervidly exchange facts about themselves, chuckling to himself at how quickly shock factor becomes the unit of currency, each party competing for the title of most outrageous family member.

'Yeah, they kicked me out of school for smoking pot in the music cupboard. Half of the staff were on stronger prescriptions than that, it was ludicrous, although Mum didn't quite get my point.'

'Really? How terrible. Your grandfather and I had a fabulous crop in the summer of 1978. We had a great little set up in the outhouse. We went through seven pairs of scissors trimming the buds. *Seven!*'

'Would you like to come and see the lake?' Ella asks Arthur, another layer of shyness seeming to have crept into her tentative smile.

'Sure.' Arthur smiles back. Of course she wants to give Anna and Grayson a little space to get to know one another. It's only natural. They've years of ground to cover.

'Won't be long.' she directs to the pair of heads huddled conspiratorially, wiry white curls meeting their youthful counterparts in a clash of mischief and fond memories.

'Oh, good,' Anna remarks as she watches them retreat across the grass out of earshot, 'She's finally taking the bull

407

by the bollocks.'

'How do you think he'll take it?'

'Take what?' Anna squints at him. He sighs, giving her a direct look. 'Just fine, I'd imagine. He's far too polite to make a scene. I think he'll be quite pleased, actually.'

'Yeah?'

'Yeah. Because, of course, now you're morally bound to look after us in our old age. No more meeting our fates cold and alone, bodies discovered by mere chance days later as a passerby notices a strange smell emanating from an open window. Now we can look forward to someone dressing our bedsores and counting out our pills for us. We certainly got the better end of the deal. How do *you* know, anyway?'

'You just told me.' he sniggers.

'I did *not!* You tricked me. That's not fair at all.' she laments, brows knitted together in sulk.

'Nah, it was pretty obvious. There's an old picture in her jewellery box, her and two lads at a table in those paper crowns you get in Christmas crackers. She's staring at one of them like a lovesick puppy. I knew it was him as soon as I saw him.'

'That doesn't automatically make him your father, though.'

'Well, no, but he obviously *is*.'

'Mmm.'

'Were they together?'

'Not that I knew of. But I was a bit preoccupied, to tell you the truth. When I worked it out, it didn't surprise me one jot, though.'

'Is he nice?'

'Oh yes. Far too nice. She'll terrify him.'

***

Ella and Arthur walk away from the hotel, down the hill in a companiable silence and stop at the lake, which shimmers under the mid-afternoon sun. Arthur breathes in deeply, taking in the taste of the air, a world away from the metallic air of London. The day is warm, the only sounds the rustle of the leaves as a calm breeze sways the greenery back and forth, clouds moving across the pristine blue sky like slow balloons.

'Wow,' he breathes enthusiastically, 'What a spot. Is it safe to swim?'

Ella nods, 'It is. But I don't. Tessa used to, though. She reckoned it kept her mind sharp, the cold water.'

'You never fancied trying it?'

'No, not really. I never really understood it. I mean, there's a heated pool inside,' she says, gesturing behind her and wrinkling her nose, 'Without any eels lurking in it.'

'Fair point.'

Ella sits down onto the grass, folding her legs in front of her and Arthur follows suit. They gaze out across the lake for a few moments more, Arthur still mesmerised by his surroundings, a child-like expression painted across his face, as though he can't quite believe that a view like this can really exist. He catches Ella watching him and feels sheepish, having outed himself as the city boy he has always been already.

'So, what do you think?' she asks.

'That's a daft question,' he replies quickly, 'it's amazing. It's basically a bloody mansion, isn't it? And all this *space!* Honestly, Ella, it's so elegant, all of it. You've clearly done a fantastic job.'

Ella laughs. 'I meant Grayson. What do you think of Grayson?'

'Oh!' Arthur exclaims in surprise, 'Oh, well… He seems great. I've only just met him, obviously, but they looked like they were getting on like a house on fire, didn't they?'

'They did. It wasn't her I was worried about, though.'

'Me?' he turns to her in disbelief, 'You thought I wouldn't like him?'

She shrugs.

'Why wouldn't I?' Arthur continues, puzzled. 'I mean, I know I'm not exactly an extrovert, but I like to think I'm friendly enough?'

Ella sucks her teeth. 'You are, you are. Of course you are. I didn't mean anything like that. Ah, God,' she says, covering her eyes, 'I wish I still smoked.'

Arthur turns to stare at her, only just noticing the nervous energy she is emitting. He had been too distracted by the grandeur of their surroundings to have noticed before. He watches as her long, slender fingers, direct gifts from her mother, release her eyes and begin to pluck out tendrils of grass.

'Ella,' he says gently, 'Is everything okay?'

She takes a deep breath, vibrating with the effort of holding back her tears.

'I've made such a bloody mess of this.' she says, her voice plummeting a register, full and sad.

'A mess of what?'

She shakes her head and swallows, gesturing wildly with her hands before giving up, unable to articulate the things she needs to say or to find the best manner in which to say them.

410

He shuffles across the grass, closing the gap between them and puts an arm around her. Of course she's emotional, she must be all over the place; it's a big day for them all, her son and her mother in a room together for the first time. She's bound to be feeling overwhelmed.

'It's alright,' he tells her, pressing his forehead against hers, 'It's all fine. Everything's going just fine. Everyone's happy.'

Her tears spill over, then, and he feels her body tremble and shudder beneath his arm. She turns towards him, the tips of their noses touching, and squeezes her eyes shut. Their proximity is both tantalising and excruciating. He finds his heart jump-starting as he feels the warmth of her exhale on his lips.

They stay like this for a few more seconds, gently rocking backwards and forwards, until her eyes suddenly snap open and she pushes him away and grips his hand in both of hers.

'He's yours!' she blurts out, 'Grayson, he's your... you're his... he's your son, Arthur!'

He feels the air escape from his lungs. His ears begin to ring as he stares at her in confusion, his eyes searching hers for any hint of a trick, a laugh, a joke. But he doesn't find one.

She tilts her head to one side and tears trickle from her eyes as she rasps, 'I'm so sorry, Arthur. I should have told you. I wanted to tell you, before this. At first I told myself I had to be sure, sure that you weren't married with a family that this might wreck, sure that I wasn't just bringing trouble to your door for no good reason... after that, I told myself I had to be sure about your character, that you were a good person, that you'd be something positive in Grayson's life... and well, after that, after that it was just pure cowardice. The more I

411

got to know you, the more my feelings crept up on me, things I thought were in the past suddenly became my present, too, and I could never find the words… Then I thought that when you saw him, that would be it, you'd know, I wouldn't have to ever say it, but…'

'He's… he's mine?' Arthur whispers, 'I'm a father?'

Ella nods, loosening her grip on his arm, leaving angry red finger marks on his speckled skin.

'I'm sorry,' she says again, 'I didn't know how to… I should have told you sooner.'

He takes a deep breath, letting the information sink in for a few moments, trying his level best to quell the panicked array of thoughts that threaten to ambush the moment. The appearance of his crippling self-doubt is as reliable as ever, as his brain revolts and clamours to spew out reasons why he is unqualified for this role, why he'd be useless and lacking.

His thoughts turn towards his own father and the strange relationship they'd had, bordering on estrangement in his younger years until much later, when Teddy and Oksana had left and he realised he had backed the wrong horses. Then, he thinks of Louie and the father he had never had chance to become. Would he have flopped or excelled? Perhaps it would have been the making of him, but they would never know. Lastly, his thoughts turn to Grayson, who taught them to play their guitars and had been the one to take the boys to their football games. Grayson had been the only real example of fatherhood that Arthur had known.

He considers himself as a teenager and tries to imagine the scenario of Ella arriving at number thirty to tell him she was pregnant, and how he might have reacted. The truth is, he has no idea. He's certain that his mother would never have let him hide from his responsibilities, but that didn't necessarily mean that Ella would have been any better off. He remembers the confusion of the years after they lost Louie, the way his life had shrunk and turned pale and anaemic with his grief and decides that she had probably done the right thing. Sure, he'd missed out on a lot of things he ought to have been party to. But equally, she had removed the opportunities for him to fuck it up for all of them.

For the first time in his entire life, he finds that he is able to steady the thumping of his heart and drown out the anxiety. As he takes Ella's hand into his own and looks into her eyes, he realises that he has unexpectedly stumbled upon a reason to believe in the good in himself. One half of that reason is trembling beside him and biting her bottom lip, and the other is back up the hill, made up of equal parts of both of them.

He certainly never expected that, in his fifties, he would be given an opportunity to start again like this. This is a gift, he realises: people to love, who might love him back. After all, there is nothing more certain than death. Everyone is marching towards the same destination from the moment they take their first breaths. But now, he might not have to do it alone. The benefit of having spent most of his life alone already is that he will only appreciate them even more. And in that moment, he decides that that is exactly what he will spend the rest of his life doing, whatever shape that might take.

He squeezes her hand in silence and pulls her back towards him, where she rests her head on his shoulder. He brushes away the hair stuck to her cheeks, slick with tears, and kisses her forehead, before burying his head in her hair and letting his own tears escape.

'Will you stay for a bit?' she whispers.

He swallows hard before telling her, 'I'm not going any-where.'

The End

A note from the author

T hank you wholeheartedly to you and every other person that took time out of their lives to read this book. It started out as a lockdown project to ward off the lonely evenings and quickly became an obsession that I couldn't shake. At the time, I never imagined that it would ever see the light of day, let alone be bought and read by other people. I am beyond grateful.

If you enjoyed Number Thirty-Two, please consider leaving a review of it on Amazon or Goodreads. These reviews are invaluable to authors as they help to get the book in front of more pairs of eyes.

For news about the release date of my second, upcoming novel, *Tramp,* you can go to my website at cassiesteward.com and sign up to my mailing list for updates.

Acknowledgments

Thank you, wholeheartedly, to every single reader who has taken a chance on a debut author by reading this book. It means the world to me.

Thank you to my mum, Lulu, and my dad, Mikey. You have supported me in all areas of my life since my first day on earth and the writing of this book has been no different. I couldn't be any luckier to have you. From the seed of an idea and the initial few chapters I cobbled together (with very little idea of the direction it would go in) all the way through to the final draft, you have been there to read and give feedback on every single version there has been of Number Thirty-Two. I would never have managed to get this story out into the world without both of your help.

My Auntie, Julia Slack, who came on this writing journey with me. We started writing our books at the same time and held hands throughout the process, sending our drafts back and forth for months on end until somehow, we both had finished novels. I'm so glad I had your hand to hold, even though neither of us really knew what we were doing!

That brings me to the author Keith A Pearson, whose brilliant books I have long enjoyed and admired. Keith challenged Julia via e-mail to write 10,000 words to see if they could become a book. In doing so, he unwittingly set the wheels in motion for what was to become a finished novel for each of us. Thank you so much for all of your invaluable advice. It's amazing what a few kind words from a stranger can become – you have changed our lives. I also should add that the ending of this book is only the way it is thanks to your brilliant feedback.

Thank you to my editor, Claire, who did such wonderful things to this book during her part of the process and showed me what it really could be with a proper polishing. I learnt so much from you. Thank you to Nuria who designed my cover, which I love so much! Thank you for being so patient with all of my strange requests for revisions (rainbow effects and borders, I'm sure I was very annoying!)

Thanks also to the people who beta read for me in the final stages and provided feedback that helped to shape the story, especially (Auntie) Helen Coxhill, Karen Legge, Steph Harlow and Joe Cartwright. Thank you Beth, who so kindly gave up her time to teach a complete novice about how to market a book.

Writing is a solitary thing, but only until the first draft is finished. After that, it's such a team effort and I'm grateful for the help of so many people. If I listed everyone who had helped me along the way, these acknowledgments would be an entire book by themselves!